Australian author **Ally Bl** strong coffee, porch swing beautiful notebooks and so inquisitive, rumbustious, sp her exquisite delight, and sh stories so much she'd write them even if nobody read them. No wonder, then, having sold over four million copies of her romance novels worldwide, Ally is living her bliss. Find out more about Ally's books at allyblake.com.

Juliette Hyland believes in strong coffee, hot drinks and happily-ever-afters! She lives in Ohio, USA, with her Prince Charming, who has patiently listened to many rants regarding characters failing to follow their outline. When not working on fun and flirty happily-ever-afters, Juliette can be found spending time with her beautiful daughters and giant dogs, or sewing uneven stitches with her sewing machine.

CINDERELLA ASSISTANT TO BOSS'S BRIDE

ALLY BLAKE

HOW TO WIN A PRINCE

JULIETTE HYLAND

MILLS & BOON

First published in Great Britain 2023
by Mills & Boon, an imprint of HarperCollins*Publishers* Ltd,
1 London Bridge Street, London, SE1 9GF

www.harpercollins.co.uk

HarperCollins*Publishers*, Macken House, 39/40 Mayor Street Upper, Dublin 1, D01 C9W8, Ireland

Cinderella Assistant to Boss's Bride © 2023 Ally Blake

How to Win a Prince © 2023 Juliette Hyland

ISBN: 978-0-263-30659-0

12/23

Printed and Bound in the UK using 100% Renewable Electricity at CPI Group (UK) Ltd, Croydon, CR0 4YY

CINDERELLA ASSISTANT TO BOSS'S BRIDE

ALLY BLAKE

MILLS & BOON

To the gorgeously wondrous
Amy Andrews, Clare Connelly and Jennifer St George,
my fellow founders of www.HowtoWriteLove.com,
the online course that we created with the heartfelt
intent to share all we have learned in our years spent
writing romance novels. I am ever grateful to
be basking in their collective glow.

CHAPTER ONE

THE DAY HADLEY MOREAU resigned as executive assistant to her billionaire boss, she wore black. And not just any black—the kind of black that made a woman feel as if she were made of pure steel: fitted black tuxedo pants, black toenails peeking out of black peep-toe pumps and a high-necked black silk shirt with an oversized bow at the neck. The press of it against her throat, against the hard pulse of her jugular, was a reminder not to say anything that might give him even the slightest indication that he could change her mind.

"What the hell is this?" The infamous, the inimitable, the *impossible* Ronan Gerard looked up at Hadley from his seat at the head of the table in the Big Think Founders' Room, the back of the chair curling behind his shoulders like a not-so-subtle imitation of a throne.

"I think you'll find it's a letter of resignation," said Hadley, her voice crisp as she glanced pointedly at the piece of paper clenched in Ronan's claw, while every cell in her body remained braced for his response.

Ronan's gaze hardened; his nostrils flared. She could feel the sweep of his displeasure as it blew about the room like a tornado. And yet his lips remained tightly closed.

Say something, she thought. For, the moment he said something, she could say something back. And snap, crackle, pop:

their sharply honed repartee would siphon the electricity from the air.

And yet…crickets.

No *Don't be ridiculous*.

No *You're not going anywhere*.

No *Stay, please, I can't do this without you and, more than that, I don't want to*.

Fine. There was as much chance of Ronan Gerard saying those words as there was of Big Think Tower growing wings and flying away.

But what about the standard *"why?"*

That had to be eating at him. How a person could choose not to work for Big Think Corp would make no sense to Ronan Gerard. His company was his everything. It was his life, his passion, his obsession. Nothing mattered to him more. Nothing.

Hadley gave him a smidge longer to respond, in case he was building up to something. Despite the current statue-like comportment, she knew he was gathering steam from the muscle ticking in his jaw, the shadows in his crisp blue eyes. She'd made a career of understanding the man's most minute tells, after all, so that she might give him what he needed before he even knew he needed it.

Then again, Ronan's refusal to give, to soften even a little, was but one of the reasons why this day had finally come.

When it became clear she'd have to be the next to speak, Hadley notched back her shoulders and looked to her tablet—a super-fast prototype developed by Big Think, and one of many things she'd have to leave behind. "I'm sending you a link to Pitch Perfect employment agency to source my replacement. High-end corporate is their niche."

She glanced up to see if *that* got a reaction, but the man was the human version of a storm cloud in a snow globe:

dark, brooding, threatening thunder but safely encased in an impenetrable barrier.

So, she went on. "As noted in my letter, I'm offering a generous eight weeks' notice—the first four to finish any outstanding work and to train your new assistant. The next four, you will pay me as a contractor to project manage the Big Think Ball to completion. I've provided an amount I believe to be fair compensation for that role."

At *that* Ronan stood, slowly. He was pure restrained power in a bespoke suit as he pressed back his chair with a level of calm that had Hadley's heart thudding against the tight bow at her throat.

If he tried to negotiate, to push for more time or lower compensation for her work, she was ready to fight him. In fact, a good fiery debate would make this so much easier. Their disagreements always did: benign release valves that kept things from spilling over into some comment, or action, they couldn't take back.

Only, he remained silent, merely making his way round the table. Slowly, his eyes on her—those unfairly perceptive, deceptively warm, midnight-blue eyes—the paper still clenched in his fist.

If he thought this "prowling panther" move might make her waver, cower, he had another think coming. She held her ground. Held his gaze. Held tight to the myriad reasons why she could no longer work for the man—the ones she'd happily admit to, and those she never would.

Until she noticed the uneven knot of his tie.

The man, for all his skills, had never mastered that one. As always, the impulse to go to him, to fix it, to make sure he looked as perfectly put together on the outside as he was on the inside, flooded through her. Instead, Hadley's thumb began tracing the tattoo that ran around the base of her right ring-finger: a bow of thin black string, a talisman. A reminder to remember always to trust her instinct.

The same instinct that told her it was time to move on.

Only, Ronan noticed the move; his gait paused, his dark gaze dropped to her hand. Just as she'd come to know him over the past several years, and despite her best efforts to preserve a safe level of opacity, he'd found ways and means to come to know her too.

His blue gaze lifted to hers, locking on, seeing a knowing glint. A single eyebrow rose in question, making it clear he knew she did not feel nearly as cool as she was making out.

Oh, buddy, she thought, heat rushing through her, a thready pulse now beating at her temples, *you have no idea*.

In fact, maybe she ought to tell him every last reason why she had to leave. That would wipe that assured smile from his face—the thought of which was nearly enough for her to let it out.

But that was never going to happen.

For, while Ronan Gerard was stubborn—a stubbornness born of extreme privilege—Hadley was more so. Only, she was street-smart stubborn: gritty, wily and survival-level stubborn. Yes, working for a successful company had given her the taste and means for the finer things, but deep down she was still the scrappy kid who'd grown up sleeping in her mother's car, or on a couch belonging to her mum's latest boyfriend.

Remembering *that*, Hadley left her tattoo alone, gripped her tablet in both hands, pressed her toes into the points of her shoes and stared the man down, even as he continued his prowl down the length of the room.

Neither of them said another word until he stopped. The delicious notes of his aftershave, the questions in his hard blue eyes that he was mulishly refusing to voice and the uneven knot of that damn tie vied for attention in her head.

"You're really doing this?" he finally asked.

His deep voice and velvety tones washed over her like a winter fog. She only just managed to keep a shiver at bay.

"You're really leaving me."

A note of sorrow, of disbelief, light but there, had Hadley's gaze whipping from the knot of his tie to his eyes and their gazes tangled. For a breath, moments, memories and history curled between them like a whisper, like a wish.

But, no. She was done wishing. Done putting herself in a position that would only end in pain as, in her experience, such things always would. It took every fragment of those street smarts to keep her voice even, her expression composed, as she said, deadpan, "I'm not leaving *you*, Ronan. I'm resigning. From a *job*."

A muscle jerked in Ronan's cheek and she thought perhaps she had him. That she'd cracked the smooth, polished, marble armour he wore like a second skin. But then he breathed out slowly, the tautness in his jaw easing as he slid his hands into his pockets and leant back against the desk, before flicking at some speck of nothing on his jacket.

As if that was that. As if he'd said all he would say on the matter. As if the last seven years stood for nothing.

And the tension swirling between them—the tension that was always there, watching, waiting—only grew, till it felt as if rope was winding about her ankles, her thighs and her chest, threatening to crush her.

"Okay, then," said Hadley, when the tension became too much. Cynicism dripped from the words, giving her away. "If that's all, I'll head to HR to lodge my resignation, to make it official and set in motion next steps."

Then, because it would stay with her all day if she didn't, Hadley hooked her tablet under her arm, stepped in, grabbed the knot of his tie and yanked it into place.

The insides of his knees bumped against the outsides of hers. The warmth of his skin pulsed towards her fingers. His aura—dark and delectable—clouded around her. She told herself that she was fixing his tie because it was best to ease back on such tasks, rather than go cold turkey. Not that she was *addicted* to straightening the man's tie. Not at all.

She tightened the thing a smidge more than entirely necessary.

"Better?" Ronan asked, lifting a hand to run his fingers over the knot, as if tracing the place her fingers had been.

"Infinitely," said Hadley.

Then, with one final acute glance at those knowing blue eyes, she stepped back, spun on a high heel, walked out of the room and shut the door behind her with a very slight bang.

To think his day had started with such promise, Ronan thought.

First, an email from Paris, informing him of his nomination for the International Humanitarian Award for his company's inroads regarding renewable energy and disease control. A hell of a thing for the son of a man who'd earned his fortune greasing political palms by the way of oil and coal.

While also providing him with possible leverage with the one man he'd been trying—and failing—to bring into the Big Think fold for years? Cattle baron, beloved by all sides of politics and one of Australia's most influential figures, Holt Waverly was famously tight-fisted when it came to spending his money or political cache on anything beyond the scope of his tightknit family. Waverly was proving to be the ultimate ungettable get, but Ronan wanted him on board as a benefactor, or even as a supporter, with a ferocity he couldn't quite explain. Yet every phone call, every request for a meeting, every pitch, had thus far failed in courting Waverly's favour.

Ronan had been imagining how a prestigious award focussed on Big Think's future-proofing success might tug on the sun-weathered heartstrings of a man with three grown daughters—with grandkids surely on the way soon—when Hadley had sauntered in.

Her dark hair had been flicked and falling over one eye, lips slicked in red, channelling Bette Davis or Greta Garbo— knockout Hollywood glamour with an underlying thread of *don't mess with me or I will cut you*.

To say the woman had sapped his breath from his lungs as thoroughly as if he'd been sucker-punched would be an understatement. To say she'd done so every day for several years was on him. At least he'd learned how to manage it: with constant vigilance and by bracing himself for impact.

Managing had been a necessity, for Hadley was a weapon—*his* weapon. At least that was what he'd always thought till that morning, barely a moment after he'd collected his wits, when she'd dropped her bombshell.

"I think you'll find it's a letter of resignation."

And every feeling of promise, every damn thought, had been crushed by the fallout.

Now that the aftershocks had settled, the ripples faded to a swirling red mist and a mid-grade tightness in his neck, he had moved onto trying to figure out what the hell had set her off, so that he could fix it.

Fixing things was what he did. Putting things to rights. For that, he needed Hadley. And he always got his way in the end.

"Earth to Ronan? Hey! *Gerard!*"

Ronan, back in his seat at the head of the table, found his way through the red mist, and looked up to find his business partners—Ted Fincher and Sawyer Mahoney—taking up their usual spots in the Big Think Founders' Room. Ted was in his father's ancient, beaten-up lounger, with Sawyer sitting backwards on whatever chair he'd found.

The Big Think Founders' Room was not the elegant haven of thought and creativity—the kind of place Aristotle or Da Vinci would have found inspiring—he'd imagined when Big Think Tower had been no more than a collective twinkle in their eyes. This room, in which bright minds made game-changing decisions and where billions were earned and spent, veered more towards the eclectic simplicity of the university dorm lounge in which they'd first met.

Proof, perhaps, that Ronan did not always get his way. Which was not the reminder he needed right now.

"Did he hear a word we said?" Sawyer said out of the side of his mouth, glancing at Ted as he grabbed a hand ball from the bowl he kept on the table and began juggling it with his left hand.

Ignoring Hadley's offensive sheet of paper for now, Ronan said, "I'm assuming you were nattering about window treatments. Or your next book club pick."

Sawyer—quicker off the mark than Ted, whose phenomenal scientific brain was likely computing what window treatments might be—said, "The latest Brené Brown, naturally."

A smile flitted at the edge of Ronan's subconscious but did not penetrate, for his head was full—of Hadley. And not in the way it usually was. Instead, he wondered what the hell had happened to bring her to the point of leaving.

She was a fighter. She never pulled back from saying her piece. If she had a gripe, she let it be known. It was a big part of why she fitted so well. For the inner circle didn't have time for politeness, or vacillation. Humour, yes; the work they did was serious enough to require respite. But never hesitation.

And Hadley had been a part of Big Think for as long as it had existed. Her supernatural ability to take their wild ideas and plan, delegate and make them happen was stitched into the company's very fabric.

Yes, the two of them spent more time sniping at one another than not, but that was part of the magic, the kinetic energy, the push-and-pull that fuelled him. Her resistance to half-heartedness reminded him, daily, of his mission to do better. To *be* better.

So, what the hell had gone wrong?

When he realised Sawyer was actually filling Ted in about the latest book he'd read, Ronan growled, "It's been a hell of a day already, so let's just get on with it."

"But we wait for Hadley," Ted noted, glancing towards the door to the spot where she usually stood.

Ronan had always imagined she saw herself as their bodyguard, ready to bite anyone who dared attempt to enter the inner sanctum. Now he wondered if she'd had one eye on the exit the whole time.

Growling again, this time at himself, Ronan snapped, "No waiting. Let's get on with it."

"But Hadley has the agenda," said Ted.

Ronan looked at his laptop, realising Ted was right. At which point he coughed out a laugh, not even an inkling of humour in or around it.

"You okay over there?" Sawyer asked, head cocked, as if he realised this wasn't a Ronan-juggling-a-hundred-things-at-once level distraction but a whole other thing.

"Peachy," Ronan shot back. Then closed his eyes, a headache pressing behind his left eye.

"You sure?" Sawyer asked. "Because you look like you just heard Wall Street fell down a sink hole. Or Tom Ford stopped making suits."

Hell. He had to tell them. For, while Hadley was his, the others leant on her constantly and had long since adopted her into the fold.

Strike that—Hadley was not *his*. Though Ted and Sawyer leaned on her constantly, she officially worked for him alone, as *his* executive assistant. His right hand. The voice to his thoughts. The strong arm to his determinations. The veil people had to get through to get to him. And if she left…

Something shifted in his chest. No, not his *chest*—his base instincts. He felt rumblings of impending disaster, like the earth quaking before a volcano blew its top.

That settled him back into his body like nothing else. Big Think was not about to go bang. It was too big, too important, too necessary. Which was why Hadley had to stay.

Ronan curled his hands into fists, his nails pressing into his palms, and ground out, "Hadley is not here, as this morning she gave me a letter of resignation. No concern of yours. I'll sort it out—"

"I'm sorry," Sawyer interjected, both hands out in front, as if pushing back Ronan's words. "Did you just say Hadley *quit*?"

Ronan nodded.

"She quit?" Ted asked, now fully engaged, rather than having half a mind on whatever scientific breakthrough he was currently working on. "Why?"

Sawyer asked, "Has she been headhunted? If so, we match it."

Ronan shook his head. "It's not that. People have tried, for years. I've shut every one of them down, matching any offer and then some."

"Of course you have. You're Ronan Freaking Gerard."

"Then why?" Ted tried again.

To that, Ronan gave no response. For he'd not actually asked. Had he instinctively known he wouldn't like he answer?

Ted, well-used to asking questions and getting answers, asked, "How much notice has she given? Does it give us time to change her mind?"

"What does her contract stipulate?" Sawyer added, before Ted's and his gazes both swung back to Ronan.

This Ronan did know, and it wasn't pretty. He'd readily have prevaricated if he'd believed the situation required it, but in the end went with knowledge being power.

"There is no contract," Ronan stated. "There never has been."

Sawyer sat forward, and carefully placed his hand ball on the table. "I know I'm stating the obvious here, but what the hell, Ronan? *No contract?* We don't do handshake deals. We don't move an inch on any project without having the legals in place. Your rule."

A nerve fluttered under Ronan's right eye.

Sawyer was right, of course. But the way he and Hadley had come to work together had been born in such fraught and complicated circumstances, choosing delicacy over conformity had seemed the right thing to do. And he'd never regretted that choice. Not for a moment.

Now, not having circled back to that felt like the most colossal error of judgement in his life.

"As to Ted's question, Hadley has given eight weeks' notice and she has agreed to train her replacement."

Sawyer shook his head. "The Sawyers of this world are replaceable. The Ronans are dime a dozen. The Hadley Moreaus are *not*."

"Don't you think I know that?" Ronan seethed, only to hear the strain in the words that echoed back at him. And it had nothing to do with how hard he'd worked not to be some cookie-cutter suit a man from his background and social position might have chosen to be. But the point was taken.

Hadley was wholly unique. Her background had not naturally eased her into the work she now did, but she was tenacious, whip-smart and highly motivated. Like a T-1000

Terminator, knock her down and she'd come at you more determined than before.

He tried picturing some other person running these highly sensitive meetings and coordinating his precariously balanced calendar. They'd require a key to his home, his passwords and his medical history. He ran a hand up the back of his neck, which felt as if it had come out in a sudden stress rash.

Then he tried picturing some other person leaning in, fixing the knot of his tie, and he recoiled...physically.

A day at Big Think without Hadley—without her work ethic, her ability to get stuff done—felt inconceivable. How to fix it? More money, time off, a contract, an island in the Bahamas? The truth was, Ronan would give her whatever it took to change her mind.

With that, the final vestiges of red mist curling about his mind dissolved. Ronan leaned forward and looked his partners down. "Rest assured, this is not over. Now, we need to move on. If you remember, we have a company to run. A company that is bigger than any one of us."

Ted looked concerned, Sawyer compassionate. Ronan refused to acknowledge either.

"Forget the agenda. Sawyer—updates on the Centres for Physical Therapy. Go."

Sawyer narrowed his eyes Ronan's way a moment longer, before his enthusiasm for his pet project took over—an ode to the treatment he'd received after breaking his leg in a career-ending football game years before.

Then Ted waxed lyrical about an elegant new vaccine created to combat the cancer-causing Epstein-Barr virus and now ready for trial.

All the while, Ronan found his gaze shifting constantly to the empty doorway. While trying to imagine some other person taking her place was impossible, imagining Hadley was as easy as breathing.

He imagined her standing in her usual spot, tablet in hand, expression absorbed, the whole of her impossibly chic.

He imagined her looking up, her gaze finding his and lingering, a beat longer than it should. Those dark eyes of hers searing right into his soul, making him start to believe he might actually have one.

Ronan looked down to find his hand was resting on the paper she'd handed him, smoothing out the creases. Breathing in deeply, he could all but sense a waft of her perfume lifting from the page, rich, warm and sophisticated. Circling him. Mocking him. Dragging him under.

"So, I can let Adelaid know it's a go?"

Ronan came to as Sawyer said, "Fingers crossed. Petra just agreed to curate a collection in New York, so we might be home by Christmas, or just after."

Christmas, Ronan thought. A week before the Big Think Ball, which took place on New Year's Eve. After which Hadley would be gone…for ever. Unless he found a way to make her stay. Which he would do. For he *was* Ronan Freaking Gerard.

"Ronan?" Sawyer nudged. "Dinner at Ted and Adelaid's? Or are you busy Christmas Eve?"

Busy with *family*, Sawyer meant, though he didn't say the words, knowing they could be akin to a match to a tinderbox where Ronan was concerned.

He would try to carve out time to see his mother before the holidays. His father could go to hell and stay there.

This was his true family. Not the one he'd been born into—where recrimination and cocktails took pride of place on the on the family crest—but these good, smart, enterprising, fiercely loyal men and the women who'd recently swept into their lives, bringing with them balance, expansion and the space to let go of old wounds.

"Add it to the calendar," Ronan said, then remembered there was no one in the room to do that for him.

Ronan's jaw set so hard, he nearly cracked a bone. *Impossible*, he thought yet again. Hadley could lodge all the damned forms with HR she damned well liked. Ronan was not letting her go.

Hadley stood outside the Gilded Cage, waiting on the team they'd hired to help turn it from a nightclub to day-and-night event space, opening the way for high teas and the luxurious lunch crowd.

It was a job she could easily have outsourced, only the Gilded Cage was one of Big Think's most special properties, Sawyer and Petra having become engaged to one another there—twice.

And she'd needed to get out of the office.

The more time that went by before Ronan finally said something, or looked at her in some way that tugged at all those dark, hidden, yearning places inside that she was so desperate to leave behind, the greater the chance she'd change her mind.

She'd made a bargain with herself when she'd come to him all those years ago, cap in hand, asking for a job: one year. One year to learn all she could learn, then take those tools and create her own opportunities, never again beholden to anyone.

Only, she'd not expected to relish the work, to love the pace and the pressure, or to luck out with such monumental financial security. And she'd not expected *him*: his brilliance, his work ethic, his intractability that called to her own.

So, she'd stayed. And it was the only time she'd ever broken a promise to herself. The only time she ever would.

When her phone rang, Hadley jumped.

It was Sawyer's wife, Petra.

Checking the street to find still no contractor, Hadley answered, "Hey, what's up?"

"Ah, so I was just talking to Sawyer and he seems to think you're leaving Big Think."

Hadley rustled her fingers through her hair. She hadn't considered this—the speed of the Big Think information web. She would have liked to have told Petra and Ted's wife, Adelaid, herself, for over the past couple of years they'd become friends. She could only blame the rareness of lasting female friendships in her life for the slip.

"Say it isn't so," said Petra.

"It is so," Hadley avowed. "I handed Ronan my letter of resignation this morning."

"You gave an actual letter. Of resignation. To Ronan. In person. And lived to tell the tale?"

"I did."

"Wow. I mean…wow. I've always known you were a marvel of a woman, but that's impressive. The freaking cojones on you."

Hadley found herself laughing at Petra's response. A most unexpected thing, considering how tightly wound her insides still felt.

Then again, her friendship with Petra and Adelaid had been *the* most unexpected part of working at Big Think. Was that something else she'd have to let go upon leaving the company? Her insides twisted all the more.

"Did he melt down?" Petra asked. "Or did he go all stoic and manly. Or did he finally crack and drop to his knees and tell you he could not do what he does without you and insist you had to stay?"

"Stoic." Pure Ronan—unreadable, impenetrable, impossible. "With no insisting I had to stay."

"Excuse me? He's *letting* you *go*?" Petra asked on a gasp. "Just like *that*?"

Hadley fixed the hook of her structured bag over her elbow and moved up onto the stairs outside the club so she wasn't blocking the footpath. "There was no *letting*. I am not his to let. I resigned. I gave ample notice. That's that."

"Wow. You are stone-cold, my friend. Brilliant and brave, and bolshie as hell, but stone-cold. I am in awe.

"Hang on," said Petra, then after a few beeping sounds continued, "We have Adelaid. Adelaid, have you spoken to Ted?"

"Not since he left for work," said Adelaid breathily. Hadley pictured her fair flyaway hair fluttering and falling about her face, vintage maternity dress fluttering about her knees as she dropped awkwardly into a seat somewhere. "Why? What did I miss?"

"You won't believe what Hadley just did to Ronan," Petra teased.

There came a beat, then Adelaid squealed, "Really? Oh, that's brilliant! And about time!"

Hadley breathed a little easier, knowing her friends weren't pulling back or taking sides. The fact that they were romantically attached to the other Big Think founders would have given them every right.

Though, it turned out, Adelaid wasn't done. "Thank the gods we can all now stop tiptoeing around the two of you. The longing looks, the accidental touches, the sexual tension…. Big Think Tower could have run on the electricity you and Ronan produce. So, how was it? Incendiary?"

Belatedly, Hadley realised Adelaid's misunderstanding; the absolute assuredness that she and Ronan had…

Hadley's heart thumped against her ribs hard enough to bruise as she blurted, "Wait, no! You've got that all wrong. We're not—I haven't—he would never—"

"Adelaid," Petra kindly took over when Hadley found herself in a glitch loop. "Hadley *resigned*."

Adelaid's pause was weighty. "From *Big Think*?"

Hadley was still too shaken by Adelaid's attestation that they'd all been "tiptoeing around" to speak in recognisable sentences. Though Adelaid was wildly fond of classic romance movies, so chances were she was projecting.

"But you *are* Big Think!" said Adelaid, doubling down. "The first day I walked into the place, there you were, coming at me across that big, scary foyer, so terrifyingly glamorous. Then you looked me in the eye, and as good as told me I belonged there as much as anyone. I could have hugged you forever."

Hadley swallowed, for Adelaid had unwittingly pressed on a bruise. It had taken Hadley years to feel as if *she* belonged there. The men had gravitated towards one another, naturally, like calling to like. While she'd slipped in through a crack, then hung on with all her might.

The irony was it had taken for her to finally understand her value, trust her instincts were on point and know her innate abilities were without peer, to then realise that for all those reasons she had to leave.

Because life wasn't fair. It was built that way. And she'd been born into the faction that got the short straw, eventually; always.

"How did Ronan take it?" Adelaid asked. "Did he beg? Plead? Offer an eye-watering raise? The jet? A small country?"

"He didn't even try to talk her out of it," Petra stage-whispered.

"Seriously?" Adelaid asked. "That man! I often think about how much he could do with a really good shake."

Hadley knew the feeling. Over the years she'd wanted to shake him, rage at him, poke him, pinch him…and other things. Things she imagined in the dark, in the quiet, in the space between sensible thoughts. All the ways she might get through to the man, to show him what was right in front of him.

Had resigning partly been a version of that—a kind of wake-up slap? If so, it had failed. For he'd stood there, looked her in the eye and given her nothing.

"You know what?" said Petra. "Ten bucks says he's sitting back in his lair right now, hatching plans and schemes to get you to stay. Possibly stroking a fluffy white cat in a slightly menacing manner while he's at it."

At that, Adelaid burst into laughter. "I can so see that. He has all the hallmarks of a Bond villain who took a wrong turn somewhere and ended up doing oodles of good instead."

As the other two went back and forth, coming up with more and more versions of Ronan as great villains of history but with a good streak, Hadley mused at how right they were.

That was the great paradox regards Ronan Gerard. He might be stubborn, gruff and entitled but, beneath the polished exterior, his motives were pure.

Ronan knew full well how easy it would have been to follow in his father's footsteps. Constantine Gerard had grown obscenely rich and well-protected, despite decades of nefarious dealings and unspeakable behaviour, by choosing to see the rules of business as meant for other people. Yet Ronan had made a deliberate decision to use his money and influence to enact real change in the world.

Big Think Corp was the *pièce de résistance*. A veritable funnel of grand ideas and lightning-quick action that had poured more investment into medical breakthroughs, renewable energy, disease control and community-led services for those in greatest need than any other private group could.

Yet his father's shadow remained, pushing Ronan to do better, be better. To the point Hadley wondered if there would ever be a time when Ronan could look himself in the mirror and say, *I am enough*. Whether he'd ever be able to outrun the demons that chased him.

Unluckily for her, it was that sliver of darkness, the knowledge of where he'd come from that could never be denied, that called to the darker conflicts that lived deep inside in her. Add the fact that he was utterly gorgeous, and knew it—all big and broad and bear-like with that strong, striking face, those entrancing dark-blue eyes and a voice like warm molasses—and how could she not have fallen deeply, painfully, regrettably in love with the man?

Or maybe it wasn't love. Maybe it was some inherited self-destructive streak—this constant, living ache she felt behind her ribs; the vivid dreams that left her shaking, sweating, spent; the way her body surged, her blood sparking, her belly tightening to the point of pain any time they were in the same room.

It was a miracle she'd not thrown away her career, her self-respect, all of it, for the chance to be with him just once. It was her mother's MO when it came to the men in her life, after all. She could see her mother's face, full of hope, despite all evidence to the contrary, thinking *What if he's the one?*

Only now things felt as if they were coming to a head.

Since Adelaid had swooped in and stolen big, brilliant Ted's heart—and Petra had finally realised she'd had Sawyer's heart in the palm of her hands for years—the dynamics at Big Think had changed practically overnight.

Leaving Ronan as the sole man at the helm for whom the

company was his *raison d'être*. And—not that he would never admit it—Ronan was struggling. Working longer hours, meaning she did too. Pushing back more and more against her ideas, which she knew was his way of getting the best from her.

All of which meant the gravitational pull that had existed between them from day dot had grown stronger still. As if, without Sawyer and Ted there to act as foils, Hadley was hurtling towards a black hole.

No wonder she'd hit breaking point. And Hadley Moreau had zero intention of breaking. Not for him. Not for anyone. Giving her no choice but to do what her ever-hopeful mother had never been able to and be the one to walk away.

Her phone buzzed and, at the thought it might be Ronan, her skin tightened all over. Lifting the phone from her ear, she checked the screen and saw it was the contractor, saying he was close.

And, while to all the world she might still present as Hadley Moreau—cool, sharp, and focussed, like a machine—inside it stung that Ronan was yet to message, yet to call. Yet to say a damn thing! The ache that his continued ambivalence brought on, and the disappointment in herself for still wanting more, was so strong she could taste it on the back of her tongue.

Hadley blinked to find the contractor coming up the street, waving. She waved back and cleared her throat. "I have to go. Work beckons."

"Even now she's Little Miss On Top of Things," Adelaid said on a sigh. "You are my idol."

"Whatever happens from here, you've got this," Petra added. "Elephant in the room, our partners are invested in Big Think too, but we support you and we love you. No matter what."

"Thank you," Hadley managed, holding in the feelings swarming through her—emotions she was not equipped to handle.

They both rang off, leaving Hadley feeling unusually wobbly in her high heels.

She pulled herself together as the contractor arrived and was at about ninety percent capacity as she showed him round the space.

Her mind kept whirling back to Adelaid's words: *thank the gods we can all now stop tiptoeing around the two of you.*

All of us.

All this time.

Both Petra and Adelaid had asked about Ronan's reaction—both expecting it to have been spectacular. But neither had asked her *why* she was leaving. Was it possible they *all* somehow knew? That they'd seen the writing on the wall long before she had—Ronan included?

"Hadley?"

Hadley shook her way out of the fog and moved to the contractor, concentrating as he talked through ways he imagined they could switch things up with as little disruption to business as possible. Knowing she had to be at one hundred percent from here on in to get done everything she needed *done*.

Before she left Big Think—and Ronan—once and for all.

CHAPTER TWO

HADLEY ARRIVED A smidge late to the next Big Think founders' meeting in the hope she might slip in, run the agenda then slip out again and get on with the mountain of work she had to get through in the next three and a half weeks.

There was also the fact that somehow she'd managed not to find herself alone with Ronan since her announcement which, until that week, would have been unheard of. It made her wonder if he'd been avoiding her too. Which was ridiculous, considering nothing mattered more to the man than his company, and he'd work alongside an ogre if it meant the company's success.

Mind spinning into knots, Hadley didn't notice the room was empty until she was inside. She checked her watch. Had she got the time wrong? Or had they had the meeting without her? For all that that would be the case in the not-too-distant future, the very thought that Ronan might have…

"Hadley."

Hadley whipped round, the bell sleeves of her floaty white top spinning out, her leather skirt squeaking she spun so fast.

"Ronan," she said on an outshot of breath that sounded far huskier than she'd have liked.

For there he was, standing in the doorway. Her doorway. Well, not her doorway, but the one that felt like her doorway as that was where she stood for all their meetings—never quite in, never quite out.

And now, with Ronan's large, dark presence filling the doorway, she wasn't sure where she stood at all.

Not moving out of his way instantly was her first mistake. And once she hadn't, she couldn't, lest it seem that she was backing down. Where Ronan was concerned, she'd learned to stand her ground.

Looking up was her second mistake. For he was close—dangerously close. Close enough for her to see how deeply furrowed his brow was, and allow herself to wonder if that was her doing. Close enough to note every hair that shadowed his hard jaw, and a new tightness there, the planes of his already gloriously carved face looking like pure granite. Close enough to scent the subtle notes of his aftershave and to feel the warmth of his skin and the subtle shift of his breath against her hair.

Nearness wasn't uncommon, considering how closely they worked together: heads bowed over one another's desks; in and out of cramped cars; sitting together in planes and airport lounges; sharing hotel suites; their feet knocking against each other's at restaurant tables. She'd found ways to move past him, to protect her space, to glide through his world while still making as much impact as she could on the business she loved.

Only now it *felt* different. As if, since her resignation, the dynamic had shifted. There was an extra crackle in the air, the sense that things were not quite stable. And this time, instead of gliding out of his way, she held her space, owning it as if she had some final thing to prove.

"Hadley," he said again, only this time his voice was softer, rougher, as if he'd had to push the word free.

Even in her high-heeled ankle boots she had to look up,

as if assenting to the way his gaze roved over her face, in much the same way hers had roved over his. As if both were checking to see what might have changed in the rare hours they'd spent apart.

"Yes?" she said.

"Can we just—?"

"Move!" a voice said from behind Ronan.

Ronan took a step her way till there was no space between them at all. His hands reached out, taking her by the upper arms, pressing her back against the wall as he shifted to cover her, to protect her as Sawyer, with his big, jock energy, hustled into the room behind him. Ronan's chest brushed against hers, his thumbs swept down up and down her arms and his stubble caught on her hair.

And then he was gone, following Sawyer, patting him on the back and asking after Petra and their New York plans, leaving Hadley standing against the middle of the back wall, her cheeks flushed, her chest heaving, her hair floating over her face.

It took her a good three seconds to come back into her skin, only to find that she was trembling, not with surprise, but with flutters of desire. Because, despite the speed of the interaction, she'd have bet good money Ronan Gerard had just taken the chance to sniff her hair.

When, even to her squirrely mind, that sounded ridiculous, she quickly ruffled her hair back into place, moved away from the wall, back to her spot by the door, and gave herself a good, strong talking to.

Enough with the projecting, she told herself. Painting her feelings and the reactions pulsing through her body onto Ronan was wholly unfair. All it had done was put her in the position whereby she had to give up the best job she would ever have so that these feelings didn't eat her alive.

Hadley looked up as Ted lumbered into the room, pushing his glasses higher onto his nose. His expression turned sweet and his ruddy eyebrows raised, as if asking if perhaps she'd changed her mind. While both Sawyer and Ted had bothered to track her down separately—asking if they could do anything, *anything at all*, to change her mind, then hugging her and wishing her all the best when she'd made it clear they could not—Ronan had not. Not once.

Hadley shook her head. And, when Ted reached out to touch her arm in consolation, she felt like weeping. As Ted made his way to his usual chair, Hadley made every effort to feign cool, sharp unaffectedness, even while her insides still roiled, fumed, and fluttered.

Things were bound to feel strange as she dealt with mentally and emotionally disentangling herself from the fabric of this place. From Ronan, and the space he took up in her day-to-day life. Until the day came when the ties could be cut with a single, final, painless snip, sending her floating off into the ether, untethered and alone.

While it had been quite some time since she'd been alone, it was a place she knew well. A place less likely to break her heart.

"Hadley," Ronan called, his voice a gruff bark from his seat at the head of the table. Then, "Agenda." It was as if nothing had happened in the doorway. As if the air hadn't crackled like mad. As if he hadn't looked at her face as if he'd missed it.

Pressing all that down into the deep, dark, hidden place in which she kept all such moments, Hadley pulled up the agenda on her tablet. Then, after only a moment's hesitation, she moved past all the other bits and pieces, going straight for…

"The Big Think Ball."

Of all the projects she'd had a hand in at Big Think, the ball was Hadley's baby. It had been the first big idea she'd floated after joining the company. Having worked in hospitality since she'd been sixteen—catering, waitressing and hustling for tips behind numerous bars—it was one area she knew more about than the phenomenally well-read men she worked for.

It was also Big Think's biggest PR event of the year, one that brought more press than vaccinating a village for free, or the patenting of a new electric motor ever had. It also raised a great chunk of the funds that allowed them do both, much to Sawyer's delight, Ted's discombobulation and Ronan's perpetual disillusionment that people didn't simply see Big Think's brilliance and leap on board.

When she'd first broached it with Ronan a year or so after she'd started working with him, she'd been fully prepared for a "no." For he was quick with those, if something didn't fit within the parameters of his vision. When it had taken him about half a second to say, "Go for it," as if he'd been awaiting the day she'd stand up and ask for what she wanted, she might well have fallen for him then and there.

Now, Ronan waved a hand, as if giving her permission to start there if she must, and her feelings ran more to umbrage.

Ignoring Ronan completely, she made eye contact with the others before referring back to her tablet. "We have several weeks till the night of the ball. The theme is locked in—this year it's the 'Yellow Brick Road'. We scored a huge coup, landing Australia's favourite musical-theatre export as the MC. The tables sold out within minutes of going on sale. We are still accepting auction items, as my intention is not only to break our record for funds raised on the night, but to obliterate it."

She looked up to find Sawyer juggling hand balls, and

Ted looking out of the window. And she could happily have throttled the lot of them then and there.

They were brilliant, all three of them, in their own specific fields. But—as often happened with brilliant men—they had long got away with lacking basic life skills, such as listening to anything that didn't directly concern them. And she wondered if they had a single clue as to the hustle *she* put in behind the scenes in order for their company to run as efficiently and effectively as it did.

Gritting her teeth, her gaze swept to Ronan, fully expecting him also to be otherwise engaged, only to find him watching her intently, a finger running back and forth across the seam of his lips. And she fast found herself caught in the tangle of that dark-blue gaze.

This was where she would usually narrow her eyes then look away, or he would blink slowly then shift focus to talk to Ted or Sawyer. And both of them would act as if the moment had never happened. Only this time neither one of them moved. It was as if they were playing some new game of chicken.

Heat prickled at Hadley's skin as a bubble seemed to descend over them both, him trapping her with the pinpoint focus of his thoughts till she felt awash with warmth, with want. With so many feelings, she lost track of what she'd been saying.

No, a voice popped up in the back of her head. *Your words are important. Make them listen.*

Hadley frowned then dragged her gaze to her tablet. She scrambled for just the right thing to force them to pay attention, till she remembered a nascent idea she'd been playing with.

Big Think might own some of the world's coolest hotels and most successful scientific and tech labs—heck, they had their own jet—but the people in this room were its greatest assets. Big, burly Ted with his phenomenal brain, ginger beard and Clark Kent glasses. Sawyer, with that killer smile and the kind of charisma that could convince a nun to cartwheel.

And then there was Ronan. Never had there been a man with a greater sense of purpose and the means to make things happen. And, if that wasn't seductive enough, he looked like a Greek statue—all thick, curling hair, broad shoulders and devilish hooded eyes that could make a woman's knees melt at twenty paces.

Each on their own was a force to be reckoned with—together in the same room, on the *same stage*, they would be magic. Add the fact that, with this idea of hers, she'd be pushing all three out of their cosy little comfort zones, the more she thought about it, the more she loved it.

"As our grand finale at this year's ball," she said, lifting her voice to a neat shout that had Sawyer flinching, Ted blinking her way and Ronan settling deeper into his throne as if this was a side of her he particularly enjoyed, "We will be auctioning the three of you lugs off to the highest bidder."

Ted's eyes grew comically wide behind his smudged glasses. Sawyer lost track of a ball, the thing bouncing off to the other side of the room.

While Ronan… Ronan looked at her as if she'd just thrown a glove at his feet. But, rather than shoot the idea down, or smoulder with intense disapproval, the corner of his mouth lifted, creating a crease in his right cheek, as if he knew exactly what she was doing. She could all but hear the rough edge of his voice as he thought: *game on*. And the thrill that shot through her proved something was very wrong with her.

"What exactly do you mean by 'auction'?" asked Sawyer, eyes comically wide. "Like a *bachelor* auction?"

Ted held up both hands in surrender. "Ah, not a bachelor. So, I'm out."

"Ditto," said Sawyer. "Already found my special someone. Which leaves Ronan. He is the prettiest of the three of us. You've been so uptight of late, mate, sending you on a date could only do us all some good."

Hadley suddenly imagined some sophisticated, well-bred, well-off woman dropping gob-smacking coin to take Ronan on a date. Needless to say, the spitting green angst roiling in her belly was not something she was proud of.

"You'll take one for the team, won't ya?" Sawyer asked.

Ronan blinked once, that smile still hooking at the corner of his mouth, though his eyes had turned feral. They were gleaming, predatory and still on Hadley as he said, "What if I did have an excuse?"

"Right." Hadley snorted. Then, before she could stop herself, she said, "Like you have a 'special someone' out there that *I* don't know about."

At that, he lifted an eyebrow.

And Hadley felt the impact like an arrow to the heart.

What she'd *meant* was that she looked after his calendar, his dry cleaning and his grocery shopping. She'd even been tasked with sending break-up bouquets in the early days, something she'd refused to do after the third. Not only because it played with her already messed up heart, but because—as she told him point-blank—a good man must face up to the consequences of his actions.

She'd *know* if he was dating someone because it was her job to know.

Only Ronan was looking at her as if she had skin in the game. And the game of chicken continued. She could hear the crackle of electricity in the backs of her ears. Could feel the buzz of it in her veins. This strange new standoff played out between them, right out in the open.

When it felt as if every ounce of air had been sapped from the room Ronan cleared his throat and shifted in his chair, and Hadley had to stop herself from punching the air in victory.

"I was not, in fact, suggesting a *bachelor* auction," she said, gaze shifting easily over Ted and Sawyer, leaving Ronan well alone. "I'm not about to pimp you out. I am friends with your partners, for Pete's sake, so you can all settle down."

But the idea, or a version thereof, did have real, money-spinning merit.

She went on. "How about this? Whomever wins the auction gets a one-on-one with the founder of their choice. A pitch meeting, or a tour of the facility at your side. The chance to see behind the curtain. Something clean-cut, wholesome and brand-happy. For some strange reason, people are constantly at me for access to you lot, so let's make them pay for the privilege. Magnanimous and highly competitive... It would be the perfect big finish."

Her big finish. Ronan would be on stage, looking larger than life in his custom-made tuxedo, all broad shoulders and generational polish, squinting grumpily and gorgeously into a spotlight as she turned her back and walked away for the very last time.

Ted and Sawyer murmured preliminary approval, mostly out of relief, she reckoned. But that was enough for her.

"It's decided, then," she said. "The Big Think Founders' Auction it is. Now, I have photographers coming in Wednesday for new marketing imagery to advertise the ball."

"I'll get out my fancy suit," said Sawyer, tugging at the collar of his snug polo shirt.

"No suits," she said, for she'd had a few left-field ideas

there too. This being her last ball, it was not the time to hold back. "And Sawyer, Ted—don't shave till after."

Ted gave her a thumbs-up, while Sawyer grinned as he rubbed at his scruffy cheeks. "I'm down with that. But what about Ronan? Please say he needs to wax—full body."

Ronan, now tapping something into his laptop, held up a single finger in response. Sawyer burst into laughter and finally the room felt normal again.

Until Ronan's gaze once again found Hadley's and the tension came back with a vengeance. "What do you need from me?"

While some part of her so wanted to take his words another way, she knew he meant for the photo shoot. "Light grey suit. Snow-white shirt. Silver tie. And don't let them take a single photo till I've checked the knot."

At that, she remembered fixing his tie the other morning—the feel of his knees pressing against hers, the scent of him in her nostrils—and felt all kinds of off kilter.

"So that's it from me," she said, fussing as she tucked her tablet under her arm. "I've emailed you the rest of the agenda, all items you are big enough to look after yourselves. Okay?"

Fully aware none of them would dare contradict her, she shot each a beatific smile then walked out of the room, wobbling only slightly as she passed through the doorway, remembering Ronan filling it as his gaze had roved hungrily over her face not many minutes before.

At the lift, she shook out her arms, her legs and her hair, shaking off any lingering sensations that were not of imminent use to her work—meaning any lingering sensations linked to Ronan. The touch of his hands on her arms, the tilt of his mouth as he read her like a book, and the look in his eyes that made her wonder if perhaps this wasn't as one-sided as she'd convinced herself it always had been.

Muttering to herself to get a grip, Hadley swiped her security fob over the sensor and headed up to Ronan's private floor where he kept an apartment, a gym and the kitchen for his personal chef. His gargantuan private office was there too, as was hers. They faced one another with a large open space in between, but were close enough so she was within shouting distance.

Not that she had anything to complain about there, for her office was gorgeous. Large and airy, it had plush rugs, a lounge suite, private dressing room, top-notch tech with the most beautiful pale-gold tiled ceiling and dark teal wallpaper that made the space feel like something out of a gothic novel. She'd designed every inch of the space herself, and loved it more than chocolate.

Though, secretly, she'd loved her first office too, back when Big Think had been little more than a dream and her "office" had been a tiny desk pushed up against Ronan's in a small ground-floor corner of a converted warehouse in Richmond. Ted had worked in a lab across town; Sawyer had had a couch, but had been mostly on the road, drumming up contacts even then, meaning headquarters had mostly been just the two of them.

It was where she and Ronan had built their close working habits, cooped up together in that intimate space, making plans and building something amazing. With limited funds and gigantic ideas, there had been little room for civility, hurt feelings or privacy. But it had suited them both—in the mud together, clawing their way towards something great.

But now, having exceeded every possible dream, Ronan was still restless, still hyper-focussed, still reaching for something. While Hadley felt as if she'd given all she was willing to give before she lost herself entirely.

The lift door opened and Hadley breathed out, reminding

herself that melancholy would do her no good. She had to focus on the ball: the photo shoot, how it might lean into the theme, and now the auction. Plenty to keep her mind busy.

As Hadley neared her office, her assistant, Kyle, got up from behind his desk in a flutter of paper and puppy-dog enthusiasm.

"Any news?" he asked as he jogged behind her towards her office door.

By that, he meant had she changed her mind. Though born with St Bernard Syndrome—aka resting sad-face—Kyle had looked even more down-hearted since she'd given him the news of her imminent departure.

Hadley waited for him to catch up and shot him a half-smile. "Plenty. I've figured out how we are going to close out the ball."

She touched her thumb to the security pad and her smoky-glass office door swished open. Even though it had been a couple of years since they'd moved in, she felt a frisson of disbelief and pride that this space was actually hers—she an ex-waitress, high-school drop-out, daughter of a hot mess of a single mum who'd struggled her whole life to make ends meet.

Kyle dropped his tablet on the coffee table by the book-shelves before heading off to make them both coffees from Hadley's espresso machine, while Hadley popped her tablet on its charging pad and sank into her peacock-blue leather wonder of an office chair, sighing as it settled beneath her.

She sprayed a little water on Cactiss Everdeen: the mini-cactus Adelaid had given Ronan when he'd hosted a dinner party a while back, which Hadley had taken, knowing Ronan would forget it existed the second it was out of his sight.

Then she looked across to the open door of her office and beyond, to where the doors to Ronan's empty sat open across the way. For all the security—the thumbprints and personal fobs—he left his doors open more often than not. They'd both positioned their desks so that they could see one another, all that way away.

She startled when Kyle placed her coffee in its porcelain cup onto a leather coaster on her desk.

"You okay?" he asked.

When Hadley realised her hand was rubbing at the spot over her ribs right over her heart, she dropped a fist on the desk.

"Two things," she said.

Kyle held up a finger before hustling over to where he'd left his own fancy Big Think tablet. He sat, stylus aloft, and nodded.

"The grand finale of the Big Think Ball will now be a non-bachelor bachelor auction."

"Brilliant," said Kyle. "And whom are we auctioning?"

Hadley paused, looking at him pointedly.

Kyle shook his head. "Sawyer, Ronan and Ted. Of course! The Billion-Dollar Bachelor Auction. Love it."

"Only, we're not calling it a *bachelor* auction, as it's not a bachelor auction, because two out of the three are no longer bachelors."

"True that," said Kyle with a sigh. "Only, it's totally a bachelor auction, right?"

Hadley smiled, then felt a need to rub her ribs again when it hit her how much she'd miss working with Kyle. Easy, breezy and light, their relationship was the exact opposite of that with her boss.

Kyle grinned. "So, we sell them off in a completely G-rated, sophisticated, professional manner, while totally playing up their bangable-ness, because, hello, elephant in the room."

Hadley didn't dignify *that* with a response, but agreed wholeheartedly. For, while the ends absolutely justified the means, thinking about Ronan and that term had the wires in her brain short-circuiting.

"The second thing?" Kyle asked.

"It's time we start looking for my replacement."

Ronan swung his keys in his hand as he took the lift to the private garage below Big Think Tower, as if the smack of metal against his palm might unlock some insight into how the hell he could change Hadley's mind.

There'd been a moment—before the meeting that morning—when he'd sensed his chance to say something, before Sawyer had barrelled into the room and broken the spell.

No, he thought, scowling, there had been no *spell*. That made it sound transcendental, or magical, when it had merely been a moment alone. One on one, for the first time in days. Which was entirely his fault, as he'd absolutely been avoiding her—but only because he wanted to say *exactly the right thing* that would get her to rescind her resignation.

Problem was, he'd yet to come up with a reason that didn't sound as if he was commanding, or demanding, or rolling over and begging. Which was utterly infuriating. He was never this unsure—ever. But he needed to get this right so that they could get back to the way things had been.

Because it had *worked. They* had worked. Yes, they pushed one another's buttons, and their working relationship was far more hot-tempered than was in any way normal. The blame for that lay squarely in both corners. As a boss, he was no peach: his standards were high and his patience thin. While Hadley was tenacious and had a famously short fuse.

Their motivations, though, were perfectly in sync. She was a true Big Think believer, and had never let him rest on his laurels, even for a second. Since he'd known her, she'd made him do better, be better, every single day.

So, why the hell did she want to give all that up? Whatever the reason, there had to be some way to lure her back. Something she wanted. Something only he could give her.

Several rather specific ideas slithered, unbidden, into his head built on memories of a million moments when their eye contact had held far longer than usual. Times in near-empty lifts when they'd stood close enough their arms had brushed, and brushed again.

As always when he had such thoughts, he acknowledged them, then pushed them aside. For he would never act on them. He had infinite wells of self-control and would empty every single one if that was what it took not to be that man. Not to be anything like his father.

The lift doors opened and, as he stepped into the garage, his phone rang. He answered without checking, growling, "Ronan Gerard."

"What the hell is this I hear about you making a play for Holt Waverly?"

Ronan pulled the phone from his ear as if burnt, and saw *Don't Answer!* in lieu of his father's name on the screen. *Damn it.* If anyone had some nefarious radar that alerted him to the extremely rare moments when Ronan might think about him, it was Constantine Gerard.

While the urge to drop his phone and crush it underfoot was strong, Ronan tapped into the self-control he was so proud of, moved his phone to his other ear and said, "I'm well, thanks. And you?"

"Don't sass me, boy," Constantine Gerard barked back, his gravelly voice sending shards of aggravation through Ronan's nerves.

It had been some years since Ronan had done a single thing

his father had told him to do, and he said not another word as he slid into his car, the soft, cream leather sinking under his bulk. The phone connected to the Bluetooth as Ronan gunned the engine and arced out of the private garage.

"How's Mum?" Ronan asked.

"She's fine," his father ground out.

She'd better be, Ronan thought.

As if the man had a clue. His parents' relationship—Constantine's simmering anger, his mother stoically taking it as payment for her comfortable life—had messed him up for a long time, until being out in the world had shown him how damaging it all was. But the scars remained.

When Ronan said nothing for long enough—sassy or otherwise—Constantine lost patience, as Constantine tended to do. "Holt Waverly is a no-go area."

That was the second reason why cultivating a relationship with cattle baron Holt Waverly appealed to Ronan: his father had famously fallen out with the man a decade before, over some land grab gone wrong, and had felt the cut of it ever since.

Ronan kept his attention on the traffic, which was heavy, and the sky above—a deep cerulean blue. "In case you hadn't realised, Big Think is not your company, and therefore its dealings are not your concern."

Ronan could all but hear his father's sneer. "Its mast bears my family name." There came a pause to let that sink in. "Waverly is a hard bastard. He'll eat you alive and you won't even know it's happening."

In direct contrast to the rising tension, Ronan gently tapped the indicator, checked his mirrors and changed lanes. "Appreciate the input, but we already have a list of people deemed unsuitable for investing in our projects, and Holt Waverly is not one of them."

His father's silence evidence the irony had not been lost on him.

For a second Ronan considered following up by telling his father about the award. But he couldn't be sure if he'd tell him to chafe the older man, or in the disturbing hope his father might actually be impressed. Old habits died hard.

Then his father scoffed, "Who put this supposed list of yours together? That girl—?"

"Don't," Ronan snapped as ice slid through his veins. "Don't even think about it." Don't even think about *her*.

Tolerance all used up, Ronan's voice was lifeless, cold, as he said, "I have an appointment. Say hi to my mother."

His father cleared his throat. "Son, that's not why I called. I—"

Ronan hung up, but not before the word "son" rattled against the sharp edges of his brain. Spying a gap in the lane over, he pressed his foot down, the acceleration shoving him back in his seat, his grip on the leather steering wheel painfully tight.

That girl.

The nerve of the man. The audacity, to dare to refer to Hadley at all. And force Ronan, in penance, to relive all that had gone down, as if it had happened days, not years, before.

It had been at a party—the first, in fact, back when his company had been little more than an idea. They hadn't even had a corporate name as yet, but word had been out that brilliant young scientist Ted Fincher, football star and Australian of the Year Sawyer Mahoney and Constantine Gerard's son were about to hit the world of philanthropy in a big way.

Ronan had used that momentum to pull together a soft launch. His father had been there, of course, along with his cronies. Which meant Ronan had spent much of the evening making sure the drinks trays discreetly avoided his father's corner of the room so that things didn't take a dark turn.

Then Ronan had seen his father make a beeline for the kitchen, just before the launch speeches were about to begin, and something, some instinct, had made him follow.

He'd imagined catching his father and reversing him back into the room so that he would witness his son's big moment, knowing that the party, the launch, was as much about that as it about anything else.

It had taken him a few seconds to note the starkly clean silver benches, the abandoned plates of food, and the fact that the space was devoid of kitchen staff, as if some dark wind had swept them from the room.

Then...sounds of a scuffle...movement. His father looming over someone trapped against a bench. And his father's voice, like gravel over a sore throat, with a level of aggression even he'd never heard before.

Which was when Ronan had seen *her*.

He'd noticed her doing the rounds earlier: one of the caterers, tall, graceful with spiky dark hair over a stridently beautiful face. But it was the cool gleam in her dark eyes, the way she'd intentionally avoided serving anyone who dared to chat her up, that had stuck with him.

Good for her, he'd thought, a big fan of autonomy, of temerity, of pushing against expectation—before adding *keep an eye on her*, her in this room full of entitled men, to his list of things to do to make sure the night ran smoothly.

And now she was pinned down in his father's arms. The part Ronan had never been able to process, even after all these years, was that for a microsecond he'd imagined it was mutual—his father being known for his bullish charm, for his tenacity, and for the women. Till her dark eyes had shifted when she'd seen him, searing him. They'd been filled with mortal panic.

Ronan's hands slipped on the steering wheel at the memory, a sheen of sweat having sprung up all over him, and he moved out of the fast lane, easing back on the accelerator.

His father was a classic bully—in the work place and at home—an absolute master of quick, cutting, emotional abuse. For Ronan, it was all he'd ever known. It had been the foundation of his childhood. But until that moment Ronan had never seen evidence of *sexual* violence.

Ronan had left his own body then; his breath had sapped from his lungs at her fury and her fear. And the shell that had protected him his whole life, protected the familial connection to his father, had snapped free. *He'd* snapped free.

A fury had filled Ronan that night, primal and painful, as he'd flown across the room and hauled his father away. The older man's arms had flailed, pots clattering, the sweep of salt and pepper hair falling messily over his eyes. Dull eyes. Rotten eyes. Eyes that had once been the exact colour of Ronan's before drink and age had seeped in.

When his father had fled, Ronan had swallowed down the bile filling his throat and faced the stranger in their midst.

Her gaze—*Hadley's* gaze—had been pure energy. And rage—as if she'd been a second away from kneeing the old man in the balls, had Ronan not intervened. She might have managed it too. And yet, for all the trauma of that moment, the family mess that had ensued, not a day had gone by when Ronan did not feel deep relief that that he'd walked into that kitchen when he had.

Slowing to a stop as the light turned amber, Ronan ran a hand over his mouth. He and Hadley did not talk about that night; at least, they hadn't for years. And yet it coloured every conversation, every disagreement, every moment they were alone.

Was it that way for her? He'd been there when it had happened. He'd witnessed her in her most vulnerable moment. Was it possible, when she looked at him, she sometimes saw his father too?

He'd asked, "Are you okay? Can I help in any way?" When he'd got nothing, "What's your name?"

She'd glared at him then, all spit and fire. "Why on earth would I tell you that? I'm done with this job, so no point trying to get me fired."

"Fired?" Ronan had reared back. "I'd never…" His father—his monster of a father—had no doubt told her exactly that, as some kind of leverage against resistance. *Hell.*

He'd placed a hand on his heart then—at least on the region where a man's heart ought to be, a non-Gerard man—and said, "I only want to help. If I am able. If you'll allow me. I'm Ronan Gerard."

"I know who you are," she'd spat. "Your photo is on every screen out there."

Ronan had winced. Right; of course: the launch. Speeches lauding his education, his ambition, his connections, were no doubt happening right then. It had all suddenly felt so self-serving, incestuous—old money calling on old money—as if he'd been swept up in the way things had always been done rather than how they could be done. It was a mistake he'd never make again.

Then she'd begun to pace, fists clenched, shoulders up around her ears, raging at the sky, making it clear she was angry at *herself* for what had happened.

Which had been enough to bring Ronan's focus back where it needed to be: on *her.*

Riding a wave of pure instinct, he decided she was tough

enough to handle difficult truths. He'd explained who his father was, how the man worked—that Constantine would find a way to blackball her, so she should be prepared.

Then Ronan had offered her whatever help she needed—a car to take her home, a glass of water, a Scotch—or to follow her in a separate car to the closest police station, where he would back up her account all the way. If she needed a recommendation for whatever job she wanted, she could count on him.

That night, she'd refused it all. Had made it clear that she didn't need or want anyone's help. That, unlike everyone else in this ivory tower, she was more than capable of looking after herself. She'd found it in her to thank him for his intervention, then she'd ripped off her apron and the ID badge on her shirt, tossed them on the bench and was gone.

Leaving Ronan shaken, sickened, emotionally spent, empty to the core…and done with Constantine Gerard.

Then the following Monday, Hadley Moreau had walked into the Richmond warehouse in which he and the boys had been renting a small space at the time.

How she'd found him, he had no idea. The guts, the daring, the determination it must have taken for her to turn up there the way she had… He'd never seen anything like it.

Ted and Sawyer had actually been in situ that day and Ronan remembered it had been almost comical—the laughter, the clatter of laptop keys and even the creak of the exposed plumbing had gone quiet at the intrusion of the lanky stranger.

"Hey," he'd said, his voice raw as Hadley had walked up to his desk, her knuckles white where she gripped the handle of her bag, highlighting the first of a range of delicate tattoos he'd learn over the years she sported—a forget-me-not string around the base of a finger.

ALLY BLAKE

49

The relief at seeing her again had given him a rush of adrenaline that had pushed him back in his chair.

Then he'd remembered himself and stood, his hands in his pockets so that she'd feel safe. "Is everything okay...?"

He'd paused; remembering her name, having seen it on her catering uniform ID, but not presuming to use it till she gave it to him willingly.

She'd nodded, chin lifted, jaw tight. Then she'd held out her hand. "Hadley. Hadley Moreau."

Ronan remembered nodding, as if her name had already been etched into his psyche. As if all roads had led to this moment. And, when he'd taken her hand in his, a spark had shot through him, spearing him, earthing him.

Change was coming.

Scratch that: it had been right there in front of him.

She'd told him she'd been listening at the party and—if it hadn't all been smoke and mirrors—she liked what she'd heard. That she needed work, after having had to leave her last job. She'd told him that she was a hard worker, a fast learner and that she took no crap. Then she'd asked what she could do to help.

And help she had, more than any one of them could have imagined. She'd fast become the glue that held them all together through the exponential growth of the company, administering billions of dollars of investment and spending and dealing with three big stubborn personalities.

Now she was leaving...for good.

Talk about change coming. It had been nipping at his heels for a while now, with Ted working from home half the time while looking after his daughter, Katie, and Sawyer away with Petra's work almost as much as he was off spreading the Big Think word.

Nipping at his heels? More like taking the legs out from under him.

If Hadley stayed, he could deal with the rest. If she left...

She *couldn't* leave: it was that simple. If he couldn't have *this one thing*, then what the hell was all of his money, honour and influence even worth?

Even as he thought the words, he knew it was discomfort talking. It felt as if the company he'd given his life to was getting away from him. He'd tied his identity to its ethos, its triumph, and, without the grip he'd had on the place from inception to prosperity, who the hell was he?

Eventually the quiet whir of the engine humming beneath him, and years of practice maintaining control over his emotions, took the edge off the unspooling thoughts that were not taking him to any place good.

The truth was, he and Hadley were now very different people from they'd been that night. They'd both worked hard to put it behind them. But, even while they never spoke of it any more, that night had stuck to them like a wound that had not quite healed.

For Ronan, it was the guilt at not having been brave enough, strong enough, to call his father out and to cut him off long before that night. And he knew Hadley had never come to terms with having had to rely on him to give her the leg up to the life she had now, even if she didn't know it herself.

Perhaps she did know it. Perhaps that was why she was leaving—because she realised didn't need him anymore. That she never had.

Ronan swallowed down the lump in his throat and zipped through traffic once more till he took the turn-off towards home.

If he was the only one still committed to Big Think with

the same ferocity with which they'd all started, then he'd simply have to go up a notch.

"Call Holt Waverly," he commanded his car display and, while the phone rang, he prepped in his mind the message he would no doubt be forced to leave when the man did not pick up.

But he would not stop trying. While things might be changing—and all too soon things might be completely un-recognisable from those early days—he was still Ronan Gerard: ambitious, steadfast and inevitable.

CHAPTER THREE

HADLEY HUMMED ALONG with the Nirvana playing in her ear buds as she entered the code to let herself into Ronan's house.

She dumped the mail she'd fished out of his letterbox by the security gate into a bowl on the hall table—mostly flyers despite the custom brass sign on the letterbox requesting otherwise. She noted in her tablet that the flower arrangement needed replacing, then headed down the wide hall, her Doc Martens clomping against the marble tile.

The first time she'd seen Ronan's house—seen the high ceilings, the vast rooms, the darkly elegant décor, the golden chandeliers and the opulent antique furniture—her eyes had nearly bugged out of her head. For she'd never imagined such luxury existed outside of movies.

And she'd seen nice houses. Between "boyfriends," her mother had cleaned houses for a while, back when Hadley had tagged along before she'd been old enough to go to school. Till her mother, desperate and broke, had been caught filling her pockets with hidden cash, and they'd been off in the car again.

That was where she'd first learned to bargain—with herself, with the universe, with any gods that might be listening. Had vowed to work herself ragged, to make smart choices, to leave behind no mess, if the universe agreed not to mess with her for fun.

Now Hadley walked through Ronan's home with ease, humming, making notes on her tablet as she went, checking Ronan's wine cellar—a light-and temperature-controlled room off his kitchen—so she could tick off the required bottles he wanted for his table at the ball. It was not a job she'd delegate, even to Kyle—not quite yet.

A flutter of anxiety kicked at her belly. There was so much information to pass on before she left—not just about the job, but about Ronan. How to support him. How to push him. How to *handle* him.

She could just leave it up to them to find their own way. Ronan might actually find relief in the absence of their niggly fights. Of the tension that crackled between them. Of her insistence on having complete autonomy in her role.

He might also miss the ease of their shorthand. Miss the way she never let him coast. Miss *her*.

Was that even possible? Anytime they'd teetered towards anything even resembling closeness, intimacy, he'd pulled back. Sent another wall crashing down between them. As if he was still trying to prove to her that he had infinite self-control. That she was safe where he was concerned.

When "safe" was never a word she'd use to describe her feelings for Ronan. She felt hungry, exasperated, enlivened, valued. He made her *feel*. Period. The song in her ears hit a cacophonous crescendo, thankfully cutting off *those* thoughts before they got their claws into her as she entered the huge kitchen, her favourite room in the house. It was far too big for a single man with a private chef, with cleverly canted skylights sending shards of buttery dusk sunlight over the creamy surfaces, the bronze fittings and wood-panelled walls.

She plucked a grape from a bowl of fresh fruit on the corner of the bench, tossed it in the air, caught it in her mouth and...

"Hadley?"

Hadley coughed as she swallowed the grape whole, the rubber of her soles screeching against the floor. Her gaze tracked the room frantically, to find Ronan standing half-in half-out of the doorway leading to the pantry.

"What are you doing here?" Hadley asked, running a hand through her messy waves and down the casual, swishy and rather short mustard-yellow dress she'd thrown on, because after this she was heading to a movie night with Adelaid and Petra, which they'd forced her to attend upon pain of death.

A beat slunk by, as if Ronan was tracking her every move, before his deep voice rolled her way. "I live here."

"Could have fooled me," she muttered. The man spent all his time these days in his apartment at Big Think Tower, like a beast holed up in its gothic castle. "Didn't you have—?" her mind went to his calendar "—an osteopathy appointment this evening?"

"I cancelled."

She pulled herself upright. He *never* cancelled. She cancelled for him. It was her job. For a few more weeks, at least.

"But your neck..." she pressed.

"I came home for a swim instead."

"Of course you did," she ground out, for she'd wasted more time than she really had sweet-±talking her way to getting a last-minute appointment with an impossible-to-land practitioner.

"Why are *you* here?" Ronan drawled, his voice low and warm from the shadows.

A sharper memory slipped through—the rich lady asking the same of her mother, the stolen cash gripped in her fist, the understanding that her mother had done something bad and, by association, so had she.

Hadley stood taller.

"It's my job," she said flatly, "To check your cleaner is

doing their job, to organise, to have your front gate serviced, to keep your cellar stocked. None of which you'd do otherwise."

"True," he said, with a slight lift of his mouth.

"For the next three weeks at least," she added, knowing it was a low blow. But she needed him...needed him to *say* something, anything that told her he realised this was for real.

Ronan came out of the pantry, shut the door with a soft snick then proceeded to move round the bench towards her. Was this it? Were they finally going to talk about this like grown-ups?

Which was when Hadley realised he was wearing nothing but a towel draped low on his hips.

Late-evening sunlight slanted through the kitchen windows, tracing his chest—golden-brown and rippling with muscle. His shoulders were broad and strong. His appendicitis scar caught the light when he breathed, slashing above one hip, the operation from before her time.

His feet were bare. One toenail was black as if he'd kicked it at some point or dropped something heavy on it. She found herself grateful for the imperfection.

He lifted a hand to his wet hair and raked it off his face. A drop of water made its way over his shoulder, over his pec, curling round a bare nipple before sliding down his abs and losing itself in the arrow of dark hair leading...

She was staring. Staring and *salivating*. Hadley lifted her gaze to his to find his dark-blue eyes glinting. And it had nothing to do with late sunlight and everything to do with the fact he'd caught her checking him out.

This was when he'd usually stiffen, sniff in a breath and look away, as if such a heated moment had never happened. Only this time he stayed, his smile growing. And Hadley felt a wave of warmth rush through her, sweeping into her cheeks and burning her thoughts to a crisp.

At which point *she* spun on her heel and walked out of the room. What the hell had that been about? And why—why now?

"Hadley," he called, only this time his voice was rich and thick, lit with the full understanding of every thought bouncing about inside her head.

She stopped and squeezed her eyes shut. She took a deep breath, steadied her features and turned. "Yep?"

"Where are you going?"

"Movies."

"I meant, why the rush?" A beat then, "You have a date?"

For a second she considered lying. She'd do it too, if it meant saving her skin. The niceties were for those who could afford it.

"I do," she said, watching his expression, the flicker in his jaw, the fist tightening at his hip. Then she added, "With Adelaid and Petra."

At which point she saw it dawn on him that she'd been messing with him. Deliberately, knowing she could.

His smile this time was different. Harder, somehow—lit with understanding and intent. He took another step her way.

She swayed a little, as if having less than five metres' distance between them while he was dressed—or undressed—like that was a dangerous thing.

What did she think might happen? That she might leap on him? Or melt into a puddle of lust? Sure, she'd managed, by the skin of her teeth sometimes, not to step over that line as yet; surely she could hold out now?

Hadley pressed her toes into her boots, held her tablet to her chest and ambled round the island bench towards him. Her eyes were on his face, not…the rest. Not that that helped. For it was that strong, beautiful, masculine, perfectly carved face that starred in her every fantasy.

She held out her tablet and showed him the page she'd brought up with the bottle of wine she'd chosen. "I was making sure you had enough. For your table, at the ball. You do."

He nodded. "Anything else I can help you with?"

So many things…such as the tickle at the back of her knees, the dryness of her mouth and the heaviness at her centre.

For a moment, a sliver of time, Hadley wondered what he might do if she said those words out loud. But, where he'd spent the past several years proving himself a safe person for her to be around, she'd spent them protecting herself emotionally. So she didn't say a thing, and with that came a jolt of soul-deep regret.

She hugged her tablet to her chest and looked him in the eye. "So, the Billion-Dollar Bachelor Auction. Great idea, right?"

A muscle in his hard jaw clutched. "Please tell me that's not what you're calling—"

"Of course not," she said, a quick grin flashing across her face. Ah, how she enjoyed goading him. Poking and prodding till she was gifted flashes of the man behind the mask. "Just between us."

"Wonderful," he murmured. "And, yes. It's a fine idea."

"Great," she said, deflating with relief. "I've tweaked it a little more. I want to encourage regular benefactors who already have access to you guys to have the ability to bid on behalf of groups who'd never be able to afford such an opportunity. To give a leg up to those who'd usually never see the chance." *People like her.*

By rights, considering where she'd come from, she ought never to have found need to set foot inside the front door, much less have an access-all-areas pass to the entire kingdom. But, after losing her catering job the night everything had gone to hell, with rent due and prospects lean, she'd seen her chance and taken it. And together they'd flourished.

Which was why she adored Big Think so very much. The piles of money, the fancy balls, the namesake tower were all set dressing: the glitter and sparkle that lured in investors so that Big Think could help as many people as humanly possible.

Something in Ronan's gaze made her wonder if he knew why she felt so motivated about this idea. If he too was thinking back to that fateful night, the dark shadow that both bound them and kept them apart.

Then he leant against the bench and his towel slipped. He caught the towel at one hip with a scrunch of a fist, but not before Hadley's breath hitched, the gasp echoing around the huge space. When his gaze snapped to hers, electricity arced between them like a living, breathing thing.

Their gazes tangled, hot and hungry. If her chest was rising and falling as deeply as his own, then a few more breaths and she might well pass out.

She was not alone in this…this purgatory. She knew his tells, and for once he was doing a terrible job of hiding them.

They were alone, in his house. On a warm, dusky evening. And he was already half-naked. What might he do if she closed the distance, placed her hand on his chest and felt the give of his warm, hard skin? How might he react if she grazed her teeth over that spot where his neck met his shoulder?

Would his chest lift beneath her hand as he dragged in a ragged breath? Would he tip his head, giving her better access? Would he tremble as his effort at keeping her at arm's length finally crumbled? Would he let go of the towel and wrap his arms about her, hauling her close?

Or would he even allow her to get that close before finding

some reason to move? Would be bring down the metaphorical wall that continually slammed into place between them?

Then Ronan said, "I do hope you're not imagining I might dress like this for your meat sale."

Hadley blinked and realised her gaze was on his flat belly, drinking the jut of his hipbone, the hunk of muscle by his clenched fist.

Her gaze shot to his, expecting to find a smirk tugging at the corner of his mouth. But instead his face appeared grim, haunted even, as his eyes slowly roved over her. He took in the kick of the short skirt halfway up her thighs. Her ankle-high Doc Martens. Her legs in between.

By the time his eyes made their way back to hers, her breath was tight in her throat. For that face—rough-hewn, dark-featured, carved by the gods—was so beautiful, so heart-breaking, so deeply private. And for a few long, heady breaths she was so filled with yearning, with want, with barely banked flames seeming to lick inside her chest. Before they shot down the backs of her thighs and back up again, till she could feel the molten flicker at her core.

Then he shut it down, hard, like a door slamming over his features. The very same door he'd used when she'd resigned and he'd not tried to stop her.

"Found what you came here for?" he asked, his voice raw, cavernous, pained.

She nodded. For she had—and so much more.

"Good," he said, then moved to walk past her. Right past her, tightly past her, considering how spacious the kitchen was.

The knuckle of his clenched hand brushed hers, a handful of skin cells barely making contact. And her senses scattered and sparked at the rare touch.

And then he was gone, padding out of the kitchen and into the house.

Somehow Hadley made it out of the front door and to her car on legs made of jelly.

She made it down his driveway and out onto the road. With distance, she felt more confused than ever. More messy, wretched, frustrated and confused, sure that in the great balance she was right and he was wrong.

About what, she wasn't as sure.

"Realising I sound like a broken record but…do we wait?"

Ronan looked up from his phone to see Sawyer straddling a chair, a hand ball twirling on the tip of his finger, his eyes looking towards the doorway of the Founders' Room.

"We wait," Ronan insisted.

Sawyer flinched dramatically. "Sheesh. And there I was, thinking perhaps you'd finally admitted to yourself that Hadley is leaving."

"She still works here. So we wait."

He'd been away the past couple of days, a last-minute trip to Sydney to meet with some long-term benefactors. The kind of trip Hadley would usually join, but he'd used it to give himself some breathing space, in the hope of coming up with a plan that didn't end up with him aching for her, in his kitchen, half-naked.

And a plan had come.

Stay: that was all he had to say. One simple word. Only, every time he thought it, it took on connotations he didn't mean. Or, more to the point, connotations he'd prefer not to highlight.

Stay…because I need you.

Stay…because I can't imagine doing this without you.

Stay…for me.

Ronan pictured her in his kitchen the other night, dressed in that floaty yellow dress with its loose V-neck, the skirt flirting with the tops of her thighs and, below, those fifties-era silk stockings she favoured with the fine vertical lines dissecting the backs of her long legs as she'd walked away.

He'd watched her for a long moment before she'd seen him, floating around his kitchen to the music in her ears, no walls up, no worries, no pretending to be anyone other than who she was. He'd let himself imagine them in another life, if they'd met some other way, with no dark history between them, and it had made his heart thunder with unspoken possibility.

Then, in the moment she'd realised he was not exactly dressed for visitors, her gaze had turned liquid-brown, her tongue darting out to touch her bottom lip as she'd looked at him as if she wanted to lick him up and down.

It had hit him—this was no crush lapping back and forth between them. It had been building from a much deeper place. It was innate, earthy, simmering for such a long time that, if let loose, it could consume them both.

And he could not allow that. For he was born of a rotten heart. For all that he'd managed to use that knowledge to forge a business that had gone against all expectations, beneath that bolshie, tough exterior Hadley was far too precious, too hopeful, for the likes of him.

"Got it," said Sawyer, snapping Ronan back to the present.

Sawyer gave a double thumbs-up, then moved to lie back on his couch, lift his damaged leg to the arm rest, and put a cushion over his eyes.

While Ted frowned at Ronan as if something had just occurred to him.

"Problem?" Ronan asked.

Ted said, "Anyone had any luck getting her to change her mind?"

Sawyer shifted the cushion just enough to see over the top.

Ted went on, "Because I can't imagine a non-AI, actual living human being who would be able to do what she does." Then, belatedly, "For you."

"Without being reduced to a quivering puddle in the corner," Sawyer added helpfully.

"Exactly," said Ted. "It's as if the two of you were made for one another."

At that, Sawyer coughed out a laugh; Ted's non sequitur clearly tickled him greatly.

"And," said Ted, warming up now, "Have we ascertained *why* Hadley is leaving?"

"Not as such," Ronan admitted.

"There was that night, years back. The broom closet…?" Ted looked at Ronan as if he was something interesting he'd just found in a Petri dish. "Or was it a cloak room?"

"You're right," said Ronan, shifting on his seat. "Let's get on with the meeting."

But Ted's focus was honed now. "In the past you've tried to convince me I am mixing up my memories which, granted, has been known to happen—nerd brain. But I can *almost* swear I saw the two of you a few years back, at the first Big Think Ball, coming out of a cloak room together—or was it a broom closet?—looking…"

The room held its collective breath, till Ted said, "Dishevelled."

"How much coffee did you drink this morning?" Sawyer asked Ted as he pulled himself up to sit, shooting a glance at Ronan which told him Sawyer knew way too much. "Not sure I've ever heard you say this many words in one sitting that didn't have 'genus' and 'family' involved—"

"It was the cloak room," said Ronan. And Ted and Sawyer turned to stone. Ronan sat forward slowly, till all the air in the room built with such pressure it felt as if they were in a balloon fit to burst, then said, "But nothing happened."

"But…" said Ted, like a dog with a bone, or a scientist with the sniff of evidence in his nose.

Ronan held up a hand. "You do remember how Hadley and I met?"

With Hadley's permission, Ronan had filled them in on the bare bones about that first day. He'd assured her they would be discreet, but also determined that as his business partners they deserved the whole story before taking on an unknown.

Ted nodded.

"Then you understand why nothing happened in the cloak room. Or any other time. Nothing untoward has ever happened between Hadley and me. *Ever*."

Ted nodded again. But then his nostrils flared and he held out both hands in front of him, as if about to explain some complicated chemical equation. "I understand what you're saying. But I can't see the correlation. And it's just… I love you guys and want you to be happy. And I wonder if something happening in a cloak room is what you both need in order to be happy."

Ronan rubbed a hand over his jaw, wondering how the hell he'd ended up in the middle of this particular conversation.

"I can't…" he said, then stopped. "We can't…" Nope, that wasn't it. "What if leaving is what Hadley needs in order to be happy?"

And that was the kicker. The one great stumbling block that had kept the word locked in the back of his throat.

Ted's mouth opened, then closed, his shoulders slumping, defeated. While Sawyer gave Ronan an understanding half-smile. At which point Ronan grabbed his phone and pretended to be wholly engrossed in its contents. All the while, his mind tripped back in time and place to a certain cloak room.

It had been the first Big Think Ball. They'd all been on a high at how well it was going. The money had been coming at them thick and fast, meaning their first big project, Ted's pet project, would be funded for the next decade and they'd have more to spare for further projects.

He remembered the laughter in Hadley's eyes, the wide stretch of her lush mouth, as she'd dragged him into the cloak room so that they could avoid a particularly boorish bene-factor who'd been trying to convince the two of them to join his wife and him for "a little swing session" once the ball was done and dusted.

When suddenly, enclosed in the darkness, their breaths loud, their laughter ricocheting off the close walls, they'd realised how close they were. And how alone.

In the dark, all his other senses had felt heightened. Her body heat had been just within reach, the taste of her per-fume on the back of his tongue.

Then either he'd moved, or she had. Likely both—drawn together by that nameless, sightless, irresistible impulse they'd managed to keep locked away in the light of day. His hands had unerringly found her waist. Hers had slid up the back of his neck before sinking into his hair.

Then he'd felt the tremble in her fingers, felt a frisson of vulnerability, and it had taken him back to the moment they'd first met. When he'd found her in a hotel kitchen, his father's rough hands on her, her lovely face contorted in fear.

And he'd pulled away from her as if burned. One moment his desire for her had been a living, breathing thing—beck-oning, calling, screaming at him to take his damn shot with the woman who filled his head day in, day out. The same woman who was pressed up against him, clinging to him, sighing for him.

The next, he'd felt drenched in shame.

It was then he'd finally had to admit, if only to himself, that his attraction to her was real. That it existed outside their first meeting, outside the work they achieved together, and lived within him every damn day.

It was also then that he'd promised himself that he would never act on it—never. For he'd never forgive himself if he took advantage, in any way, of the situation in which they'd found themselves. The one thing that truly separated him from his father was his complete self-control.

Now, it was as if her leaving had torn something open inside him—some place in which he'd buried every feeling, every rush of attraction and every *"what if?"* until every waking moment had been consumed with such feelings, such longing, he'd have had to leave the state in order to feel some relief.

Was *that* why she was leaving? Had she worked out, before he had, that distance would be the only answer?

Hadley. *Hadley, Hadley, Hadley.* Maybe she was right. If he didn't hear her name in his ears, taste her scent on the back of his tongue, see her face every time he looked up from his desk, maybe he could get over it. Over her.

Over it all.

He glanced up to see Ted and Sawyer in deep, whispered conversation. And, despite himself, he listened in.

"He's clearly *not* happy," said Ted. "He seems miserable. Has done for months."

"He's okay," said Sawyer. "A lot is going on, that's all. He'll figure it out."

"But we could do something about it," said Ted, his stage whispers getting louder now. "Adelaid thinks he's one eye-twitch away from turning to ash. She has friends. She could set him up."

Sawyer seemed to consider this. "You might be onto something. I wasn't kidding the other day—the love of a good woman would do him no end of good."

When Ronan's glare felt so hot it was in danger of burning the insides of his eye sockets, he rubbed both hands over his face and let loose. "I can get my own women, or woman, if and when I so desire. What I need right now is a proficient assistant who's not intent on selling me off like I'm a hunk of meat, and who can do the damn job without arguing about every little damn thing!"

At which point, Hadley stepped into the Founders' Room and froze. Her eyes were wide. Her lush mouth was pulled tight. Her dark hair was gloriously mussed—*dishevelled*, even—sending Ronan's synapses into a mass of sparks and blinding light.

Then a slickly dressed young man moved in behind her, lifting his hand in a sharp wave. "Hi," he said, expression unfazed despite the tension rippling through the room.

"Hi…?" said Sawyer, a small smile on his face, the only one of the group who thrived amidst chaos.

"Sawyer Mahoney, Ted Fincher, Ronan Gerard…" said the younger man, pointing each of them out. "It's an honour."

"And you are…?" Sawyer asked.

"Jonas St Clair," said the young man, before sweeping his hand across the sky and saying, "Aka, *The New Hadley*."

Hadley, colour high on her cheeks, chest rising and falling while she looked at Ronan as if she'd like to flay him where he sat, said, "Looks like you just got your wish."

Hadley sat knock-kneed on a pale-pink velvet ottoman in the middle of the ladies' bathroom on the twentieth floor of

Big Think, her teeth wrapped around her thumbnail as she tore it to shreds.

So many emotions roiled through her, she struggled to pin down which to deal with first. Embarrassment at Jonas's first impression of Ronan, no doubt having heard his declaration just before they'd walked into the room. Hurt from the words themselves. And the ache of knowing that Ronan didn't mean them, and had clearly been lashing out because it was finally hitting him that she was leaving, for real.

In the car, on the way to the movies after the altercation in Ronan's kitchen, she'd called Emerson Adler—the founder of the Pitch Perfect employment agency and asked if she had any leads as to her replacement.

Turned out Emerson had been just about to call. While she knew any number of brilliant candidates, she'd been struggling to find one with just the right skill set to take on Ronan Gerard. She'd admitted she'd been beginning to wonder if he might be her white whale, till she'd hit on Jonas St Clair.

The next day, after discovering Ronan had gone to Sydney without her, without even telling her he was going, Hadley had instantly set up a lunch meeting with the mysterious Jonas at a café off Collins Street.

"Ms Moreau?"

Hadley had looked up to find a guy in his late twenties dressed in a sharp suit with a lavender tie and matching pocket square. On his feet, he wore spats.

"Hadley, please," she'd said, lifting off her chair to offer her hand.

"Jonas St Clair," he'd offered.

His handshake had been perfect—strong, but not a power move. Ronan would like that.

"And may I say, before I am forced to slip into professional mode, you are a vision of sartorial splendour." Jonas blew a chef's kiss then let his hands drop, as if swiping the moment away.

Hadley had laughed, liking him instantly, and not only because he'd liked her outfit. She liked his gumption. He instantly came across as sharp, bolshie, forward, focussed and unafraid. A frisson of destiny had come over her.

Two affogatos and a spate of stories about his mean, rich old grandmother later, she'd offered him a one-week trial on the spot.

"Hadley?"

Hadley looked towards the door of the bathroom. "Mm-hmm?"

The door bumped before opening a smidge, and Jonas's face sneaked into the gap. "Are you decent?"

"I try."

Jonas opened the door a little more. "I've been around enough money people in my life to not be surprised by anything. Is it okay if I come in?"

"Sure," she said.

Jonas sat on the edge of the ottoman, leaving a perfectly respectful amount of space. "So, that was a heck of an introduction."

Hadley deflated. "I should have warned you that you might not be welcomed with confetti and home-made cake. My leaving has not yet quite sunk in with the powers that be."

"By that you mean Ronan?"

Hadley nodded.

"Making me even more sure I'll have big shoes to fill."

"So, you're not coming here to say 'thanks but no thanks'?"

"I'm the middle child of five kids with filthy-rich parents, both of whom are completely self-obsessed. Messieurs Mahoney, Finch and Gerard? I can cope with their whims and vagaries because that's my normal. And will, for the chance to work here." Jonas glanced around, taking in the décor and the elegant fittings. "For as long as I get the chance."

Hadley knew exactly how he felt.

She reached out, squeezed his arm then used it to pull herself to stand up.

For all that Hadley had felt overwhelmed with how much information she'd have to impart to her replacement, in that moment she realised there'd never be enough time to tell him everything. So she told him the big stuff.

"Don't pander, ever. Be yourself. Push back if you disagree—they'll cope. And never forget where you are. This place…what we do here…it's beyond special. More than you can even imagine."

"Done," Jonas said. Then pressed himself up to stand too. "And, if I feel the need to hide or kick something, I now know the place to go."

CHAPTER FOUR

AFTER THE MEETING was done—the three partners some-how having achieved less than before they'd started—Ronan headed straight to his private office, preparing to lock him-self away and make decisions that would change the world, on his own if he had to.

Yet he couldn't settle. Every part of him felt twisted in the wrong direction as he tried to unpick how everything had gone so very wrong.

Learning Sawyer had clearly been onto him, and for some time, had been a jolt. But Ted? Ted who rarely saw anything past the edge of his glasses unless it lived in his house or wriggled under a microscope? So much for keeping his con-flicted feelings for Hadley under wraps.

Then there was Hadley herself. Two solid days apart and he'd been itching to see her, to hear her voice. So much so, it had taken everything he had not to call in on his way back from the airport to hash things out, once and for all.

Only the fact that he couldn't imagine her opening her front door and him not wanting to pull her into his arms and kiss her had sent him to his apartment at Big Think to lose himself in work instead.

The look in her eyes when she'd walked into the Found-ers' Room as his words had reverberated around the small space, the hurt: he could still feel it like a fist lodged between his ribs.

He was losing control more and more, when control was his base state, his foundation. This wavering was proving difficult to accept.

Thoughts roiling, pulse beating hard in the side of his neck, Ronan started at the disruptive knock on his office door. His *closed* office door that he usually left open so that he could see Hadley at her desk.

The knock came again—succinct, but resolute.

Hadley.

He breathed out hard, swiped a hand down his tie, rolled his neck and said, "Enter." And found himself sitting up straighter, bracing, as ever, against all that she was.

A swift swish of the door, and in she came, looking heartbreakingly beautiful in a loose white shirt tucked into high-waisted cream trousers. Her usual sharp silhouette seemed to soften more each day, as if she was unhitching herself from some character she'd been playing at Big Think and morphing into her true self.

She was also looking at anywhere but him as she walked up to his desk, as if she too was braced against all that he was.

Ronan sat forward, hands steepling on his desk, conciliatory, not combative.

Her gaze finally found his. She was fire and ice, heat and hurt, and concern for him. As if she knew his outburst had been the result of the fact that he was struggling too.

Then with a soft laugh, more of an exhausted outshot of breath, Hadley looked up at the ceiling and said a silent prayer to whatever gods might be listening. Then she looked back at Ronan and demanded, "Be nice."

Ronan opened his mouth to ask why.

But then she shouted, "Jonas! Get in here."

And in wandered the young man in the sharp suit. With his neat hair, manicured nails, good posture and confidence to spare, he took a quick sweep of the room, as if memorising everything he saw, before he moved to stand next to Hadley.

"Since we didn't get the chance for a formal introduction…" said Hadley, alluding to the fact Ronan had ordered the room cleared of non-essentials while they'd spoken of private matters, which had resulted in Hadley taking Jonas by the elbow and dragging him from the room a minute after they'd entered. "Ronan Gerard, this is Jonas St Clair."

"St Clair," said Ronan, his voice low.

"Pleasure to meet you, Mr Gerard," said Jonas, holding eye contact. Then, moving a step towards Ronan's lounge, looking at the bookshelves and artwork, he asked, "I assume that's a real Renoir."

"It is."

"My grandmother has claim on a couple. Though I'm certain at least one is a print she had framed after a show at the Met."

Ronan, surprised to find himself surprised, sat back in his chair and said, "St Clair—as in the shipping St Clairs?"

"That's us," said Jonas, swinging a charmed smile Ronan's way, alert, and deliberate. The kind that came with privilege, ease and a healthy dose of knowing it. The kind of smile Ronan had seen in the mirror his whole life.

Ronan's gaze slammed back to Hadley, to find her watching him, a small smile on her face. Her eyebrow lifted, a shoulder with it. Almost as soon as they'd started working together, they'd developed their own language, a kind of shorthand that went beyond words.

He'd miss that.

Refusing to let that thought move to its natural conclusion—that he would miss her—he forced his mind to settle.

This was his moment. His chance to put his foot down and stake his claim. But the mess of a conversation he'd had with Sawyer and Ted, in which *he'd* proposed that leaving Big Think might make Hadley happy, had made him realise what had been stopping him from stopping her from going.

Whatever Hadley wanted, he wanted for her, even if that meant saying goodbye.

As for Big Think, on that score at least, he had the final say. He could be a total arse and tell St Clair to get the hell out. That he would choose his own assistant, thank you very much. But Hadley would never have brought him here unless she was sure.

She knew she'd found her replacement. Not a new her, but a new *him*. Meaning this wasn't some game she was playing. This was *really* real.

Feeling himself spiralling, Ronan ground his feet into his shoes, pulled his burdens tight around him like armour, then pressed himself out of his chair and slowly made his way round the desk till he stood before this Jonas St Clair person. St Clair was, he noted, a good two inches shorter than his own six feet three inches—which he liked. He held out a hand.

Jonas kept eye contact, smiled and shook. It was steady, sturdy, strong, and then done. *Damn it*; it was the perfect handshake.

"Jonas," said Ronan, feeling at least one of the wide-open locks tumbling about inside him click back into place. "Welcome to Big Think."

Hadley's sigh was subtle. And, if Ronan wasn't mistaken, held the slightest hint of a shake, as if she too knew how real this had now become.

"Give me half an hour to show him around," said Hadley. "Give him the tour. Introduce him to as many people as he can handle."

Jonas, hands in suit pockets, smiled as if he had no limits.

"After which I'll pass him over to HR," Hadley went on. "Then I'm all yours for the rest of the day. Okay?"

"Okay," said Ronan, then leaned back against his desk as Hadley led Jonas out of the room.

Leaving Ronan attempting to get any work done with Hadley's voice saying *all yours* swirling around inside his head.

Hadley felt a sense of lightness she'd not felt in a long time, if ever. As if she'd swallowed helium or walked through a cloud of nitrous oxide.

It was partly due to Jonas and how well he already fitted in. Partly due to the fact that Ronan had accepted Jonas with such grace. But mostly due to the fact that she and Ronan were no longer circling one another like feral cats.

She'd left Jonas with Kyle, who was as anxious to make a good impression on Jonas as he was excited to have a new play mate. Then she'd headed back to Ronan's office to find him on the couch in front of his gargantuan bookshelves, feet up on the coffee table, talking to someone on the phone.

He beckoned her in with a finger and waggled the same finger at the other couch. She sat where she'd been sent, dumped her tablet on the couch beside her and then, after a moment, kicked off her towering cream heels and put up her feet too.

Ronan stopped mid-sentence, gaze locked onto the sight of her wriggling toes and bare feet rocking back and forth. Then with a glance her way he shucked off his own shoes and put his socked feet beside hers, then went on with his conversation.

Hadley laughed, and felt lighter still. For this was far closer to the normal Hadley and Ronan than all the dreadfulness of the past few weeks: multi-tasking, manically productive, and intuitively making space for one another.

Though, rather than pull out her tablet and get work done till he was ready, Hadley took the rare chance to catch her breath. She slipped a little lower in the chair, let her head fall back against the headrest and closed her eyes. She let the smooth tones of Ronan's voice wash over her as he talked through a possible investment with one of their finances guys in a lab he'd toured whilst in Sydney.

When Ronan rang off with his usual, "Later," Hadley opened her eyes.

"You all right over there?" Ronan asked, the tip of the phone resting on his chin, his dark-blue eyes on her.

Having given into the light-headed lethargy that had come over her, she gave him a slow smile and said, "Yep."

Ronan's gaze darkened a fraction more as he let his phone drop to the couch. "Nothing you need? A cup of tea? A biscuit? A blanket?"

"Nope."

Ronan nodded. Then he breathed out hard through his nose, his gaze tangling with hers, a slight and very welcome smile lifting the corners of his mouth. "Where's Tweedledee?"

Tweedle...? Ah. The Big Think Ball the year before had been a Mad Hatter's Tea Party theme. Drowning their guests in wistfulness and whimsy made for higher donations, she'd found.

She tilted her head to see round her feet. "By that you mean...?"

"St Clair."

"Right. And Tweedledum would be...?"

"Kyle."

"And who am I in this scenario?"

"You're Alice, of course. Soon to be heading back through the looking glass."

Hadley's heart gave a little squeeze at how true that was. But she found a smile and said, "Does that make you the Queen of Hearts?"

"I think we've pushed this analogy far enough," he said, then tapped her foot with one of his.

"Fair enough," she said, tapping his foot back.

Only when her foot rocked away, his followed so that they sat, feet touching, with the room quiet, the heightened animosity and awful tension that had swirled around them the past weeks disappearing like mist in sunshine.

Then his foot started to rub against hers. Infinitesimally, but enough that there was no denying what he was doing. And she let him. Because it just felt so damn good not to be fighting or hiding. Just to be with him, this man who'd filled up so much of her life that she honestly couldn't picture what that life might look like once she'd left.

The thought of a week, a month, more, without seeing his face or hearing his voice, doing what they did so well, was suddenly so big a thing to face, she curled her toes to rub back against his. Friction, sweet and sensuous, sent sparks shooting up her leg till she felt as if her insides were filled with Christmas firecrackers.

Then Ronan's mobile rang, buzzing on the couch beside him. Which meant it was likely family, if they had that kind of access, as most calls went through her office. But he didn't even glance down.

Instead, he shook his head, once, twice, then smiled across the table as he blew out a hard, sharp, telling breath. A blatant acknowledgement, his first *ever*, that he was feeling what she was feeling. That there was something there between them.

Emotion clogged the back of Hadley's throat, and the backs

of her eyes began to burn. For, while she'd *yearned* for such a moment, a sign that she wasn't imagining this mutual spark the way her mother so often had, she was just so relieved that they were actually talking again that she was terrified of screwing it up.

Hadley slowly pulled her foot away and dropped it to the floor. Then, with a tremble in her hands, she grabbed her shoes and shucked them back onto her feet.

"Get that call," she said, shooting him a quick glance to find him watching her, his gaze lit with understanding, with unchecked heat. *Oh, mercy.* "Then give me ten minutes to grab the proofs from the photo shoot, and the December projections, then I'll bring them back for your approval. Deal?"

He winced. He hated monthly projections. He thought them a waste of time, when his plan was always to exceed them. But she hoped it might help her get the proofs from the photo shoot past him. She'd heard from Adelaid's friend, Georgette, who worked in PR for Big Think, that Ronan had baulked at having to sit on a hay bale as opposed to being behind a desk, looking all Master of the Universe chic, which was how his shoots usually went down. But Hadley was certain she was onto something special with this one, so he'd have to deal with it.

He gave her a short nod, then reached for his phone and took the call.

"Ronan Gerard," he said as she walked the ocean of space towards the door of his office.

She felt his eyes on her the entire time, those warm, glinting yearning eyes, and it was a miracle her knees didn't give way.

"Shall I get cracking, then?" Jonas asked from his spot in the doorway of the Founders' Room. And, for all that Ronan had taken a liking to the kid, there was no denying the lingering sense of resentment that his presence meant Hadley's absence.

Right when they seemed to have found their way back to something close to normal, Jonas was stepping more fully into her role.

Ronan waved him away.

"Bright, that one," said Ted once Jonas had left. Then he dropped to his hands and knees to look for one of Sawyer's hand balls he'd tried to juggle in the middle of the meeting. Sawyer was in New York with Petra and his younger sister Daisy—something to do with art.

"He's no Hadley," Ronan grumbled. Then, hearing the pang of hunger in his voice, he pulled himself up. Since the truce they'd broached in his office, a meeting of feet in lieu of a handshake, he'd felt as if a hole had opened up inside him that he couldn't fill—not with food, not with work, not with grumbling at his co-workers.

"Unflappable," Ted added, now packing away the electronic gadgets he'd been mucking about with—something to do with new remote medical-treatment tech one of his teams was close to testing. "The fact he knew about competing tech in Germany—he might have saved us months and millions."

Ronan grunted his agreement and wondered where Hadley was. What she was doing. When he'd see her again.

His phone buzzed on the desk, snapping him out of the fog. A glance at it showed it was his mother calling.

He called her once a week, on a Monday when his father was at work, listening hard to her tone to see if maybe this was the week she'd had enough. If this was the week she'd finally hardened her heart to the man who'd terrorised them both throughout Ronan's childhood. Though, it had never seemed as if she saw it that way—for she clearly loved the man, accepting that her husband worked hard, needed to let off steam, and Ronan should be so lucky to have had the opportunities he'd had.

But she never called him. Not since he'd cut off his father. Bar the one time, after Big Think had taken off, when his father had used *her* to try to get Ronan to attend some event that would bring him caché.

It was no wonder he'd hardened his own heart enough for the both of them. If that was what love was, then he wanted nothing of it. Best to encase his heart in lead and leave the thing to petrify. Trusting in his head, and his gut, had served him well.

Till Hadley Moreau had waltzed into his tiny office in Richmond, so dauntless, so game, and he'd felt his heart smack against its constraints. Restraints he'd kept very much in place ever since. For, if his mother taught him anything, it was that his heart was the very last organ he should ever trust.

Ronan glanced at his phone again, and considered letting it go to voice mail, but could not. Just in case this was the day.

"Mother," Ronan said, running a hand over his forehead.

At that, Ted, who adored his own mum, looked up and gave Ronan an encouraging thumbs-up. Then he pointed to the door, in case Ronan wanted privacy.

Ronan shook his head. He'd make it quick. "All okay with you?"

There was a pause, then, "Of course, darling. Fit as a fiddle. It's about your father."

"What about him?" Ronan asked, his voice tight, gruff. "What has he done now?"

"Don't be like that, darling. I know the two of you do not see eye to eye, but some things are more important than silly old grudges."

Ready to spell out any number of "silly old grudges" he

was happy to hold onto, he stopped when he heard a hitch in her breath. A hitch that clanged through Ronan as if his spine was a series of bells. Adrenaline spiked. His palms sweated the way they had as a kid when his father had come home from work asking for a Scotch.

"Mum, what's wrong?"

Ronan felt Ted move in closer, pulling a chair up beside him, quietly being there.

"I'm sorry," his mother said. "Sorry to be the one to tell you, but your father… He said he's been trying to talk to you, but you're so busy. And you're both so very stubborn. Your father is sick. Very sick, in fact. It's cancer. Darling, your father is dying."

CHAPTER FIVE

AFTER A RATHER fabulous morning during which Hadley had let Jonas run a brilliantly successful meeting between herself, Kyle and Georgette, as they finalised the winners from the Yellow Brick Road photo shoot, Hadley decided to check in on Ronan.

Enough time had passed since the footsie incident that, knowing their history, they could happily pretend it had never happened. Not that she'd forgotten a single part of it; not the relaxed way he'd shucked off a shoe, the rub of his foot against hers, nor the seductive smile. She might well dine out on that for quite some time.

Whistling as she walked—a little *Somewhere Over the Rainbow*—Hadley sashayed into Ronan's office with a quick rap on his open door. To find Ronan's chair turned towards the wall of windows behind his desk.

"Gerard," she said. "Question." When he didn't turn, she called, "Ronan?"

His chair squeaked, as if he'd only just heard her. Then his chair slowly turned.

Her stride faltered and her heart tripped and stumbled when she saw the look on his face. The hunch in his shoulders. The rock-hard set of his jaw. The redness around his eyes.

"What… What's wrong?" she asked, slowing.

Was it Sawyer? Ted? Ted's baby? Was it Big Think? Was it him? Was he…?

She was disaster planning, something her mother had been all too good at—figuring her way mentally through every possible terrible outcome so that she might be prepared. Hadley used to think that was simply what a person needed to do to survive. *What happens if I screw up? Have I saved enough money? Can this company truly be for real, or will it turn out to be some front and I'll have to be ready to disappear at a moment's notice?*

Time, the comfort of a decent wage, workplace respect and Ronan proving time and again that he had her back had helped Hadley realise that—for the lucky ones—it didn't have to be that way.

But now, seeing Ronan so distraught made her want to barricade the door then go to him, drop to her knees, take his hands in hers and kiss his knuckles till he felt ready to tell her what had happened.

But that wasn't her role here. A foot rub did not change that.

"Ronan," she said, and this time her voice was cool. *She* was cool. She could face anything. "Tell me what happened."

Then he blinked at her, *saw* her, and something in his face seemed to soften, just knowing she was there. And whatever thoughts she'd had about being *cool* fled in an instant.

Screw it, she thought, and before she even felt her feet moving Hadley went to him, She dropped into a crouch by his chair, taking him by the hand said, "Ronan, you're scaring me. Talk to me. Please."

"It's my father," he said, his voice like razor blades over ice.

And Hadley flinched—literally—her body reacting physically to his quiet declaration.

What the hell had Constantine Gerard gone and done now? Embezzled? Sure. Have a secret family on the side? She wouldn't put it past him. Arrested for sexual harassment...or worse? God, she hoped not.

She turned his hand over in hers and ran her fingers down his palm in a way that used to keep her mother calm any time they'd lost yet another place to live.

Flashes of relief, then craving, then self-reproach flashed across Ronan's eyes—as if whatever had happened had stripped him of his ability to hide behind those beautiful, dark guarded eyes.

And while that hunger, and that rare showing of vulnerability, did things to her—warm, slippery, effusive things—she put them aside, compartmentalising. Another long-learned survival mechanism.

"Why are you leaving me?" he asked. But she knew he was deflecting—a survival mechanism of his own.

"Tell me about your father," she said.

"I can't."

"Why? Because of what happened all those years ago?" She shook her head. Old news. It had nothing to do with them, or with why she was leaving, if that's what was worrying him.

He swallowed. It was! It *was* worrying him—partially, at least. Because she'd given him no other reason, he'd gripped onto the big, bad one he'd yet to truly face. No wonder he'd been so elusive, so hard to read. If anyone would make Ronan lock down, as if the world was at DEFCON 1, it was his father.

"Families are complicated," Hadley said, her ankles starting to burn. She was wearing the wrong shoes for this. She pulled herself up to stand and let go of his hand, his fingers slipping through hers, leaving sparks in their wake. Then, knees a little wobbly now, she sat against the edge of his desk.

"I could have written my mother off a hundred times—the choices she made, the mistakes, the men she put her faith in to save her from herself…"

Hadley shook her head, wondering where on earth she as going with this. But the way Ronan looked at her, drinking in her words as if they were an elixir and he a man dying of thirst, meant she had no choice but to go on.

"Did *I* make the right choice, indulging her? Not putting my foot down? I'll never know. What I do know is that I was not responsible for her behaviour. She was the grown-up."

She kicked the edge of Ronan's chair. "Your father, his actions, were all locked in long before you came along. You are not, and never have been, responsible for his actions. Or for taking up the slack in the world by being right all the time. We do the best we can with the tools we have at the time. It's all we can do."

When she finally came to a stop, her words rang between them, echoing around the large space. She felt a lightness in her chest, a kind of giving, and a release, for some of those revelations had been new to her.

Ronan stared at her, as if struggling to believe that her thoughts on the matter could be true. He was struggling to see a world in which he was not striving, reaching, pushing to do better. To make up for the fact that Constantine Gerard was such an awful man.

"What's happened with your dad?"

Ronan rubbed a hand up the back of his neck, then, he gazed at her mouth, then her neck, then her eyes, then looked away and said, "My mother called this morning. He's dying."

Conflicting feelings rushed through her, and she gripped the edge of the desk. "Dying how?"

"Cancer. Stage four. Melanoma—spread to the lymph nodes. Liver. Brain."

"Oh," she whispered, imaging brutish, bullish Constantine Gerard succumbing to the ravages that must be going on in his body right now. And finding herself unmoved. Because she was a terrible person, with not an ounce of forgiveness in her body? Or because all the empathy she had was being given to the man's son?

"I'm sorry." Ronan sniffed lifting himself higher in the chair so that he was upright. Shoulders back, he shook off the doldrums. "You don't want to hear this."

"Yes, I do."

"But…" He stopped. His gaze was even more wretched, the conversation heading danger close to touching on how they'd met. As if he'd borne the weight of it all this time. Which he had, because she'd let him.

She couldn't let him do so any more. Not alone. It was long past time they talked it out.

"What happened to me that night," she said, "was awful. Humiliating. Scary. Your father had been trying it on for hours—whispers as I passed, hands reaching for me. I told him to stop. Made it perfectly clear. Yet it only escalated until he followed me into the kitchen, and demanded the others leave or he'd have them all fired on the spot."

She'd started out feeling certain that this was the right thing to do, but now her chest began to tighten as she forced herself to remember.

"Hadley…" Ronan said. Was he begging her to stop? No. His tone was different from any she'd heard before. As if he needed to hear it, to face it, to accept it. As if only then might he be able to move on.

"I faced him," she said, looking out of the huge windows of Ronan's office, Melbourne in all its gothic beauty displayed below. "Feet braced, like one of my mother's better boyfriends had taught me, thumbs untucked in case I had to take a swing." A swing! At Constantine Gerard. "But he had me against the bench before I could even raise my hand."

A shift rent the air as Ronan lifted himself from his chair slowly, taking care not to startle her. Then he moved to sit against the desk beside her, giving her space, but also putting himself in an equal position.

Of which she was glad because, now she'd started, it seemed she couldn't stop.

"His breath was hot against my face, his eyes wild, inhuman. And then he was gone… And you were there."

Hadley breathed out hard and looked sideways.

But Ronan was looking out of the window now, his own hands gripping the edge of the desk. There was no sense of heroism in his expression. No, "you're welcome" in his posture.

"I'm so sorry," she said, remembering how the conversation had started. "Your father is dying and I chose this moment to—"

"I wanted to hit him so badly," Ronan said. "My fist was clenched, ready. I remember feeling so angry, I was surprised my skin wasn't tinged green. But then I saw the fear in his face, and felt my own fear reflected back at me. Terror was his move, not mine. So, I did the worst I could do, on my terms. I washed my hands of him. Told him I was no longer his son. Told him if he ever came near you, or if I even heard a *whisper* of him touching another woman against her will, I'd go to the press. I'd write a book. I'd tell the world every detail."

Hadley breathed out, knowing his truth as well as if it was her own. "Hell of a bluff," she said. "Though you'd never have gone through with it, in case it hurt me."

At that, Ronan turned to face her, only now he looked calm. As if he'd weathered the worst of the storm. And his eyebrows flickered north in agreement.

"Did we do the right thing that night, letting him go?" Hadley asked.

Ronan glanced at her mouth, then back to her eyes before repeating her own words back at her. "We do the best we can with the tools we have at the time. It's all we can do."

And Hadley could not remember a moment when she had loved the man more: his empathy, his strength, his determination to carry the weight of the world. He was such a good man, made more so by the fact he had no clue just how good he was.

Considering how combative they'd been of late, she couldn't be sure things had truly settled. She might not get the chance to be this close to the man again. So she took her fill of him, counting his lashes, the whirls in his thick, dark, mussed hair, the shades of blue in his dreamy eyes and the rises and valleys in his beautiful face.

"Can I do anything?" she asked. "Anything to help?"

Ronan's gaze, which had been searching her face as she'd been searching his, as if they were both too raw to hold back, tipped back to hers. Then a sad smile tugged at one side of his mouth. "This is helping."

She nodded. "It's okay to feel all kinds of things right now—conflicted, sadness, remorse. The wish that he might have been a different kind of man."

All feelings she'd had to reconcile when her own mother had passed away.

"Okay?" she said.

And he nodded. Then his hand moved, his little finger nudging hers in a show of solidarity.

An electric shock skipped up her arm, landing in her chest, making her gasp. It was like the firecrackers and the foot rubs, only a hundred times more. By the flare of his nostrils, the jerk of his arm, it was clear he'd felt it too.

In the past this was where one or the other of them would have made the smart choice and moved, deflecting with a joke or a grouchy demand. This time, the only movement came from Ronan's finger hooking over hers.

Desire flooded through her like a waterfall after a snow melt. When Ronan's gaze lifted to hers, a hot, hard blue, she couldn't have looked away, not even if the city outside the window had burst into flames.

"Hadley," Ronan said, his voice rough, her name a lament. His face was still ravaged by his recent news, but his eyes… They were lit with yearning, with heartache, with desire. For her.

There was no wall in place. No pretending this wasn't happening. There was just Ronan.

And, before she knew it, Hadley found herself leaning in towards him.

Or maybe he leaned in towards her.

Slowly, incrementally, the distance disappeared, as if both were caught in some magnetic vortex, spinning inevitably into the space between.

Only to come to an inevitable halt, noses almost touching, breaths intermingling. The inimitable force of mutual desire held them close, the poles of their shared history still pushing hard to keep them apart.

Hadley's heart beat madly against her ribs and, like a disoriented bird fluttering against a window, her chest rose and fell so fast she began to feel light-headed.

Kiss the man! a voice cried in the back of her head. *You're leaving soon. Don't spend the rest of your life not knowing.*

When she lifted her eyes to his, he was watching her, his gaze warm and wild with want. And, unlike their near miss in the cloak room all those years ago, with the safety of the darkness enveloping them like a shroud, the wall of windows lit them up with sharp, summery sunlight.

Ronan lifted his other hand and used it to push her hair from her cheek. Then he moved in just a fraction, his cheek now brushing so close to hers, her eyes fluttered closed. She could feel his warmth, the prickle of his stubble, the sweep of his lips against her cheekbone.

She breathed him in deeply and felt him do the same to her. Her world all breath and warmth, and the burn of anticipation.

Fully clothed, leaning on an office desk, in the bright light of day and not even kissing—it was the single most erotic moment of her entire life.

Which suddenly made her want to cry.

What was she *thinking*? Her feverish brain managed to remind her he'd just learned his father was dying. She might as well have plied him with a bottle of tequila, for all that he was in a state to make sane decisions. She would not, could not, take advantage.

Hadley ducked her head.

Ronan groaned, as if in mortal pain.

"You're dealing with the most awful news, Ronan," she somehow managed to say. "Distracting yourself won't make it go away."

Only then did Ronan pull back—physically and emotionally. He ran both hands over his face. "You're right. You are. I'm sorry. I—"

"Stop." She was not going to let him apologise for something she wanted. Wanted with an ache that might never leave her. But she pushed herself away from his desk, turned to him and pulled him into a hug. Which, as his friend—and she was his friend, they'd been through too much to pretend otherwise—was what she ought to have done in the first place.

"Call him. Don't call him," she said, while trying not to

swoon from the hard feel of him in her arms, "Whatever you decide to do, I'll have your back."

"Thank you," he muttered against her neck, his arms sliding around her till it was hard to know where she started and he began.

It hurt, physically, to pull back. But what choice did she have? Then Hadley somehow managed to walk out of his office on feet that felt like lead.

Hadley's foot bounced up and down, thumbnail caught between her teeth, as she watched Ronan work at his desk all the way across the hall from her own.

This was, officially, her last week as his executive assistant. The last week she could go *anywhere she liked* in this building she'd helped design. The last week when she would have access to the inner sanctum. The last week in which to pass on wisdom to Jonas. The last week in which to leave her mark on the place.

But all she could think about was Ronan.

She wondered if he'd called his father. If underneath the back-to-normal exterior he still felt as ragged and conflicted as he'd looked the other day. If he kept thinking about how it had felt to lean into her, skin brushing, breaths intermingling, millimetres, moments, from a kiss.

He sat back in his chair, lifted the end of his tie, gave it a look, then laughed at something said by the old university friend she'd patched through to his speaker-phone a few minutes before.

Even from that distance he was utterly compelling—dark, charismatic, exuding pure power. But the knot of his tie was just off-centre, which had her swallowing down a lump in her throat.

She shook her head, hard enough her hair caught in her

lashes, then turned her chair so she was facing cool-as-a-cu-cumber Jonas instead. He lounged on her office couch, one foot hooked on the other knee, his phone to his ear, a hand waving nonchalantly through the air as he yakked it up with an epic new Big Think supporter who also happened to be his godfather.

Hadley had had to hustle hard to make those kinds of connections, especially in the early days. Jonas did not. And she was glad of it.

Jonas hung up then sat forward and noted down the promises made in the call, so that a contract could be sent out as soon as possible. Then he asked, "What next?"

What next? Great question. Especially on the heels of the second wind that had come over her.

She had a few days left to make that hustle. To do whatever was needed to leave Ronan in the very best place to do his job. For, with Sawyer away, Ted spending more time with Adelaid as her not-that-easy pregnancy progressed, Ronan's father's illness forcing him to face parts of his life he'd spent years putting aside, and her imminent departure, life had been pushing back in a big way.

Hadley stopped jiggling her foot as it hit her what she had to do.

Ronan and his father had been in a messed-up place long before she'd come along. A father figure, Constantine Gerard was not, not in the way Ronan had needed him to be. But there was one man out there who was. A man born of privilege who'd earned his true reputation by working hard but, most importantly, by putting his family first.

She turned to Jonas. "Do you know Holt Waverly?"

Jonas blew out a long, slow whistle. "I know *of* him, of course. The man's a legend. But the dusty, cowboy chic, father-to-daughters thing, it's all rather outside my realm."

That was just what Hadley had been thinking.

Ronan had been going after Holt like a bull at a gate—all chest-beating machismo. Hadley had tried, and failed, to convince Ronan there was another way—that, as a father of daughters, Holt Waverly might respond to a more feminine energy.

"Why?" Jonas asked.

Hadley had her tablet open now, the keyboard up, fingers tapping like crazy. "Because it just became my mission in life to make that happen."

"We are *built* on a promise of future proofing!" Ronan thundered as Sawyer's image on the wall screen of the Founders' Room, connecting from wherever he was staying in upstate New York, flickered and stuttered. "How is this even happening?"

Sawyer's face had paused, mouth open, brow furrowed, the connection clearly lost. Again.

Ronan grabbed the hand ball he'd been squeezing and tossed it at the wall next to the screen, right as Hadley walked through the door, missing her head by inches.

She ducked, before shooting him a look that said he'd better watch out. But he was already half out of his chair, hand hovering mid-air.

"Seriously?" she asked.

"Apologies. That ball was meant for Sawyer."

Hadley looked to the screen, where in the half-screen beside Sawyer's comically frozen face, sat Ted in his home office, arms outstretched as his daughter, Katie, came rushing in, before attempting to climb onto his shoulders while shouting, "Dada, Dada, Dada!"

Ronan slammed shut his laptop without bothering to say goodbye, and the vision went to black before the Big Think Corp logo morphed elegantly onto the screen.

"Things going well?" Hadley asked.

Ronan growled. For all that he'd had the briefest sense of reprieve the week before, since his mother's phone call everything seemed to have unravelled all the more. Unravelling was not in his tool box. This was a serious company, with serious concerns, and he was not in the mood to deal with this circus.

The fact that he'd woken up on Monday morning, knowing it was to be Hadley's last week, had not helped.

Hadley, who'd crouched before him and taken his hands when she'd found him after his mother's phone call. Who'd looked him in the eye and insisted, vociferously, that his father's actions had nothing to do with the two of them.

Hadley, who'd lit up like a firework when his finger had touched hers. His finger, for hell's sake—his *pinkie* finger. After which she'd looked at him with such longing there'd been a fifty-fifty chance he might have self-combusted on the spot. Thankfully he hadn't, giving him the opportunity to discover her hair smelled of flowers, her skin felt like velvet and, when they were as close as they'd ever been, her crackling energy coursed through him as if it were his own.

Hadley, who'd been the one to pull back, to make the shrewd choice, right when he'd lost the will ever to deny her anything ever again.

Hadley, who—if he'd asked—would have sourced better Wi-Fi for Sawyer. And video-chatted with Katie so Ted could give the company five kid-free minutes. Sure, Jonas could probably wiggle his nose and make it happen too, but it wouldn't be the same.

Nothing would be the same again.

"You okay over there, boss?" Hadley asked, remote in hand as she switched off the screen.

He sat back and watched her—all spare movements and

quicksilver energy as she shifted Ted's chair and tidied Sawyer's bowl of hand balls. The tips of her dark hair swung just below her chin, with that "just got out of bed", mussed quality that did things to his inside. He watched her heart-achingly lovely profile—those long lashes, full red lips, tip-tilted nose and that stubborn chin. The shiny dress that whispered at her waist and swirled about her ankles, making her look like a movie star.

Busy work done, she looked up and caught him staring. She stood up straight. And from one breath to the next the temperature in the room seemed to go up a degree, or three.

"Not even slightly okay," he grumbled, answering her question. Or was it some other questions rattling about inside his head? Who knew? "I need consensus on the Hobart deal, and Sawyer's connection was completely up the spout."

"Did he mention the snow storm?" she asked.

Ronan thought that perhaps he had, but it had bounced off the other thoughts filling his head. The "it's Hadley's last week" thoughts that had him feeling tetchy as all hell, even before the damned video call.

"Now," she said, clasping her hands together, a beatific smile settling on her stunning face, "How much do you love me?"

Ronan stilled so suddenly, his heart might have stopped for a second or two. For, while he knew she wasn't being *literal*, her words caught at some raw, unprepared place inside of him.

Grateful he was not actually expected to answer, Ronan sat back in his chair when Hadley went on.

"I've booked the jet, you see," said Hadley. "For this afternoon. To take you to Adelaide…for a meeting with Holt Waverly."

At which his heart restarted with a vengeance.

"You don't have to say anything," she said, wafting a hand over her shoulder as she ambled from the room. "Think of it as a parting gift, from me to you. Just be ready for the car to the airport in two hours. Oh, and Jonas will go with you on this one."

"Hadley…" he said, unable to hide his shock and awe.

"Don't argue," she said. "Jonas will be fantastic. Just think—lots of lovely bonding time for you both on the plane."

And with that she was gone, like a wisp of smoke. And if Ronan hadn't been in love with her before…

He stopped that thought with two hands around its neck, smothering it before it had the chance to take breath.

Holt Waverly.

He searched his ego, needing to ferret out any slivers of envy that he'd not landed the meeting himself before they took root, and found there was none—not a jot.

If he'd ever had a sign that he could not be more different from his father—a sign that, no matter what happened from here, that wound was healed—that was it.

And Hadley Moreau had gifted him that.

"You ready?"

Hadley looked up from her computer, her eyes taking a moment to focus on Ronan leaning in her doorway, hands in pockets, feet crossed at the ankle, pale-blue, button-down shirt stretching across his mighty chest.

"Ready for what?" she asked, her pulse leaping just because he was there.

"Work trip," Ronan said, his tie knot so far to one side, she'd have guessed he'd done it deliberately if she didn't know him so well. "Come on. Time to hustle."

She blinked. "I'm not going. Jonas is."

"Change of plan," he said, an eyebrow raised, cheeky

smile flashing across his face with such suddenness, such utterly unfair gorgeousness, her lungs threatened to collapse in panic. It was as if the thought of finally meeting with Holt Waverly was akin to an iron infusion. "Let's do this, you and me, one last time."

Then he tapped the door frame and walked out of the door.

Of all the things they'd done, all the travel and glamour and success, their hustles, when they ventured off in search of locking in a new business partner, had been her favourite thing: packing light, staying in glamorous hotels, the private jet, the long, tiring and extremely intimate days when she and Ronan spent every minute together. And when a meeting went well, the two of them tag teaming in perfect sync, glittering with clever banter and the shiny lure of their beautiful Big Think brand, it was like nothing else.

One last time.

While the thought of it was like a shiny lure—especially considering how much admin she had to get through that day to make sure Jonas would be ready to take over—it was just not a good idea. Not after the footsie thing. And the nearly kiss. As for the fact Ronan had completely undermined her by changing the plans she'd made, well, that was just not how they did things around here.

Hadley belatedly hopped out from behind her desk, jogged to the door of her office and called, "Wait!" but Ronan kept on walking.

She passed Kyle, who was busy tapping away at his computer, and hissed, "Where's Jonas?"

Kyle shrugged.

"Ronan, wait," she called. "I'm far too busy. And Jonas needs to learn how to do this."

Ronan stopped, turned and said, "I don't care."

And something in his voice—the certainty, the pig-head-edness—made her see red. "I'm not going."

"Yes, you are." Then, "You made this happen, Hadley, when I could not. Now you have a plane ride to explain it to me, in detail. Besides, as of this moment, you still work for me. Meaning I get to say what work is more important. And, right now, that is Holt Damn Waverly."

That glint in his eye, the fighting words, switched on her stubborn gene like nothing else. It called to the clash of wills that had fuelled the push-pull of their relationship for years.

Saliva filled her mouth and her heart beat hard but steady against her ribs. And Hadley realised that ribald frustration was far easier to deal with than feelings, yearnings, and vul-nerability. And maybe, just maybe, leaning into that was the only way she'd get through the next few days intact.

"Fine," she ground out. "I'll go."

"Great," said Ronan, turning so that his jacket swished around him as if he were a freaking musketeer. "This will be an overnighter, so book us a suite. Somewhere memora-ble for out last hurrah."

With that, he waggled his eyebrows before disappearing into his office.

"Yes, *boss*!" she yelled. "Whatever you say, *boss*!"

Then she looked around her, glad they were on his private floor so she didn't look like a lunatic to anyone but Kyle, who was grinning and shooting her a double thumbs-up.

CHAPTER SIX

"WHERE THE HELL are we?" Ronan asked as they ran into the lobby of the motel and shook off the rain that had already drenched them the moment they'd stepped off the Big Think jet.

Then, when their car had dropped them at their accommodation, they'd had to weave their way around big rigs filling the motel car park in order to reach reception.

Yep, *motel*. The Big D Motel to be precise—a single-storey, flat-roofed truck stop with its own service station attached, some way off Sir Donald Brandman Drive.

Hadley felt a frisson of pleasure at the shock in Ronan's eyes as he took in the dried flower arrangement, the yellowing lace curtains and the mission-brown laminate reception desk where sat a squat little Christmas tree, the edges of its fronds changing colour.

"This," said Hadley, her arms open before her, as if showing off something fantastical, "is our lodgings for the evening."

"I don't understand."

"Sure, it's not our usual kind of place…" she said, really feeling it now.

Their "usual place" meaning some opulent, two-bedroomed suite in some ridiculously expensive six-star hotel, including a welcome hamper they never opened. All paid for by Ronan, not Big Think, who was determined never to have anyone look his way and say, *Chip off the old block*.

She went on. "When you demanded I choose somewhere memorable, I remembered staying here once with my mum, when I was seven or eight. Having only ever lived in mum's car, if not her next new boyfriend's place, I'd never stayed in a motel before, and at the time I thought it was so posh."

When Ronan's gaze made its way back to her, she batted her lashes angelically. Knowing he wouldn't dare call her out, given the story about her poor mum.

His eyes narrowed, dark and penetrating, and if they'd been able to shoot lasers they would have burned her to a crisp on the spot.

Thankfully, a bump came from the curtains behind Reception and Hadley turned to find a woman shuffling in behind the desk.

Reading the woman's name tag, Hadley smiled and said, "Dorinda, is it? I'm Hadley Moreau, and this is my wonderful, forgiving boss, Ronan Gerard. I called ahead earlier to book two rooms in your fine establishment for tonight."

The woman blinked at Hadley's enthusiasm, before her gaze moved over Hadley's shoulder to find Ronan who was looking around the space as if he'd woken up in Oz.

Dorinda, on the other hand, had taken one look at Ronan and gone catatonic, forcing Hadley literally to wave a hand in front of the woman's face.

"Two rooms?" said Dorinda, cheeks flushed, hands fretting as she hastened to find their booking. "I'm sorry, love, but we have you down for one."

Hadley's own smile dropped away. "One?" she asked, her voice lifting rather terrifyingly at the end.

"One room, twin beds. If that helps?" Dorinda's eyes

moved once more to Ronan, her expression making it clear she thought two beds would be a travesty.

Hadley's cheeks warmed as she felt Ronan move up closer behind her. "If you could change the booking to two *rooms*, that would be great. They don't even have to be anywhere near one another. Opposite sides of the complex is just fine."

"No can do," said Dorinda, clicking the inside of her mouth. "It's Monster-Truck-a-Con week. Only way you got this room was a last-minute cancellation."

So much for her big protest move. Seemed they'd have to go six-star after all. Not a sentence she'd ever thought she'd utter, but such was life with Ronan Gerard.

Hadley opened her mouth to thank Dorinda…

"Not a worry, Dorinda," said Ronan, reaching past Hadley's shoulder, the cuff of his jacket scuffing her wrist as he accepted the clunky key.

Hadley turned, caught his eye, and found it hot and hard.

Then, "Come on, Hadley, time to get moving if we want to settle into our lovely room before heading off to that big, important meeting we've been trying to land for literally years."

"But…" Hadley looked at Dorinda, who was watching Ronan leave with love hearts dancing around her head. Then she held out a flat hand and, to Hadley, said, "So you'll be paying the security deposit, love?"

Hadley dragged the small overnighter she always kept ready to go in her office over the chunky door frame that led to her room—*their* room—to find Ronan had already claimed the bathroom.

She took in the pastoral paintings on the stuccoed walls, dark-brown carpet and ancient printouts of local menus in a hand-made folder on the bedside table. And the twin beds with their red-and-gold quilts and mismatched Christmas-themed pillows propped up against the headboards.

Exhausted from her devilish dealings, as well as trying to fit six months of work into the past few weeks, Hadley fell face-first onto the bed closest to the door. As always, preferring to have the exit within reach.

Wincing when it squeaked, she rolled onto her back and a spring dug into her shoulder, after which she started laughing. For it was all just preposterous: her job, her life, her leaving…so much drama. All to end up back in the Big D Motel, wearing a dress that cost more than the accommodation, the delicate fabric now stuck to her limbs like wet tissue.

The sound of a running shower had her whipping her head towards the bathroom. A shadow moved past the slit of light below the door. The thought that Ronan might be naked had her sitting back up.

Sharing a glam suite was one thing; this was a disaster in the making. She found the TV remote, turned it on then changed channel till it landed on some reality show she didn't recognise. And she turned it up, loud.

A few minutes later the bathroom door swung open and Ronan stood in the doorway. He filled it, all big, broad and fuming. Once again, he was wearing nothing but a towel.

She rolled her eyes and turned her back.

"You're on my bed," he grumbled, striding towards her.

"I didn't hear you call dibs."

"And yet. I'm taking the one closest to the door."

She was about to say, *"How about you take the one in some other hotel I can still book,"* but when she glanced back, and saw the deep furrow in his brow, she decided that was not the hill she'd choose to die on.

Instead, she hopped off the bed, walked around the end, and sat on the other—all the while trying her best not to get too close to all that warm skin gleaming with dampness. "So, we're doing this now?" she asked. "Just walking around half-naked?"

"Seems so," he hissed, grabbing his wet jacket from the back of a chair and showing her the creases. Creases which a six-star hotel would have steamed out for him in half an hour.

"Ronan…" she said, her tone apologetic.

He shot her a look over his shoulder while he rifled through his things, coming up with nothing remotely wearable.

"Ronan," she said again, standing, moving round the bed. Only he chose that moment to stride towards the other side of the room, where his trousers lay over the back of a plastic chair, and nearly bowled her over.

Feet planted, Hadley instinctively reached for him, both hands landing on his chest—his bare chest. And, when momentum tipped her backwards, one hand grabbed frantically for his shoulder and the other dove around his waist.

When the world stopped moving up to meet her, Hadley swayed to balance, only to find herself wrapped around her half-naked boss.

Ronan loomed over her, big, bold and discombobulated. His gaze was hard, his hair a mess. His mouth a thin line. Her hungry gaze took in sculpted muscles, a smattering of dark hair and meaty shoulders, hulking and rounded from the weight he bore every day of his life—all honest, brute strength. His pupils were the size of pennies.

"What the hell is going on with you today?" he asked, his voice like sandpaper rubbing over her skin as he raised her back to vertical.

"Fair question," she muttered. One she couldn't possibly answer without utterly giving herself away.

With that she slowly disentangled herself. Slowly. When the hand at his shoulders brushed along his neck, and through the curls of his hair, it was enough to send ripples of heat through her arm to her belly.

When she was free of him, and standing a good pace back, she found him breathing as if he'd just run a marathon. Eyes closed, expression grim, he looked feverish. He looked...*unmade*. A big, beautiful human mess.

Because she'd been a human limpet? Or because he was so angry with her he could barely find the words to tell her?

"Ronan," she said yet again, her voice quiet but strong, "Ronan, open your eyes."

Whatever he heard in her voice, it was enough for him to comply.

"Okay," she said, holding out both hands in conciliation, "So things have gone a little Wild West the past few weeks. And maybe, booking this place, I leaned into that a little more than I ought. But it is what it is, and we are where we are. And we have a couple of hours till we meet Holt Waverly, which I know is important to you."

His nostrils flared, the skin of his chest was blotchy and pink, the fist at his hip holding his towel in place rigid and white. As for his towel, well, it had a ridge where she was sure it had not had before. As if...

Oh, my.

Hadley's gaze shot to the ceiling, to the wall and then to a safe spot in the middle of Ronan's forehead. Because the man wasn't angry—at least not *only* angry; he looked as though he was about to implode with the effort not to...stand erect.

"So, this is what I suggest we do from here," she said, having to stop and lick her bone-dry lips. "Let's forget what just happened, with the all the gripping and the holding and the wet skin... I have somewhere in mind where we can grab lunch. And we can buy some dry clothes. And then let's go make Holt Waverly an offer he can't refuse!"

She finished her speech by punching the air, as if her skin wasn't zinging, her heart racing, her entire body scorching with the knowledge Ronan was hard for her. The fact that they were in a small, slightly whiffy room with rather low ceilings and the sound of truck brakes outside helped—just—to stop her from doing anything completely stupid such as asking if there was anything she could do to help his *situation*.

"Okay," he said.

And it was enough to set Hadley into action. She spun, bustled over to her suitcase, grabbed a clean outfit, then, eyes front, slipped past him to rifle through his bag. She came up with a pair of jeans and a T-shirt that brought with it the soft, warm, musky scent he exuded after a night's sleep. A little light-headed, she tossed them over her shoulder. "Put this on, for now."

"Yes, ma'am," he said, a smile in his voice, and she didn't dare turn in case he took her at her word.

Having gathered her own back up outfit, she slipped into the bathroom and closed the door, leaning back against the cool wood, eyes closed, legs shaking. Then she shook herself from top to toe, before changing fast enough to set some kind of record.

Once dressed, she called, "Ready?" while checking herself in the mirror, and wiping under both eyes, pinking up her cheeks with pinching fingers and ruffling her damp clumps of hair that would turn to wild waves by the time they dried.

A minute later, he knocked. "I'm ready."

She gave her reflection a good talking to before squaring her shoulders and heading back out into the main room, where Ronan stood near the door, looking painfully good in grey T-shirt and jeans. Everything was back in place, where it should be.

Pity, she thought. Then, *What? No! Be good. From now*

on, be good. This is your last work trip together to land his white whale. Nothing else matters. Nothing.

"I'll call a car, then," said Hadley, her voice far too high. "We can do this. You and me."

His gaze was unreadable, as though he'd flipped some switch while she'd been in the bathroom that had put some invisible distance between them.

She nodded and grabbed her handbag, as he opened the door, only to look up as she reached his side.

He was looking down at her, feeling dangerously close, as he murmured, "As for forgetting the way you clung to me back there, all damsel-like? Never gonna happen."

With that, he gave her a little nudge out of the door and shut it behind them.

The rain had stopped. Ronan stepped onto the path in front of the row of squat rooms, the sun now beating down on the wet ground, and stretched out his arms, breathing in the petrol-scented air as if he'd stepped into a forest glen.

That glint of excitement was back. The thrill of the chase was creeping up on him. The Ronan Gerard charisma was ramping up, and fast.

This was going to happen today. He was going to do the thing he'd wanted to do for as long as she'd known him. And she'd made it happen. Meaning, when she walked away, she could do so without feeling as if she'd left anything undone.

Then he turned to face her, a ferocious grin on his face, and said, "Come on, Moreau, let's get this thing done." If Hadley's knees gave way, just a little, she collected herself in time to hop in their waiting car.

Holt Waverly was as advertised.

Ronan took him in—he was tall, rangy, ruggedly handsome and spare in shape and movement. When he tipped his hat off his head, it left a crease in his hair. On closer inspection, the dint, perfectly matched on either temple, appeared permanent.

"Now, that's a man," said Hadley on his left, her voice low and more than a little awed.

Ronan's gaze shot to hers to find her watching Holt cross the glossy hotel foyer, but he knew, as a man knew such things, that she was messing with him. She was giving him something else to focus on rather than how badly he wanted this to work out—*needed* this to work out.

As if feeling his attention, she looked his way, all fierce, dark eyes, pursed red lips—a true vision of loveliness.

Her expression changed, eyes narrowing: *you've got this.* Then, as her certainty, her faith in him, gave him wings, she moved to stand in front of him, right up in his personal space as she reached up and fiddled with the knot of his new tie.

"There," she said after a few long seconds of yanking, twisting and smoothing, during which he had to grit his teeth and think about the dreaded monthly projections, so as to not find himself in the situation he had that morning beneath the thin, scratchy motel towel.

"Much better."

"If you say so," he ground out.

Across the foyer—the hotel far fancier than the place they were staying in—Waverly's gaze locked onto his, as if measuring him up in half a second flat.

"Holt," Ronan said, holding out a hand. The off-the-rack shirt and suit they'd picked up in a mall on the way were pulling at his shoulders, ever so slightly too small when compared with the custom-made—but dripping-wet—gear back in the motel. "Thanks so much for seeing us."

"Ronan." Holt nodded, grasping Ronan's hand in his, the grip all bone and sinew. And hard enough, if Ronan hadn't been expecting it, he might have winced.

But by then Holt's gaze had slipped sideways, a wide, sunny smile stretching across his weathered face.

"You must be Hadley," Holt said, his voice a growling rasp of a thing, as if it too had had too much sun. "I thought you said you'd not be joining us."

Then he opened his arms for a hug.

And Hadley—who, as far as Ronan had ever seen, was *not* a hugger—*blushed* as she stepped into the older man's arms and took it.

"Last-minute spot of good luck," she said, pulling back and gifting the man a wide, blindingly beautiful smile. "I even dragged this one to Jensen's for lunch earlier, and ordered the Waverly steak, exactly as you suggested."

Holt's famous bright-blue eyes creased into a thousand lines at both corners. "And...?" he queried.

"Utter perfection. Turns out it's not all cowboy boots and slow-motion rides through clouds of red dust—you know what you're doing out there on the station."

The older man laughed, clearly delighted.

While Ronan watched on, a downright third wheel, yet loving it. The things this woman could achieve by sheer force of will, the way she surprised him every day, gave him a hell of a thrill.

He must have made a sound, for Hadley glanced his way, giving him the final moment of that smile before she blinked furiously at whatever expression she saw on his face. And then it was gone, leaving him momentarily blinded.

"Now," said Hadley, "lunch was hours ago, and I'm famished. Shall we?"

Holt nodded and Hadley ushered the men after her, waiting until they were in step, then she dashed off on a pair of prohibitively high heels faster than they could keep up without hitting a jog.

Ronan noticed, with a flash of heat, that along with the little black dress she'd picked up along with his suit she'd sourced those stockings she favoured, with the fine black seam gracing the backs of her long legs.

He looked at Holt, in step beside him, to find the older man's gaze now laser-sharp, as if casing the room for predator and prey, and not quite sure how he'd ended up there.

Ronan laughed softly. "Why do I get the feeling Hadley flummoxed you into doing her bidding?"

Holt shot him a look, eyes narrowing. "Because you've been in my shoes."

Ronan laughed again. "*Touché.* You do know *I've* been trying to set this up for an embarrassing number of years?"

Holt smiled knowingly.

"So, how did she do it?" Ronan asked.

"She's a mercenary, that's how. Got onto my youngest, Matilda, via some common connection. Tilly is a total soft touch. Through her, she got onto me. And in a three-minute phone call managed to bring up the fact she'd never known her father, and admired my closeness with my own daughters, and how their futures must keep me up at night. Somehow tugging on the only three heartstrings I possess."

Holt shot Ronan a look. "Then, once I was putty in her hand, she talked about you. About your vision, your determination, how you put your money and time and energy where your mouth is. That beneath the slick facade, you are a good man and, if I didn't hear you out, then I wasn't nearly as clever as I thought I was. And so, here I am."

There was not a single thing Ronan could say to that which wouldn't make him look like an absolute goose.

"She's a keeper," the older man said as Hadley waltzed into the elegant hotel restaurant as if she owned it. She gathered a waiter and a bar tender, both of whom followed her as if in a trance while she chose just the right table in the corner of the hotel restaurant.

All Ronan could say was, "I'm well aware."

The fact that he couldn't keep her—that all too soon he'd be letting her go, and that she'd said all those things about him—tumbled him like a rogue wave, knocking loose every one of the thousand dangerous thoughts, warm feelings and intimate moments he'd experienced with Hadley over the years—the ones he'd resolved to keep locked down deep inside.

And, barraged by a tumult of emotions while wearing a too-small, shop-bought suit, that was how he had to nab Holt Waverly. If he pulled it off, it would be the coup of a lifetime.

In the end, Ronan didn't have to pull anything off at all, for he'd been invited to the Hadley and Holt Show.

While watching Hadley snare any man in her thrall had never been a comfortable place for Ronan to be, he knew that she was doing exactly what he paid her to do: smoothing the way, for him.

She asked after Holt's three grown daughters, and talked about different cuts of beef the way a sommelier would talk of wine, while Ronan sat back, watched and learned. For this was a master class. She did not leave any stone unturned. The student had become the teacher.

The bigger question was why? Was she going above and beyond as an apology for booking that ridiculous motel room? Because this was their last such trip? Or because she knew just how much he wanted this to land?

And she knew. Because she *knew* him—every flaw, every foible, every weakness. And yet she'd told Holt Waverly that he was a good man. She'd said those actual words. And…and he couldn't get past it. She *knew* him and believed he was good.

Just as he knew her.

No one watching her now, holding her wine glass just so, all panache and effortless cool, would believe she'd had such a tough start. But he could see it in how hard she worked, how she double-and triple-checked herself to make sure not to mess up, in the biting repartee that made her compelling company, but also kept people at arm's length.

He'd seen any number of men succumb to her beauty and try to match wits only to watch, with no small amount of enjoyment, as she'd squished them like bugs. Not that she'd been pure as the driven snow. She'd dated along the way—a couple had lasted weeks, if not months—but none had stuck. An outcome that had left him fiercely relieved, even if his dating history had sputtered much the same way. His job was so constant, so consuming, he'd needed her at his beck and call.

He'd needed her... He just needed her.

For all that he'd grown up with every advantage, she reflected the best and worst parts of him: slow to trust, hyperambitious and compulsively alone. It was almost as if they'd been destined to stand in one another's path, so as to be forced to face their own weaknesses. To own them, to use them for good. Without one another, they might both have suffered from arrested development.

Was that why she was stepping back? Had she evolved past all that? Was she finally at a point where she believed herself deserving of a different life? A life filled with time, daylight, space and breath? A life devoid of such relentless, unforgiving pressure?

Ronan breathed out hard, then did something he'd never once done, opening a sliver in the lead case around his heart. So that he might imagine a life without Big Think. He tried imagining long weekends, lazy mornings, and coffee for the sake of coffee, not as a life force. Tried imagining a life lived beside someone else.

But he could not. It was a big, grey blank. Normality a terrifying unknown. As if he'd guarded his heart against invasion, against tyranny, for so long, it was too late to be any other way.

He closed himself up quick smart and the lead casing around his heart held tight. His life's mission—the need for restitution—was unfinished. And he did not see a time when it would ever feel otherwise.

And yet the *feelings* that had earlier been knocked loose, all added up to one thing, one great, big, deeply hidden truth.

He'd never known anyone like Hadley Moreau—acerbic yet kind, unsettled yet strong, warm, engaging and spellbinding yet truly elusive. Her duality thrilled him, spoke to him, unnerved him, touched him. Hadley was under his skin, in his bones, wrapped around every part of him in ways he could not see himself to undoing.

He wanted her. He wanted her to stay. He wanted her in his arms. He wanted her so badly, his chest hurt. He wanted her so deeply, he dreamed of her and yearned for her.

All that with an emotionally stilted heart; a locked down, shut off, shrivelled thing. Despite all the years during which he might have evolved along with her, he remained ill-equipped, unworthy.

And she deserved far better—far better—than a Gerard. So, he would have Big Think, and he would lose her.

So be it.

"Ronan?" Hadley's voice broke into his reverie and he blinked to find her watching him, her voice loud, motioning with her eyes that Holt had asked him a question.

Holt, seeing that Ronan's gaze had been so steadfastly focused on Hadley, cleared his throat and said, "I was sorry to hear your father is unwell. How is he doing?"

Unprepared, the question hit hard. Ronan's mouth opened and closed; akin to a fish flapping on the shore. Heat rose up his spine, gathering in his throat, tightening till he fought the urge to loosen his tie.

A hand landed on his thigh—Hadley's hand, squeezing, pinching really, rather hard, till it yanked Ronan fully into the present moment.

He said, "It's no secret that my father and I have not been close for some time." Then wondered where the hell that had come from.

When he looked at Hadley, her eyes were sharp, questioning, then, after a beat, encouraging. Her grip softened; her thumb stroked over his knee.

Go on. You can do this.

Ronan went on. "We have wildly different values, my father and I, when it comes to business, politics, social contracts…" *Women. Family. Respect.* "And yet it's been difficult, knowing he's unwell."

Holt grunted.

While Ronan wondered if opening his heart for that tiny sliver of time had rent some permanent change. Had it let something in, or let something out?

Either way, path chosen, Ronan followed the flow. "I envy you—how close you are with your family. I think that's what partly led me to create a kind of family at Big Think."

Hadley's hand jerked, before it slipped away.

"I also know," said Ronan, "that your legacy is important to you, Holt. Not your public legacy—" that was his own father's *raison d'être* "—but what you leave behind for your family. The example of a life lived with passion and purpose, as well securing opportunity, comfort, and health for them all. That is why I believe you and I are such a good fit. Your goal is our goal, only on a global scale."

"To save the world," said Hadley, stating Big Think's simple yet ambitious mission statement.

"A hell of a big call," said Holt, leaning back in his seat. If he crossed his arms, Ronan knew they were doomed. But his fingers danced on the table top—thinking fingers, curious fingers.

Ronan smiled and said, "Gargantuan." Then, "Care to help?"

When Hadley once again squeezed Ronan's thigh this time, it was a manic *squeeze-squeeze-squeeze* of excitement, as good as a high-five. Only far too close to sensitive nerves that were sitting up and begging for more.

His hand landed on hers and stilled it just as she turned her hand so that her palm slid against his, fingers tangling, a perfect fit.

They had been a phenomenal partnership, enjoying unheard-of success. A crack team. All of which felt diaphanous and transitory, compared with the warm, strong, tangible fingers curled into his.

When Hadley's gaze caught on his, a slice of heat cut right through him, bringing with it a wave of inevitability. And he felt his heart thump once, then twice, against the seam he'd opened earlier, pushing hard against its decades-old constraints. Knocking, wanting to be let out.

So, he let her go, dragging his hand away and steepling his fingers on the table. Hadley's fingers curled against his thigh another second then slowly slipped away.

Holt picked up his glass and swirled it a moment before lifting it in front of his face.

Ronan lifted his own glass. "To legacies to be proud of."

After a long, laden beat, Holt sat forward and touched his glass to Ronan's, then Hadley's. "To our families, both born and made, and their futures."

And Ronan knew—as truly as he'd known anything—that Holt Waverly had just decided to get into bed with his company.

CHAPTER SEVEN

HADLEY WAS BUZZING.

If success was an aphrodisiac, it was no wonder she'd spent the past several years with a near-constant itch when it came to Ronan Gerard.

Now, in the back of the car taking them up the motorway, Ronan filling up the back seat beside her, she flinched every time he breathed. Her body rolled towards him every time he shifted. Even the tips of her fingers vibrated with the need to flick away all her excess energy.

Was she really ready to give this up?

Not the hyper-awareness of the man beside her, for that was exhausting, and destined to continue shredding her heart until it was nothing but dust, but the rest? Having a plan, planning a plan and achieving a plan—that stuff was addictive. It was like a happy-ever-after every time.

When the car pulled into the motel car park, the Big D sign sending blue and red light over the windows, Hadley had the door open before the car had even rocked to a stop.

"Wait up," Ronan said.

But she had too much energy. And she was within sight of their room, key in hand, and couldn't wait to get out of this scratchy dress.

A hand clamped down on her wrist.

She stopped, a high heel scrunching on the gravel, and

turned to find Ronan, his gaze on the place he held her. His was jaw tight, his nostrils flaring, his thumb cruising over her wrist.

"I said, wait."

"Well," she said, her heart suddenly in her throat, "I didn't want to wait."

He looked up then, light spilling over his back creating shadows in his hard-cut cheeks, the dip of his throat, the bulk of his shoulders pressing against the confines of the cheap suit, and she couldn't quite see his eyes.

She flicked an eyebrow in question. "Well, I'm waiting now. What's so important you have to tell me in a motel car park?" she asked, her voice miraculously cool, considering how warm she felt, how electric.

He watched her a moment longer before he seemed to realise his thumb was running up and down the edge of her wrist. He let her go as if burned. Hot and cold; it was always like this—the two of them sparking like crazy, then...the icy chill of rejection.

And that was why she could happily give up the rest. Because there was only so much of that a woman could take before the constant waves of expansion and shrinking made her crack.

She was about to turn, when he said:

"Thank you." He looked up. "Thank you."

Hadley's next breath hitched in her chest, then caught, pressing into her collar bone like a fist. "You're welcome. But, while I warmed him up for you, you're the one who caught him. And it was beautiful, Ronan. Because it was real."

He watched her, rubbing at the hand that had held hers. "I didn't only mean for tonight."

"Oh."

"I meant for all the nights. And the days. And the weekends. For the years you gave to…" A beat, then, "The years you gave to Big Think."

Hadley swallowed. Ronan might often be brutally efficient with his words, having been taught that words had power—that they could cut as easily as they could lift–but he'd also been raised to be polite.

But this felt weightier than mere courtesy. It felt thick, heavy and deliberate. It felt like goodbye.

"Of course," she somehow managed. "It's—it was my job."

Ronan's gaze darkened; she could tell, now her eyes were getting used to the contrasts of the light. He dropped his hands to his sides as he took a couple of slow steps her way. She felt herself sway towards him, as if caught in his magnetic wake.

His voice was deep, rough, as he said, "Waverly told me what you said."

"Said?"

"That convinced him to meet us." He glanced up at the sky, which was clear now the clouds had moved on, but there were no stars to be seen, considering the light pollution of the Big D Motel sign. "He said you told him that I was a good man."

Hadley's chest tightened. *Oh, Ronan.* So much was happening to him; the shape of his business, and the family he'd built, changing faster than he could keep up with. And now his father was unwell, adding old poison to the mix.

"You want to know what I actually said?" she said, taking a step his way.

He dragged his gaze from the sky and looked down at her. His eyes were dark, his jaw tight. His chest lifted and fell. His eyes moved back and forth between hers, as if he wanted to know the truth—her truth—and would stand right there, in the motel car park, till she'd laid it all at his feet.

A small shiver wracked her body at the intensity in his

gaze, and at the fact she was really about to say this out loud, no sarcasm or safety net.

"I told Holt Waverly that he might like the world to think he was a tough old cowboy, but anyone who looked hard enough could see he was a conservationist at heart. A man who wanted the outback air to be as fresh and wholesome for his future grandkids as it was for him."

She took a breath. *In for a penny...*

"Then I told him that, in just the same way, he might imagine you're a sharp, intense, fiercely competitive businessman who happened to focus on future-proofing technologies in order to make a pretty good living. Yet the only reason your name meant anything to you was if it helped you help people. That your motivations are pure. And whether you had a hundred dollars, or a billion dollars, you'd find a way to do the most good with it that you could."

Hadley finished with a small shrug and wished that the lights beaming down on his back were less...motel-bright.

"Hadley," Ronan said, his voice rough. The air seemed to shift between them, to thin. As if whatever wall he'd kept between them for all these years had simply dissolved away.

"Ronan," she said, her voice husky in the night air. "I know you want us all to think you're bullet-proof. But you're as much of a mess as the rest of us. Only rather than wallowing, or fighting it, it's your superpower. Once you realise that, then you'll truly be unstoppable."

Had he moved closer, or had she? For suddenly his finger was at her chin applying the gentlest pressure. Lifting her face so that she had no choice but to look at him.

His dark brows had lowered over his deeply soulful eyes. But not in confusion, or frustration; there was sweetness to his expression, a kind of pained acceptance as his gaze roved over her face.

Hadley's next breath in was a gulp as she struggled to contain the feelings flooding through her. Her heart ached for him, and because of him. The base state of being that came from loving him.

Loving him.

Because she loved this man. How could she not? It went all the way back to that first night. It hadn't been the way he'd leapt to her defence, or offered whatever help she'd needed, it had been the fact he'd trusted she was strong enough to decide for herself what was best.

If she'd never met him, she'd have been okay. She'd have hustled and worked hard, scraping out space for herself in the world.

But *with* him, she'd flourished. Flourished from his trust in her, the lack of pretence in the way he treated her, the acceptance of her oddities, the ease with which he'd let her into the inner sanctum, gifting her a place in the family he'd created. With him, she'd been able to stretch her wings. To make mistakes, certain she had a cushion to fall back on.

She hadn't been a slave to her circumstances—she'd had the luxury of choosing exactly who she wanted to be.

If he was now a better man because of how much she'd pushed him, she was a better woman because of the belief he'd had in her.

"Thank you" wasn't even close to enough.

Hadley looked into Ronan's face, that bold, beautiful face, then she lifted a hand to his chest. She felt the hard, steady beat of his heart against her palm. Her fingertips found the edge of his tie and she curled it into her hand and used it to tug him closer, while she lifted up onto her toes and pressed her mouth to his.

She'd imagined kissing this man so many times. Imagined them coming together like two storms—the hardness of his jaw beneath her reaching hands, the clash of teeth, heaving breaths, all lust and speed, thunder and lightning.

But the moment her lips met his, the whole world seemed to gentle. Her thoughts slowed. Her heartbeat became a whisper.

While his finger at her chin shifted. Was he pulling away? *Please, no.* No, he was moving so that his hand, that big, strong hand, could cup her face, his thumb sweeping over her jaw, tilting her face so he could better angle the kiss.

And, oh, that angle as he kissed her back; slanted, warm and mesmerising. His lips slid over hers, lifting away then tasting her anew in a sweet, lush, quiet exploration. Savouring, luxuriating and gentle, so gentle, her body feeling as if it was filled with stars.

Her fingers curled harder around his tie, her knuckles brushing against his shirt. And her breath caught, the sweetest hitch, as he slid a slow arm behind her back, pulling her close.

A whimper cracked the silence—his? Hers?—a deepening of the kiss the only answer.

She slid her arms around his neck as she pressed higher, her body curving against his. She tipped her head so they were like quotation marks, tucked perfectly into one another's shapes.

And as his hardness brushed against her belly, and the whimper became a moan, Ronan's hands began to move over her, diving into her hair, fingers digging luxuriantly into her waist, sending waves of liquid desire washing through her.

Needing breath, needing air, she pulled away with a gasp against his ear. And it must have set something off in Ronan, as he lifted her bodily and carried her backwards towards their room, all the while kissing her anew in lush, drugging sips and licks as he took her down, down into some hot, molten, boneless place.

Then she was on her feet again, and there was the clink of keys as they stumbled into the room. The heavy slam of the door snapped them apart.

Hadley stepped back, the ugly brown carpet catching on her heels. The sound of traffic was muted by the soft furnishings, the room lit by a sliver of light coming through the blinds and a big red-fringed desk lamp they'd somehow left on.

Ronan looked a right mess; his shirt askew, his hair all over the place. His tongue ran back and forth over his lower lip, as if missing the taste of her already, a move she was entirely certain he had no idea he was making.

And a single spark of self-protection flared inside her. She was in charge of her own destiny. She could still put a stop to this. She could walk away in one piece.

Meaning she'd leave without knowing this, knowing *him*. A travesty big enough to swallow every other worry whole.

And so she made herself a bargain.

One night—one night to let go, let loose, let out all the feelings and wants she'd kept trapped inside her all these years. One night of not worrying about how the universe might trip her up for daring to want things she couldn't have.

And she wanted one night with Ronan Gerard more than she wanted air.

She shucked off her heels, kicked them across the room, then reached for the zip at the back of her neck, only for it to catch on the cheap fabric. She tugged again, but it wasn't going anywhere.

She swore blue murder and Ronan, a deadly-serious expression on his face, came to her, turned her on the spot then worked at the catch till it yanked down a few inches, enough so that he could he pull the dress off one shoulder.

His mouth came down on the tender tendon where neck

met shoulder, before his hand followed, sliding over her collar bone and dipping below the neck line to trace the curve of her breast. As if he'd imagined doing just this so often, he could have done it with his eyes closed.

When his fingertips brushed the swell once more, she reached back, hooking her hand behind his head, and held on tight so that when his fingers brushed lower, sliding beneath the lace of her bra to whisper across her nipple, she didn't melt into a puddle at his feet.

Knowing that was imminent, she pulled away and turned in his arms, gripping his cheeks as she kissed him, harder now, more frantic. There was nothing gentle about it anymore. He made his way down her neck, scraping, lathing, till his teeth were tugging at the loosened neckline of her dress.

When the scratchy fabric and the heat rolling threw her threatened to turn her into flames, she reached back, grabbed the edges of the zip and yanked. The zip opened enough that she could shimmy free.

Her dressed pooled at her feet and she stood before Ronan, in her black lace bra and matching underwear.

The world seemed to pause for a moment to take it in before, with a growl, Ronan had her back in his arms. He tugged at the lace edge of her half-cup and leaned her back as he took her nipple on his mouth. Her leg wrapped around his, her hands clawing for him as he feasted on her as if she was all that was keeping him alive.

Her mind spun; her senses were in an uproar. Every part of her clamoured to get closer to him. Hadley yanked at Ronan's shirt while he tore his jacket from his back. Then his hands were on her while hers were on his belt, tugging it free, loosening the fly while his hands moved to her backside, cupping her and hauling her to him.

The feel of that hard length had her moaning, mumbling

for more…and, please, now…just as the backs of her knees hit one of the beds and she fell backwards with a bounce. The old springs bounced her back up, so that her eyes sprang open, to find Ronan standing over her.

There was no towel this time. His shirt flapped open, a couple of buttons missing, by the looks of it, and his trousers were low on his hips, the fly wide open. The jut of him against his underwear had her coughing in shock.

Which brought on a smile. Pure devil. Then Ronan reached down, slowly, and rearranged himself while she flopped back on the bed, arm over her eyes lest she literally pass out from lust.

The bed dipped at her feet as he walked his hands along the sides of her calves, stopping to touch, to feel, to trace the bones and muscles, with hands and mouth, sending goose bumps springing up all over.

When she opened her eyes it was to find him on his knees, his eyes on her belly as he kissed his way down her sternum, watching in rapt concentration, his gaze hungry, as her body followed his touch, rising and undulating as his hand moved lower.

Humming now, as if in his happy place, Ronan's finger ran along the edge of her underpants, dipping below the trim before pulling out, again and again as his finger moved from hip bone to hip bone. He teased her till she began to writhe under his touch. Then his cheek lifted in a smile as he lifted the elastic and let go with a soft snap.

She hissed, her skin so sensitive, it was all pleasure and pain. Till Ronan hooked his thumbs into the sides of her underwear and without finesse yanked them over her hips, down her thighs, over each of her feet, before tossing the scrap of fabric over his shoulder.

But his gaze never left hers as he settled lower, moving

so that his breath was a warm puff against the neat patch of curls between her legs. His hands on her hips, thumbs tracing the bones in small circles, before moving down her inner thighs and gently encouraging them apart.

Shivers swept up and down her body. Shivers that threatened never to stop. Hot and needy, she let him move her where he pleased, marvelling at the fact that this was happening, while also marvelling that it had taken this damn long.

Ronan's gaze travelled up her body, his expression wondrous, worshipping, taking in every centimetre as if committing her body to memory, before his gaze found hers.

"May I?" he asked, his thumbs now tracing the fine, sensitive skin at the very tops of her inner thighs. Up and down, back and forth, whispering against her curls before moving away. And only the fact that she was panting now stopped the laugh from escaping her mouth.

"Yes!" she said, for it was not the time for quips. She knew he'd not go further without a clear directive. "Yes, a thousand times, yes!"

And that was all it took as, with a growl, he buried his face between her thighs. His nose bussed that most sensitive of spots, again and again, his fingers moving ever closer, parting her slowly, before his tongue took over with tender laps, then long, luscious licks, dipping inside her then circling her centre, not quite touching—a deliberate dance that was pure agony and ecstasy.

And all the while the vibration of his happy hum only added to the intensity as his deep voice trembled through her, his lips clamping over her, and he began to suck.

Her body bucked, her hands reaching to hold his head in place. Her nerves pulled taut, as if a single twang might snap her in half. But instead the pleasure within her only built and deepened as Ronan's mouth moved over her in deep, consistent draws, pleasure coursing through her with hot, hard, flashes of pure joy.

When she made to sit up, to move, to slow him...anything but this agonising intensity...his palm pushed her back to the bed, his thumb brushing over the tight nub of her nipple again and again, mimicking the tempo of his mouth.

"Ronan," she said on a sob, on a sigh, on a rush of pleasure that pierced her core.

"Tell me what you want," he said in warm rush of air over her centre, before he was back, doing what he did so well only faster, harder.

What did she *want*? What bargain had she made? She barely remembered her own name.

"You," she managed after a second, an aeon...who knew? "I want you."

With that, Ronan's tongue licked up her centre in a long, slow, hot stroke. And then everything tightened, the entire universe contracting to the base of her spine, and held there a moment, for the whole of existence, before the second big bang spiralled into the ether in waves of heat, light and blessed relief.

Ronan paced the cracked concrete outside the room, finishing off the phone call.

Once Hadley had fallen asleep, snoring lightly, as if succumbing to deep psychic exhaustion, his watch had alerted him to a missed call from his mother.

He'd gone outside to listen to the message, which was as much and as little as he would allow himself to do for now. For he was doing the best he could with the information he had.

He then listened to the half-dozen other messages that had come in—for it seemed life had gone on as normal while they'd been holed up in their dodgy little room. Then he stared at his phone for a long while, twisting it over and over in his palm as he tried to reconcile those two worlds. The pleasure and the pain.

Then he slid his phone into the back pocket of his too-small suit pants and headed back into the room.

Where he found Hadley lying on her stomach, the sheet covering her from hip to toe, one arm flopping over the side of the bed, the light from the dusty red lamp warming one side of her face. A lock of dark hair lay over her cheek, curling about her mouth.

Ronan pressed the heel of his hand to his chest when his heart gave a great, big kick. As if it was no longer knocking on the encasement but trying to kick the thing down.

He sat on the edge of the bed, the mattress dipping under his weight, and reached for her. Then, remembering he'd been outside for some time, he pulled his hand back and rubbed it till his fingers were warm.

Only then did he trace a light finger over her cheek, sweeping her hair aside, then down her back and along the edge of her ribs, the swell of her breast. His chest tightened as she rolled into his touch.

The eye not pressed into the bed fluttered open, narrowed, then widened, then shut tightly.

"Hey," he said, laughing.

Smiling a soft, sweet, unfettered smile that hit him right between the ribs, an armour-piercing arrow denting the encasement round his heart, Hadley lifted her head and tucked her chin on her forearm. She was so beautiful, he could barely breathe.

"Hey," she said, her voice rough. Her eyes fluttered closed when his hand swept down her back, fingertips tracing the fine bumps of her spine and the curve at the top of her backside where the sheet draped, but not quite, till goose-bumps scattered over her skin.

Then he leaned over her and pressed a kiss to a mole between her shoulder blades and she let out a soft moan.

He slid to the floor then, to his knees, so that his face was level with hers. She blinked languidly, her eyes pitch-dark. He leaned in, waited for her to lift her head and kissed her until heat gathered at his core. Kissed her till she moaned again.

Then she rolled onto her side, and what could he do but kiss the breast she'd presented to him?

Her hand dipped into his hair, tugging as he spent a good deal of time getting to know her left breast before he licked his way along her ribs. Then she fell back onto the bed, face down, with a hearty sigh.

While he'd gone hard as a rock. He could have spent all night licking her skin, kissing every part of her and then doing it all again, for the taste of her remained on the back of his tongue and he wanted more. He was addicted, for life.

So he grabbed the edge of the sheet and whipped it away to find her naked, completely and utterly. Her long, lean curves were like a dream. His dream. A dream he'd never, ever thought would be made real.

He shifted his knees apart, the growing urgency pressing against the zip near the point of pain. But he didn't want to leave her, to stop touching her, stop kissing her. Not yet.

He kissed his way down her side, a groan lodging in his throat when he reached her backside. The twin cheeks were soft and pink in the low light. His body now thrumming, his ears whumping from the rush of blood within, he grazed her, learning her taste, every taste, in the hope he'd never forget it.

Mouth moving lower as she began to roll under his touch, sweet, heady sighs escaping her mouth, he smoothed his hand down the dark vertical line of the vintage stockings she preferred. Only…

"What the hell?" he rasped, lifting up. For those weren't stockings: they couldn't be, for she was arse-bare.

His fingers gently pinched, searching for silk, only find nothing there.

"Ow," she said, alert enough now to lift onto one elbow and look down at her legs. Her breasts were level with his mouth, warm and pink from the blanket on which she'd been lying. "Pluck all you like, but that's a tattoo."

He laid his hand flat on the back of her thigh, then ran a finger down the thin vertical stripe, then back up again, stopping at the small black bow tattoos that sat just under each butt cheek.

Hell. All that time she'd been walking around with those bows, right there, and he'd never known. If he had…

If one day he found out Hadley Moreau had been put on earth to keep him in a kind of emotional purgatory, then he'd believe it. Only this wasn't punishment. This was nirvana.

"Are there more?" he asked.

One eyebrow kicked north.

"Show me," he said, grabbing her hips and turning her over.

She fell back on the bed, all husky laughter, and he'd literally never heard a sound he loved more. Then he leaned over her, face close, as if studying her scientifically. He knew about the string on her right ring finger. Taking her hand, he ran his tongue along the raised black mark.

After which she pointed the way to the tiny, fine-lined steam-punk dragonfly between her breasts, and he pressed a sucking kiss to the spot, which had her fingers digging into his hair.

He kissed, licked and ran his thumb over the several more she pointed out—all dainty and private; all stories, he was sure. Stories he still hoped she might one day tell. Till once again he found the small bow inked into the back of a thigh and he kissed her there, feeling the slight raise of it against the tip of his tongue.

Her intake of breath—sharp and hot—was enough for him to continue. He ran the tip of his tongue down the long line of her leg till she rolled fully onto her stomach, her hands gripping the sheets, her backside lifting off the bed.

When his mouth moved to her thighs, she reached back, her hand running own the hard ridge, pressing against his zip. "Ronan," she begged.

He didn't have to be asked twice. He moved off the bed and found his bathroom bag with the pack of condoms, then, having held himself together as long as he possibly could, whipped off his trousers and sheathed himself, then moved onto the small bed as best he could.

"Are you *now* thinking a suite would have been better?" he asked, his knees barely fitting on the bed as he slid his hand beneath her belly, then lower, tracing her centre till she gasped.

"Not for a second," she said, lifting to her knees and guiding herself back. Her chest flat to the bed, her face turned sideways. Her eyes closed, her body flushed, warm and pliant, as if he'd turned her boneless.

"Now, stop talking and take me," she said. "Now."

Holding on, mentally and physically, for all he was worth, lest the mere sight of her had him spilling over before he was even inside her, Ronan's hands spanned her hips. He guided himself into place, sending waves of insane pleasure up his thighs and into his balls. He rubbed his tip against the notch, caressing her, circling, till her mouth was open and gasping.

When the scent of her hit the back of his throat, warm, sweet and ready, a wave of the most brutish pleasure gripped him. Self-control at its limit, he pressed forward, just as she pushed back, and filled her to the hilt.

And there they stayed, breaths held, lost in a moment of pure pleasure, surprise and utter reality. They were here; this was happening. And Ronan could have died in that moment and believed he'd lived a pretty darned fine life.

It took every ounce of self-control to pull out in a long, slow sweep. She cried out at the lack of him, before he lodged himself deep inside her once more. Then he did the same, again and again, feeling more inside his own skin than he ever remembered feeling before.

He thought not with his head, but with instinct, feeling as if he could hear the movement his blood and feel the path of every nerve.

When she began to roll back against him, her fist clutching the sheets, her breath hastening, he matched her movements. The pink of her skin matched the heat rolling through him. The tension in her face matched the pleasure gripping him, searing him, turning his spine to fire.

Needing to feel her in every way possible, he curved himself over her, a hand sliding between them to roll his thumb over her nub in gently insistent circles that had her gasping. His next stroke angled differently and stars sprang up on the edges of his vision as pleasure built like a coming storm. With the next slide her body stilled and quaked beneath his, and he kept on, not stopping, holding her there, holding himself back, until her shivers subsided.

Then she reached between them, her fingers sliding over his, holding him there as she came again, a bucking orgasm that had her inner muscles tightening around him. And nothing could have stopped the light spiralling through him, slamming him towards some place high, hot and tight, before he shattered into a thousand pieces.

He came down to find them both breathing hard, their hands still touching, their bodies still quaking.

He eased himself free then laid her down, tucking himself against her back, curving his arm over her ribs, his heart kicking madly when she reached for his hand and tucked it into her chest.

The sweetness, the intimacy, rocked him. It was like nothing he'd ever known. Had never known he wanted. And now...now he knew there was no other way.

When she let go of his hand, it took everything in him not to grab it back. But then she turned, facing him, their noses almost touching.

He counted her tangled lashes and the creases in her full lips, which he salved with a swipe of his tongue. Then she kissed him, lushly, wantonly, with everything she had.

They kissed for some time, saying things with taste and touch that neither of them seemed able to say with words. Then afterwards they both washed, made their way back to the same small twin bed and fell asleep in one another's arms.

A pre-dawn mist had descended over the city as the car took them back to the airport the next morning, adding to the unusual quietness in the back of the car.

Ronan had woken that morning to Hadley's hand stroking him, long, leisurely sweeps of her hand that had had him bucking into her grip before his eyes had even opened.

After which she'd rolled him onto his back and straddled him, one of his condom packets between her teeth. She'd sheathed him with protection, then with herself, and they'd rocked silently, hands moving over one another, reaching for soft, wet kisses before spiralling over the edge as one.

Now Hadley flicked through her tablet, moving appointments, editing her notes on the Holt Waverly meeting, prepping bullet points for a press release for when their deal was finalised, before sending it to Jonas with a contented sigh. As if nothing had changed at all.

Ronan sat back and watched her, a growing certainty leeching into his bones that if they landed back in Melbourne without talking about it, without making sense of it, that would be it. A night out of time, never to be spoken of again. They had a history of avoiding the hard stuff if they could, after all.

But what to say? Why now? *What* now? *Now that that's happened, I can't imagine a world in which it never happens again?* What, exactly—motel sex? Or was this a chance to redefine things between them, given they'd never actually defined them at all?

He ran a hand down his face, imagining her response— the glint in those clever dark eyes, the tilt of those unforgiving lips. He'd be as good as begging for rejection. Willing it—after having been treated as an afterthought his entire childhood by a father who only saw Ronan as a mini-version of himself, and by a mother who only saw his father—would be nonsensical.

He was not a man who begged—not ever—and he wasn't about to start now. She'd already said all the pretty words about him being a good man, but it still wasn't enough for her to want to stay. *He* still wasn't enough.

Suddenly they were pulling into the private tarmac, the Big Think jet appearing out of the thinning gloom, and Ronan's chest felt tighter still.

He *willed* her to look his way. But instead she looked out of the car window as they slowed, then slid her phone and notebook into her bag and readied herself to alight from the car as it slowly cruised towards the wing of the plane.

Right, if she *didn't* look back before hopping out of the car, that would be it. He'd spent the past several years telling himself he didn't have feelings for her; he could do it again, surely?

And if she *did* look back… Ronan's heart kicked so hard, it took his breath away.

Her hand moved to the door handle.

Then her fingers pulled back and she turned and looked at him over her shoulder with a swing of her dark hair and an upward tilt of her red lips. The memory of their night together, was alight in her eyes. She was so damned lovely, it physically hurt to look at her.

This was it. A chance to do better than he had before.

"Don't go," Ronan said, his voice rough.

Hadley blinked, then glanced towards the jet. "But they're waiting—"

"Don't go," he said again, his voice rough. "Don't leave Big Think. Don't leave…" He was going to say "me", only that wasn't what this was about, was it? Damn it, he needed to get his head on straight.

"Ronan," she said, an understanding smile kicking up at both corners of her mouth. "If we'd wanted our last trip together to be a memorable one, I'd say we succeeded, but it's time for us to go."

Then she was out of the car, door slamming as she headed towards the jet.

Ronan was out of the car too, running after her, his original jacket flapping at his sides, crushed and still slightly damp. "Hadley, wait."

She stopped and turned, exasperated now. "The engine is running." But there was something else: tightness about her eyes, a melancholy.

"I decline your resignation."

She held a hand over her eyes, blinking against the weak sunlight. "Because of *last night*?"

"What? No. Of course not." Not the falling into bed part, at least, but all that it had exposed. "Hadley, you know how valued you are by the company. By me…and Ted and Sawyer. I know I should have said it sooner—instantly, in fact—but your announcement… To say it was unexpected is a massive understatement. I didn't handle it as best I could. If there's something you're missing, something you want…"

This time both eyebrows rose.

And Ronan held out his hands in frustration. "This has nothing to do with last night."

Hadley shook her head, then looked out across the tarmac as though searching for the right words. "I think you'll find you have that backwards."

"Meaning?"

"The only reason last night happened is *because* I'm leaving. You'd never have let it go that far otherwise." She watched him then, waiting to see if he might deny it.

But he could not…because it was true.

Disappointment flashed across her eyes, and something akin to pain, before she turned her back on him and headed for the steps leading up to the jet.

Ronan ran a hand over his jaw, finding it tight enough to crack bone. This wasn't going the way he'd wanted. None of it was. But he was where he was in life because he never backed down.

"Hadley," he called once again, jogging to catch up with her.

"Ronan!" she said, throwing up a hand even as she upped her pace. "You cannot purport to want to save the world while wasting this much jet fuel."

Then she stopped, spun on him and said, "Look, this trip was about so much more than Holt Waverly. It was about you struggling with what must be deeply challenging feelings regards your father's news. Me taking one last chance to push back when you tried telling me what to do. Our last night together…" She swallowed. "It was just one night."

Her voice was strong, but her eyes… They were dark, misty and awash with more emotions than he could rightly name. Then she shook her head hard, turned and jogged up the stairs and was inside the plane.

Ronan followed, locking down the emotion roiling inside him as he greeted the crew, dumped his gear and found his usual seat. He turned to look over his shoulder, finding Hadley across the aisle and back one seat, already back to frowning at her tablet.

Only as the plane rattled its way through the low-lying fog before smoothing out once they breached the clouds, did it occur to him that Hadley had said the only reason they'd fallen into bed together was because she was leaving. That *he'd* never have let it go that far otherwise.

What was her excuse?

CHAPTER EIGHT

HADLEY HAD NEVER ONCE, in the entire time she'd worked at Big Think, finished her day at five o'clock.

She'd not wanted to—she'd been desperate to learn everything she could, to prove and improve herself, and then the place had become a part of her.

After their flight back from Adelaide, Ronan had taken her at her word and let her be. Meaning she could spend her last days reliving their night away—the scrape of his teeth over her collar bone, the feel of him between her thighs, on the tarmac, him asking what he had to do to get her to stay— or she could lose herself in the work. Now on this, her last official day as a Big Think employee, her desk was tidy by five o'clock, her to-do list complete.

Now what?

Sit there a while and pretend she had things to do? Or go home, watch *Grand Designs* and eat a party bag of Twisties then go to bed, blaming the ache in her belly on overindulging.

She let her head fall to her desk and groaned. The bargain she'd made—one night… It was laughable that she'd believed that would be enough. That scratching her seven-year itch would put an end to all her feelings. Now her mind was filled with the man, trying to think up ways she could twist her bargain, but every outcome ended up with her heart dying a slow death.

She would not be that woman, taking scraps, building castles in the sky. Her poor mum had tried that—looking for a man to save her from herself, again and again, as if expecting a different outcome—only to become smaller and smaller with every romantic failure.

So, no. Just, no. No bargaining required.

Hadley pressed back her chair, picked up her small packing box with Cactiss Everdeen balanced atop, and made her last ever trek to her office door. When her legs began to shake, as the gravity of what she was doing really took a hold, she reminded herself she was not *leaving* leaving, not quite yet.

She'd sequestered a smaller room in an empty wing on a lower floor to use until the Big Think Ball was done, but this beautiful space, that she had designed so meticulously, now belonged to Jonas.

The man himself was sitting on the corner of Kyle's desk, which had been draped in copious amounts of Christmas tinsel, Christmas music playing lightly from his speaker.

"Leaving already?" Jonas asked.

Kyle moved out from behind his desk to take the box, and his eyes flickered when he saw how little it contained.

"I'm all done," said Hadley, her voice huskier than she'd have liked.

"Great!" said Kyle, slipping a hand through one elbow, Jonas the other. "Then, you're coming with us. We have plans that include multiple cocktails."

"No, I have to…" She looked towards Ronan's door to find it closed. If that wasn't a kick to the heart, what was?

If she went home, she'd just relive her night with Ronan over and over again. The way he'd watched her in the car to the airport, the confusion in his eyes as he'd run after her on the tarmac.

"You know what?" she said. "Plans sounds perfect."

* * *

Ronan turned down a hallway on a floor of Big Think he was sure he'd never seen. The lights lit up as he moved through the space, thus saving power, as the area was mostly empty; the rooms built in order to cater for future bright minds they would invite to use the space rent-free.

If Hadley had deliberately chosen an office as far from his as possible from which to project-manage the upcoming Big Think Ball, she'd succeeded. If she thought that would stop him from looking for her, well, there she'd been mistaken.

After their conversation on the tarmac and how certain she'd been on leaving things be he'd had to respect that. He'd given her space, and time, to settle into her new role.

He'd also not wanted to look like some desperate six-teen-year-old with a crush, even though that's how he felt: moody, caught up in daydreams, and in a near constant state of arousal.

It was untenable. Not at all congruous to running a multi-billion-dollar company. Meaning he had to do something to take the edge off. Seeing her the only fix.

Nearing the end of the hallway, he heard music—sultry, smoky jazz that might have had a holiday theme. He saw light under a door, picked up his pace and, once there, slowly pushed open the door to find...

"Whoa."

A jewel-blue office chair with a caramel-coloured jacket slung over the back sat oblique to round glass desk covered in papers and fabric samples. On a side cabinet sat a bunch of plants in bright pots, including a strangely familiar cactus. A speaker pulsing notes into the air sat atop a top-notch coffee machine, alongside a small fake Christmas tree laden with rose-gold tinsel and tiny pale-blue lights.

"Ronan?"

Ronan spun to find Hadley in the hall behind him, holding a small carton of milk. A pair of glasses were perched on the end of her nose—those were new. Her hair was pulled back in a squat ponytail—that was new too. As was her outfit—skinny jeans and a loose, floral top that seemed to verge on translucent but not quite.

"Hi," he said, his voice rough. In fact, every part of him felt slightly wrong, as if seeing her again after a few days apart had knocked him sideways.

While she appeared perfectly cool, chilled, unfazed to the point of nonchalance. As if she had settled into her new role without a single speed bump. Which was *just great*.

"Did you need me for something?" she asked, eyebrow raised.

Hell, yes, he needed her for something. For many things. Standing there danger close, drinking in her fine features, breathing in her perfume, he could think of a dozen ways he needed her.

Not that he would say any that out loud, having taught himself the art of self-sacrifice far too well.

"Nothing in particular," he said. "I just happened to be in your part of town so thought I should swing by. See if you needed *me* for anything."

Her nostrils flared the slightest amount, but it was enough for him to wonder. To imagine if maybe he wasn't alone in missing this…this energy he gleaned simply from being near her.

"I have all I need here, thanks," she said. Then held up the carton. "Bar milk; which I borrowed from my new neighbours down the hall. A small start-up Sawyer brought on board. Nice guys."

She moved to slide past him, the brush of her elbow against his shirt setting off a shower of sparks in his belly.

Eyes rolling internally at his own ineptitude, muttering to himself to pull it together, he followed her into the room—feeling a little dizzy from the knowledge of how much he missed having this in his life every day.

"Coffee?" she asked, holding up the milk.

It yanked him back to their first year working together, when getting him coffee was something she did. Then one day she'd told him he was a big boy and could get his own damned coffee, and from that point the lines had been drawn. From that point, their past had seemed as if it had been finally put behind them their working relationship had been more partnership than boss and employee. Or so he'd thought.

"I'm fine," he said.

Hadley set to making herself a cup. "Jonas and I have been in touch several times a day, and he seems to have everything in hand. I truly think he might be some kind of savant. Or a robot, built specifically for that job. I'm sure he's much easier to work with than I ever was."

Ronan grunted his assent. Jonas was doing fine; better than fine. He was instinctive, efficient and happy to work all hours. He'd also been coping with Ronan's moods with an easy smile, as if he knew Ronan would wake up one day and decide he was done with being a grouch.

"And how's...? How's your mother?" Hadley asked, choosing the easier route.

"As expected," he said, her last call carrying an urgency that Ronan visit. That any chance of reconciliation was depleting—fast.

But that wasn't why he'd tracked Hadley down. Wasn't why his pulse beat in his neck, and his mouth felt too dry, or—

"What took you so long to come find me?" she said, her hand pausing on the dial of the espresso machine. Her head was down, as if she'd tried to stop herself from asking, but the weight of it had become too much.

And he heard it, like an angel's song: the wanting, the missing. The slight flare of her nostrils assuring him he was not alone in feeling the sensory bombardment that being in the same room together.

The song changed, a slow number that brought up images of speakeasies, smoky basements, and people wrapped around one another in dark corners. Or maybe that was all him—his desire for her like a living thing crawling over his skin, tugging at his clothes. Making a mess of his voice as he said, "You knew where I was."

He knew, almost instantly, that it was the wrong thing to say. "Hadley—"

But she cut him off. "One of the start-up guys down the hall is from Amsterdam, and it got me to thinking of the first trip we took together. With Ted. To visit your new lab there."

Ronan breathed out. "I remember."

"Do you remember the dinner at that hole in the wall? So much food. So much wine." Her lips quirked at the memory.

"I do," he said, his gaze dropping to the movement—to that mouth. He remembered how it had felt against his. The heat of it trailing over his chest. His belly. Lower.

"Do you remember the walk back to the hotel?" she asked, turning to lean back against the cabinet, her fingers gripping the edge. "When we stopped on the bridge to watch the barge make its way down the river?"

Ronan remembered. He remembered the breeze playing with her hair, though it had been shorter then. He remembered thinking how incredibly lucky they were to have her on their team. He remembered thinking he'd have gladly given that up if it meant he could wipe away the way that they'd met.

Ronan pushed away from the door. "You wore a red dress that night, first time I'd ever seen you in a dress. And these earrings—long, gold—that brushed your neck when you moved."

Hadley's chest lifted, her tongue swiping quickly over her lower lip.

And he felt himself go hard all over. As if, despite all those years spent using some freakishly competent inner strength to hold himself back, he'd lost the knack completely.

For he also remembered her turning to look at him, a smile in her eyes that had soon been overtaken with heat, with invitation. All of which he'd no doubt returned in kind. Because he'd wanted her, even then.

Yet it was a fraction of the want he felt now. This felt urgent, as if it was tied up in his very life force. He took a step her way, then another. Till he was close enough she had to look up to hold eye contact. Then he reached up to take her by the chin, tugging his thumb over that full bottom lip.

"What took you so long?" she said, her breath washing cool air over his damp thumb. And he knew she was no longer talking about the past few days, but about their entire relationship.

"I didn't trust myself to know when to stop."

"But I trusted you," she said, then her tongue darted out to touch his thumb. Before she leaned closer and took it into her mouth.

Skin shocked by a thousand pricks of sensation, brain a cloud of need, Ronan pulled his thumb free and cradled her face in his hands.

Where their first kiss had been a beautiful surprise, this felt decided. There was no heightened emotion, no adrenaline kicking them into gear. This was Ronan, holding Hadley, because it was something they both very much wanted to do.

When his fingers brushed her cheekbones, she sighed. When he leaned down to kiss her forehead, her eyes fluttered closed, and he pressed a kiss on each eyelid, velvet-soft, a promise to be gentle with her. To repay that trust.

Then her hands ran up the front of his shirt, her body lifting, her head tilting, and he pressed his lips to hers. Sparks, heat and a sense of something new poured through him. Like New Year's Eve in slow motion.

Her hands, making their way over his shoulders, up his neck, into his hair, made a slow exploration that matched the languorous pace of the kiss. A kiss built on sensation and instinct, longing and connection. A kiss he wished could last forever.

His hands moved into her hair, catching on the hairband holding it back, dislodging it so that her waves spilled over his fingers, and her moan as his fingers found her scalp turned things slow to needy quick-smart.

All pressing bodies, and needy hands, he lifted her thigh to his hip. To roll against her centre, so she could feel just how much he wanted this.

She gasped against his mouth. He smiled at the sound. Then he nipped her full bottom lip before sucking it into his mouth. The heat roiling between them deepened, till he could barely see past the fog in his head.

The coffee machine whirred angrily as it turned itself off and Hadley jerked, turning towards the sound. Ronan took advantage, turning her all the way, his hand sliding across her belly, drawing another gasp.

Nudging her hair aside to kiss the back of her neck, he slipped a finger beneath the beltline of her jeans, then another, before opening the button with a snap as he pressed his hand into her trousers, her zip opening for him as he dipped his fingers between her legs to find her ready...for him.

Her arm slid around his neck, using it as an anchor as she opened herself to him, warm and wanton as he gave her all that he craved.

A finger slid along her seam, parting her, finding that nub then circling, circling, consistent, relentless. Even as she jerked away he found her. Even as she curled into his hand, chasing the relief, he didn't let up.

He would give her anything she wanted, all that she needed. She only had to ask.

When he bit down on her shoulder, then gave her neck a long, slow lick, mirroring the move of his hand, she cried out his name.

Then there was no more finessing, just long, sure, deep strokes as she came and came and came. He held her to him through it all. Till finally, she stilled, her mouth open, her face contorted in the most beautiful vision of pure ecstasy before she broke, waves of pleasure wracking her body.

But he kept on stroking, luxuriating in the way she trembled, her joy soothing the ache inside of him. When a sob escaped her mouth at the same time as her hand gripped his neck harder, he let her set the pace. And she rocked against his hand, gentling, slowing, caressing, hunting those final flourishes till she was limp in his arms.

As the fog slowly cleared, Ronan found himself braced against the cabinet, legs apart, Hadley a rag doll in his arms, soft jazz floating from the speaker, with the door to her new office wide open.

None of which had registered from the moment his mouth touched hers.

"Ronan?" she said when he moved an inch, her voice husky, holding none of its usual mettle.

"Can you stand?" he asked gruffly.

She straightened up. "Kind of." Then she turned, her hand reaching between them.

But Ronan moved back, rearranging himself as best he could. The speed with which he'd lost track of his surroundings, of any consequences, sat uncomfortably in his gut. That, and he felt so over-sensitised, one touch and he might blow.

Hadley's eyes questioned him: still dark, a little wild, and vulnerable in a way he'd never seen in her. All of which only added to his sense of unease, none of which was her fault.

So he stepped in, took her chin and kissed her again. Thoroughly.

"Next time," he said, shifting to give the hard ridge between his thighs a little room, if not relief. Because more than relief he needed to know there *would* be a next time. It was get him through.

As it turned out, it was the exactly right thing to say, for Hadley grinned before laughter escaped her lungs in a burst of pure joy. "I can live with that," she said, then shook her head, as if she too was happy to have a promise of more. Then she said, "Off with you, then. For I am a busy woman and I have work to do."

Ronan ran a hand over his hair and straightened his shirt, while Hadley watched his movements with a hunger he'd remember till his dying day.

Moving to her door on less than stable legs, he shot her one last look. One that had her teeth biting down on her bottom lip. Walking away from her then, with her hair a mess, her jeans still snapped open, her shirt half-hanging off one shoulder, was the hardest thing he'd ever done.

But he knew that the work he'd done, the self-sacrifice he'd perfected, had led to this, had led to her.

He knocked his knuckles on the door frame in goodbye—for now. Then he took his time making his way down the hall, glad now that she'd chosen a room so far from the rest of the world.

Not only because he needed time to make himself decent, but because it made this…whatever it was…feel as if it was private, untouched by all that they had once been.

How long it might feel that way, he couldn't possibly know. How long before he saw her again was up to the universe. But, for now, he'd take it.

In the end, he didn't have to wait long, for that night Hadley came to him, late, once the building had emptied. His staff having long since gone home, the only sign he wasn't alone in the world the whir of the cleaning staff somewhere nearby.

He heard a sound and looked up to find her in the door of his office, holding the heels of her shoes in one hand, twirling her security pass with the other, the one that still gave her access to every part of the building.

He hadn't told her to keep it because he'd hoped this might be the result, but because as far as he was concerned, she could go where she wanted, do as she pleased, and hold the keys to his kingdom for evermore.

"Hey," she said.

"Hey, yourself."

She padded into the room, closing the door behind her, then kept on coming, dropping her shoes, one by one.

Ronan made to stand, the need to be near her, to touch her, taking him over. But she shook her head and he settled back in his chair. He was glad to be sitting, as his legs might well have given way when she pulled her shirt over her head, letting it trail to the floor. Then she snapped open his very favourite pair of jeans in the history of jeans, stopping only long enough to step out of them before letting them pool where they landed.

The low light of his desk lamp poured over her, mixing with the twinkle of city lights behind him. He was dying to kiss her lean curves, the swell of her breasts, the edge of her nipples just peaking over the top of her half-cup bra, the dip at her waist, the dark shadow showing through the soft floral underwear at the apex of her thighs....

Pulse trumpeting in his neck, his belly, *everywhere*, he dared not blink as she rounded his desk, pressed a hand to his chest and straddled him. Then asked, "Is now a good time?"

He swore his response before lifting up, a hand delving into the back of her hair and pulling her to him for an open-mouthed kiss that had him fast forgetting his own damned name.

It was a good while later—spent, drenched in sweat, his shirt open, his trousers at his ankles, his tie somehow half-hanging off his neck—that Ronan came back into his own skin. His toes strained to hold his weight, his body bent over Hadley who was splayed out naked on his desk and his own primal, rawness still ringing in his ears.

The cool of the office must have trickled over her skin, as she shivered, goose bumps shooting up over her arms.

He reached down, and lifted her into his arms. He kicked his trousers from his ankles, carried her to the lounge chair, then sat with her curled in his lap.

Body loose, skin slick and pink, she lifted her head and looked him in the eyes. And the emotion there was so raw, so rich, it should have shocked him to his core.

But instead it seemed to meet something inside him. Some twin emotion that he could not name, only feel. A rush, a roar, a truth he'd been avoiding rose inside of him, but he stamped it down unsure that he could handle it. Unsure that he deserved it. A familiar smoky darkness rose inside him then, the kind that all the spectacular sex in the world could not quite snuff out.

Till she lifted a hand to his face, her eyes wide, telling him to stop thinking so hard. then she kissed him on the mouth once, hard, then pulled herself up and away. She found her clothes and stepped into them. When she found her underwear, she was already dressed, so she tucked it into her back pocket.

Then she shot him a glance, taking in his rakish tie, his socked feet, the jut of his erection ready to go again after having watched the way she put herself together, her movements so spare, so elegant.

She whistled through her teeth before biting down on her bottom lip in a way that said, "next time", without her having said a thing.

Then she picked up her shoes and walked out of his office.

And so it went, over the next few weeks.

They had no trouble finding one another—in stairwells, in the car park, in her office or his—as if they each had in-built compasses, permanently seeking one another out.

Sometimes it was quiet and slow; sometimes a raw, fast coming-together. Other times there was laughter and whispers in darkness. Ronan liked those times best, for it harked back to late nights in his office in the *before*, trips they'd taken to a hundred cities the world over, drunk on exhaustion and success. But not enough to act on the underlying sexual tension that had seasoned their relationship from the beginning.

When Ronan discovered she liked it when he talked, he articulated the feel of her skin beneath his hands, the taste of her on his tongue, how much he loved the flush on her neck as he touched her there… He couldn't believe he was saying the actual words he'd been thinking for so many years. He wondered why the hell they'd wasted so much time. And quieted the niggling, questioning voice, asking what he might yet to do to ruin it all.

Then, suddenly, it was the week of Christmas. And, just around the corner, the Big Think Ball.

CHAPTER NINE

IT WAS STILL a week until Big Think Ball—or, as the rest of the world called it, Christmas Eve. The whole crew—bar Petra, who was still in New York—had gathered at Ted and Adelaid's new Mount Martha home—a glorious, woodsy gabled mansion with the most beautiful outlook over the bay beyond.

"Drink up!" said Adelaid, forcing after-dinner eggnog into Sawyer's hand, then rubbing her lower back.

"You're not going to pop, are you?" Sawyer asked of Adelaid, before happily downing the drink. With Petra away, he was sleeping over. Then, *"Are you?"*

"Relax, Ted's a doctor," Ronan growled from his position by the fireplace, frowning at his phone as he tried to change the *Christmas for Kids* playlist crooning through the hidden speakers to anything else.

"Of *chemistry*," said Sawyer, slight panic in his voice.

Ronan's laugh, all deep and husky, sent shivers down Hadley's spine. As if he knew she was watching him, he glanced over to where she leant against the door to the kitchen. The heat in his gaze so sharp, so focussed, she felt it pierce her heart.

She spun into the kitchen, where she bumped Adelaid away from the sink and took over loading the dishwasher.

"Thank you!" said Adelaid. "I have to pee so bad." Then she was off, waddling to the bathroom.

Hadley took a moment to grip the cool of the kitchen bench, because the evening had been a lot. Wonderful, yet bittersweet. For once she left Big Think, it might well be the last such gathering she would ever be invited to attend.

Then there was the constant fear she and Ronan would give themselves away. Despite Adelaid's earlier attestation that *everyone* had been walking around eggshells for ages, waiting for Hadley and Ronan finally to crack, the others had never seemed to notice. And Hadley wanted to keep it that way. Her final week was going to be emotional enough without having to deal with any extra noise.

Besides, no promises had been made, no plans. Only short trysts. Lovely trysts—hot, sweet, tender and delectably intimate. As if, having known one another so well for so many years, they had nothing to prove and nothing to hide. But only inside the walls of Big Think Tower.

All of which made the whole thing feel beautifully tenuous. Like sunlight refracting through droplets of morning mist clinging to a freshly made spider's web, a single shake of a foundation branch and…it would be gone. As if it had never been.

"Okay," said Adelaid, sweeping Hadley out of the kitchen and pressing her back into the sitting room. "Ted can finish this up later. It's party time."

Scooting around the humungous Christmas tree, laden with wildly inappropriate ornaments Adelaid had collected over the years, Hadley waited for Adelaid to get comfortable on the plush ten-seater couch before finding a place at her side.

When toddler Katie made a beeline for her mum, Ted, standing behind the couch, swept her up and over his shoulder till she giggled uproariously.

"Thank you," Adelaid mouthed, her gaze sparkling with love.

Hadley's heart clutched. Ted's and Adelaid's tenderness towards one another was so obvious. They just let it all hang out, as if there was no fear that one day they'd blink and find it had all been a beautiful mirage.

Was that why Hadley was so fearful of anyone finding out about how she felt, Ronan included? Her mum had put so much faith in love being some ultimate answer, only for it to sideswipe her again and again. And again…

"Hadley," said Adelaid, and Hadley flinched.

"Hmm? Yes?"

"I've been meaning to say. The *Wizard of Oz* photo shoot—genius. Truly."

Hadley smiled her thanks. It had come together even better than she'd envisaged. Forgoing the boys' usual corporate spit and shine for unexpected whimsy, had led to fantastic media take-up.

"What *Wizard of Oz* shoot?" asked Ted, now holding Katie on one hip.

Adelaid gaped affectionately at her husband. "To think how I've been educating you as to the wonder of vintage films. You, Sawyer, Ronan…hay bales…."

"Ah. How was that related to the *Wizard of Oz*?"

"Did you not see it?" Adelaid asked. "You, my big, beautiful, clueless, brilliant, tawny bearded wonder, were the lion. Which is spot on. You took one look at me, and *bam*! Instant courage."

A smile tugged at the corner of Ted's mouth. "True, that."

"While you…" Adelaid reached out with a foot and lightly kicked Sawyer in the shin.

"The Scarecrow," said Sawyer, clicking his fingers at Hadley. "I did wonder when they gave me a tartan shirt and torn jeans."

Adelaid grinned. "People have always underestimated you, Sawyer. They think you're all biff and buff. But our Petra always knew you were razor-sharp."

Sawyer's smile was a mix of "aw, shucks" and fierce love

for his absentee girl. Hadley's heart kicked so hard against her ribs, she winced.

"As for *you*, Ronan Gerard," drawled Adelaid, waggling a finger at him as he stood near the fireplace. "Hadley nailed you best of all."

At that, Hadley stilled, while Ronan did a full spit-take into his drink before coughing into a closed fist.

Sawyer, showing exactly how sharp he was, glanced from Ronan to Hadley and back again, before saying, "Ronan's the yappy dog, right?"

"Toto!" said Katie.

"That's my girl," said Adelaid, reaching back to grab her daughter's foot. "But, actually, Uncle Ronan is the Tin Man. The one with no heart."

It took Adelaid a little longer than the rest to get the sense that all the air had been sucked from the room. While Hadley's throat seized up. For she'd meant the exact opposite. But how to tell him, without giving herself away? How to assure him that his heart was the best part of him?

"No, no, no! Wait." Poor, sweet Adelaid, famous for speaking before she thought, blanched as her hand fluttered to her chest. "You know full well that's *not* what I meant."

"So, I'm *not* heartless?" Ronan asked, raising a single eyebrow.

"Gosh, no! I meant you do present as a gruff, alpha, silver-spoon tycoon, figurehead of a behemoth company."

Ronan raised both eyebrows at that, comically so, and he crossed his arms dramatically, clearly playing with Adelaid now. She knew it too, by the colour that returned to her cheeks, and the gusts of breathless laughter she struggled to contain.

And, while Hadley knew that those words had pressed hard into soul deep bruises the man carried like a badge of honour, in that moment, Hadley had never loved him more.

"I do hope there's a 'but'," Ronan encouraged.

"But…" said Adelaid, now deep into a mass of giggles, giving the occasional, "Ow, ow, ow…" as she held a hand to her side. "Beneath the shiny exterior, you, Ronan Gerard, are *all* heart. *That's* the point. Right, Hadley?"

Hadley stilled as the group turned to face her, waiting for her response. Of course that was the point. But if she said yes…?

Ears buzzing, she turned to Adelaid. "I'd thought I'd been more subtle than that. This being my last ball, I've wanted it to be special. To really say something. For me, the shoot says that while Big Think has been a place dreams are made of—you guys didn't land the road to some magical place, you built it."

The silence that came over the room was different this time. It was thick, warm and fuzzy, and Hadley had no idea what to do with the emotion coming at her from all corners.

"Oh, Hadley," said Adelaid, hauling her in for a half-hug, her belly somewhat getting in the way.

While Ted placed a hand on Hadley's shoulder and gave it a squeeze.

Sawyer shook his head. "Why are you leaving us, Hadley?"

"Leave her be," said Adelaid, as she alone knew how conflicted Hadley was. "She just gave the perfect Big Think family Christmas toast, so let's raise a glass."

Adelaid grabbed her glass of pineapple juice from the coffee table then lifted it in the air and said, "To bravery and bright minds and big strong hearts. And to friends who become family. To Big Think."

Hadley lifted her glass of bubbly, and only when she took a sip did her eye line shift, finding Ronan.

He was watching her, his expression fierce.

Only it wasn't his heart she was thinking about in that moment—it was her own. And the fact that it had been in his hands for so long, she wasn't quite sure how it would cope when she finally took it back.

What if she didn't take it back? What if she braved up and stopped getting in her own way? If his heart was as strong and as capable as she knew it to be, wasn't it just possible he just might surprise her?

Later, once Katie had been put to bed with the promise of dreams of sugar-plum fairies and reindeer bells, and after Petra's surprise arrival at the door in a whirlwind of happy cheer—a true Christmas Eve miracle—Hadley ducked outside, needing air not quite so thick with all that loving, happy emotion.

The warm summer wind tugged at her hair. The fairy lights pinned to the wrought-iron lace of the porch eaves scattered golden light over her arms as she leaned against the railing, watching moonlight twinkling off the bay beyond. Voices, song and laughter hummed inside the house behind her.

"The Tin Man. That's one I've never been called before."

Hadley didn't turn. She didn't need to. She'd felt Ronan coming long before he announced himself.

He shut the door behind him. Then moved in beside her, resting his elbows on the railing. "Though I'm sure it's not the first time you've called me something no one else would dare."

Hadley shot him a look.

Ronan's gaze landed on hers, deep, dark blue: her favourite colour in the whole world. He shifted, crossing his arms on the railing, so that his fingers of one hand were near enough to touch, before he asked, "So what's next for the Wizard?"

"The…?"

"The one behind the curtains who really makes the magic happen."

Hadley breathed in deeply, taking in the night air; Ronan's assertion knocking about inside her like a pinball. "I have options. Emerson, from Pitch Perfect, has sent through a dozen interesting offers."

"I bet."

"But I think I'm going to cave-dwell for a while. Sleep in, garden, see a movie at an actual cinema—the kinds of things I imagine normal people do for pleasure."

He hummed with understanding. "Is that why you're leaving? To have a 'normal' life?"

She shook her head, but he stopped her with a finger brushing against her arm. A light caress, in contrast to his hard gaze as he watched the place where their bodies met.

This man with his hard, shiny outer shell and his warm, kind, generous heart. The heart he refused to acknowledge, as if it made him weak, instead of it being his greatest asset. He'd seen her naked, he'd seen her cry, he'd seen her enraged and giddy with joy. Hell, the moment they'd *met*, he'd seen her at her very worst and had told her he was on her side.

Not only did he deserve to know the truth, he could handle it. After the last few weeks that they'd spent together, she was sure of it.

The muffled voices in the house lifted, and a new song began. Hadley thought of the joy in Petra's eyes when she'd seen Sawyer coming at her like a steam train, and Adelaid's expression as she'd tucked herself under Ted's arm, his hand resting protectively over her pregnant belly.

Then she angled a little Ronan's way and said, "When I started working for you, I barely knew myself. I was so desperate—for security, for comfort, for independence. I'd have fought for those things, tooth and nail. Only, with you they came so easily, and in such abundance, and I just stopped fighting. Stopped fighting for what I wanted next, in case I lost what I had."

"What was it you wanted?"

Hadley lifted a hand to Ronan's face, cradling his hard jaw and running her thumb over his cheek, the rasp of his day-old stubble sending goose bumps up her arm. Then, heedless of who might be watching, she leaned in and pressed her lips to his.

His hesitation was brief, before his eyes slammed closed and he kissed her deeply, like a man drowning. He turned to pull her into his arms, as if he'd been craving her all night long.

When they finally pulled apart, lips clinging for a tenuous final moment, Hadley's eyes fluttered open, their breaths loud in the night air.

"I wanted that," she said simply. "I've always wanted that. Only wanting and not having does tend to wear a person down. And I didn't want to be worn down. I want to…garden, and see movies, and sleep in on Sundays."

And here was the kicker. Oh, the lies she'd told herself in an effort at not making the same mistakes her mum had made. When the truth was she wished she could have her mum back, long enough to just hug her. And tell her she was enough.

"And I want to have a family, or at least *be* a family. Not because I work with someone, but because we chose one another, and made promises to one another, and meant it."

She took a deep breath.

"What I want is to love. And be loved." Rather than making her feel weak, saying it out loud made her feel invincible.

"I'm in love with you, Ronan," she said, unable to help the catch in her voice. "And that's why I had to leave."

There—that was it. That was all of it. Having shed the load she'd been carrying for so long, she felt limitless. As if she might float up and away. But she didn't want to float away. She wanted Ronan to respond.

He did, by leaning back, just enough for moonlight to spill between them. Enough to let in the warm night breeze where before there had been only him.

Well, she thought, *that's a response all right.* Cheeks warming, stomach churning, she reached out for him, curled her fingers into his shirt and gave him a shake. "Say something, damn you."

It worked.

"You've got me wrong," he said. "You've got me *all* wrong. I can't."

"Can't what, exactly?"

"I just... I can't."

And that was it. That was all she got.

While in the background voices sang loudly, joyously, *I Saw Mummy Kissing Santa Claus*, Ronan's jaw turned to granite, his blue eyes onyx dark. She wasn't even sure the man was breathing any more. It was as if he'd morphed from a potent, decided, hot-blooded man into a suit of armour, impenetrable and cold, before her very eyes.

What had she *thought* would happen? Honestly? That he'd fall to his knees and declare his undying love for her? He'd known how she felt. He'd had to—some semblance of it at least. The rich vein of sensual tension coursing between them, teetering on the border between flirtation and vexation, had been the keystone of their relationship.

And now he *"couldn't"*? Couldn't what? Couldn't *love her*? Why not? What was wrong with *her*?

No, that wasn't it. She'd been with him, *really* been with him. He worshipped her. What he meant was that he *wouldn't* love her. Wouldn't even allow for the possibility. Because that would mean he'd stopped fighting against all the demons in his own damned head.

Which made her not worth *stopping* fighting for.

Hands shaking, insides crushed, she took a step back, then

another, distancing herself from Ronan, from the yearning that still curled inside her. For, while her heart felt pummelled, her feelings all awash, there was pride there too.

Pride in how she'd taken the leap. Pride that she'd stopped hiding from herself. And she wasn't about to lose that by begging.

While Ronan might be brilliant, might be deeply committed to being a better man—might well be the love of her life—she wanted more. And, no matter how many times she failed, she'd not stop reaching. Because she was her indomitable mother's daughter, after all.

Hadley said, "Merry Christmas, Ronan. I hope you get whatever it is that you do want."

Then she stepped in to press a kiss to his cheek and felt him expand towards her. Felt the tension in him, as if he was struggling not to haul her close. Because wanting her had never been his problem—believing he deserved her had.

Heading inside, she said her goodbyes to a chorus of, "No!" and, "Stay!" She hugged each friend, a little harder than she usually might have, then headed out into the sultry midsummer's night.

With no plan, no destination, no driving goal—only herself to hang onto.

She had him wrong. Hadley had him all wrong.

Ronan knew he had a heart…it was just a battered, bloodied mess of a thing. Beaten into submission young, his parents' example of what relationships looked like having sent it cowering into the deepest recesses of his chest.

What was left of it, he kept under lock and key, protected and safe, so that he might eke out just enough empathy and hope to do the kind of work he had to do. Until there was nothing in reserve for anything else. Anyone else.

Not nearly enough to give Hadley what she'd asked of him. To give her what she deserved.

Hell, he'd been so selfish, taking all that he could of her these past weeks.

And all the while Hadley had loved him. *Loved* him. She'd said the actual words. Hadn't she? The more he replayed her declaration inside his head, the more it began to feel less and less real.

Attraction, yes—God, yes. Understanding, intimacy, friendship built over years of knowing one another—absolutely. The truth was, he adored her. If he had to be stuck on planet Earth with a single person, he'd choose her, hands down.

And there *had* been a moment, a pause in time, after she'd said those words and an explosive warmth had bled the hairline cracks in the iron casing around his heart. The same cracks that being with Hadley these last weeks had brought on.

But *love*? Surely she knew him better than that. For, to him it might as well be a cyclone, the kind one had no hope in hell of curtailing. The kind that made a person feel helpless, out of control. Was she surprised he'd shut down? Tin Man? Try Fort Knox-level bank vault.

"Hey."

Ronan flinched hard, his neck pinching. Then he turned to find Ted ambling up to him, hands shoved into his pockets, feet bare on the wooden porch.

Ronan rolled out the tension pulling at his shoulders, breathed into the ache in his gut and managed to say, "Hey."

"I've been sent to find out if you're planning on coming back inside any time soon. Or are you keeping an eye out for Santa?" Ted leant down to see out from under the roof, where starlight poured down on the dark greenery between their house and the bay, creating an eerie glow.

Voice ragged, Ronan said, "I think it's best I head off. Can you give Adelaid my apologies?"

Ted gave Ronan a look. "Not in the mood for sing-alongs? Now Hadley's left?"

Ronan's instinct was to deflect. To self-protect. But his armour had taken a beating and he found himself saying, "Something like that."

"Mmm. Can't be easy for you, mate, with her gone, me working from home, and Sawyer away with Petra a lot of the time. You could have made it hard for any of us to make the changes we did. And, considering the investment we've all ploughed into the business, you'd have had every right. But you've been a prince among men—Adelaid's words, not mine."

Ronan breathed out, the weight of Ted's words gushing through the cracks in his armour—bigger now, and too many to mend.

Ted glanced at Ronan. "I'm sorry if we've let you down."

At that Ronan baulked. Did they really think that? Was that what his descent into gruff moroseness over the past couple of years had led them all to believe? Did Sawyer think that? Did *Hadley*?

"Ted," he said, his hand landing on his old friend's back. "Big Think was my breathtakingly ridiculous dream. When you two lumbered into my life, I lured you into my plan. *Any* time I've had with you at my side has been my fortune."

Ted's mouth crooked into a smile. "I think you'll find we were happy to be lured. Without *you*, we'd have both flubbed about in mediocre careers."

Ronan's mouth twitched, but more out of habit than any feeling of mirth. For his whole body ached, as if he'd come down with a sudden flu. "Highly unlikely. But thank you for pretending otherwise."

Ted's smile grew, for he knew his worth. His work would

have been ground-breaking with or without the others. Just as Sawyer would have found stratospheric success in any field he'd tried. While Ronan…

Ronan's instinct was to claim brilliance regards the scaffolding he'd created, and the clever people he'd forced to join his cult. Except Hadley's earlier words, regarding the Big Think dream, and the family he'd built, forced him to acknowledge that he was more than the sum of his parts.

Ted reached out and slapped a hand on Ronan's back. "Now come back inside when you're ready. And stick around. It's nice in there."

With that, Ted ambled indoors, ducking to fit under the door frame. Leaving Ronan feeling freed. As if he'd been holding onto a lead balloon his whole entire life, and had finally let it go.

After the horror show with Hadley, he *also* as if his insides had been hollowed out. But he'd rebuilt himself from less before. He could do it again. So long as he stuck to the promise he'd made himself all those years ago—to protect those under his care—at all costs.

And protecting Hadley meant compelling her to see that loving him would never be in her best interests, then so be it.

CHAPTER TEN

THE NEXT WEEK went by impossibly fast. As if Hadley had clicked her heels together three times and it was the night of the Big Think Ball.

"Holy Dorothy," said Jonas as together they stood in the entrance to the ballroom at the Elysium Hotel. It was not long before the guests were due to arrive and the gang was all there, taking in the custom-made light show of creamy dappled light shimmering and shifting over the walls, ceilings and floors—images of trees, fields and floating orbs of witch-light drifting in and out of focus. While at their feet golden swirls of light—less yellow brick, more buttery dreamscape—swept from the entrance, through the ballroom then up onto the stage.

A rush of satisfaction slid through Hadley, warming the edges of her still stone-cold insides, like the tiniest flame still trying its best to survive an ashen fireplace.

"Oh, Hadley, it's perfect," Petra, a world-class art curator, pronounced.

"That's saying something," said Sawyer, drawing Petra in to kiss the top of her head.

"I assume proper measures have been taken to ensure no one will experience vertigo?" Ted pondered as he watched the lights move across the high, gilded ceiling.

Adelaid smacked her husband on the arm. "Stop being Science Boy and just appreciate the gorgeousness."

Kyle laughed. "Good luck besting this next year, Jonas," he said, before dragging Hadley's replacement off to do a final tech check.

The others followed, moving into the ballroom, pointing out all the deeply charming touches.

While Hadley breathed out, suddenly deeply exhausted. Since driving back to Melbourne on Christmas Eve night, she'd been keeping herself going by willpower alone. Now the end was here, and there was nothing more she could do, she could quite happily have found an empty room and cried.

A rush of tingles skittered over her skin and a moment later Ronan moved in beside her, his gruff voice scooting up her arms and into her chest as he said, "Hadley. This is phenomenal."

"Thank you," she managed, the first words she'd said to him since Christmas Eve.

Not because she regretted telling him how she felt. That had been a revelation. The tough, insular young woman who'd been ready to scratch and fight the world for her place in it, had found such faith in her own decision-making ability, she'd let herself fall in love. And that was a hell of a thing.

Which didn't mean it didn't hurt like hell not to have all those big wonderful feelings returned.

Hadley braced herself and turned to face him. Her heart stuttered when she saw how hard he looked. His gaze tight, his stance rigid. It was as if he'd clad himself in new heavy-duty armour, several layers deep.

But this wasn't the time to worry about Ronan, or herself. Tonight was about raising funds to pay for projects Big Think had not yet even dreamed of.

Holding her tablet in front of her like a shield, she said, "Okay, report time. As it stands, donations have already exceeded projections. We've sold more tables than ever before.

And, once the Founders' Auction goes ahead, I honestly believe we will have raised more money than we did the first and second years combined."

Ronan finally looked her way. And as her eyes met his, the one place he couldn't hide no matter how hard he tried, she saw *him*. His sorrow and his struggle. His desire and his demons. His obstinance and his aspiration. And, as if some flood gate had been accidentally left open, her love for him swept through her like a rogue wave.

It was too much. She didn't even bother making up an excuse, merely spun and walked away. But where could she go? The She the hordes were gathering at the front door. And she had actual important work still to do. So, she turned back, only to stop again.

"Can I help you?" a soft voice asked.

Hadley looked to her right to find she'd stopped outside the cloak room, of all places, considering what had happened— or nearly happened—the night of the first Big Think Ball.

That moment swept over her with such aching clarity. She and Ronan, tossed together into the dark. Her hand running up his lapel, the rampant thudding of his heart proof that she wasn't alone in her desire. The way, even in the near-darkness, she'd felt his gaze drop to her mouth.

Even though nothing had happened, that moment had unlocked the possibility. It had been the tipping point after which everything had changed, leaving her in a permanent state of yearning.

"Hadley?"

Blinking her way out of the fog of memory, Hadley looked up to find Ronan standing a few feet away, brutishly handsome, all potent power constrained beneath the confines of his sleek tux.

When he walked towards her, desire sprang to life inside

her, curling and unfolding throughout, as if all it needed was the mere hope of rain to bloom.

Unless… What if she stayed? Let him speak? Maybe he'd just needed more time?

"Hadley," he said again when he neared. His voice was low, intimate and ragged. His gaze was hot and hungry.

She couldn't breathe for the anticipation.

He took another step towards her, his hand reaching…

"Oh, brilliant!" a voice called out. One of the young photographers—all of whom had been recommended by Sawyer's little sister, Daisy—hired to cover the event.

And the moment was shattered, like a pebble hitting a pane of glass.

"Photo op!" said the photographer, lunging towards them, holding an old-school flash camera to his eye.

"Wait," Hadley said, needing a moment to collect herself.

For this was not Oz; it was real life. There would be no magical transformation in the Tin Man. Ronan would remain the king of stubbornness. "We should find Sawyer and Ted, while you're all nice and pressed. Before you get food on your ties."

Then she glanced at his bow tie, to find it was crooked—infinitesimally, but still. She felt Ronan notice her noticing in the way his body stilled, his chest lifted. In the way he held his breath, as if waiting for her touch. Waiting for her to turn into him, step between his shoes, breathe deeply of his warmth and his skin, her fingers brushing his shirt as she fixed his nearly perfect tie. It was the same sweet foreplay dance they'd been performing for years.

She glanced up to find him watching her, an eyebrow lifted.

Then, fingers tingling in disappointment, she left his tie alone, and turned to face the photographer. "Second thoughts, take the photo."

"Great!" said the photographer. "Scoot in. Nice and close."

Hadley scooted in, a ripple of awareness shifting through her as Ronan's hand landed on her lower back.

"Now, smile!"

For some reason she could never explain, rather than grit her teeth and force a smile, Hadley looked up at Ronan, to find he was looking down at her. Her emotions went into freefall. Time tumbled over itself. Multiverses, what-ifs, chances missed and opportunities avoided coalesced into that moment. Their shorthand went haywire as she read so much in his eyes that he didn't have the language, or the capacity, to say.

Click-click-click.

"Gorgeous!" the photographer declared, then bounced off towards the ballroom.

"Gerard!" a voice called.

Hadley blinked back into the moment, and looked up to see the doors at the far end of the long entrance hall had opened, the first of their guests arriving in a wave of glitter, sparkle and black tie.

As if they shared the same consciousness, Hadley and Ronan stepped apart and the Big Think Ball began.

The rest of the night flew past like a beautiful dream until it was mere minutes before the Billion-Dollar Bachelor Auction. The big finale. Hadley's last hurrah.

She checked the account on her tablet, a wad of emotion lodging in her throat when she saw that in the past half-hour they'd reached her blue-sky target and exceeded it by over a million dollars.

Scrolling down the lists of donors—most anonymous, some not—she stopped. Her throat closed up at the sight of one name in particular. She looked up, searching for Ronan, her instincts finding him in an instant.

Miraculously, he was alone, standing at the side of the room, watching the evening unfold. While she'd managed to avoid him for much of the night for her own mental health, there was no way she could now.

"Ronan," she said, as she approached.

He turned, his dark-blue eyes lighting up.

Telling her heart to calm the heck down, Hadley held up the tablet. When he saw the total, he coughed out a husky laugh. "Seriously?"

She nodded, a smile catching at her mouth.

The smile turned to laughter when he suddenly reached for her, picked her up and spun her round. Those nearby looked and laughed, surprised and delighted.

When Ronan slowed, Hadley slid down his body, her hand running down the back of his neck and over his shoulder. As her heels hit the floor, their gazes caught, locked in a private moment, heat and history coursing between them.

Stronger now, Hadley was the one to step away. "There's one more thing. The donation that put us over the edge…it was from your father."

Ronan reared back as if slapped. "What the…? No. He'd never."

"He did." She showed him the relevant donation in bold: Constantine Gerard and Associates.

Ronan lifted a hand and ran it over his face as he peered out over the crowd, as if looking for hidden danger. "I can't accept it."

"You can," said Hadley, reaching out and taking him by the arm, squeezing till his gaze returned to hers. His armour now gone, as if that had been a mirage and it had taken too much energy to keep it in place. Then, "You *have* to."

"But why?" he said. "Why now?"

"An olive branch? An apology? His way of finally telling

you he sees value in what you are doing? The only way to know is to ask him."

It was just as likely Constantine Gerard was messing with his son, as he always had, but this moment was not about *him*. It was about Ronan giving himself permission to make peace—with his father's actions, his father's past, his father's blood running through his own veins—so that he could truly move on.

Maybe then he could could allow himself to love. But not until he loved himself.

Hadley traced her hand down his arm till she took him by the hand. His fingers curled instantly, protectively, around hers.

"You are not your father, Ronan."

"I know," he said, his voice deep, ragged.

"You are not your father," she said again.

"I know," he growled, louder this time. Loud enough that the air from his words tossed her hair from her cheeks.

"Then you know that this money is bigger than all of that. Take it and do good with it. Because you can."

The orchestra struck up a chord and Hadley glanced distractedly towards the sound, to find couples moving around the dance floor, eyes to the sky, laughing and cheering as the light show changed to make those dancing appear as if they were being rained on by golden dandelion dust.

When she looked back, it was to find Ronan looking down at where their hands were joined. He turned her fingers over till her palm faced up and he ran a slow thumb down the centre, sending a hot flush up Hadley's arm.

Then he used that hand to tug her closer and said, "Dance with me."

"But the donation…"

"Will be put to good use, as you rightly proposed. Now,

put work aside and dance with me. In this amazing space that you created."

Slipping her tablet into the pocket she'd had built into the voluminous skirt of her designer dress, she nodded and let Ronan draw her closer still. Then he led the way to the dance floor. His hand was tucked over hers, as if he never wanted to let her go.

But he *was* letting her go, in every sense. She no longer worked for him, and he refused to give into his feelings for her. Which meant this moment, this dance, was to be their full stop.

Which was why she refused to read anything into the heavy glint in his eyes. Or the thud of his heart as he turned her into his arms. Or how tightly he held her—one hand tucked between them, the other low on her back as they swayed to the strains of *Moonlight Serenade*, dandelion dust floating down on them from above.

Hadley let her eyes drift closed, and let herself love him, one last time.

A smatter of applause brought Hadley back to the present far too soon, to find they were still swaying while everyone else was facing the stage, cheering as the MC made his way to the podium.

The MC's velvety voice crooned into the microphone. "Now, for the moment we've all been waiting for. It's time for the Founders' Auction!"

The crowd—dappled in gauzy light, giddy with money, and warmed by excellent booze—cheered uproariously and made their way back to their respective tables.

"Hadley," Ronan said as Hadley too began to move away.

She tilted her chin towards the stage. "Go on," she said. "You're on. Go charm their socks off. Time to bring it home. For Big Think."

Ronan looked to where Ted and Sawyer—looking dapper, dashing and winningly chagrined—were making their way onto the stage. Hadley drank the man in while she had the chance: his thick, dark waves, that strong jaw, those languid, deep-blue eyes, and that big, strapping frame built to hold up the entire world.

She loved this man. She had done for a very long time. Only what she'd come to realise these past weeks was that she wanted to be loved with the same intensity, the same certainty, the same vulnerability. There was no half way. No wishing and hoping it might turn into something more.

And, if Ronan couldn't give that to her, then she had to let him go.

"Go on," she said, giving him a light shove. It toppled him off-balance but he caught himself quickly. He turned back with a glint in his eye, a flicker of the fight she'd been waiting for, before the crowd swallowed him up, the surge of enthusiasm pressing him towards the stage.

Hadley didn't wait to see if he made it.

She turned on her heel, the crystalline colours refracting off the moisture in her eyes, the music, the laughter, bouncing off the bubble she created around herself as she floated towards the exit.

Plucking her phone from the other pocket, she sent a quick text to Adelaid and Petra, letting them know she was okay. She wished them both Happy New Year. Then she walked down the long hall, past the cloak room, through the wide front doors of the hotel and into the night.

Ready to start the New Year as she meant to go on—her Big Think era behind her.

Spending the day after the Big Think Ball—known to the rest of the world as New Year's Day—on *Candy*, the Big Think yacht, had been a tradition for the men. A chance to ease sore heads and reflect on the year they'd put behind them, before starting the new one with bigger goals than ever before.

It was also one of several traditions that had fallen by the wayside as first Ted then Sawyer had found others in their lives to consider first.

So it was somewhat of a surprise when Sawyer had knocked on Ronan's front door at the crack of dawn. "Great. You're here. Worried you might be sleeping it off in the Tower."

Fair, Ronan had thought, since he'd practically moved in there. But spending the night in that building, after the way Hadley had left without even saying goodbye? He couldn't have thought of anything he wanted less.

Heading out to sea, Sawyer at the helm, Ted lay back on the plush couch that ran the length of the cabin below, nursing a rare hangover due to the number of people who'd insisted they drink to the health of the baby near-bursting from Adelaid's belly. While Ronan sat upright, eyes ahead, head thumping from a frown he just couldn't shake.

"How long has he been like that?" asked Sawyer, after dropping anchor and joining them below deck.

Ted said, "A while."

"You think he might be broken?"

"I'm not *broken*," Ronan growled, his voice rough. Then he blinked and squinted against the brightness, to find Sawyer leaning back against the bar, arms crossed.

"Okay. Then you look like crud for no reason at all."

Ted sat up slowly and looked at Ronan. "That's putting it nicely."

Ronan felt his lip curl and glanced at the windows, wondering how long it might take to swim back, only to find they could no longer see land.

Sawyer grabbed three bottles of some healthy green sludge from the fridge, handed them over then took a seat, putting himself at the point of a triangle: the three corners of the Big Think empire.

Only Ronan very much felt as if he was hemmed in. "Why does this suddenly feel like an intervention?"

"Are you in need of an intervention?" asked Sawyer.

A muscle flickered under Ronan's eye.

"No?" said Sawyer. Then he lifted his drink in salute and the others followed suit. "Then, let's drink—to a hell of a year."

"Hell of a few years," said Ted.

Ronan winced as he tasted the health drink—no more beers, like in the early days. Everything had changed. Ronan made a sound, like the sound a man might make if he was quietly losing his mind.

He sat forward and let his head fall into his hands. He could sense Sawyer and Ted mouthing things at him over his head.

"Okay," said Sawyer. "So, now seems like as good a time as any to bring up the elephant in the room."

Don't say Hadley, Ronan begged inside his own head. *Please don't say Hadley.*

Sawyer didn't in fact say Hadley. "We've been limping along for a while now, pretending our original business model was still sustainable. But the truth is, you've been taking up far more than your share of the slack, and that's not fair."

Ronan didn't deny it. How could he? He was exhausted—emotionally, physically, and psychologically. He'd been stretched so thin, he'd somehow let the best thing that had ever happened to him slip through his fingers.

He ought to have refused Hadley's resignation the moment she'd offered it. Put an end to the ludicrous idea then and there. Instead, they'd fallen down some interminable rabbit hole that had led to this.

To him walking into on Monday morning and her not being there. Ever again.

"Big Think belongs to all of us," he managed. "Always will."

"It will," said Sawyer. "But you have to give yourself the same grace you've shown us. You need time and space, room to find a life outside of the company. What you do is important, but so are you."

So was he.

Not merely as the co-founder of a multi-billion-dollar company, or the son of a man he was trying to best, but just Ronan, the living, breathing, human being.

"You're right," said Ronan before he even knew it to be true. For Big Think had never been just about the work. It had been about community and friendship, the urban family they'd built. It had been about giving each of them the chance to shine, whatever that had meant for them.

The others had taken that chance and flourished, while he'd deliberately, forcibly, lived within the margins, the grey in between. Holding on tight to that safe space, while the brightest, most vociferous, pushiest, punchiest creature on the planet did her all to yank him into Technicolor.

He pictured her office, all the jewel-bright colours, under her glinting gold ceiling, Hadley deliberately creating a space that felt bold, and luminous and decadent. A space for talking, arguing, sharing. Big things, small things, things that only they'd cared about.

He pictured her lying back on the bed at the Big D Motel eating crisps from the mini-bar, watching some old movie with the sound of truck brakes screeching outside, the light from the red-fringed lamp making everything look a little naughty.

Hadley.

"What did he say?" said Ted.

Ronan looked at Sawyer to find him smiling. His eyes were wide, as if saying, *Jump on in, the water's fine.*

"He said 'Hadley'," said Ted, clicking his fingers. "So that's why he looks like crap."

Sawyer mimed his brain exploding.

Hadley.

Hadley, who wasn't a founder but had been in the inner circle all the same.

Hadley, who was the sole reason their big ideas came to fruition.

If Ronan was the brass, Sawyer the brawn, Ted the brains, then Hadley had been the core. The soul. The strong, steady, consistent, heartbeat that had kept pressing them forward all this time.

But, more than that, she was also *his* core. *His* soul. *His* heart. He was smitten with her, he respected the hell out of her, and he adored her. He *wanted* her so badly, it physically hurt, which he'd worn as some sort of badge of honour. If he could feel that way, and go without her, then didn't that mean he was a better man than his father could ever hope to be?

But he'd only been punishing himself, and punishing her, when all he'd ever truly wanted to do was support her, enjoy her, work beside her and admire her. To live alongside her.

But, instead of telling her all that, he'd been so terrified of showing a chink in his famously formidable armour, he'd stood there while she'd carved out that heart and handed it to him on open palms.

And he had said nothing.

"Hadley," said Ronan, her name on his tongue like water for a man dying of thirst. "Hadley loves me."

Sawyer breathed out long and slowly. "You think?"

"I know it. She told me so."

"She did?" said Sawyer, and that time he looked genuinely shocked. "Wow. Good for her. And what did you say?"

"Nothing."

"What do you mean, nothing?" Sawyer asked.

Ronan shot him a look. Only for Sawyer to sit back in his chair, his hands on his head, his eyes wide with shock. "How can a guy as smart as you be so stupid?"

Ronan wondered the same thing.

But a sense of clarity was finally coming over him, like cloud clearing over a calming sea.

She'd not left because she loved him, but because she loved him but couldn't be sure he'd ever come to realise that he felt the same.

When the very thought of *not* loving Hadley now felt incomprehensible to him. How could a person know her—know her street smarts, her sincerity, her warmth, her curiosity, her ferocity—and *not* love her?

Ronan felt time stretch and contract, swirling around him like the tornado. He'd spent the better part of his adult life believing that he was fuelled by the determination not to be anything like his father. He'd martyred his life to the mission, as if it was an act of moral excellence. But he'd achieved that the moment it had even occurred to him to try.

"Damn it," he said, launching to his feet. Then, louder, "Damn it!"

"Is he okay?" asked Ted.

"He'll get there," said Sawyer.

"Should we do something?" Ted asked, concern now edging his deep voice.

"Like what?" Sawyer asked, sounding far more chipper.

"A cold compress to the back of the neck? I don't know, I'm not that kind of doctor."

Feeling as if lightning had hit his veins, Ronan declared, "I'm in love with Hadley."

"We already knew that, right?" Ted whispered, while Sawyer put a finger to his mouth.

"It's why we niggled and snapped and drove one another crazy. Why I stayed at work so late all the time. Why her office mirrored mine. She left because while working for me it would never happen. She quit so we could…"

So that they could *be* together. Which was incredibly unfair to her. Why shouldn't he have been the one to leave? Well, he couldn't, because it was his company, but then it was hers too, as much as it was anyone's.

"You done?" Sawyer asked.

"Hmm?"

"You've been standing there, looking like you're in the midst of the rapture, for a few minutes now. Just let us know when you're done so we can get the heck back to land."

"Oh, I'm done. In fact, I think I know how to fix it all."

"Great!" said Sawyer, sweeping to his feet, only to wince when his leg old injury made itself known. Then he was off, taking the steps a little more carefully.

Then came the distant sound of the anchor winching back into place, the rev of the engine and off they went, in a tight circle that sent Ronan and Ted rocking sideways before the boat shot off, back towards shore.

"Can't he go any faster?" Ronan ground out.

For, when a man like Ronan Gerard realised what he wanted the rest of his life to look like, he was not about to sit back and wait for it to happen.

First to Big Think Tower, so that he might put things in order there. He did not want to leave anything to chance.

His feet took him to the Founders' Room, only to pull to

a screaming halt in the doorway. For Hadley was sitting on his "throne" at the head of the table. His hungry gaze drank in her denim overalls over a black tank-top, her face free of make-up. Her forehead creased, her thumb playing over the bow tattoo on her finger as she stared out of the window to her right. A big box of stuff on the table at her elbow.

She looked soft, unguarded and utterly lovely. How he'd managed to go this long without falling to his knees and declaring himself, he had no idea.

And yet, Ronan didn't move, didn't even breathe, standing in *her* spot in the doorway, trying not to blink funny in case she disappeared.

But something alerted her to his presence anyway. That something that had always meant they knew where each other was in any room.

She sat up, blinking furiously. A finger wiped under each eye. Had she been *crying*? *Hell.*

"Hadley…" he said, moving into the room.

"Ronan," she said, standing and fussing with the packing box. "I'm sorry. I came in to clean out my makeshift office, thinking no one else would be here. I'll finish up and get out of your hair."

"It's no problem," he said, his voice calm, his movements slow; hyper-aware of how easily, and how quickly, he could screw this up. He'd proven himself more than capable of that already. "Take your time. Truly."

"What are you doing here?" she asked.

"I had some pretty important business to attend to," he said.

"Oh," she said, trying to act as if it wasn't her business now, but he could see she was itching to know. Because his business *was* her business and had been from the day she'd walked into that old warehouse and demanded he give her a shot.

He reached into the back pocket of his jeans and pulled out the handwritten document—the one he'd just scrawled, then copied and sent to their in-house lawyer—and slid it along the table. It spun as it moved, stopping so that she had to walk a step closer to pick it up.

"What's this?" she asked, bending to look but not touching, as if it might bite.

"It's a partnership agreement. Go on," he said. "Read it."

She watched him a moment before her eyes dropped back to the paper. Curiosity won out, as always, and she unfolded the paper and read the words.

Words offering her a quarter share of the company.

Ted, Sawyer and he had agreed, without reservation, on the ride back to shore to give up equal portions of their own shares in order to bring Hadley into the fold, if she was amenable. With remuneration going back to day one of her tenure with them.

He waited for her to absorb it. For Hadley, he'd wait as long as it took.

When she looked up, her eyes flickered with shock, confusion and a good measure of disbelief. "I don't understand. How is this possible? *Why?*"

Ronan knew she meant *why now*. Once she read on she'd find the arrangement as not dependant on her actively working for the company if she still decided to leave. It was merely the agreement they ought to have put before her all those years ago, if he'd not been so intent on treading carefully, carefully, when it came to impeding on her autonomy.

He moved slowly down the edge of the table.

"Why the offer?" he said. "Because Big Think was not Big Think before you came on board. It was a collection of egos and promise, of talent and gumption. Then you walked in the room, took one look at us and knew exactly what we needed in order to coalesce. You brought form and finesse. And without that, without you, we might never have found our way out of that Richmond warehouse."

He swallowed, needing to have every wit about him to get the next part right.

"As for why *now*? Because I've come to realise that I've spent the past several years not letting you know how deeply I value you, in case you saw through me and saw everything. Which was unforgivable. And unfair."

"Everything?" she asked, pink rushing into her cheeks, her fingers gripping the agreement till it crinkled. When she noticed, she quickly set to straightening out the page.

Which gave Ronan a burst of hope. It wasn't an instant yes, but it might not be a no.

"Every thought," he said, "Every feeling. Every secret wish. Every ounce of longing. You knew that you riled me, you knew that you pushed me, you knew you made me want to be a better man. But I couldn't have you know that I adored you. That I dreamed of you. How despairingly I wished we'd met under different circumstances so that I might have asked you out, come to know you over a glass of wine, taken you home and kissed you senseless under your porch light. The way normal people go about such things."

A small sound escaped her mouth, halfway between a sob and a sigh. He'd put her through the wringer but she was strong enough to take a breath, to think, to decide for herself.

She looked down at the document. "This offer…" she said.

"Is without conditions. A quarter-share, if you want it. We are all in agreement. We all think it's way past time."

Ronan forced himself to stop moving towards her when she was just out of reach even though he wanted to touch her, so badly. But this was business, and he needed her to know that one had nothing to do with the other.

"Initial thoughts?" he asked, his voice miraculously dry, even while his heart felt as if it were beating in his throat.

"There goes early retirement," she muttered, a glint of fire bursting behind her dark eyes.

And Ronan laughed. It was as if a valve had burst open, and once he started laughing he couldn't stop. He laughed so hard his cheeks hurt. So hard he bent over and gripped the table, the relief akin to being filled with helium.

And Hadley joined him. She gave a short gasp of laughter at first, then great rolling barks that had her clutching her side as if she had a stitch.

Then their laughter eased, falling away to soft sounds on both sides, till their gazes tangled and the room filled with a sizzle of electricity. As if they'd just realised it was the two of them alone in the room. The only ones in the entire building, in fact.

Then she said, "Why? Why couldn't I know that you dreamed of me?"

"Because then you'd have to examine your own feelings and surely decide that you couldn't waste your time on a man such as me. A Tin Man with a useless heart."

Hadley blinked. Then she took a step his way, the first since he'd entered the room. Then she took another step, and another, then lifted the hand holding the sheet of paper and placed it on his chest...up and a little to the left.

"Not useless," she said, her voice low, quiet. "Bruised. In need of time to heal." Then she took his other hand and placed it over her heart. "I know, because like calls to like."

He curled his fingers around hers, before lifting her palm to his mouth and dropping a kiss on the soft cushion of skin.

Her head dropped back and she sighed. Which he took as a good sign, and kissed his way down her wrist, following a row of freckles inside her forearm before he reached her elbow. He ran his thumb into the bend, over the constellation tattooed into the soft skin, and she bit her lip.

"Hadley," he said. "Look at me."

She did something truly rare then; she did as he asked without questions. And he saw it in her eyes: her love for him, radiating like a moonbeam. How had he never seen it before? Had she hidden it that well, or had he been too stubborn, too scared, to see it for what it was?

He pulled her hand back to his chest and said, "I'm going to tell you something now. And I want you to promise me, in advance, that you will forgive any blunders, because I'm running on gut instinct here. Okay?"

She squinted at him, head shaking back and forth. "I make no such promises."

Fair enough, he thought with a grimace. She was far too savvy for that. So, he started with the hook.

"I love you, Hadley Moreau."

At that she ceased shaking her head. Her eyes opened wide. "I'm sorry, but did you just say…?"

Ronan held up a finger and said, "Let me get through this."

She snapped her mouth shut and nodded, her eyes big, dark and focussed on his. Her body now trembled under his touch.

"I remember the day you walked into my office, so clearly," he said. "Skinny jeans, Doc Martens, several earrings glinting up one ear. Like Audrey Hepburn had had a baby with a biker. Serene yet utterly terrifying, practically daring me to turn you away. It wasn't just that siren face of yours that gripped me through the middle, or that core of steel that glows, fiery hot, from within. It was the way you refused to be wholly impressed by us. As if we had to earn your respect. Exactly what I needed before I knew I needed it."

Hadley laughed then, a cough of joy that she couldn't contain.

He took a breath. "But there was that whole thing with my father…"

She shook her head. "You know where I stand on that score."

"I do," he said, "But it took me a really long time to accept that. Likely because, every conversation we had from that day on, I could hear my heart clanging in my chest any time you neared. And I knew how lucky we were to have you. So I chose to park those feelings, as wild and unexpected and new to me as they were, to a man who prided himself on being contained."

"Ronan, I…"

He placed a finger over her mouth. "Nearly done."

Hadley was really trembling now. Or maybe it was him. Either way, so long as they held one another up, he knew they'd be fine.

"Then you kissed me, outside the Big D Motel, and invited me into your world in a way I'd never dared hope possible. Right when I was on the verge of losing you."

He shook his head. "I never claimed to be a smart man when it came to matters of the heart; in fact, I'd quite happily state that on that score I'm a complete dunce. I'm sorry it took me this long to own how I felt, how I *feel*, about you."

He lifted both hands to cradle her face. "I love you, Hadley Moreau. I've loved you for longer than I remember loving anyone or anything. And if I'm not too late, if I haven't acted in such a way that means you can't trust my words…"

Hadley curled her fingers into his shirt, yanked him to her and kissed him hard. Then her eyes squeezed shut and she threw her arms around his neck and kissed him harder.

And Ronan knew this was it for him. He'd never love anyone the way he loved her. He was done, gone, smitten. He was hers. For ever more.

He pulled back and kissed her once more, a place marker, then said, "Marry me."

"Ronan," said Hadley, rearing back and shaking her head, all laughter and joy. But again it was not an outright no.

So, again, he said, "Marry me."

She pulled up the piece of paper still clutched in her hand. "How do I know you don't just want me for my money?"

Ronan pulled her closer, her softness sinking into his hardness, and her eyes glazed over as she felt it too. "I guess you'll never know."

She smiled, her eyes flitting between his. And he saw it—the moment when they were finally, *finally*, in complete sync. Her breathing evened out, her gaze lit with a healthy measure of *about time, you damn fool*.

Ronan said, "This my pledge—I am yours, if you'll have me. Yours to organise, to bait and debate, to nudge and mould and push, so that I never rest on whatever laurels I might think I have. Do with me as you please."

Her eyes narrowed as she leant back, trusting him to catch her if she fell. And her smile…her smile was like an arrow right through his now fully unencumbered heart.

"So, who's going to tell Jonas that he has to move out of my office?" she asked, her eyes sparkling.

Ronan was as relieved as he was glad. The rightness of it flowed through him like breath. "I'll leave that up to you."

"Fine, but I'm keeping him for myself, meaning you'll have to find yourself another assistant."

"Is that right?"

"Already regretting your offer?" she asked.

"Not even slightly," he assured her.

She settled herself against him, the trembling having stopped now that they were wrapped around one another. Now she felt strong, supple and warm. Now she was shift-

184 CINDERELLA ASSISTANT TO BOSS'S BRIDE

ing subtly, back and forth, rubbing herself against him, the friction making it hard for him to… Well, hard, basically.

"Does that mean you accept our offer?" he asked.

"I do."

"And you're coming back to work?"

"I am. But not only because you gave me part of your company," she said, her fingers now playing in his hair.

"That's fine. I didn't give you part of my company in order to make you stay."

He leaned down then, arms wrapped around her waist, and kissed her, sealing the deal.

"I love you, Ronan," she said simply when she came up for air.

"I love you more."

"Not possible."

We'll see, Ronan thought as he turned and lifted her onto the table.

And gave in when she pulled him down over her. For when a man tells the woman he loves that she can do with him as she pleases, it behoves him to follow through.

EPILOGUE

"COME BACK HERE," whispered Hadley, taking Ronan by the hand, before looking around, and dragging him into the nearest room, which happened to be a cloak room.

He didn't complain. In fact, he rarely complained these days. Having this woman in his life, truly in his life, made that life a rather wonderful thing.

In the semi-darkness of the cloak room, several things occurred to him at once; the fact that the first time they'd nearly kissed had been in such a space, and that on this day, their wedding day, did tradition not state that he wasn't meant to see his bride until the big moment? Both of which were soon smothered by having her near.

He hauled her close, figuring *why not*. But she pressed her hand to his chest, stopping him at the last.

"Here," she said, then reached up and fixed his tie. His gaze drifted over her face, that heartbreakingly lovely face, while her fingers fidgeted at his neck.

"I do have attendants you know, either of whom could have told me if my tie was not straight."

"Pfft. As if they'd notice. And in all the years I've known you, you've never been able to get a tie right," she said, giving the knot a final yank.

Ronan slipped his arm around her waist slowly, so as not to startle her, his voice dropping a note as he whispered against her ear, "Did it ever occur to you that I might be completely adept at tying a tie? I just liked the way it felt having you near, fussing over me."

Hadley's hands stilled, her dark gaze locked onto his. "Is that true?"

Arm now fully around her, Ronan spun her till she was backed up against the wall of coats. And she didn't stop him. She was too busy calculating. When her eyes once again found his, they were glinting.

"You are such a rogue," she said.

"And you are such a bossy-boots," he shot back.

Fight flared in her eyes before she said, "You love that about me."

"More than words can say," he agreed, his voice a growl, his need for her sweeping over him.

And when she began to melt in his arms, he had the feeling searching him out to fix his tie was as much a ruse for her as it had ever been for him.

But then she tilted her head away. "Do you hear that?"

"Hear what?" Ronan asked. Her hair was longer now, meaning Ronan was forced to gather it in a twist and toss it over her shoulder so he could press his nose to her neck.

"Knocking," she whispered.

"Ah, guys…" Sawyer's voice came through the door. "The guests are getting restless. We might want to get the party started."

Hadley bit her lip, then gave in and said, "Coming!"

"Not yet, you're not," Ronan affirmed, hand moving over her backside.

"Later," she said, pushing her hips back, laughing and shaking her head at the same time. "We have something more pressing to do right now."

Ronan pulled himself together. "Promise?"

"Today, in this dress? Let's just say I'm a sure thing."

* * *

Several minutes later, Ronan stood beneath an ivy-covered arbour at the end of an aisle scattered with soft white rose-petals. Ted and Sawyer stood by his side.

Sawyer and Petra, having secretly married while on a quick trip to Florence, had their bouncing baby boy Claude in tow. Sawyer's mum was currently cradling him in the front row, while Petra's mother, sitting beside her, made kissy cooing noises; neither woman paying attention to the proceedings at all.

One of Adelaid's many brothers was chasing Katie around, which Katie clearly thought was the best game ever, if her screams of laughter were anything to go by, while baby Cary slept in another of Adelaid's many brother's beefy arms.

Ronan caught *his* mother's eye and she gave him a watery smile.

When his father had died, Ronan had attended the private family funeral, standing up beside his mother, holding her hand when his father's surviving brother had presented a eulogy as unflinchingly damning as it was kind. Leaving the world with a fair picture as to the complex man Constantine Gerard had been.

And while he remained stoic throughout, that night, curled up in Hadley's arms, Ronan had cried.

Something that might well happen again today, if the ball of emotion lodged in his throat was anything to go by.

Then the harpist perked up, playing Pachelbel's *Canon in D*. Adelaid and Petra appeared, looking teary, smiley and delightful in dresses of pale green, walking solemnly down the aisle.

The music changed, going up a notch, or maybe that was Ronan's heart thundering madly in his ears as Hadley appeared. Her dress a column of creamy white, the material hugging her in a way that had Ronan picturing monthly projections for all he was worth. Her face was serene, her lips freshly slicked with red. Her hair, though, was somewhat dishevelled. No doubt due to their recent shenanigans in the cloak room.

Fine with him; dishevelled was his favourite look on her.

Ronan breathed in and wriggled his toes so that the vastness of this moment, all that had led up to it, did not take him out. Besides, Hadley was out there alone, all eyes looking her way. Nobody was giving her away, as she'd been adamant that the only person with the right to do that was her.

Which also suited Ronan just fine, especially as she was willingly giving herself to him. And he to her. Which they had been doing for some time now. They didn't need any legal papers to make that a reality—they had, after all, been known to do just fine till now without contracts to bind them.

And yet, here they were, about to promise their lives to one another in front of friends, family and a flock of seagulls flying over the Finchers' beautiful Mount Martha house, no doubt hoping to score some crumbs once the party moved to the grand marquee overlooking the bluff.

Ronan stepped out onto the grass and held out a hand. He waited for Hadley to take it before helping her up onto the dais.

"Hey," he said. "Long time, no see."

Hadley shot him a look, the kind that levelled him smack, bang—a kick to the heart. He'd do whatever it took to keep those looks coming as long as they both did live.

"Ready?" he said.

"Born ready," she answered, though her fierce expression showed him the thought of promising herself to him was filled with meaning that went beyond a single day.

Best friends at their sides, the sun shining down from

above, Hadley and Ronan turned to face Jonas, who of course had a marriage celebrant's licence to go along with every other qualification he had up his sleeve.

Ronan, who still had Hadley's hand in his, used it to pull her close till they were shoulder to shoulder, side by side. A matched pair.

When Jonas said the words, "Dearly beloved, we are gathered here today to see these two lovebirds finally tie the knot," the crowd went wild. There was cheering and whooping, making Hadley laugh so hard, she leant against him for support.

When she looked up at him, he stole a kiss. And she let him, lips lingering till they pulled away as one. A little breathless. A whole lot happy.

Certain it would only get better from there.

* * * * *

HOW TO WIN
A PRINCE

JULIETTE HYLAND

MILLS & BOON

For my editor, Laurie, who helped take this
long-held story dream and make it a reality!

CHAPTER ONE

BRIELLA AILIONO SNAPPED another photo of herself, hoping the angle highlighted the long dark gown her best friend had designed for this final engagement. The image was about the dress, not her, but if she'd learned anything, it was that appearances were always scrutinized. If her mother was still talking to her, Brie might thank her for the multitude of lessons she'd taught on the subject.

She scrunched her nose as she examined the image. She wasn't as bubbly as the other potential brides here, wasn't bouncy and excited for the tiny possibility she'd win the "prize" in a few minutes. She only had one princess ticket in the giant glass spinning lotto wheel up on the palace's balcony. One shot to become a princess. One shot to wear a crown.

One shot too many!

Prince Alessio's Princess Lottery was all the country of Celiana had talked about for the last year. Throughout each week, potential brides had purchased tickets and then deposited them on Sunday while cameras watched. It was a year of spectacle.

If she could have devised any other way to launch Ophelia's bridal gown and specialty dress shop so quickly, Brie would have. A standard rollout with a mixture of graphics across social media platforms, booths at bridal fairs, a well-placed billboard or sponsored "news article" were options.

Success lay down that path, in two or three years. This way, this scheme, with her standing next to all the brides in a new wedding dress designed by Ophelia as she rattled off

comments about the gown and the spectacle... Well, it meant
success was at Ophelia's door year one. And wild success, too,
not just keep-the-doors-open, scrape-by success.

And her own business was rocketing out of the gate, too.

Her marketing firm; her "little" business, the one her
parents refused to acknowledge—it had a phone that never
stopped ringing. An overflowing email inbox. Even buyout
offers. There were possibilities at every corner.

Built from the ground up with no help from her family,
it was Brie's achievement. All hers. She was making the
choices—finally in charge of her own life.

The cost was a ticket in the Princess Lottery. The winner
got a crown, and Prince Alessio as a husband.

Blowing out a breath, she looked at the image on her phone.
It was good, and the dark dress was highlighted nicely against
the wall of white and cream behind her. She stood out.

Which was the point of this marketing campaign.

"If my name comes out, I think I might just faint!"

"Me too!" the women squealed, then looked at Brie.

She raised a hand and winked as their eyes widened. Her
dress's dark hue gave off a less hopeful vibe. Though like all
Ophelia's designs, it was gorgeous.

"Good luck, ladies." Brie smiled as they walked away. She
didn't really mean the words. No one should "win" their groom.

But the palace hadn't asked her thoughts on this marketing campaign. If they had, she'd have at least pointed out that
requiring attendance on the palace grounds, if you'd placed
your name in the lottery, was a terrible plan. There was exactly one lucky winner, and over a hundred unhappy losers.

Not great optics, which was unusual for an entity whose
whole role one could label "optics."

"This is so exciting! So exciting!" The squeals echoed behind her.

It felt like she was the lone person here who didn't want to
wear a crown.

You are!

If she didn't need to be here for the final splash of Ophelia's wedding dress line, she'd have watched this play out on her small television screen in yoga pants, a T-shirt, messy bun and with a giant bowl of popcorn.

Instead, she was the standout in a sea of princess hopefuls dressed in bright cream.

"If my name comes out of that monstrosity, I suspect I'll do more than faint," she murmured, keeping her eye on the balcony where Prince Alessio would appear any minute.

"Not excited about the possibility of becoming a princess?" Nate, one of the local reporters who hadn't gotten the plum press pass the palace gave international media, asked as he sidled up next to her. "People consider Prince Alessio the most handsome prince."

There is one prince in this country—not much of a competition.

Though even before his brother, Sebastian, was crowned king, Alessio would have won that title. The spare had become the superhot heir.

Whoever ended up with Alessio would never have a hard time looking at him. He was tall and blond with brilliant green eyes, muscular shoulders and full lips. The handsome prince was not the issue she had with this public relations stunt.

The palace swore the reformed rebel was excited for this. The man who'd left Celiana for almost three years, only returning following his father's stroke, was happy. That was the story they needed. Easier to sell to the masses.

The real story was about ledgers. This modern fairy tale was the quickest way to remind the world that Celiana was once the honeymoon capital of Europe. It had already boosted the country's tourism and aided shops and attractions struggling since the global tourism economy crashed a few years ago.

In each press release and interview, Alessio dutifully discussed the woman he'd meet at the altar as though he already loved her—like that was even possible. He reminded everyone that his parents had had a marriage of convenience that turned to a great love. Then he worked back to the benefits for the country, reminding anyone watching that Celiana was the most romantic place to start your union.

A bride to right the country's travel economy...who wouldn't want to fill that role?

She couldn't fault Alessio for caring about the people of this country. Their elected leaders were more concerned with retaining power. And Alessio seemed far more concerned with the kingdom's day-to-day running than his brother.

The once dutiful Prince Sebastian, now King, was missing engagements and generally acting like a playboy, and the previously rebellious spare was stepping in for the benefit of Celiana. The role reversal for the men since their father passed was an epic story.

Or it would be, if the palace commented on it.

There were other ways, better options, to jump-start the tourism industry.

"My dreams don't involve a crown."

Her dreams had already cost her the aristocratic life she'd been born into. Cost her the family that "loved" her only when she performed the script they'd drafted from the moment of her birth. She wanted to be more than a trophy wife to some man her father wanted to do business with. She was carving her own path.

Brie's dreams were going to carry her from the small, rented office to a penthouse with a view. No one else was writing the story of her life. Nope. Briella Ailiono controlled all her publicity statements—not that she actually planned to make any about her personal life.

"Since my name is only in there once, the odds are very good I will have to fight with everyone else for a place on public transportation following this fiasco."

She shook her head and looked to the balcony again.

Where was Alessio?

He was meant to pick his bride at the top of the hour, and it was three minutes past. Maybe he was having second thoughts.

Marriage was a commitment, one that should involve love. A promise of forever between two people who cared for each other, rooted each other on.

The opposite of her parents' union.

Her best friend, Ophelia, and her husband, Rafael, had the kind of union Brie would have.

If she ever met someone at the altar.

After watching them cheer each other on, love one another in sickness, health and business ventures, she would not settle for less.

She'd spent her teen years surrounded by people who only cared about her family's wealth. It was better to be alone than to marry for power and connections.

"Care to make a comment for the press?" Nate grinned as he held up his notebook.

There were many comments she wanted to make. She wanted to call this whole thing out for what it was: a PR stunt that made the heir to the throne a prize for whoever's name got picked. The prince was a commodity instead of a man worthy of having a partner who chose him.

And it wasn't like this was a true game of chance. The lottery had gone on all year, with the press corps gleefully showing up weekly to watch women put the tickets they'd purchased into the huge crystal ball specially made for this occasion.

Each "bride" could put her name in once a week for fifty-two weeks. The first week the entry was free…a stunt to show that anyone could be the next princess of Celiana—and the reason more than a thousand women had entered the first week.

But with each week, the cost of entry rose by ten euros—donated to the arts fund Prince Alessio championed. It was a good cause, but the price was steep for a year's worth of tickets. Thirteen thousand euros was needed for a genuine chance at the crown.

That meant there were very few women who could expect to step onto the balcony today. All were from wealthy families. In fact, the final week Brie had watched less than twenty women put their names in. Those were the ones most likely to stand on Alessio's arm today. All "real" princess material.

"No one wants to hear my thoughts on this, Nate."

"It's just as well," the reporter huffed. "I doubt anything I write will make the cut anyway. The actual story is the women up there." He pointed to the front of the group—where those with fifty-two entries stood.

"So true. They look beautiful. Several are wearing Ophelia's gowns."

She grinned as she looked to Anastasia and Breanna. She'd been in the same class in school as the identical twins, though not close friends. Even as girls, their parents had made little secret of their plan to marry their daughters to the crown. Her parents had thought the plan to marry Breanna to Alessio and Anastasia to Sebastian was crass and had discouraged Brie from forming any close attachment.

It was horrible of her parents, though when the twins' mother had mentioned being fine about interchanging the girls if one was pulled as the lotto bride, Brie had cringed. The words were horrible, and the fact that the girls were picking bridal outfits for today made it so much worse.

Not that the twins had reacted. Neither had commented as Ophelia fitted them. Their silence broke Brie's heart. They deserved more than a scheming family. But the price of breaking with your powerful family, the price Brie had paid, was high. She couldn't judge others for not choosing it.

"The wedding gown thing is weird." Nate chuckled as he looked at the women all around. "It's not like the marriage is happening today."

"Agreed."

She looked at the sea of white. The contract they'd all signed when entering this fiasco had required their attendance today and the wearing of a gown fit for a bride. What were women supposed to do with the gowns after today?

It was unlikely they'd want to wear them when they met

their true love, but she supposed the royal family didn't think of such minor details.

"Black is an interesting choice."

This she was willing to put on the record. "You can print this. My dress is technically dark green, Nate." She held up the small train, letting the light hit it just right. "At Ophelia's there is a wide variety of gowns, including a selection of dresses with a modern flair."

"It certainly stands out. Though I'm not sure my editor will print that."

The green stood out. That was the purpose, but it was also her own personal statement.

"Dark colors are best when love dies."

"Ouch!" Nate bent over, pretending to take the hit to the gut, then laughed. "Guess you won't cry if your name doesn't come out today."

"I'll cry if it does!"

The last thing she wanted was a marriage of convenience, particularly one trying to save the kingdom. That was too much pressure. It was a burden even the now-dutiful prince shouldn't have on his shoulders.

"The prince!"

The cry went up from the gathered and Brie took another photo. The whole point of this was to make Ophelia's shop shine.

Going live on her social media site, Brie waved and smiled as people started joining the live stream. Sure, the national and international media were here, but Brie was an actual potential bride who'd been at the crystal entry ball every week this year. Her following had reached two million last week as people waited for today's outcome.

"Prince Alessio just stepped to the balcony. He's wearing a dark suit…"

Mourning the loss of love for himself?

Brie didn't know why that thought bothered her. After all, he seemed the ever-willing participant in this game.

She was too far away to see his face, but his walk seemed stilted. It was a hitch that she wasn't sure the cheering crowd noticed.

"We offer a wide range of suits for the suit lover in your life, too." Brie's voice was bright as she flipped the screen back to her. "He's reaching into the vat of tickets! Who will be our new princess?"

Cries of excitement echoed around her as she waved for the camera. This was finally almost over, and she'd done a good job. Ophelia's shop was on the international market now. Her appointment books were full for the next six months! Brie's baby company was entering the international stage, too.

It meant the Ailiono family would never control her life again.

"Briella Ailiono." The call echoed across the field.

Time slowed as she watched the phone fall from her fingers. No. No. *No.*

"Briella Ailiono!" Alessio called again, hoping his voice sounded steady. Every bit of today would be monitored, filmed, dissected. Those looking for a love story would swoon; those thinking this was nothing more than a charade would look for any sign that Alessio wasn't sure of the plan.

He was sure...sure that this plan would revive Celiana's wedding and honeymoon tourism industry. He was certain that the people would benefit from it, and equally certain that he owed his father's memory more than being known as the rebellious prince who'd fought with him just before the stroke that ultimately stole him away.

Marriages of convenience were the way of the royal life. And there were benefits to wearing a crown... Hopefully they outweighed the thorns for Briella.

Where was his bride? Shouldn't she be running to the front...brimming with excitement?

He knew she was here; attendance at the lottery was mandatory.

In a wedding dress.

That was an instance of dark humor gone wrong. From his brother, King Sebastian, whose word was now taken far more seriously. He was a man Alessio hadn't thought capable of cracking a joke before their father died. But Sebastian wasn't the same since the crown of Celiana had landed on his head. The dutiful son, the heir to the throne, the one who'd always known his place in the family, seemed lost as destiny finally gave him what he'd been trained for.

And that left Alessio in the role of dutiful heir. It was not a position he coveted…but if not for his fight, his rebellion, perhaps his father's blood pressure wouldn't have spiked. Maybe this wasn't the role Alessio wanted, but it was the one he owed.

"Where is she?" Alessio looked over the balcony. The crowd was dispersing, and no one looked like the happy winner.

"She was live on her social media page just as you called her name," his mother, Genevieve, said. The queen mother offered an encouraging smile, something he'd rarely seen in private after his father's untimely death.

Not that Queen Genevieve had ever smiled much. The love story between King Cedric and his queen was well scripted. Everything about it perpetuated the island's fairy tale. But like most fairy tales, the proper story lacked luster.

His mother and father had never loved each other. They respected one another, but it wasn't love. Alessio doubted his father was capable of loving anything besides the country he'd served.

It was King Cedric who'd mentioned how well the island flourished after his union with Queen Genevieve. His father had contacted Alessio, asking him to marry. That was in the "before times," when he was in his little glass shop in Scotland, working, acting, as just a man. It was the happiest he'd ever been.

His father had told him he owed it to the people of Celiana. Alessio had countered that he didn't owe anyone anything, that the future king should do it.

King Cedric said no one would believe a queen lottery. That as the heir the expectations for Sebastian were different. His father was looking for a foreign match, one worthy of the title of queen. Alessio's match was far less important since he'd never sit on the throne. It was a pointed reminder that Alessio was second in his father's eyes, heart and plans—in all things.

They'd screamed at each other. He'd said some terrible things. Things he couldn't take back now.

His father's stroke happened less than an hour after Alessio hung up the phone. The king had never regained consciousness. He'd never realized Alessio had returned home, embraced his father's plans and followed through. This world was his prison, but he would do his best to make sure Briella was content.

Somehow.

At least the stunt was working. The shops were busy. The island's hotels and hostels were booked solid. Many of the residents had opened their guest bedrooms for people wanting to visit…for a fee.

His father's final idea was saving Celiana.

And nearly a year of wedding planning would cement the country's place again.

Celiana—the home of your love story.

Becoming engaged to a stranger was unnerving. There was no way to sugarcoat that. However, for centuries royals had signed documents, wed strangers and then spent years betrothed. At least he and Briella had time to get to know each other before setting an actual date. His lottery was unique, but the idea of a union for business or the greater good of a country was ancient.

That reminder did little to calm his racing nerves as he looked over the departing crowd. There was still no sign of Briella.

He knew her. Or rather, knew *of* her as the outcast of the Ailiono family. They owned more land than anyone else on the island. Their businesses touched nearly every aspect of life on

Celiana. Not that they'd done much to help the country. The family only focused on adding to their already endless coffers.

And their daughter had done something to get disowned, something they refused to discuss. He didn't understand why she would willingly step back into this world, but maybe she'd not wanted to leave. Most aristocrats clung to power, hating even the thought that they might lose the thing they felt made them better than others.

Ridiculous.

"Her live ended as soon as you said her name." His mother's words pulled his mind away from his worries—mostly.

"Live?" He looked over the departing sea of white, again trying to imagine where Briella was and why she wasn't racing to where the royal guard was waiting for her.

"She's the marketing manager for a dress shop. She's stunning and she talks about the shop, highlighting why one should get their wedding day attire from Ophelia's. It's a brilliant campaign."

That his mother would know that was only a little surprising. Through social media, she'd followed the eighteen brides with fifty-two entries as closely as Alessio had followed the economic progress. She was in her own way vetting potential daughters-in-law. If Briella was marketing through the lotto, the queen mother would have seen her.

"Your father would have enjoyed the ingenuity. That was something he respected." The queen mother tipped her head, looking at the departing "brides."

He thought his mother missed his father, but it was like one missed a confidant, not a great love. Stepping away from the balcony, he patted her arm. Affection was not something the royal family did well.

"He'd have been proud of you focusing on Celiana's future."

No, he wouldn't.

Alessio was doing what was expected of him. That did not earn a place of pride in the royal family. His father gave everything to Celiana. Doing anything less than that was unacceptable, even if the palace walls felt like they were always closing in.

"I know he thought a royal wedding was a good idea. Ours worked...mostly." She bit her lip and offered a smile, but there was something in her voice. The unstated hesitancy sent his stomach spinning.

Briella would have adjustments to make. Life as a royal was not the glamorous stuff of magazines or the fantasy of movies. The royals of Celiana served the country and its people. The sacrifices that came with that—well, the sacrifices of a few for the many—were the bedrock of royal service. He'd run from his duties once, but not again.

"This way, Princess."

"I am not a princess." Her tone was sharp, carrying around the corner as security led her to him.

His stomach, already unsettled from the day's activities, tumbled on the sound. She didn't sound happy or excited. He'd counted on the winner being thrilled, happily standing beside him for the rest of the day's activities with a giant smile. The blushing bride-to-be. He'd selfishly even hoped her excitement would quell his anxiety that had grown stronger as today crept ever closer on the calendar.

They needed to present a united front. It was necessary to quiet the naysayers, who claimed this was nothing more than a short-term publicity stunt.

There were whispers floating through social media and a few regular news channels. The rumors, if proved true, could impact the entire country. A royal wedding brought tourism and prosperity. A royal scandal... That could undo everything.

"She was trying to flee," Henri, head of security, stated as he deposited Briella in the small alcove.

Flee?

"A runaway bride... That is quite the headline. Though not the one we're aiming for," Alessio quipped as he stepped forward.

Briella let out a soft chuckle as her bright blue eyes met

his. She was gorgeous; her long blond hair was wrapped in an intricate braid, and a near-black dress hugged her curves in all the right places.

The few times he'd seen her at court, she'd been reserved. Not a slip of laughter or hair out of place, she was the perfect Ailiono daughter. Until she wasn't. Rumors swirled about the reasons, but there'd been no concrete answers.

"Running away would be easier in tennis shoes... I might have even made it." She glared at the fancy heels poking out from under the gorgeous dress.

"One often overlooks the power of footwear." Alessio shrugged, not quite sure what to make of this conversation. The idea of running was intoxicating. During the three years he'd lived abroad, he'd felt freer than he ever expected to feel again.

"I should have considered it, apparently." She crossed her arms as her ice-blue eyes caught his.

Any words he might say evaporated as he met her gaze. He'd planned to bow to his bride-to-be, exchange a few pleasantries, bask in her excitement. He'd focus on the spectacle as he tried to make it through the next steps.

Now...now he couldn't quite find any kind of response.

Briella bit her lip then shook herself. "My apologies, Your Majesties... Your Highness." Dipping into a low curtsy, she let out a soft noise he feared was a caught sob.

That broke his heart. He might not be sure of this plan, but there were no monsters in this castle. Well, not really.

"Mother, could you give Briella and me a few minutes?"

The queen mother looked at Briella, still bent in her curtsy, and nodded. "I'll have the king delay the formal announcement and pictures a few minutes."

It was still weird to think of Sebastian as the king.

"Thank you." He slid down to the ground, catching the shock of surprise in Briella's face before she smoothed it over and joined him on the floor.

That was an ability the royal family excelled at, too. He instantly recognized the ability to conceal all feelings. And he hated that she'd learned the trick. Hated that she was using it on him.

Why wouldn't she?

"Briella—" He crossed his legs and leaned forward, making it clear that he was paying attention but giving her a little space.

"Brie." She coughed, clearing the sobs from her throat as she looked at him. "I prefer Brie. We're sitting like kids in a gym class."

"It's comfortable." Honestly, he'd sat without thinking. The position was hardly regal.

It was something he'd once have done to anger his father.

"Though before we go out, I'll have to ask you to look at my pants and make sure I have no dust on them. Pictures and all...we wouldn't want dust to take center stage in today's narrative."

"Of course not." Brie shook her head. "Dust is such an important factor for the press."

"Royalty is all about the show."

It was the first lesson princes and princesses learned. Everything is documented, speculated on, gossiped over.

"What the heck is this conversation?" Brie put her fingers on her forehead, rubbing at the line between her brows.

"The first lesson in your new life. Things that seem meaningless matter."

"This isn't a life I want."

Her cheeks darkened as she rolled her eyes. Her voice was soft, but the hint of terror came through clearly. He reached across and took her hand, squeezing it, trying to ground her.

Grounding himself.

It wasn't one he wanted, either, but that hardly mattered. She'd signed a contract. For all legal matters, she was basically a princess.

Her hand in his was warm. It felt...right? That was a weird descriptor; after all, they didn't know each other. Not really. She was to be his bride, but today, today was an unknown.

"Brie."

He offered what he hoped was a comforting smile as she broke the connection between them. The empty feeling in his palm echoed through his soul. He wanted to reach back out to her.

If you didn't want this, you shouldn't have put your name in the contest.

Saying those words wouldn't help now.

"Brie," he started over. "We have guests we need to see to. Expectations to meet."

"Expectations."

She propped her hands on her knees. In another time or place, they might have been sitting in the schoolyard waiting for their turn on the tennis or basketball court. Instead, they were in fancy clothes on the floor of his father's office—a room his brother still refused to convert to his.

"How can you possibly think of expectations? We don't even know each other. What, we just go out and role-play happily-ever-after?"

Role-playing was the name of the game. Hell, he'd expected his bride to be so excited. That way people might not notice his own discomfort. Instead, he was trying to convince her to go along with the day's duty.

"We have our whole lives to get to know one another." Not exactly comforting, but true.

"Our whole lives!" Brie stood, her dress swooshing with the quick movement. She walked past him and started pacing. "Our whole lives, Your Royal Highness—"

"Alessio," he interrupted as he stood. "It is only right that you call me by my first name, too. At least in private."

"In private. This can't be happening."

He'd felt the same many times. Yet it didn't change what had to be done. "But it is."

"I don't want to marry you." Brie planted her feet, preparing for battle.

This was not in the day's script. His mind raced; what was he supposed to say to that? The rebel buried in his soul shouted with joy before he reminded himself to keep calm. Duty was his life now.

Alessio sucked in a deep breath. That bought him seconds but didn't stop the pounding of his heartbeat in his ears. He'd spent a year figuring out how to make his father's goal a reality—a royal wedding for the country to rally around. Then another year prepping for today. It couldn't unravel. It simply couldn't.

There was no other plan. If this imploded today, Celiana's name would be in papers globally for days, maybe weeks.

For all the wrong reasons.

He could already see the headline: Princess Lottery Bust!

The success Celiana had gained would evaporate overnight. And coming home after his father's stroke, taking up the mantle of duty he'd sworn off, being the face of Celiana's resurgence...it would all have been for nothing. That couldn't happen.

"If you didn't want to be a princess, why was your name in the lottery?"

It wasn't like they'd forced people to put their names in. It was a choice. One that more than a thousand women had chosen.

She'd chosen this...just like he had. And with that came a responsibility to the people depending on them.

"To help Ophelia!" Brie rocked back on her feet as she looked toward the balcony. "To help her get her wedding dress business off the ground. It was a marketing stunt to help my friend. My name was in there once.

"Once," she whispered the word again.

One lucky ticket was what the lottery was all about. He'd parroted that line in many interviews. Alessio hadn't actually counted on someone with one free entry winning. But her reasoning was perfect.

Dutiful...but in a different way.

"That was kind of you." Alessio stepped to her side, grateful when she didn't step away. Helping her friend was admirable. And it was what she'd be doing as a princess.

Except instead of one friend, she'd help the entire kingdom.

"Kind?" Brie's sapphire gaze met his. "It was a marketing strategy, Alessio." Her body shifted and for a moment, he thought she might lean toward him.

"So is the lottery. A marketing strategy to jump-start the tourism industry. One that is working."

"And the only cost is *our* futures."

A tear slipped down her cheek and his hand rose without him thinking. His thumb rubbed away the drop, and Brie let out a sigh as he cupped her face.

"You signed a contract. Duty is why you put your name in. Duty is why you continue. We'll make it work."

"Make it work." Brie's hand rose, taking his and pulling it away from her face. She squeezed his fingers, her mouth opening as her eyes darted to their joined hands, before she let him go. "Make it work... Such romantic words."

Romance wasn't in the cards. The *idea* of romance was...but *actual* romance? That was not what royal marriages really were.

"According to the movies, Prince Charming and his bride always live happily ever after."

He wasn't Prince Charming. That ideal didn't exist. At least Brie knew that already. He wouldn't have to watch the light dim from his lottery bride as the realization struck.

"This isn't a joke."

The old Alessio would have said that this whole thing was a joke, a giant prank that was over-the-top. Unfortunately, the die was cast.

"You're right," Alessio agreed. "It's our duty to Celiana."

Brie looked at the door. Voices were mixing on the other side of it. A host of events was scheduled for today.

"What if I make you a deal?"

"A deal?" He needed to shut this down, they needed to get moving...but curiosity, and a hint of the rebel he'd been, kept him in place.

"Yes. This was a publicity stunt, and I am a marketing manager now. What if I can get tourism moving in areas not revolving around this? In six to eight weeks, if the focus is on something besides just us, we part ways."

"How would we even measure that?" As the question fell from his lips, he realized there was hope in it, hope that she might actually know a way. Hope he couldn't afford.

"The same way any business measures success." Brie rolled her eyes, gesturing into the air at nothing. Her thoughts on the Princess Lottery were quite clear. "We measure hotel bookings. The bookings need to increase in the next eight weeks—let's say by at least five percent—and tourism at our major sites needs a ten percent bump. That is doable in eight weeks or less."

Was it doable? If so… No. He needed to shut this down now.

"The contract for entry was binding. We've entered into a royal marriage contract and there's no going back."

The contract was similar to the one his parents had signed.

"I'm aware of what I signed. But if the royal family finds me an inappropriate match, you can void the contract."

She'd read the fine print.

"If I show you that I can get the tourism industry back to what it was without the need for a royal wedding, then you can find me inappropriate and end the contract."

The word *no* was on the tip of his tongue, and he knew that was the right answer, but the idea of fulfilling his end of this devil's bargain, while not having to go through with a royal wedding… It was intoxicating.

What if he could make good on the argument he'd had the night his father died without giving up everything?

But what did that mean for Celiana? If the tourists didn't come back for the royal wedding, would they come back at all?

"What if I convince you that there are benefits to royal life? That yes, the trade-off can be steep, but you can find rewarding things in service?"

Those dutiful words had been parroted so often to him when

he'd complained that he'd had no choice in the position of his birth. They were the words he should have said immediately when she offered the deal.

"So rewarding you ran away."

Touché.

"I came back."

She raised an eyebrow and shifted, like she wanted to call out the statement, poke at it.

"I can show you another way. A better way." Brie crossed her arms.

He saw so much of the man he used to be in her. Trapping that energy felt wrong, but duty still came first. It had to... didn't it?

"Without a scandal that destroys the kingdom or my brother's reign." His fight had led to so much damage already; he would not add to it. He couldn't.

Brie bit her lip before nodding. "If we can't do it without those things, then I guess I meet you at the altar." She held out a hand. "Deal?"

"Deal." For the first time since returning to Celiana, Alessio thought there might be a way to earn his freedom. Maybe.

"All right, first steps." She pulled out her phone and took a deep breath. "Do I look like I've been crying?"

"No. Your cheeks are a little flushed, but that's all. Why?"

"We have to tell our followers what we're doing. Rule one of marketing, don't miss prime opportunities. And flushed works. People can think you swept me off my feet."

She held up her phone and looked at him.

"Do you blush when you're swept off your feet?" he asked.

"No one's ever tried."

That was a shame. A woman who stepped in for a friend, who was so determined to chart her own course, deserved someone who'd sweep her off her feet. If her plan worked, then she'd get that chance.

Why did that give him an uncomfortable feeling?

"All right, Prince Charming, here we go." She pressed a few buttons. "Smile!"

He wasn't sure if the order was for him or her.

"Surprise!" She waved at the camera. "Guess who's here with me."

Brie stepped beside him, and he wrapped a hand around her waist. Her hip brushed his, but she didn't remove his hand.

"I guess you all get to follow me on my path to being a princess now!" Her voice was too bright. Too happy. "It's going to be a blast." She waved and disconnected the live.

"We'll get better." Brie blew out a breath as she glared at the phone.

"I thought that was fine."

She stepped away, just out of arm's reach. "That's why I'm the marketing manager. We came off stilted. *I* came off stilted. I'll make a post later about nerves and seeing royalty. It will be okay."

He suspected the *It will be okay* was meant for herself. Still, it was time for the next stage.

"We can practice with the guests here." He offered her his hand.

"Right." Brie slid her hand into his.

She looked up at him. Her full pink lips were so close, so perfect. Her hips shifted, pressing against him. It was an odd moment, one that his former self would enjoy too much. The old Alessio might even have joked that one sealed such deals with kisses.

Kissing Brie… His mind tumbled through the thoughts as the air in the room seemed to guide them together.

The crowd let out a cheer on the other side of the study door, breaking whatever magic was spinning between them.

Brie breathed out. "Ready or not."

"Ready or not." Alessio squeezed her hand, grateful that it was this woman standing beside him. Grateful that fate might have given him another chance at freedom.

CHAPTER TWO

HOW HAD THE day gone so off course? She was meant to be home, not reminding herself to not flinch as camera flashes popped off. Brie's feet were ice blocks, and the idea that she had to step into the room, pretend to be a happy princess-to-be, made her stomach twist. This wasn't the plan.

This evening was supposed to be about celebrating Ophelia's successes and planning the next steps of her future. She needed to focus, find the next steps. That was what Brie did well.

Yes, she was standing next to Alessio. After making a deal with him and nearly kissing him. Kissing… Her mind wanted to wander back to that moment. Even with all the calls and camera flashes, it was that moment her brain wanted to replay. He'd nearly kissed her.

At least she thought he was going to kiss her. Brie had very little experience with that. Well, none actually. She'd not lied when she told Alessio no one had ever tried to sweep her off her feet.

Her family had kept her sheltered, which was a fancy word for controlled her. The few men who'd asked her out after her escape had wanted access to the Ailiono family. She'd gone on exactly three second dates and no third.

The romance books she devoured described the moment before lips connected. The light touch of his fingers. The scent of sandalwood and cedar. The hesitation and excitement.

All those things were present. Except Alessio smelled like the ocean, fresh and free.

The prince, who'd joked about shoes and runaway brides, was rigid now. It was the dutiful Alessio beside her. The one who'd returned from overseas, never discussing what he'd done, assuming the burden of expectation.

Except she'd seen the hint of resignation in his eyes. It was a look she'd worn so often in her family's home. It was that look that made her ask for the deal, which he'd agreed to far quicker than she'd expected.

Maybe he acted like the dutiful prince, but she thought the rebel was still there. He yearned for freedom as much as she did.

Alessio leaned his head against hers. "Take a breath, Brie." The words were barely audible, but his arm slipped around her waist.

Her lungs screamed as she inhaled fresh oxygen.

"It's role-playing, remember."

His soft voice insinuated itself to her soul, reminding her of what was at stake. They needed to look happy today. In a few weeks, they could start pulling away in preparation for ending the engagement, but today… Today they needed to look happy.

His fingers gripped her waist, comfort washing over her as he held her tightly.

She'd never liked men to touch her like this. It felt possessive… It was possessive, at least when her father did it to her mother.

But Alessio's grip, his hand placement, felt more like protection, security in the storm. It was peaceful.

Protection? Security?

Brie didn't need protection or security. She took care of herself. She'd learned quickly that the world didn't care for rich kids. Even if they'd been cast out. She'd been on her own for years.

It was difficult, but she'd found her way. She'd graduated,

opened a marketing company, found her own footing. She was an independent woman.

Still, Alessio's touch felt nice. Too nice. It reminded her of his fingers on her cheek and the gentle touch of his thumb on her wrist.

She should reclaim her space, but she couldn't make herself do it. In fact, she had to fight the urge to lean her head against his shoulder as the barrage of questions started. That would be too much. It would look overdone, even if it was a natural action.

"Are you excited?"

No. She knew her smile wasn't enough to respond to the reporter's question.

"Any thought to the royal patronages you'll support?" Another question popped off before she could answer the last.

Thank goodness.

"Not yet." She'd never considered the fact that Alessio might call her name. She'd refused to think of the possibility she might be a princess. The odds were not in her favor...and that was the way she'd wanted it.

"Do you think your family position played any role in your selection?" The reporter's smile wasn't quite a smirk, but she felt Alessio's hand tighten on her waist.

"It was a fair drawing. Are you suggesting otherwise?" Alessio's voice was casual, but she heard the bite behind it.

Which was good, because she knew the answer to that question was that if her family had had their wish, she'd have married at nineteen. It was a choice they'd not even bothered to run past her before making.

"Will your wedding dress be by Ophelia or a royal designer?"

Finally, a reporter's question she could answer...sort of.

"I'm positive that I will wear one of Ophelia's dresses when I marry."

Alessio's fingers tightened on her waist. It wasn't a lie. If she ever married, and Brie was far from sold on the institution, she'd wear one of Ophelia's designs. However, Ophelia's designs would not grace the royal chapel.

At least not on Brie.

A twinge of sadness pressed into her chest. Ophelia's work deserved to be in the royal wedding. If Breanna or her twin sister had won the prize, Ophelia would at least be in the running to design the gown of the decade.

But when Brie didn't wed Prince Alessio, when the ruse was over... She doubted the next royal bride would choose the best friend of the woman who refused to play the part of the lotto bride.

The idea of another woman meeting Alessio at the altar sent a mixture of emotions through her soul. She couldn't quite determine the mixture. It should be relief...should be acceptance. Those were present, but the sadness lingering in the recesses of her body shocked her. Alessio deserved more than a royal union focused on what it brought Celiana.

Would they let him marry for love? Probably not. But at least it wouldn't be the spectacle of a lottery bride. That would be some consolation, right?

"Prince Alessio, do you think your father would be happy with your lotto bride?"

He shifted. Not much. Not enough that she thought anyone in the room noticed. If his arm wasn't around her waist, she wasn't sure she'd have noticed, either.

"I'm sure King Cedric would have been pleased."

They were words. That was the best she could say. It was his interview tone, the one she'd heard so often over the last year. But there was a hint of uncertainty, too. Maybe it was the camera flashes or the casual mention of the man Alessio had called King rather than Father.

Brie slipped her arm around his waist. He was providing her comfort in this sea of uncertainty; she could do the same. And it would look good for the cameras.

His eyes locked with hers and she smiled.

"We forgot to examine you for dirt," he said.

The words were quiet, but she saw a flash of the playful Alessio. That was the magic they needed to tap into.

"If that is the story of the day, remind me to say I told you so." He winked.

If that was the story of the day, the first episode in this marketing adventure was a loss. But he was smiling, and she was looser, too. So she winked back.

"Fair."

For a moment, it was easy to pretend they were a genuine couple. A few minutes of comradery in the storm of whatever this fever dream was.

"How about a kiss for the camera? A proper kiss?"

Her mouth fell open before she clasped it tight and forced a smile back on her face. Kiss. Of course the cameras wanted a kiss. This was a spectacle, after all.

And what was a romantic spectacle without a kiss?

Her fingers shook as she tried to prepare. The idea of kissing Alessio didn't bother her. If he'd dropped his lips to hers a few minutes ago, she might even have swooned a bit. The man was handsome, funny and more relaxed behind closed doors.

She wanted to know how the man beside her, who'd wiped a tear from her cheek, who'd joked about dust and looked like he might like to run away from all this, kissed.

That curiosity was something she'd need to deal with later, without an audience.

But kissing Alessio for the camera, letting the world see her first kiss, felt wrong. A first kiss held power. It contained so much possibility.

Except there wasn't any possibility in their situation.

"I think my future bride has had enough excitement for the day." Alessio's formal tone hung in the room.

What if he doesn't want to kiss me?

Why was that thought banging in her head? This was a charade. A charade. She needed to remember that.

"Are you saying that kissing her Prince Charming would be too exciting?" Lev, a royal commentator who spent most of his time finding fault, however minor, with the royal family, raised a brow.

Prince Charming.

How did the title sound so different when it fell from Lev's mouth?

Lev had spent the last year calling the bride lottery a stunt. He was even hosting an informal betting pool on his website for people to wager how long the royal engagement lasted. The largest bet was placed for three months from today.

The fact that Lev was here was a signal. The royal family wanted to smother his suggestions. Rather than exclude him, they'd made a point of inviting him. If she'd marketed this union, she'd have made the same suggestion.

Media was a game and it was one she was quite skilled at, one that was going to grant her freedom from this trap.

Still, she hated that when she won, it would prove the man right.

"I am quite the kisser. My bride-to-be will certainly swoon the first time our lips connect." The words were said with an over-the-top flair.

Anticipation coated her skin, but she could play into the moment, too. "So sure of yourself."

The audience chuckled, smiles draping everywhere as they clapped for the couple. Good, they were back in control of the narrative. Those that controlled the media narrative won.

Only Lev frowned as he typed something into his phone.

This wasn't real. She knew that, but she hated the look on the gossip reporter's face. She hated that, even unintentionally, they were playing into his expectations.

Brie lifted on her toes, pressing her lips to Alessio's cheek. The connection was brief, over before she could really think it through.

More than a few calls echoed throughout the crowd for her to do it again, but it was Alessio's reaction that fascinated her.

His jade eyes held hers. The questions and camera flashes

evaporated. For a moment, they were the only two people in the crowded room.

"Alessio." His name escaped before she leaned her head against his shoulder.

The day was too much, just as he'd said. The questions, the spotlight, the way the life she'd known had shifted in the space of seconds when Alessio pulled her name.

She was reacting to the day, to the hope of a way out...not to him.

"Shall we get a drink?"

"Please."

Alessio held up a hand. "Briella and I are going to seek refreshments. Enjoy the party. There will be plenty of time for questions during our courtship."

Alessio didn't release her as they walked away from the journalists. His arm was light on her waist. It was a reminder of the role they were playing, and that if she stepped away, everyone would comment.

First lesson—things that seemed meaningless mattered.

She took a deep breath, all hopes of calming herself evaporating as Alessio's scent invaded her senses again. The man was gorgeous, a literal prince... Did he have to smell like heaven, too?

Brie had never allowed herself to fall in lust—not that there'd been many options. Just because she was horrified that her name came out of the giant glass tumbling ball didn't mean she couldn't acknowledge the man beside her was hot.

Right?

Alessio was tall, attractive, kind. There were worse men to play pretend with. Her mouth was dry as she looked at him. His jade gaze met hers and her belly flipped. The man was the definition of *gorgeous*.

A table layered with treats came into view. The decadence reminded her that she was in the palace, next to Alessio as his bride-to-be. She shouldn't need the reminder. She needed to focus, start thinking of her plans and their next steps.

She'd spent her youth looking attentive at boring family functions while drifting away to her own mental space. Even in this ruckus, she should be able to do it. But as his fingers stroked her side, it was impossible to focus on more than his touch.

"This is lovely."

Hints of sugar, lemon and a host of other flavors skipped through her senses. So many sweets finally overtook the delicious scent that was Alessio.

Pastries overloaded the table. Rather than hiring one caterer, Alessio had asked each bakery to deliver a few dozen of their best desserts. That way, everyone got to claim a piece of the day. It was a marketing coup.

"It is." He smiled and looked at the table. "What kind of dessert do you like best?"

"I don't know." She laughed as she looked at the sweets, hoping to cover her uncertainty as she stared at the table. She'd not run in aristocratic circles in years, but she knew the game. Smile, look attentive, even when you feel like falling apart. Muscle memory had been reinforced by years of Ailiono training.

Her mother had not permitted Brie to have sweets as a child or teen. Her family raised her to be...to be exactly where she was, actually. However, her parents would never have attempted to marry her to one of Celiana's princes. Alessio and Sebastian had crowns, but the man her family had wanted her to wed had power. He was a business partner of her father's, a scion of industry with no regard for the women who stood by his side.

Her father's arrangement was for Brie to be his third wife. His third wife and nearly thirty years his junior, she would be the definition of a trophy bride—a young woman he could mold into his "perfect" wife. Only, she wouldn't gain her freedom like the other two had.

Rationally, she knew her mother no longer controlled the

food she ate. That just like the outfits she wore, Brie could now choose her food. She was allowed to make her own choices.

She'd not graced her parents' impressive doorstep in almost seven years, but this action... She'd tried so many things since being disowned, but never sweets. Each time she looked at one, considered it, she'd heard her mother's screaming voice, and the urge to taste something had died away.

She didn't have to stay in this restrictive world. Brie had a path out. She could do this.

"I prefer lemon and lavender treats," Alessio said as he handed her a plate, then started putting things on his while making small talk with the person in line before them.

The plate was tiny, embossed with the royal crest at the top and the bottom. Brie knew it only weighed a few ounces, but it was lead in her hand.

She'd overcome so much. This shouldn't be that hard. But still her finger gripped the plate like it might fly from her hands. Her ears buzzed, and she knew people were watching. The longer she stood here, the more likely someone would make this a moment out of their control.

Alessio put a chocolate petit four, a lemon bar and a lavender cookie on his plate, then turned. His eyebrows pulled together as his gaze fell to her empty plate.

"Brie?"

"I don't know what dessert I like." It was such an inconsequential thing, something that wouldn't bother her if she wasn't surrounded by dozens of cameras, in the palace, suddenly engaged to a prince.

She might even make a joke about being a twenty-six-year-old sweet virgin. And she would laugh to cover the past and how it made her different from her peers. She would joke so she didn't have to remember that her family only wanted her if she played by their rigged rules.

"These are my favorite. Try one." He put the cookie on her plate, his fingers tracing along her wrist.

Her breath caught on the connection. Heat raced up her arm as his touch grounded her. She wasn't alone.

"And I do not know what this is, but it's lovely." He set another treat on her plate, leaning forward and pushing a piece of hair behind her ears.

He leaned close, ocean breeze coming with him. Her nerves were still racing, but now they focused on the handsome man's lips brushing her ear.

"You don't have to eat them. Or you can."

She knew the touches, the small talk, even the refreshment table, were designed for the day. It was all a perfect marketing tool for the country and the royal family. If she'd overseen the event, there were a few changes she'd have made, but whoever had planned the occasion was an artist.

And yet, part of her wanted to believe he was caring for her, that the concern sweeping his features was meant only for her. Truly for her. She wanted to believe that if the participants all fell away, if the fancy dresses disappeared and he was in lounge pants and she was in comfy pants no one should see, he'd still care.

Brie smiled. "Thank you. You don't have to hold my hand through all this."

But it's nice.

"You are my bride-to-be." He leaned a little closer. "And the cameras are watching."

Cameras.

The cameras would be focused on the caring prince performing actions for others…not for her.

The press corps surrounding Brie's apartment didn't surprise Alessio. The swarm must have descended as soon as he announced her name. He knew the families with fifty-two entries for their daughters had scheduled security for today, anticipating such an occurrence.

Actually, all the families that could afford the high cost of a year's worth of entries had security. Brie's neighbors were undoubtedly unhappy...and worried.

They needed to fix this. Maybe she could spin this into a "move into the palace with me" post. Yet the public didn't have access to the royal quarters, so there wasn't much of a tourism trap there.

"What the hell!" Brie leaned against him as camera flashes assaulted the tinted windows.

"You won the Princess Lottery." Had she really not expected people to be here?

Brie somehow got closer to him. Her body was warm against his. Maybe it was silly to be so happy with the simple action. But she felt nice against him. They were partners in their goal, two souls from powerful families that craved freedom.

And if it didn't work...if they had to wed to protect Celiana...they'd find a way to make do. Maybe his parents hadn't loved each other, but respect was more than many got.

If there was another way to aid the generations of bakers, shop owners, bistro and hotel operators who based their businesses around honeymooners, reaching for it wasn't selfish. Right?

Alessio had been the rebel. He'd been the runaway unhappy with his role as second fiddle. Stepping in as the dutiful one felt weird, and he wasn't quite sure he was doing it right.

"This is...this is..."

He understood her being at a loss for words. Alessio had grown up in this life, and it was still a game he felt like he was failing at most days.

"It's royal life. The start of it at least. And the role you agreed to play."

Brie's blue eyes flashed. She was gorgeous, and the day was long. The blend of emotions sent desire through his soul. And he ached to protect someone from the world that had finally beaten him.

After all, she hadn't chosen this. Not really. She'd submitted one entry, one tiny slip in a sea of hopefuls, one chance for the crown that would sit on her head forever.

"Only until I get a plan in place that brings more than honeymooners." Brie sighed as the driver pulled as close to her place as the crowd allowed.

"If you can make that happen, then yes. It's temporary. But it might be a good idea to at least consider that it's forever." He paused before adding, "Trust me. If it doesn't work and we meet at the altar, you'll feel better having at least considered it."

If he'd made himself believe his little glass shop was temporary, maybe closing it wouldn't have broken him as much.

"I refuse to think of that until it's absolutely necessary" She pushed away from him, her top teeth digging into her lip.

"Fine. But for now, you're a princess-in-waiting. And the world needs to believe that you believe that." The flash of anger turned to frustration as her bright eyes found his.

"Right. Control the narrative." Brie pulled the bottom of her dress to the side, readying herself to step out.

His life was a series of narratives. Some of them were so well spun, even Alessio wondered what was real and what was the official palace line. It shouldn't bother him that she was speaking in the same tone, but frustration pooled in his soul.

"It's not just about narratives. It's about the country and duty and making sure everyone is safe, even if it means giving up something of yourself."

It was like his father's ghost had spit the words out. They were words the old Alessio would never have spoken.

"Soon you'll have a plan for this country that will bring it more than just honeymooners. And I'll be a blip in the royal family's memory."

Not in my memory.

No matter how long he lived, he wouldn't forget the woman who had marched in after being offered a crown and made a deal to get out of it. How often had he craved the same thing? If her plan worked, he might get back the life he'd had. The life he craved.

Most people only saw the glamour of the crown, not the pain behind it. And now he had the beauty beside him.

"So, what are we going to do?" Fine lines appeared around her eyes. Her lips tipped down before she plastered on a smile. "Move me into the palace?"

He hadn't expected her to suggest it, but he was glad she had, so he didn't have to.

"Yes. You move into the palace. You can make a video telling everyone."

"I was kidding, Your Royal Highness."

Your Royal Highness.

Her back was straight, and she was ready for battle. That was good. Celiana needed strong female role models. And even if they didn't meet at the altar, she'd impress people.

"Brie—" Alessio gestured to the crowd "—you won the Princess Lottery."

"We have a deal, Your Royal Highness."

"Do you plan to call me Your Royal Highness whenever you're frustrated? Not that I'm complaining… Well, not really. It will make it easy to determine when you are cross." He tapped his head. "Mental note made."

"This isn't a joke."

He agreed, but humor helped in difficult moments. It relaxed people. He'd been good at it once upon a time. That man seemed to want to emerge around Brie. He'd have to wrestle him back into the mental cage he thought he'd thrown away the key to.

The crowd was getting impatient.

"You can't stay here. It's not safe." He gestured to the sea of people.

Most of them just wanted a picture of the royal couple. They wanted to tell their friends and future grandkids where they'd been when Prince Alessio and Princess Briella arrived at her home.

But there were others. People who despised the monarchy and people who blamed the hard years on the royals.

It wasn't fair. Celiana was a constitutional monarchy. King Sebastian was little more than a figurehead. But the royals were the faces of the country. They were the attraction that drove tourism. Real-life fairy-tale creatures, they played a role with perceived, if little actual, power.

And the last few years had been hard. The economic downturn had hit nearly every sector and there were more than a few disgruntled citizens. And even if there weren't, that didn't mean that a future royal bride should live unprotected. Even one who never planned to wear the crown.

She sighed but didn't wilt. Her eyes roamed the crowd, and he saw acceptance register.

It was good, but it tore at him, too. Acceptance was part of the royal life. He and Sebastian had learned at an early age that their wills, their desires, all came at least second to the needs of the country. It was a lesson Brie would face again and again, too. Particularly if they wed.

His choices had evaporated the moment his father had his stroke. But hers... Until today they'd been wide open. The ease of life, the ability to just run to the store or go to work... all were gone for her, at least for a while.

"You're right. I can't stay here."

Brie's words pulled him away from his unsettled thoughts. He had to focus on the present. The past was lost, and the future was a reminder that his life was scripted now. *Focus on the here and now.*

"We'll pack up some of your stuff now, then I can send the staff to get the rest."

"Sure." Brie nodded. He could see that a fight was brewing in her eyes, but she was ceding the ground on this. A battle won.

"Princess! Princess!" The calls echoed as security opened the car door.

Brie raised a hand, smiling as she moved through the crowd, ignoring the questions and moving as quickly as security created the path for them.

She shut her apartment door behind them and crossed her arms. "This is too much."

"This is what winning the lottery looks like." The rules were clear. Each entry was a contract. By putting your name in the crystal ball you agreed that, if chosen, you became a princess.

"I'm aware of that, Alessio."

"She entered *for* me." A woman stepped from what had to be Brie's bedroom. "I am so sorry."

"Ophelia." Brie ran to her friend.

She held on tightly, and Alessio was grateful she had someone to pour herself into. And he was jealous there wasn't anyone who'd do the same for him. He glanced around the apartment, looking for a way to give them privacy, but it was too tiny.

"I shouldn't have agreed to the marketing strategy. This is a nightmare." Ophelia's voice shook as she looked to Alessio.

Before he could say anything, Brie squeezed her friend, then stepped back. "Not ideal, but at least this fiancé is cuter than the one my parents lined up."

"Closer to your age, too." Ophelia's laughter mingled with Brie's. "But this isn't the time for jokes."

She'd been engaged? That didn't make sense. The Ailionos made huge engagement announcements. Her parents' engagement party had cost more than his parents' wedding.

And she wasn't in contact with her family. Her family had disowned her...at least according to the not-so-quiet rumors.

Engaged.

The word tapped against his brain.

His life was a series of long days, but he was officially overloaded.

"Engaged?"

"Not important."

He wasn't aware he'd spoken until Brie waved it away. But he saw her shoulders tighten—so it wasn't unimportant. Another question for another day, then.

If there was a spurned ex waiting, well, he at least needed to make sure security knew. That was the reason for his curiosity. The only reason…

He almost believed that.

"I came to see if you wanted me to spirit you off the island. Not sure how, but Rafael and I planned to work that out later. Bringing *him* makes that harder."

Ophelia tilted her head as she looked at Alessio, sizing him up. He didn't shift under her judgment, but that didn't mean he didn't want to.

"Not impossible. Just harder." Ophelia raised a brow.

"No escape needed." Brie shook her head and moved to his side. She was close to him but careful not to touch him. There were no cameras here, no reason to pretend they were starting the journey of falling in love.

"I have a plan." Brie nodded to the door where the crowd was audible. "And my plans always work out."

Ophelia opened her mouth but said nothing.

But he could hear the concern. No one got everything. But this…this he wanted Brie to achieve. For her peace…and his.

"I'll get the dress back to you tomorrow, if that works?"

Her friend crossed her arms. "I assume the palace will purchase it. They often put high-profile outfits in the fashion museum." Ophelia's eyes held his, daring him to contradict her. "I think this one counts."

"Ophelia—"

"Send the bill." Alessio looked at Brie. "After all, it would be expected."

"Of course." There was a look in her eyes. Did she wish he'd said something else?

No. They were just tired.

"I will send the bill first thing in the morning, Your Royal Highness." Ophelia stepped to them and pulled Brie into her arms.

"I meant what I said," she said to Brie. "Say the word and

I will find a way to get you out of this." She kissed her cheek, then stepped back.

"Thank you." Brie took a deep breath. "Alessio, while I gather a few things, can you make sure security helps Ophelia get to her vehicle without being accosted by the crowd?"

"Of course."

Brie moved to her room.

Before he could open the door, Ophelia put her hand on his chest. "She's had a lifetime of hurt. You do not get to add to it. So, if you hurt her, crown or not, you *will* answer to me."

The threat wasn't needed, but he was glad Brie had someone in her corner.

"Understood."

"Good." Ophelia nodded then listened as he gave the security team directions for her safety.

As soon as Ophelia was out the door, he heard Brie shout from the other room.

"Alessio!"

He moved as quickly as his feet would carry him. Had someone broken in? Sebastian had once had a girlfriend who was stalked by individuals hoping to capture a picture to sell to the press. A few had even broken into her place, foolish hope of quick money outweighing rational thoughts of jail time.

Brie's apartment would be easy to get into, and the lotto bride picture would be worth thousands!

The small apartment was sparsely furnished. The only photos appeared to be of her, Ophelia and a man he guessed was Ophelia's husband. The apartment was close to public transportation, and was the kind of place university students and those just starting in their careers chose.

It was not a place one expected to find an Ailiono. Her room at the Ailiono mansion was likely larger than this space. What was she doing here?

"I made a mistake letting Ophelia leave." Brie's hands were on her chest, and her eyes were tired. The weight of everything seemed to press against her.

"Oh." Alessio wasn't sure what to say. "I thought you weren't escaping."

If she left immediately, would they ask him to draw another name? How selfish was he for considering that? When they broke up in a few weeks, he could pretend to be heartbroken. But today…

"I told you I could prove this stunt unnecessary."

"You did, but it's a lot. You know it and I know it." Alessio knew his voice was too tight, but while he wanted to believe in the possibility, reality was difficult to avoid for a royal.

"I meant that. I'm not running." The last sentence was tight, and he could see her shift slightly.

Not yet.

He'd run. He knew the look. But she was here now.

"Brie—"

"It's the dress," she interrupted, gesturing to herself. "The dress," she repeated as her eyes fell to the floor.

He wasn't sure what the issue was.

"It is gorgeous."

He marveled at the deep green, and the low neckline with a simple necklace. She was beautiful, but the dress turned her into a nymph, a mythical creature almost too beautiful to touch.

"Yes, it's beautiful. Some of Ophelia's best work, but I'm buttoned into it."

She turned, and he saw tiny buttons starting at the base of her neck, all the way to the top of her incredible butt.

He swallowed the burst of need pushing at him.

She looked over her shoulder, pulling her braid to the side. "Can you, please?"

"Of…course."

Stepping up, he lifted his hands and started undoing the delicate pearl buttons. Her skin appeared by centimeters. A tiny mole on her shoulder, a freckle in the middle of her back. He'd never been turned on by so little, but Alessio ached to run his finger along the edges of skin he was revealing.

He would not betray this moment. She'd asked him for aid so he would ignore the fact that he wanted to trail kisses across her back, wanted to strip the dress down. He cleared his throat as he refocused on the buttons. The rebel prince pushing against the dutiful man he needed to be.

"You all right?"

No.

"Fine." He breathed the word into being. He made it to the middle of her back and let out a sigh of relief.

"Is something on my back?"

"No." The word did nothing to stop the pulsating bead of need in his soul. It didn't clear the thoughts or the desire; if anything, the fuse seemed to speed up.

"You're perfection." Alessio's finger slipped, connecting with her bare skin. Desire blazed through him. What would she do if he kissed her? What would she taste like?

Fire? Passion?

"Think you can take it from here?" Alessio barely got the words out.

"No." Brie looked over her shoulder. "I mean…it's just, the pearls are sewn on by hand. It's so delicate. I can't see the buttons. I wore it to highlight her ability, given that you required a wedding dress."

"Actually, that was Sebastian." Alessio let out a sigh. This was a topic he could use to alleviate some of the need clawing through him.

Brie spun. Her hands clasped the top of the dress to keep it in place.

All hope of ignoring the desire evaporated. Her chest was pink…with frustration…or might she be pulsing with need, too?

His body ached as he made sure to keep his gaze focused on her face, when all he wanted to do was worship her with his lips. His tongue…

"Your brother?"

Focus, Alessio. Focus.

"He's still learning his words carry more weight. The Princess Lottery was my father's idea, the reason I came back." That was close to the truth.

"You came back for this. I might have stayed—" Her blue eyes caught his. "Where were you?"

"Not in Celiana." He didn't discuss those years. The happiness, the freedom...

"Right." He started to push his hands into his pockets before adjusting his stance. "Sebastian... Well, he thought the idea wild and hasn't kept his thoughts quiet."

"He's different." Brie looked at Alessio.

"The crown is heavy." That was another topic he wasn't going to discuss. Sebastian wasn't the same. He skipped duties. He seemed uninterested in the role he'd practiced for since birth.

"Good thing we aren't getting married... We might have to answer each other's questions." Brie pursed her lips.

Not necessarily.

That was a sad truth of royal life. As long as you looked happy to the outside, you could do almost anything behind the walls of the palace.

"Sebastian joked that I should have everyone arrive in wedding dresses, and before I knew what happened, they wrote it into the contract. Luckily, most people rented their gowns."

"Rented?" Brie's mouth fell open.

"Yes." He made a twirling motion with his finger, and she turned as he restarted his undressing mission. "I worked out a deal with one of the chain bridal gown places in America. The women could rent their gowns, then ship them back. If one of the women with a rented gown won, the chain would get to dress the princess on our wedding day."

"That was very kind." She bent her head, and his fingers slipped again.

The contact between his fingers and her bare skin lasted less than a second. It was no time at all and forever all at once.

"I think..." she started, but didn't continue for a moment. "I think I've got it from here."

"Of course." His feet screamed as he stepped away. "I'll…" Words were difficult to muster. "Should I pack anything in the living room or kitchen?"

"No."

He headed for the door.

"Alessio?" Her cheeks were pink; her lips pursed. Brie's hands clutched the bodice of her gown. She started toward him, then stopped.

"Yes?"

"Thank you." Her smile was soft. It wasn't a brilliant, excited grin or joyous beam, but it filled her eyes. "Today was a long day."

"Tomorrow is the start of the next chapter." Whether that ended in their freedom or at the altar was still too early for Alessio to know.

"I look forward to showing you how we save Celiana without sacrificing our own happiness."

"I hope you do." He stepped out of her room to give her space. Privacy was something in short supply within the palace walls where she'd be living—at least for a few weeks.

And maybe forever.

CHAPTER THREE

ALESSIO STOOD IN front of Briella's door. He needed to knock. It was nearly nine in the morning; time was moving fast. His bride-to-be was a stranger. They didn't need to know each other's secrets, but they needed to know enough to put on a good show.

That was all people really wanted. It was a sad truth he'd learned as soon as he was old enough to understand the news articles printed about his family. A smiling family was best. The press could translate any frown into a generational fight in an instant. Truth was only good if the gossip was boring.

And the gossip was never boring.

Brie was part of this now whether or not she wanted it—at least for a while.

The hint of his old self was rooting for Brie.

But the man standing in front of her door this morning was Prince Alessio, heir to the kingdom and man at the center of the Princess Lottery scheme.

The scheme could very well result in Briella Ailiono meeting him at the altar. The further he got away from her enthusiasm, the more he figured that would be the outcome. Maybe she was a marketing genius—he wanted to hope so because no matter how much he'd run through the deal last night, Alessio had found no ideas to help her.

Celiana was a kingdom built on honeymoon tourists. When they'd vanished, so had much of the prosperity. The tourism board had run a few ad campaigns, but none of them had resulted in much. The honeymooners had stayed away...until the Princess Lottery.

The morning was already slipping away, and he'd yet to greet her, yet to see the woman who might very well be his wife. In the palace, everything was scheduled. And on the schedule for the day was "Get to know the lotto bride."

His secretary had actually written those words. *Lotto bride.* It was a descriptor that would follow Brie for the rest of her days.

Unless she pulled off the unthinkable. Then she'd get her freedom...and so would he. Maybe he could go back to Scotland. He'd sold his shop, but he'd opened one once before and he could do it again. Except living incognito after being the international face of the Princess Lottery wouldn't work.

It had barely worked the first time. Every once in a while, people would recognize him, but he'd been able to play off the doppelgänger idea. After all, no one expected a prince in a glass shop.

It could work again—but he'd have to have security. It was something he probably should have had before. But his father had refused to provide it since he'd "walked out on duty."

Alessio squeezed his eyes closed. No. He couldn't give in to that fancy. Even if she had figured out a brilliant plan, there was no guarantee. He'd tasted freedom once. Giving it up had destroyed a sizable portion of his soul.

Brie could hope. Alessio couldn't afford it.

Today was about preparation, informing her what she should expect.

Everyone would snap pictures of her.

Language lacked descriptors for Brie's beauty. She was ethereal. Unbuttoning her gown last night was nearly a spiritual experience.

His subconscious had spun that moment into heated dreams. He was attracted to her. How could he not be? But it was her strength that echoed through his heart. How many women would challenge a prince the moment they met him?

He needed to knock, start the day's agenda by going over the rules, the expectations. He had to explain the bars of the gilded cage that was hers now.

How was he supposed to do that?

"You look weird hovering in front of her door, brother." Sebastian's tone was relaxed. Jokey...unbothered.

Unbothered.

That was once the descriptor applied by his father to Alessio. Sebastian was dutiful. The obedient son. The one who did what was expected...until his father passed.

Now the man was unbothered by everything. Despite the crown on his head. It was infuriating. But given that the last argument Alessio had had with the king of Celiana resulted in his brother's coronation, Alessio had sworn not to argue.

Bury the emotions. Deal with it privately.

"Good observation, Sebastian." Alessio turned, wondering what would happen if Brie opened the door to find the king and her fiancé facing off.

"Aren't your rooms connected?" Sebastian leaned against the wall.

"Yes." His brother knew that; he was just pointing out that Alessio didn't have to be out here. But he did. He was trying to make Brie feel less trapped.

"Trying to work up courage?"

He wanted to deny it, but what was the point? He'd been caught. And he needed courage. Though that wasn't all he needed.

Part of him, the rebel prince who cried out in her presence, wanted to open the door, pull Brie into his arms and see if the heat burning between them last night was still there.

"Did you need something?"

"I'd like to remind you that no one forced you to follow through with the king's plan." Sebastian looked at his fingers then back at Alessio.

The king's plan.

"You're the king and you didn't have any better ideas." Alessio didn't like the hint of bitterness in his tone.

The royal family's only actual power was influence, but it was influence his brother seemed inclined to ignore for as long as possible. Their father was gone; if they didn't step up, who would?

"Maybe you should have worn the crown."

Alessio laughed. "King Cedric is rolling in his fancy tomb hearing that."

His father had spent his life pointing out Alessio's flaws. Getting away had been so healing. It was ironic that he'd finally become the prince his father wanted.

If King Cedric was here, I'd still be free.

"You wear the crown well." It wasn't the truth, but maybe one day it would be.

"We both know that's a lie." Sebastian knocked on Brie's door.

"Wai—" Alessio's mouth froze as his brother rapped his knuckles again.

They waited a moment, but Brie didn't answer. His stomach hit the floor. Surely, she hadn't fled...

"Rattling you is fun. Hard since you came back. But fun." His brother winked. "Your bride-to-be was in the kitchen at four thirty. She's now installed in the media room in the east wing."

"We only have one media room," Alessio grumbled as he started toward where his fiancée was hiding.

Four thirty.

He was an early riser by necessity. If he wanted any time to himself, he took it before the world woke. He'd go for a run or a swim a little after five thirty and have breakfast by six fifteen.

However, when he owned his life, Alessio regularly waited until eight or nine to begin his day.

Stop thinking of that.

It was the past. Focus on Brie. On the here and now.

"She's under your skin."

"She's…"

Alessio pushed his hands into his pockets then pulled them out as words refused to come to mind. Brie wasn't under his skin; it was the thought that her idea, her plan, whatever she'd figured out, might actually work. There was the rush free- dom brought, the hint that maybe the life he'd had could be his again.

Still, he did not get ruffled, not anymore. That was Sebas- tian's role.

Alessio was cool, calm and dutiful. The prince everyone expected…the one the island needed.

"There is one thing we should discuss before you greet Briella *Ailiono*."

The inflection on her last name gave away the issue. "Her family."

"So you've thought of it, too?"

Not really. Not in the way that seemed to echo off his brother. He'd seen her panic yesterday at the dessert table. Heard the jokes that cut too close to her soul about an engage- ment to a man evidently many years her senior.

Her family had let Brie down. He understood that. She'd flown from her cage and landed in another. Just like him.

"She's estranged. The entire court knows that." The reasons for it were for Brie to acknowledge, not him.

Her panic at the dessert table yesterday had made Alessio see red. That she'd panic at such a thing implied the control she'd endured growing up.

Luckily, he'd kept his cool for the cameras.

"Do you know why she's estranged?"

"No. But it hardly matters. If the Ailiono family has issues with this union, they will go through me."

Brie was smart and kind—the woman had entered the bridal lottery solely to help her friend, and had protected Ophelia last night, too. Maybe those weren't qualities the Ailiono family valued, but they were ones he did.

Sebastian's head snapped back. "Going toe-to-toe with the Ailionos might not work. They have more power."

"More land, more money...power—they probably think so. But no one has ever really tested that." Alessio didn't wish to break that ground, but if Brie needed it... Well, the royal family would offer her protection. There had to be some bonus to wearing a crown.

"You'd challenge the Ailiono clan?"

"If necessary." Maybe it was weird to feel so protective of Briella. But it was the least he could do. She was under his protection for as long as she was his fiancée...and for forever if they met at the altar.

"You don't have to marry her."

"Good. Something we agree on." Brie was smiling as she held the door open.

For once Alessio wished the palace staff didn't keep the door hinges so well oiled.

"Brie. You look lovely this morning."

Alessio dipped his head, unable to keep the smile from his lips. She was gorgeous and so sure of herself. Once more his heart swelled with the idea of freedom. Of escaping...with Brie.

Except that if they escaped, it wouldn't be together. His happiness deflated a little on that realization.

"I've breakfast in here for you, Alessio. There is enough, if you'd like to come to the presentation, too, Your Majesty."

"Sebastian." The king tilted his head. "You are to be my sister-in-law after all."

"We'll see about that."

"I *like* her." Sebastian nodded to Brie, then turned to Alessio. His brother didn't hide his chuckle as he walked away. It was still weird to hear Sebastian laugh.

"A presentation?" Alessio stepped into the media room and felt his mouth fall open.

One side of the room looked like a miniature studio with a ring light, green screen and laptop set up. The other side indicated she'd found the library and carted what looked like dozens of books.

How long had she been awake?

"Did you get any sleep, Brie?"

"I did." She smiled, hesitating before adding, "Thank you for asking."

The hesitation before her thanks nearly broke his heart. It was a simple question. A kind one. And he could tell that no one usually asked.

No one asked him, either. How he wished they shared more in common than family trauma.

"How?" He blew out a breath as he surveyed the media room.

"I slept here." Brie grinned. "The couch is surprisingly comfortable."

Alessio shook his head. "I haven't slept on a couch since I was a teen trying to make King Cedric mad."

He couldn't even remember the argument now. There'd been so many with his father. But the result was Alessio sleeping on the same couch Brie had for almost a month until he had finally relented on whatever the fight was about. Which was why he didn't remember the reason. He only remembered the fight his father had won.

Though since he was back in Celiana, his father had won that one, too. Not that he'd ever known it.

"Why do you call him King Cedric?"

Alessio took the coffee from Brie's hand, her fingers brushing his. The lightening he'd experienced at her touch last night reappeared immediately.

He took a long sip, before asking, "What else would I call him?"

Brie's eyes widened.

"I fear I said a princely thing."

"A princely thing?" Brie moved to the small table where fruits, scones and breakfast meats were laid out. "What does that mean?"

Alessio made up his own plate then followed her to the couch. "Oh. It's a thing that makes people realize Sebastian and I aren't normal. That our upbringing was…unique."

Unique was as good a word as any.

"I called him King Cedric because that was his title."

In his mind it made sense. He knew others viewed their parents differently. He cared for his mother, loved her. His father, on the other hand… He'd respected his devotion to Celiana. If a little of it was ever directed toward him— Alessio shut the thought down.

His father had done the best he could for the country, but he'd seen Alessio and Sebastian as extensions of his duty more than as sons.

"Alessio…"

Brie's eyes held a look he knew was pity. He didn't need it. Didn't want it—particularly from her.

"Presentation time." Alessio clapped his hands. "We have a wedding to stop!"

A wedding to stop.

Those were words Brie desperately wanted to hear, so why did they turn her skin cold?

Alessio, the rebel turned dutiful heir to the throne, was a mystery. He'd spent his teen years avoiding royal duties, arriving almost late to events and ducking out early. It was typical teen behavior—but as a prince the press had labeled him a rebel. And he'd seemed to lean in to the role.

Brie mentally shook herself. This wasn't a mystery she needed to crack. She needed his support, which he seemed willing to give. But he'd dodged every deep question she'd asked.

That didn't matter. It didn't.

A yawn gathered at the back of her throat, and Brie forced it away. There wasn't time for exhaustion. She'd worked through the night. Literally. She'd taken catnaps on the couch, woken and restarted.

Brie had pulled all-nighters at university. Her parents had cut her off just after her first semester, when she'd made it clear she had no intention of marrying her father's business contact. From that moment, the payments for school all fell to her.

But for the first time in her life, she could make her own choices. So she'd taken out a loan and made it her goal to graduate in three years instead of four. Working as a barista on campus, studying on every break and going on less than five hours of sleep most nights nearly broke her.

Her family had hoped she'd break, that she'd come crawling back and do what they wanted. Follow their plans. But doing that meant never getting a say in the choices of her own life.

Was that what had happened to Alessio? Why he was back? He'd spent three years abroad, and the royal family had said nothing of his whereabouts. It was like he'd vanished to another dimension, only to reappear when his father, the man he only called King Cedric, suffered his stroke.

The royal family had welcomed him back. They'd pretended like the years away never occurred. Her family would do the same if she bowed the knee and agreed to marry a business contact or foreign heir, if she added value to the family firm. It wasn't as if the Ailionos needed more.

Part of her did wonder about the conversation, if there was any, around the dinner table last night. Her mother had made her thoughts on the Princess Lottery clear when a reporter asked her about it at a ladies' charity event. It was an event Brie knew her mother didn't want to be at, but appearances were what mattered.

According to her mother, the lottery was gauche and in poor taste for the royal family. She'd said that no one would treat the lotto winner like a real princess and that she thought the whole thing ridiculous. She'd not commented when asked about Brie's participation.

"What was your favorite dress Ophelia made?" His question broke through her tired brain.

"The one I wore yesterday." Brie grinned as she pulled up

the presentation slides. "I know white is tradition, for some pretty horrid reasons in my mind. Purity." She made a face. If that was important to a person, then fine, but it wasn't important to her, and that should be fine, too.

"A little old-fashioned, true. The color of a gown should be a bride's choice, for whatever reason she likes. Of course, it needs to be coordinated with the groom."

"So he gets a say?" Brie raised a brow. She had no plans to meet Alessio at the altar, so the argument was pointless, but she couldn't seem to stop herself. "I thought the day was about the bride?"

"But what if she wears orange, and he's in blue? A color clash in their photos! Forever, Brie. Think of the pictures!"

Brie shook her head as the laughter bubbled up. The silly Alessio was here. The one that sat on the floor with her yesterday. The one she needed beside her for this campaign to work.

"That is ridiculous!"

"It is." Alessio leaned toward her, and her eyes fell to his lips. Round, full...so close. "But it made you laugh."

A joke. It was perfect. He'd not questioned her statement on bridal purity. Instead, he'd made a joke about color theory. It was silly and there was no judgment in his voice.

Not that there was much to tell about her love life. Brie had never been with a man, and at twenty-six it made her feel awkward sometimes. But that was better than the alternatives.

She was an Ailiono, which meant everyone who'd asked her out wanted her because of her family. No one wanted her for her, and she wasn't willing to give her heart away for less.

Maybe once she made her own way, found her own path. But deep down she worried she couldn't run far enough to be free of the Ailiono name.

"I love the deep green, the buttons. I obviously can't wear it for my wedding day, though." She saw his lips twitch on the words *wedding day*. The giant white elephant in the room.

"If we marry, you can wear any color on our wedding day. The jade highlights your eyes, gives you a fairylike appearance. And acknowledges your strength, your ability to step away from tradition. But I must know the color so my tie coordinates."

A lump pressed against her throat. What was she to say to that? He'd told her to prepare in case they married, in case she couldn't pull it off. And for just a moment, she let herself visualize marrying Alessio.

He'd be so much better than any man her family would choose. But he wasn't her choice. Not really.

It was just years of loneliness reacting to his silliness and an acknowledgment of a kindred soul. He was a man caught in the same storm of family expectations.

The memory of him unbuttoning her dress flared in her mind. Her body had ached for release. Her brain had screamed for his lips to trail the path of the buttons. Her body had shuddered as his fingers brushed her skin. If he'd asked to kiss her...

She cleared her throat. Time to put away intrusive thoughts about the man before her. The prince. Her fiancé.

Her fake fiancé.

"Let's get the show started."

Alessio turned his focus to the smart board she had hooked up to the laptop. "All right. Show me what you've got."

Brie saw the hint of hope and the moment he cleared it from his face. He wanted to believe this was possible, but he wasn't willing to fully give in to the thought. Would that hurt her plans?

She wasn't sure.

"All right, so you ran the bride lottery to rejuvenate tourism, correct?"

"My father pointed out, just before his stroke—" Alessio paused, made a clicking noise with his tongue, then started again. "We were once the honeymoon capital of the world, Brie. Many of our shops, our bakeries, rely on the tourist traffic."

"You're right," Brie conceded.

It was an issue she'd acknowledged in her research last night. The number of families that relied on revenue from honeymoon tourists was far larger than she'd realized.

And the tourism bounce the Princess Lottery had brought was real. In fact, she'd spent a solid hour last night running numbers and trying to control the panic building in her soul. The country clearly needed the fairy tale.

But that reliance was also a weakness.

"I might have looked for another option, maybe. But then the Ocean Falls Hotel—"

"Closed last year," she interrupted.

This was her presentation. Focusing on failures was a recipe for disaster. She'd listened to more than one professor drum on the need to focus briefly on the past then force the client to look at the future, at the bright picture you wanted them to see.

She continued, "The upgrades needed to bring the historic building into the twenty-first century were too much for the current owners. I've heard rumors of a corporation stepping in. So it might reopen."

She hoped it did, even if she'd never stayed there. The Ailionos did not stay in regular hotels, and once she'd been cut off, she couldn't afford a night. But she'd listened to tourists in the bistro talk about the murals and salt baths. The closure was a devastating blow to the local economy.

"Your family are buying it?"

Could they still be called her family? She supposed she carried their last name. Their DNA created her. Her mother had spent her entire childhood using knife-edged compliments to sculpt her into the perfect Ailiono bride: submissive, willing to do whatever the family asked.

Her father was never home. His life was spent at the office or with one of his many mistresses. She was only a thing to be bartered for his power.

The only thing her parents had agreed on in the last decade was her dismissal from the family firm.

"I'm not privy to the inner choices of the Ailiono firm, but if I had to guess...yes." She shrugged.

According to reports, the hotel needed extensive renovations. The historical beauty was crumbling from the inside. Her family was one of the few with the resources to accomplish such a task.

"Tourists—"

"Do not need to be honeymooners," Brie interrupted again. "We've limited ourselves by catering only to them. All the efforts the tourism board made were to court honeymooners, not tourists in general. The island revolves around love, but it doesn't need to."

She waited, but he didn't offer anything, so she moved to the next slide. "The Falls of Oneiros, the market stalls stuffed with goods from around the world, the Ruins of Epiales, the hiking trails, the art scene, which is world-class, cuisine that is spectacular—a place foodies should flock to—we have it all here."

Brie sucked in a breath, nerves making her rush. "In short, we've got something for most kinds of tourists, and we're limiting ourselves by focusing our efforts on honeymooners. Marriages fail, even if they don't end in divorce, and return trips are few and far between."

"Such a dismal statement." Alessio crossed his arms.

"I know King Cedric and Queen Genevieve's union was the stuff of legends."

Alessio made a face but didn't add anything. Her parents' union was the stuff crafted from the worst nightmares.

"Not every marriage is a success story. And there are people who never wish to marry. They have had bad marriages and won't want to travel to an island of love. They are people who could bring their money to this kingdom but won't if we are only a honeymoon destination. That is the mistake we have made so many times. We can be more. The country *needs* to be more."

Alessio's stance loosened as he leaned forward, his hands resting on his thighs as he looked at her screen. "How?"

The urge to clap nearly consumed her. She knew this moment. She'd seen it in meetings, when a client who'd been uncertain saw her pitch and knew it had possibilities. That was when the momentum shifted her way.

She was going to gain her freedom.

Hidden under the joy was a pinch of something, a pain that shouldn't be there. She didn't want to marry Alessio. She didn't. So why was there anything besides joy?

"We—" she pointed to him, then herself, ignoring the bite of discomfort in her belly "—do all the things." She flipped to the next slide, focusing on the joy winning brought. "We use the bride lottery and our 'impending nuptials'—" she put the words in air quotes "—as the marketing. Everyone will follow us anyway, so we become tourists in our kingdom. While the world looks at us, we market everything Celiana offers. We use my social media platform and engage with people, but talk about everything but the wedding."

"Everything but the wedding?"

"Yes. We'll refer to each other as fiancé and act the part some."

"All part of the show." Alessio nodded.

Show.

It was the right word, but Brie hated it. Still, those were the roles they were playing.

He stood, stepping toward her. Her heart picked up, the annoying organ steadfastly ignoring her brain's commands to stay calm. Alessio smelled divine this morning, the smile on his lips, the twinkle in his green eyes for her...

"This might work." His hand reached for hers, the connection blasting through her.

Her tongue was stuck to the roof of her mouth. Once more her brain issued the orders to say yes. One did not fall in love fast. In lust, however... Well, that box was already checked. But who wouldn't lust after the Adonis standing before her?

"It will work." It didn't sound as confident as she'd like. "And we can start today." She moved to pull up her plans to hike the trail, but Alessio's fingers tightened on her wrist before he let her go.

She looked at him. The prince stood here now. The silly rebel was gone. This was the man she'd seen on television. It was a subtle shift: a tightening in the shoulders, a tip of the lips, a coolness in the eyes. Here stood Alessio the dutiful.

"We are not starting today."

If her breath was thready and uncertain, his was firm. There was no hint that the touch between them was driving lustful thoughts through every inch of his body.

"Alessio," she began, thinking maybe she wasn't the dutiful daughter of the Ailiono family now, but it was the role her family had groomed her for. It was a mask she could slide back on. "This is a good plan."

"It has promise."

Promise!

Before she could argue, he reached for her wrist again. Once more her body betrayed her. Her chest loosened, her skin heated and an ache to lean closer poured through her. There was a pull she'd never felt before, one she needed to ignore, no matter how much her body might yearn to explore it.

"But tomorrow is an early enough start date. You've been up all night." His fingers ran along her palm.

Pulling herself together, she stepped away from his touch. She needed to focus. "I'm used to it."

"Just because you are used to it doesn't mean that you should be." His voice was velvet. A calm water. That was what he felt like.

There was the urge to relax that pulled at her. She'd never given in to that impulse when her life was overwhelming. And if she'd given in, if she'd returned to her family, she'd have lost everything.

Brie couldn't give in now, either.

She raised her chin. "I'm not weak."

That was the word her mother had thrown at her over and over. Eat too much: she was weak. Get anything less than an A-plus on homework: weak. Rebel against family plans: weak.

"I hate that you feel the need to defend rest."

Who was he to say that? Since returning to the island, Alessio had worked tirelessly. It was all he did.

"How often do you rest? You and your brother have reversed roles. He plays and you—" She cut herself off. This was not an argument they needed to have.

Alessio raised a brow. "Don't hold back. I can take it."

My feelings never matter, so say it.

That was the underlying statement. Why was it so easy to read him?

Because they were two sides of the same coin.

"What does everyone say about me, Brie?"

"That you work yourself to the bone for Celiana. That you've changed. That maybe you should have been king."

Alessio shuddered. "I am not the king. Just a prince serving his country." He closed his eyes for a second, then opened them and offered a smile. "It's a good plan, but starting tomorrow is good enough. Rest today. You will be on the go for as long as you are in the palace."

Maybe forever. He didn't say those words, but she heard them in the quiet.

Fine. She could rest today, but there was still something else, something she'd thought about too much since her name left his lips yesterday.

Her insides quaked. She could do this…she had to.

"There is one other thing." Her voice shook, and his eyes softened.

He read people well. That was good, but it also meant he paid attention, and no one had ever paid attention to her. Not really.

"Brie?"

Say the words, Brie.

Her mind was screaming; blood pounded in her ears.

"We should kiss." She swallowed the lump in her throat before pointing to the ring light. "For the camera."

"For the camera?" Alessio looked at the setup. "Is that necessary?"

"We need to put something out today. Control the narrative. And people wanted to see us kiss yesterday. This will be a good teaser for tomorrow."

"Teaser?" Alessio blew out a breath. Maybe he didn't want to kiss her, but it needed to happen.

"There's more." He raised an eyebrow but didn't interrupt. Which was good, because if she didn't rush this next part, she might not get it out. "I want to kiss before we do it for the camera. I don't want my first kiss to be for an audience...even one we are controlling."

"First kiss?"

There was no way to miss his shock. What was she to say? The truth.

Brie did her best not to drop his gaze.

"Yes."

The word shook as it exited her mouth, and she clenched her fingers. This wasn't a big deal... Well, a first kiss might be. She'd hoped it would be—once—but those girlish dreams had died years ago.

At least she thought they had. Last night she'd nearly turned and kissed him. Kissing Alessio didn't frighten her; in fact, she wanted it. More than she'd wanted something in a long time.

And yet he just stood there, his green eyes boring through her.

"My engagement was arranged and not for long." Brie cleared her throat, not wanting to travel that road right now. "And the Ailiono name means the few dates I've been on in the last few years were epic failures."

She didn't owe him an explanation but once she started it the words tumbled forth.

"Relax." Alessio's arm wrapped around her waist, the weight of it heavy against her back. "Breathe."

She took a deep breath, looked at him, and still nothing.

"If you don't want…"

He placed a finger over her lips and dropped his forehead to hers. "I want to kiss you, Brie."

The words were soft, and hard, and her body tightened. Flutters of excitement raced across her skin. His scent wrapped around her.

"But I'm not going to kiss you."

That stung. In the softest, gooiest part of her soul. A place she never let anyone in.

"This moment deserves to be yours. As special as I can make it. So, you're going to kiss me." He opened his eyes, his lips so close. "This moment is yours, Briella. All yours."

She waited only a moment before brushing her lips against his. The touch was so light—so unsatisfying.

Closing the tiny distance between them, she wrapped her arms around his neck. If this was her first kiss, she was making it memorable. Her nerves vanished as she grazed his lips again.

His hand trailed along her back, each flick adding more heat to the internal inferno he'd awoken. His other hand lingered on her cheek, his thumb rubbing against her jaw.

Brie let her body lead as she opened her mouth. His tongue met hers and her world exploded. She pulled him closer, though she wasn't sure how it was physically possible.

He tasted of coffee and scones and life. *Life.* It was a weird description, but it felt so true. She had plans, goals, but much of her life was lived in stasis, waiting to really begin. Here, now, it felt like something so much more.

Finally, she released him. The nerves that had vanished in his arms roared back immediately. What was one to say after they'd kissed a prince? After acknowledging their lack of experience? When their entire body seemed to sing?

Silence hung between them.

"Maybe we should have videoed that." Brie let out a nervous laugh. In the realm of good things to say after a first kiss that was at the bottom of any list.

She straightened her shoulders and pointed to the media setup. "Round two?"

"This is your show." A look passed over Alessio's features, but whatever it was disappeared before she could decipher it.

"Now for the camera?" Alessio gestured toward the media gear.

Brie opened her mouth. Of course the moment wasn't momentous for him. It was only her first kiss after all, a prep for the real show.

"Now for the camera." Brie smiled, hoping it looked real.

CHAPTER FOUR

BRIE'S HEAD WAS buried in her phone as she lifted what he suspected was at least her second cup of coffee. She made a few notes on the small notebook beside her, a frown crossing her lips.

"What's wrong?"

Brie looked up, her eyes widening as she met his gaze. "When did you get here?"

"Not long ago, but you were focused."

When he was in his glass shop, people had been able to sneak up on him. He'd get lost in the moment, in the creative juices that flowed when he was working on a piece.

"You frowned. So I repeat, what's wrong?"

"Our second kiss looked too stilted. The feedback on the story I put up is less than stellar. There are comments that we look like robots."

"Oh." Alessio slid into the chair next to her. "I take it that is bad." He'd known that the second kiss was lacking, especially compared to the first.

The first. The feel of her lips on his, her body molding to his. It was magic, a kiss like he'd never experienced. He'd wanted to melt into her, spend the rest of the night worshipping her lips. Then she'd joked that they should have filmed that one.

A nervous joke. He'd understood that immediately, but it had stolen the illusion from the moment. Their second kiss, the one she'd uploaded, felt much more like two strangers—which they were.

"Yes. It's bad." Brie downed the rest of her coffee, hopped off the chair and filled her cup again. "But we're marketing Celiana. Not us." Brie blew out a breath. "Love is boring."

"Really?" Everything about the Princess Lottery seemed to indicate otherwise.

"Yes." Brie sighed like it should be obvious. "It's why your parents' love story never really made headlines."

Love story.

It was weird to hear that knowing it was false. "Their wedding kept the honeymoon industry going. That is the legacy of their love."

"No." Brie slid back into her seat. Her jeweled gaze caught his.

His breath skipped. She was so close, the aroma of her coffee and the sweet scent that was just Brie reminded him of their kiss. Their first one.

"Their legacy is the wedding." Brie shrugged, like she wasn't just dismissing the mythos of the great love the palace carefully sculpted.

Before he could add to that, she continued, "Your father had no identified mistresses."

Only the country.

"Your mother was faithful, too. Delivering an heir and…"

A blush invaded her cheeks as she looked away.

"And a spare."

The word didn't matter to him. He'd heard it his entire life. He was the spare. The one that really only mattered if something happened to his brother. It was a scenario Alessio never wanted to happen.

Brie's hand closed over his. "The point I'm trying to make—" she squeezed him and for a moment he thought she'd let him go, but instead she kept holding his hand "—is that gossip is more fun. Love—true love—is boring. Aka your parents."

She blew out a breath. "I don't know how we fake that, though. We need to be boring so they focus in on the locations."

"I do." Alessio lifted her hand, kissing the center. It was a sweet gesture, one he'd seen his father do a million times with his mother.

"That is a Prince Charming move." Brie sighed. "But I am serious."

"I know." Alessio took a deep breath. "You can't tell anyone what I am about to say."

Brie nodded.

"My parents weren't in love."

Her mouth fell open, but he didn't wait for the exclamation he saw building.

"It was an act. A well-scripted one. They cared for each other, but it wasn't love—not really." Alessio knew he was rambling, but he wanted her to understand. "They caressed a lot in front of reporters when they were first wed—at least that's what I've heard. Once the story was set, they lessened the touches, but people just figured it was normal longtime married-couple things."

Alessio ran his thumb along her palm, grateful she was still holding him. It was weird to talk with an outsider about this. "I know it sounds bad. And I know they respected each other, but behind the palace walls, they lived independent lives."

"That is perfect!"

Perfect. Not exactly the response Alessio expected. Or wanted.

"So we pattern ourselves after your parents. We act like they did. Happy is not fun to discuss."

He understood that. At the heart of the show, he'd always heard not to frown, not to make a face. A face could be interpreted, and the interpretation was always the thing that sold the story.

"So for our hike up the falls today—" Alessio looked at her hands, ones he'd need to hold, to kiss, to touch "—we act like we are falling in love."

The path to freedom wouldn't be difficult to walk. But the idea of role-playing love with Brie sent an uncomfortable arrow through his heart.

"And in the palace, we can lead separate lives for the next few weeks." She looked down and ran her hand along the back of her neck.

Then she grabbed her phone. That thing was an extension of her. "Shall we try a little live? It's early still, so we won't have as many viewers, which might make us looser."

"Sure." Alessio shrugged. "But what are we going to talk about?"

Brie bit her lip, then shook her head. "Let's run it without a script. A 'get to know you live' kind of thing. My family is off-limits. So is yours. Any other questions unwelcome?"

"I don't discuss the years I was away."

Brie nodded. "Understood. Though I'll admit that I am a little desperate to know. The only trips I took out of the kingdom were with my family, and I spent far too much of those vacations with a book in a boardroom while Dad had a meeting he couldn't—or didn't want to—reschedule. Not information I'd planned to share. And that right there is why we put things off the table."

Brie laughed and let her hand graze his knee. She set up the phone on a stack of books she must have carted down from the media room, and he watched her slide into "on" mode. Her shoulders were just a little straighter, her smile a little too full. But then he had an "on" side, too. One he needed to get into.

"Good morning, Celiana." Brie waved before holding up her coffee cup. "Alessio and I are in the kitchen, having coffee, and thought we'd spend a little time with you."

She leaned closer, making sure they were both in the frame. His arm slid around the back of her chair, and he could tell it pleased her.

After all, it looked good for the camera, though he'd done it to make sure she didn't tumble out of the tall chair. It was an unrealistic fear, but his body had acted without thinking.

She lifted the coffee cup again.

"How many cups of coffee have you had this morning?" Alessio winked before making eye contact with the phone. Was he supposed to talk to her or them? That was a question he should have asked.

"More than one, less than—" Brie put a finger on her chin "—less than six."

"Five cups, Brie!"

She grinned and her look was so infectious he nearly forgot about the camera.

"In my defense, your cups are small." She held up what looked like a regular coffee cup to him.

"If you think about it, it's unfair to judge by this tiny thing." She set it down and leaned on the counter. "I should have thought to grab one of my coffee mugs."

"I fail to see how the size of the mug impacts the amount of coffee you drink." He reached his hands across the island, letting his fingers wrap with hers.

Touching her was intoxicating, and they'd agreed that they needed to look affectionate. It should feel like acting…at least a little. Yet…it felt so natural as her fingers linked with his.

"It's the same amount by volume." She made a silly face, then stuck her tongue out at the "tiny" mug. "But then I can say that I drank two cups, and it sounds less horrendous."

"How big is your mug?"

Brie threw her free hand over her face, the drama making him chuckle. "There is no mug big enough. But mine holds basically half a pot." She beamed, then looked at the phone. "Next topic. Are you ready for our hike?"

"Sure."

He'd hiked the Falls of Oneiros several times as a child. The area was beautiful, but he hadn't visited in years.

"The Falls of Dreams." Brie sighed and pulled her hand away. "My brother, Beau, and I used to stand at the top, think of our dreams and throw a petal over the falls."

She bit her lip then lifted the cup. Family was supposed to

be off-limits. Beau Ailiono was a business scion, the heir to the Ailiono fortune, but he and Brie had been close enough once to hike and wish for something at the falls.

It was the standard routine at the falls. Oneiros, Greek for *dreams*, was where the locals came to cast wishes. Few tourists found their way there.

That would change once they visited—hopefully. The tourism industry had not courted the outdoorsy types. She was right; they had restricted their focus, and opening that up was a good thing.

Though he wasn't sure it would be enough.

"What were your dreams?"

He and his brother had never participated in making wishes when they'd hiked the falls. Their lives were planned out. The expectations known. What good were dreams when the path was already set in stone before you?

What had she thought was possible? What had she wanted more than anything?

"Freedom." She cleared her throat.

He did not know what to say to that. Freedom.

His heart clenched as he stared at her wavering smile. Freedom. One word, with so much meaning.

Freedom was something royal life did not allow.

"What were yours?"

The question interrupted his worries. At least he had an easy answer. "I never made a wish."

He felt the weight of her stare, but what was there to say? His role was determined from the moment of his birth. To wish for more… Well, that had led to the greatest heartbreak of his life: closing his shop and returning home.

"Well. That changes today!" Brie waved at the camera. "Who wants to see Alessio toss a petal?"

A ton of hearts and comments saying "Yes!" flooded the chat screen.

"All right, stay tuned." Brie leaned over and kissed his cheek, then shut the live stream off.

"Was that better?"

"Yes." Brie tilted her head, thoughts clearly evident in her eyes.

Sadness or pity? He wasn't sure, but he didn't like either option.

"You are more than the title prince."

Whatever he'd expected her to say, that wasn't it.

"Not really." He finished his cup of coffee and left the chair. Once upon a time he'd been more than the spare. More than a prince. He wanted to believe it was possible for it to happen again, but the odds... He didn't even want to calculate them.

Freedom.

The word echoed in his mind.

"You are more than your title, Alessio."

"Well." He stepped around the kitchen island and pulled her into his arms. "I am a fiancé now, too."

"I'm serious, Alessio." Brie's hands cupped the sides of his face.

He could tell she'd done it impulsively, but he enjoyed her touch. A little too much.

This didn't feel like living separate lives when her phone's camera wasn't on—when no one was looking. It felt real, and far more terrifying.

"Fine. I'm more than my title."

"Good." Brie released him, her gaze following her hands before she crossed her arms. "Now...um..." She looked over her shoulder. "I need to get ready for the hike. Good job this morning."

He playfully offered a military salute. If she saw the humor in his movements, she didn't react. And then she was gone.

"I guess people got the message..."

Brie stared out the window of the SUV. The crowd was at least three people deep even though they'd blocked the hiking path off and they had a three-hour window to hike on their own. She'd pushed for an open hike; the palace security team hadn't laughed in her face, but they'd squashed the idea with exceptional speed.

However, she didn't mind spending time alone with Alessio as she should. This morning they'd said they needed to look happy, like they were falling in love. That was the method his parents had used—so successfully that she'd had no idea. But her touches for the camera were the ones that felt off, unlike touching his knee over coffee or when she'd put her hands on either side of his face; those felt so real.

And for a moment today, she'd seen herself, felt the connection between them that was more than the lottery. She'd worn the same look as him once.

The Ailiono daughter. A piece on her family's chessboard. She'd seen the same despair when he said he wasn't more than his title. She'd still have that feeling if she hadn't left her family.

If she married Alessio, would she experience the same desperation again? Yes. It was why she needed her freedom. But after seeing his look this morning, she needed freedom for him, too. Alessio was far more than his title. He wasn't the spare, the heir only until his brother married and had children. From this point forward she'd focus on the man, not the title.

"The message you broadcast?" Alessio's hand tapped her knee. "Yes, I think that message got out."

He pulled his hand away. Technically no one could see them yet, but part of her wished he'd left it.

"True." Brie knew the crowd was here for the lottery princess, here for the story, but it was weird to see so many people. People normally avoided the Ailiono family—unless they were hoping to make money with them.

No one would describe the Ailiono family as easy to be around. Beau had been, *once*. Then he became their father's mini-me, the man set to take over the Ailiono family dynasty.

He'd abandoned her. She'd hoped he might ride to her rescue when she was unceremoniously kicked out. She'd held out hope for far too long that he might show up.

She shook the memory from her head. Beau was the perfect Ailiono family member. She wasn't. So their paths had parted.

Had Alessio and Sebastian had a good relationship growing up? What happened when Alessio left? Those were questions she couldn't ask him, though Brie was curious. Deep down, she knew they'd experienced some of the same trauma. And they craved the same thing.

He kissed the top of her head. They'd agreed they needed to touch, needed to make it look real for the camera. Her plan wouldn't work unless people focused on the recreational sites Celiana offered. That meant they couldn't give the likes of journalists like Lev things to feed into rumors of unhappiness.

People liked a love story…they loved a disaster. That was the real public relations rule. If they looked unhappy, it wouldn't matter where they went. All the world would see were the frowns.

But she didn't want him to kiss her forehead. She wanted him to kiss her lips. Their first kiss had poured through her far longer than the few minutes her lips had touched his. It was an ugly reminder of how much the second kiss was lacking.

She'd thought about that first kiss far too much, which was acceptable if she was a blushing schoolgirl. But as a twenty-six-year-old woman…

"Let's do this. Your smile ready?"

This needed to look good. Tourists were on vacation. Vacation was happy time.

"I can always find a smile." Alessio grinned, but it was the prince smile, one she might not have fully pegged as fake until she'd spent time with him. But now it was easy to see; if she could see it, so might others, too.

"We need authentic smiles."

Alessio's brows rose before he pursed his lips. "It is a real smile."

"No." Brie shook her head. "It's Prince Charming out for an outing. It's not real."

"Prince Charming is a fantasy. I am no fantasy." Alessio leaned closer to her, his lips spreading into a convincing smile.

Brie held up her hands, pretending they were a camera. "Click." She laughed as his head tilted, his grin growing even bigger. "That was a genuine smile. Focus on whatever brought that out."

"You brought it out." Alessio pulled on the back of his neck as he turned his attention to the crowd.

She knew those words had slipped out unintentionally, but her insides warmed as she watched the smile on his lips. She'd done that. It was silly to care about, but still...

"Luckily for you, I will be on the trail beside you the whole time." Brie blew out a breath and grabbed the door handle. "Showtime!"

"Briella! Princess Briella!"

"Princess!"

"Briella!"

The calls rose around her. Flashes from cameras and held-up cell phones, which she knew were recording, greeted them on the side of the path. There were makeshift barriers with lots of people stood behind them.

She'd wanted an audience; her plan depended on it. But it was still a lot to take in.

Alessio squeezed her hand as they wandered to the barrier. His smile looked genuine, full, and it eased her as she stepped into the role, too.

Alessio started shaking hands, and Brie smiled at a young girl.

"You're such a pretty princess." The girl held up a sunflower.

Brie bent down so she could meet the girl's eyes. "I'm not a princess...not yet. Just Brie. What's your name?"

"Ella. Like the end of your name. My mom owns a bakery. It's always busy now. She said last night that it was because of you."

A woman standing behind Ella let out a soft groan. "I've

told you not to eavesdrop on Daddy and I. Give her the flower, honey."

Ella looked at her mother and made a face. "But I want her to know the rest."

"Know what?" Brie asked, making sure she kept a serious face. Ella was serious, and Brie could be serious, too, though a laugh was bubbling in her chest.

"I like to play Cinderella, but now I can play Princess Briella." Her smile was so wide, so open.

Brie looked to Ella's mother. The woman had taken time out of her bakery to come with her daughter today. The country needed the tourists; family bakeries thrived on them. But the hope in Ella's and her mother's eyes sent fear tumbling through her. What if Brie's plan failed?

Ella and her mother weren't the only regular people here. Yes, the press was here, but so were many regular folks whose livelihoods were riding on Prince Alessio and Princess Briella.

Brie looked at Alessio. His gaze met hers, and he grinned before turning back to the gathered crowd. She'd sworn to meet him at the altar if her plan failed, but she'd refused to think of the possibility. And she couldn't focus on it now.

"Thank you for the flower, Ella."

Alessio placed a hand on her shoulder, and she rose. "If we want to hike the trail before the day gets too warm, we should get moving."

"Agreed." Brie smiled at the crowd, though now she suspected it was her smile looking forced instead of Alessio's.

She took his hand, her body relaxing a little with the touch, waved with the sunflower, then followed him down the path.

"I think we did pretty well there." Alessio adjusted his backpack as they started up the trailhead.

"I think so, too."

At the very least, it was a good start. The actual test happened with the video they did at the falls. Could they successfully turn the attention to the falls and not them?

"And now we hike." Alessio pulled one arm in front of him, stretching his shoulder, then did the other.

"Now we hike," Brie conceded. The trip to the falls would take about an hour. In silence it would seem like forever. "So maybe we should play twenty questions."

"Twenty questions? What is that?"

Brie shook her head. "Seriously, Prince Charming? It's exactly what it sounds like. You ask each other twenty questions, 'get to know you' style. I'll start. Favorite color?"

"Green. You?"

"Light blue. Like the water over the falls. Favorite season?"

"Summer."

They continued the questions as they walked the path. The questions were getting a little deeper but carefully avoiding anything too deep.

"Who was your first fiancé?"

She lost her footing, and Alessio's hand caught her elbow. His eyes locked with hers as he steadied her.

"Brie?"

That was not a question she'd expected.

"Sorry. Maybe I shouldn't have asked, but I assume he is not a security threat. Or is it possible he is?"

Security was important for the royal family, but she didn't think that was why Alessio was asking.

The fiancé… That was the night she'd broken with her family forever after refusing to play the role they'd carefully planned out for her. The role her mother played for her father, despite how unhappy it made her.

Kate Ailiono was the "perfect wife."

In public. Behind closed doors, *shrew* was the kindest word one could say. She was jealous of the mistresses and time spent away from the family home. The screaming matches were epic.

The only problem was Brie, and that she wasn't willing to follow in her mother's footsteps.

Time slowed as they stood together on the path. Alessio wrapped an arm around her waist as they looked over a mountain pass. Her past and the future were slamming together. Except he wasn't her future.

She never talked about Milo Friollo. Ophelia only knew because she'd helped Brie escape the Ailiono compound the night her father announced the union.

She could still visualize the man sitting beside her at the table. Milo had smiled and reached out to hold her hand. No notice had been given to her. There was no expectation that she'd do anything other than follow.

"Forget I asked. What was the last book you read?" His tone was sweet, but she could hear the bead of worry under it.

Her most recent read was on marketing to different Enneagram types. She could tell him that and ignore the other question. That was the simple answer, but she couldn't quite find the words.

Brie reached for Alessio's hand and started back up the trail. "I never talk about him."

The sentence slipped into the open. His name burned the back of her throat, but she didn't say it. Alessio walked beside her but said nothing. No questions, no pressure.

Pressure was an Ailiono family specialty. No one could make silence hurt like her family.

And yet, she'd nearly gone back—so many times. When her feet were bleeding from standing for hours as a barista with burns on her hands, and her eyes were so heavy from exhaustion as she tried to study and keep a tiny roof over her head, she'd thought of it. On her birthday, when no card, no phone call, no acknowledgment from her family came, the desire to belong again had nearly driven her home. When her rent was due and she was short… When everyone was out at bars, having fun, and she was skipping meals…

"Milo was older." That was a kind statement. The man was three times her age, a lifetime of lived experiences to her teenage self.

"Milo Friollo?"

That Alessio could guess at the man her parents had arranged for her wasn't surprising. Milo walked down the aisle more than most. And each wife was younger than the last. He'd married six months after that dinner. And there'd been another last year—wife four was nineteen…just like Brie had been.

"My father and he are business partners. Or they were. I'm not sure their professional relationship survived my flight. Though it probably did. Money is what matters after all."

Once the words were out, her brain refused to stop. "They ambushed me at a family dinner. Announced that we'd marry in six months." Her fingers flexed as the memory of Milo's touch echoed in her brain. "He married another on our wedding date. Though that union lasted less than a year."

"Ambushed?" Alessio let out a grunt.

"It's not that different from the countless other marriages made for prestige, family alliances or money. People like to pretend that we are so different from our historical counterparts, but the truth is the wealthy and privileged rarely marry for love.

"Hell, we are trying to get out of a nearly ironclad marriage contract." Brie laughed. There had to be humor, or she'd cry. "They disowned me for refusing to follow my parents' demands and somehow I ended up back in an arranged marriage." The laughter died away.

"I hope you get out." His words were barely audible.

"You hope I get out. What about you? If you could be anywhere, where would it be?"

"I don't know."

"I think you do." The heat in Brie's cheeks had nothing to do with the hike. She'd answered the one personal question he'd asked, but it appeared that he would not do the same.

They hiked the rest of the trail in silence.

"The falls!" She raised her hand, pointing to the crystal blue water cascading over the mountain's edge. The Falls of Oneiros.

The Falls of Dreams.

"It's gorgeous." Alessio let out a breath as he followed her gaze.

His lack of response to her question frustrated her, but she also wanted him to have this moment, a real one, before she turned on the camera. She grabbed two petals and pressed one into his hand as they moved to stand as close to the edge as possible.

"Do you need to get the phone out?" Alessio looked at the petal like it might bite.

"No. Not for your first wish. We'll film another, but this one… I don't know, it's tradition. You should get to do it the way everyone else does."

"Sebastian and I always knew our roles. Heir and spare—what good were wishes?"

The words broke her heart. Family expectations were hard, but he'd had expectations from the country, too.

"Make a wish. There has to be something you crave."

A look passed over his eyes and Brie lifted up on her toes. It wasn't planned, and there was still frustration bubbling in her. But she was drawn to him. She pressed her lips to his. His arms wrapped around her waist. Alessio deepened the kiss.

The mountain hummed in sync with the racing falls. The world seemed to cheer their connection.

Here and now, there was only her and Alessio. The security team had cleared the falls before they arrived and was standing down the trail, around a bend. In this moment it would be easy to pretend this was a regular date. He was a man who just wanted to spend time with Brie.

It would be easy to pretend they'd met somewhere and were regular people with regular expectations.

But pretending wouldn't get her what she wanted, the freedom she craved. Pulling back, she held up her petal.

"Ready?" She winked and gestured for him to hold up his, too.

He looked at his petal and she could see words tumbling in his eyes. A want, something buried so deep.

"Here, I'll show you how." She held the petal to her chest. *Freedom.* It was the word she'd always thought when she stood here. *Freedom.*

She let the petal loose and opened her eyes to watch it float over the falls.

"Your turn." She reached for his free hand. "Close your eyes."

Alessio looked at her, then closed his eyes.

"Lift the petal to your chest and think about what you want. What you really want, Alessio."

He did as she said, taking a deep breath.

"Now let it go."

He opened his palm, and the petal floated into the falls. He opened his eyes and wrapped his arm around her waist. She didn't think as she laid her head against his shoulder.

"See, that wasn't so hard, was it?"

His lips brushed her head. "Thank you for the experience, Brie."

Again they stood in silence. Finally, he squeezed her. "Scotland. If I could go anywhere, it would be Scotland."

Before she could ask any follow-ups, Alessio grabbed two more petals. "Now, showtime."

"Right." She'd nearly forgotten. She'd been lost in the moments of his kiss, in him.

It was good that he'd reminded her... It didn't sting. Not even a little bit.

CHAPTER FIVE

ALESSIO LOOKED AT his watch. He'd gotten a quick swim in after dinner and had the rest of the evening to himself. Brie would be in the media room. It was where she spent any free time. And today there'd been quite a lot of freedom.

Which meant he'd not seen her much.

They'd enjoyed a quick outing at a local bakery. The small trip was designed to give the illusion of dating while highlighting a local establishment. They'd stayed less than an hour, and talked to the baker and her son. He'd eaten a few cookies. Brie had—

Alessio closed his eyes. He'd been so focused on the discussion that he wasn't sure she'd sampled anything. He stopped, his mind flashing to the first day—how was that less than a week ago? She'd looked like a deer in headlights by the dessert plate.

Her mother was notorious for controlling what food passed her lips. The comments Brie's mother made to the ladies and men of the court were often downright rude. If that was what she was willing to say in public, what vitriol had Brie heard behind closed doors?

It wasn't hard to imagine. His father had leveled complaints against him at every chance. Though never about food.

It was nearly seven. That meant that if she'd grabbed dinner, she was bent over spreadsheets and crunching data that seemed to appear from nowhere.

She wouldn't look for him for the rest of the night. They

were in the palace. That meant separate spheres. She hadn't wanted to put up a video about them this evening. Instead, she was tracking what people were saying about the visit to the Falls of Oneiros two days ago and the bakery this morning.

They each wanted this to succeed, but she needed a break, too. And he had an idea that might just work. It would only take a few minutes to put it together.

He knocked on the door, waited for her call to enter, then swept the door open and pushed in the cart the kitchen staff had helped him prepare.

"What?" Brie's hair was falling out of her bun and there were smudges on the glasses she wore when working at the computer. Her oversize sweater easily fit over her knees, which she had pulled up in her chair.

"Good evening, Brie."

She looked at the tray he was pushing and raised a brow. "Good evening. I…um… I already ate."

He knew that. The kitchen staff had told him she'd gotten a chicken salad sandwich and some veggies. But no dessert.

Alessio walked over to the desk and nearly leaned in to kiss her cheek. They were in the palace. The little touches weren't needed, but that didn't stop him from wanting them.

Brie's gaze focused on his lips. Had she wanted him to kiss her?

Kissing was not the purpose of this encounter. He honestly wasn't entirely sure what this was about, but he'd wanted to spend time with her.

"I know you ate, but this isn't dinner." Her brow raised again. "Figure you gave me something special the other day, so I'm hoping to return the favor."

"Something special?" A frown touched her lips, and he wanted to wipe it away. "A wish isn't something special, Alessio."

"Why?" He walked to the cart and pushed it by the little table she used for meals before gesturing for her to join him.

This wasn't a grand affair, but he wanted her to enjoy it away from spreadsheets and numbers.

She bit her lip as she walked over and looked at the covered trays.

"Because mine was staged. I think it is important that you made a wish. You are more than a prince. You get to have your own dreams and wishes, but…"

Brie hesitated and looked at her feet. She sucked in a deep breath, then looked back at him. "But mine was for the show."

"Not the first one." He squeezed her hand, then lifted it to his lips.

"Yes, but—"

"But nothing. My first wish was mine. So little in my life is." The wish was a moment, one he got to hold deep in his soul even if he doubted it could come true.

"But now…" He pulled off the covers of the two trays with what he hoped was a flourish.

"Cookies and pie." She let out a laugh. "Not sure what I expected, but somehow sweets wasn't it."

His stomach twisted. What else might be under such a display? The Ailiono family was notorious for controlling business dealings, but it was clear Brie had been controlled in other ways. And she'd escaped.

She'd made her own way, only to find herself behind the bars of another cage.

"I know your mother doesn't like sweets."

Her laughter was bitter as it echoed against the walls. "My mother abhors treats. Anything that might add a pinch of weight to her waistline."

"Her waistline…" Alessio leaned forward on his hands. "And yours?"

"Ailiono children are extensions of their parents. Beau is my father, even if once upon a time I thought he might break away. Thought he might come with me, but…well…he didn't."

There was more to that story. But Brie cleared her throat as

she picked up a cookie. Her eyes didn't move from the raspberry lemon one.

"I was my mother."

"Was." Alessio reached for her hand. "You *were*, but now
you are Brie, Princess of Celiana, eater of whatever sweets
she chooses!"

"Princess?" Brie pushed at his shoulder. "Alessio. I know
you're joking, but it is so weird to hear 'Princess Brie.' Even
after crowds have shouted it for days."

She was stalling. So he grabbed the other raspberry lemon
cookie. He popped the tiny pastry in his mouth. The flavors
were divine.

"Your turn."

Brie looked at the cookie, then up at him. If she pushed
back, he'd stop, but he wanted her to try. She squeezed his hand
then took a small bite. A tiny bite in a tiny cookie, but a bite.

"Thoughts?"

"It's tart. Fine."

"*Fine* is not what we are looking for!" He grabbed a dark
chocolate bar and passed it to her. Chocolate was his mother's
favorite. He preferred fruit flavors.

She took a bite and then another. "All right. That *is* good."

Chocolate made her smile. Good to know!

She lifted the lavender cookie from the tin. "This looks too
pretty to eat." Turning the cookie, she pointed to the small lavender outline the baker had created in the center.

"A work of art." He grabbed its twin. "That is designed to
be eaten."

"Art shouldn't be eaten."

"No. This art should. Art is designed to give the person
near it a feeling, an experience. A painting might bring out
happiness or sorrow. A sculpture may remind you of a loved
one who passed or a brilliant childhood memory. And cookies, pastries, they are designed to evoke the majesty of the flavors. It does the baker a disservice to think it too pretty to eat."

"Wow. What is your creative outlet?"

Brie's jeweled gaze captured him. Expectation and happiness were bright as she guessed at what was truly in his soul.

"What?"

Brie set the cookie down. "What is your thing? Painting? Sculpture? Did you make the cookie?"

"No." He'd not meant to let so much out, but the words could be of an art aficionado, not an artist. He was a patron of Celiana's art scene. Even the Princess Lottery was a fundraiser for it.

Her hands wrapped around his waist, her sweet scent lighting through him. "Come on, Alessio. No one talks that passionately about art without doing something."

"Lots of people talk about art passionately."

They did. He'd stood in many a gallery with people who'd never picked up a brush but waxed on about the meaning of a piece.

"I'm sure they do. But not with the feeling you had in your voice or the twinkle in their eye. Are you a mime?"

"A mime?"

Brie pulled back, a giggle in her eyes. "Sure. That's an art form. What's yours?"

No one had ever just asked him what his creative outlet was. No one had even guessed the prince had one. In his glass studio, covered in sweat from the fires and dust from the shop, he'd looked less than regal. But he'd been happy.

"Glasswork."

"Oh. Like melting glass and bending it." Brie tilted her head, and he could see all the questions building.

Alessio nodded. "It's a little more but yes, at its base, it's melting and bending."

At his height in the shop, he'd made a few pieces a day. Most of them sold, and he had a few in his suite that he couldn't part with.

"You have to show me."

"Can't. I gave it up. Princely duties and all." There was a workshop on the palace grounds. It was his workshop. But the glass ball he'd made for the lottery was his final piece, his goodbye to the art as he stepped into the role he'd been born to play.

"That's a shame." She stuck her bottom lip out, then opened her mouth but closed it without saying whatever had come to her mind.

She put the whole tiny cookie in her mouth, closed her eyes and let out the softest sigh. He wasn't sure exactly what Brie was experiencing, but watching her was magical.

"That is divine."

"You're divine." The words slipped out, but he didn't want to pull them back. She was perfection.

Brie looked at him, and he nearly shifted as she seemed to stare right into his soul.

The world with its requirements, its worries, the concerns for the kingdom and Brie's plans—it all vanished as she dropped a quick kiss on his cheek.

"Um…" She looked at him, and he could see the shock running through her face.

She'd not planned to kiss him. It wasn't on the schedule after all.

His hands moved without thinking, pulling her back into his arms. She sighed, like there was no other place she'd rather be, then lifted her head. Their lips met and once more the world seemed to stand still.

She tasted like chocolate and freedom, and he craved every piece of her. Her fingers moved along his back, her body pressing against his. Every sense was tuned to Brie.

Brie stepped back and he let her go, even though the urge to deepen the kiss, to run his fingers over her bare skin, was crying out within him.

Her cheeks were a delicate rose as she pointed to the trays. "Chocolate. I like chocolate. The lavender is good, too. I mean, even the lemon raspberry was good."

They were shifting topics. That was probably for the best. "You don't have to lie. You didn't like it."

Brie pursed her lips and pushed a piece of hair behind her ear. "It was all right...nothing like chocolate, though."

"So we start trying out different chocolates for dessert."

If she wanted to shift the conversation away from kisses, he'd go with the flow. She'd lacked control before. There were parts of their lives that would always be out of their control, but Alessio would give her as much as possible.

"Chocolate flavors? How many flavors are there?"

"More than I can count." He wrapped an arm around her shoulder, not really intending to, but his heart skipped as she laid her head on his shoulder.

"Dessert is nice. No wonder my mother wanted me to avoid it." Brie sat up, the past breaking through the illusion of the treats.

"I wanted to show you the metrics I have. The falls have seen a large booking, and the bakery sold out. Of course, we won't have all the metrics for several more weeks. Still, the focus of the first few adventures has stayed on the location after brief mentions of us...touching."

The hesitation caught his attention, but she was already throwing things up on the smart board. Tables, charts, growth exports—all were very impressive, he thought.

He'd done his time in economics and stats classes, getting through on pure grit with a barely passing grade. Most of the time he'd spent in those classes was daydreaming ways to sculpt whatever creation was burning through his mind.

King Cedric hadn't allowed Alessio to major in art or art history. That was not a proper "princely" topic, according to the king. That hadn't stopped Alessio from spending all of his free time with the art teacher and master glassworker.

"Do you ever tire of it? Of the cameras? The questions?" Brie's questions roused his mind from trying to make sense of the numbers before him.

"No."

She spun around, horror clear on her face. "Come on, Alessio. Never? You were the rebel once upon a time. The skipper of as many engagements as possible. The royal who stuck his tongue out instead of answering pointed questions. You really never tire of it now? Of the lack of privacy? Of the rules? The regulations? The stares…the…"

He caught her fingers, holding them tightly, grounding himself in the present. Once upon a time, he'd rebelled against everything. He'd hated the cameras, the lack of privacy. Giving in to those emotions again might be cathartic, but if this effort failed… Alessio wasn't willing to hope yet.

"When I returned, I pledged myself to Celiana."

A look passed across her features. It sent a shiver through his soul. It would be her life, too, should they meet at the altar.

"It's not a horror show, Brie." He squeezed her fingers.

"It's not *not* a horror show."

That was hard to argue with. "I guess I just see it as part of the duty. Just an extension of the crown."

"Dutiful Alessio. Why the change?"

"It was time to grow up."

She pulled her fingers back, and he watched the wall crash back down between them. The openness was closing as she flipped back to her spreadsheets.

Brie could tell when he wasn't fully honest. She was the only one bothered by his surface-level answers. She was also the only one that paid close enough attention to tell the difference. Brie deserved the answer, but he couldn't give it.

It was cowardly, but that was a story he wasn't going to share with anyone. Even Sebastian didn't know the real reason he'd returned. That secret was buried with his father and that was where it was staying.

CHAPTER SIX

BRIE BIT HER lip as she looked at the email, then looked to the door. Alessio would be here any moment for breakfast. Despite saying they wouldn't spend time together in the palace, they took all their meals together now. And if he saw her frowning, he'd worry and ask why. And she'd probably tell him.

That wouldn't be a big deal if he was telling her personal things. Like what was in Scotland—or who. Or why he'd come home to stay. He could have come for the funeral and then headed back—right?

Brie let out a sigh. She wasn't actually clear on what the rules were for the heir. Maybe he'd had to return and stay. But that didn't mean he had to give up glassworking.

She'd wanted an answer but he'd refused to discuss it or give a full explanation. He was holding back. And if Alessio wasn't opening up fully, then neither was she.

Her business was precious, and this was the second possible cancellation this week for a job she'd scheduled before her name had echoed across the kingdom two weeks ago.

Fourteen days and a lifetime all at once.

The first week, two cancellations had come in saying they wished her well on this endeavor, but understood that her new duties would mean diminished time for their accounts. The email on Monday had asked if she planned to complete the jobs scheduled. It was polite, but they'd included all the account information to return their retainer.

And now this email was here. Yes, no princess in the history of Celiana had worked outside the palace. But she didn't plan to be a princess.

The stats were still up, though not as much as she was hoping to see. It had only been two weeks. That was a blip in marketing time. But with the viral marketing campaign she'd developed, she'd expected more. Or maybe she was just hoping for more. And there were pockets of dissent already, comments that they'd done nothing "wedding" related.

No bridal gown shopping. No cake testing. No venue discussions.

Two weeks. They'd been "engaged" two weeks. It wasn't like all couples immediately hopped to planning. Still, a rumor could tank this whole thing, so she'd scheduled a wedding outing to calm the waters before the ripple fully developed.

Tapping her fingers, she tried to bring her focus back to this problem. If she sent back the retainer for this job, that would mean she'd lost four jobs—so far. She blinked back the tears that were threatening. She'd built her business from nothing once. Brie could do it again.

If she had to.

Taking a deep breath, she typed out the reply thanking them for reaching out and offering to return the retainer, then deleted it. Instead, she sent a quick line saying that, while she was busy, she fully intended to fulfill all her contracts. She'd planned to take a few weeks off following the bride lottery anyway, so nothing was disrupted. She'd be in touch at the beginning of next month and let them know they were at the top of her calendar.

By then she and Alessio would be laying the groundwork for the breakup anyway.

The thought tore through her. Breakup.

This isn't real, Brie. It's not a breakup. Not really.

So why did the thought of not seeing him again bother her so?

Her mind drifted to how he kissed, how his lips felt as they brushed hers, how he tasted when she deepened the kiss.

Then her mind took it a step further. She dreamed of how his fingers tracing down her skin might feel, dreamed of his lips finding far more than her mouth.

Pushing away from the computer, she wandered to the smart board and looked at the graphs she'd developed for the latest outings. She needed to focus on those, not on the handsome prince always by her side, despite their initial pledge to not spend time together inside the palace.

The door opened, and she couldn't stop the smile as Alessio stepped in—juggling two cups of coffee.

"Good morning." He handed her a cup, and she saw his eyes flit to the pot in the corner. "Not sure I should aid in your caffeine intake."

Over the last week, he'd told her that a walk outside or a swim in the pool would be just as good a way to wake herself up. She'd visited him at the pool once. And him in a bathing suit had definitely woken something in her.

"I've only had one…no, two." She thought hard. "Yes, only two so far."

"Only." Alessio shook his head before dropping a kiss on her cheek. "You all right? You look a little off this morning."

Little got past him. It was sweet and unnerving.

Her family had never noticed little things about her. And her coffee habit was not a little thing. She'd used caffeine to keep herself up since she was in high school. It was a habit her parents hadn't minded.

Her parents felt the same way about work as Alessio did now about duty. It was what you did. To question that was unthinkable.

"Breakfast for the princess and prince. Celiana's lovers," Sebastian sang as he strolled through the door with a bag of something he tossed to Alessio.

"Muffins?"

"Homemade!" He winked as he slid onto the couch.

Alessio looked at the bag and frowned. "In other words, you

slipped your security team, spent the night with a woman and left before she woke?"

"Alessio—" Brie's voice was soft as she stepped to his side.

"No need to fret, Princess." Sebastian let out a soft laugh. "This is a common refrain we share. Unlike my brother, I waited until dear old Dad passed to learn how to slip my security detail. You should try it again, brother."

Alessio's body went rigid beside her, and she heard the bag crumple in his fingers before he handed it to her, the top of it nearly mangled.

"You are the king."

The words slipped from her lips before she'd thought them through. This wasn't her fight, but Alessio's brow was furrowed. He'd clenched and unclenched his palm three times and was fighting to keep from shifting on his feet.

How quickly she'd learned his little tells over the last weeks. She wanted to wipe away the worry. But she also understood Sebastian's need for freedom.

She'd craved it for so long, come so close to it. Surely Alessio understood, too.

"Thank you. Exactly." Alessio wrapped his arm around her waist, grounding himself as he stood just a hair taller.

"Wow, the lovers are teaming up. Interesting."

"Don't change the subject, Sebastian. What happens if something happens to you?"

Alessio shifted his feet and Brie thought he wanted to stomp them but was resisting. Was that a hint of the rebel pushing out?

"You have security for a reason," Alessio stated.

"If something happens, you can handle it. The man that returned to the island is quite dutiful." Sebastian closed his eyes and leaned his head against the couch's back. "Perhaps that is a win for everyone."

"No." Alessio's voice echoed through the room.

"Because you don't want the damn throne, either. Don't want everyone wanting you for the crown."

"Because I don't want to lose you." Alessio was vibrating.

"Weird statement, considering you were the one that abandoned the family. Didn't care if we lived or died then."

"Damn it, Sebastian. That is not—" His eyes flicked to Brie. She saw him bite back whatever it was he planned to say.

Brie reached for him as he stepped away from her. "Alessio—"

"Excuse me, sweetheart. I need a moment. I'll see you shortly." He turned, closing the door softly.

"It would have been more dramatic to slam the door." Sebastian clicked his tongue. "Not that my brother would ever do such a thing. At least not now. He used to do it as an art form. When he ran away to Scotland, the door he slammed nearly came off its hinge."

Maybe Alessio slammed doors once, but now he held the hard emotions inside. The worries, the anger—those emotions were buried under the princely cover. Happiness, joy, excitement—things that brought out smiles for others—seemed easier for him.

Brie had learned that in the little time she'd been with him. His brother, his king, knew it and was using it against him. Sebastian was dumping his own issues on the man who was doing his best for the country, for his brother.

"You shouldn't have said that." Brie's words were quiet as she stared at the closed door, willing Alessio to walk back through it.

Brie bit her lip, then turned her full attention to the king. "You shouldn't joke about him not having you in his life. My brother isn't in mine, and…" Her throat tightened as Beau's face danced in her mind. "You shouldn't wish for such things even if you don't want the crown."

Sebastian's eyes opened and color coated his cheeks. *Good.* He should think of his words and what they really meant.

She missed Beau. Their lives had separated. Or more accurately, their parents had separated them. It hurt to think that he'd not reached out to her. But he was still in their world.

Even if he'd never reached out for her, she'd never wish Beau gone. And if she found out he'd said it, she'd scream at him, demand he understood how much she needed him in the world, if not her life.

She opened the bag of muffins, mostly to give herself something to do. The tops were perfect, and she wanted to chuck one at the king. "These are store-bought."

"No." Sebastian looked at her. "Homemade."

"Nope. They're from Lissa's Bakery downtown. Ophelia loves their orange ones. I always brought her one when she was having a bad week."

Brie lifted the muffin from the bag and showed the bottom of the confection, sugar and sweet wafting up from the pastry. "The little heart made with a C&D is her signature. It represents her children, Charlotte and Delia."

Sebastian cocked his head. "Quite the detective, Princess."

"Not a princess."

"Not yet."

He was trying to rile her up. She wasn't sure why, but Brie wasn't going to fall for it.

"Your brother loves you and he worries about you. You shouldn't toss that in his face."

"Even if he would be a better king?" Sebastian raised an eyebrow as he stood up from the couch. "The man that came back is exactly who father wanted on the throne. Ironic that it's him and not me."

"Especially for that reason. You grew up the heir." She held up her hand when he went to interrupt. "I'm not saying that was easy. I am sure it wasn't. But he grew up the spare, the replacement for you, a role no sibling should have to play."

When one thought about it, the ancient idea was quite sick.

"You are both more than the crowns on your heads. He is your brother. Don't let whatever personal issue made you lie about muffins get in between that."

"Careful, Princess." He took the muffin from her hand, taking a big bite out of it. He tilted his head, like he was trying to act brave or just redirect her focus. "You seem to be falling for him."

"I don't have to be falling for him to want to see him treated with care."

That was true. But it didn't change the fact that the words *falling for him* sent a wave of butterflies through her belly.

"If you say so." Sebastian took another bite of his muffin and wandered out of the media room. Brie looked at the marketing notes she had on the board. There was work to be done.

There is always work to be done.

Grabbing his forgotten coffee, and her own, she went in search of the man she most certainly wasn't falling for.

Alessio flipped and kept his body moving. The cool water slipping over him as he skimmed through the pool calmed him. At least it usually did. His fingers were wrinkling, but he didn't care as he flipped and pushed off the wall again. Move. Just move.

Usually twenty minutes was enough to burn off any unpleasant emotions. He wasn't sure how long he'd been gliding through the water, but the fury of his brother's words still wouldn't dissipate.

How could Sebastian have said such a thing? How could he have voiced such awful thoughts?

His brother was struggling with the crown, and Alessio was the reason for that. His argument—Alessio's rebellion. Even if Brie's scheme worked, it wasn't freedom he'd get. It wasn't freedom he deserved.

Sebastian needed him, even if he wouldn't say it directly. So the palace was where Alessio would stay.

Without Brie.

He pushed off the wall as sadness overtook him. Brie didn't deserve this gilded cage; he did. Losing his brother was not an option.

This is my place.

He shook his head in the water, wishing there was a way

to wipe the pain of staying from his soul. He was his brother's helper. That was the way his father had always worded it.

Wanting to be more, his selfishness and his desire for freedom, had cost his family.

His shoulders burned as he reached the wall, but he didn't stop. He'd told the lifeguard to let him know when thirty minutes passed. It felt like that call should have come a while ago, but perhaps he was just tied up in his emotions.

That wasn't something he could let happen today. He and Brie had a full schedule, wedding dress shopping. It was an event she'd scheduled to cool the comments about them not wedding planning. It shouldn't be something he was looking forward to.

But part of him—the selfish part—wanted her with him. His partner in the life his choices forced on him.

He wanted to watch her walk down the aisle. He wanted to dance with her. Wanted to see her cut a chocolate wedding cake and eat lavender cookies. Wanted to see her smile. Wanted her beside him.

Brie made him laugh, she made him smile and she challenged him. She was fun to be around. With her he felt like the Alessio he'd once been. Not number two. Not the spare. Not the rebel that disappeared. With her he felt nothing more than a man. It was intoxicating.

Despite their unique situation, he felt like they were connected, meant to be.

Rationally he knew that was because they'd spent so much time together and because they were united in their quest for freedom.

But he wanted to believe she felt the connection, too.

Two legs appeared at the end of the lane, dangling in the water. She'd found him.

He didn't change the speed of his stroke, but his heartbeat picked up. He'd left Brie with his brother, an upset and pouty king. He'd wandered off and just left her.

Heat that had nothing to do with exercise flooded his

cheeks. Sebastian had been in the mood for a fight, but Alessio had walked away, afraid that if he gave in, all the hurt he had would spill into the open. The wounds created as the spare had driven him from Celiana…and then had driven him back. But Sebastian didn't deserve the pain King Cedric had laid on Alessio.

But that wasn't an excuse for leaving Brie. What had he been thinking?

Lifting out of the water, he felt his mouth slip open at the sight of her holding out his coffee cup.

"You left this, and it was getting cold." She leaned over and dropped a kiss on his nose. "So I drank it."

"Heaven forbid we let coffee go to waste." Brie's bloodstream must be at least 50 percent caffeine.

"So glad you agree." She beamed as she reached around behind her back and pulled out a bottle of water. "This is probably more what you're looking for after a swim, though."

She uncapped it without asking, then passed it to him as she kicked her legs in the water.

The water tasted perfect. It was what his body craved. His soul—it craved her.

"Thank you. And I am sorry. I shouldn't have left you with my brother. I was just…" His mind blanked on the right word.

"Angry. You were angry."

"He has a lot going on. The pressure of the crown. No one expected King Cedric's stroke. Despite being raised for it, I guess Sebastian thought he had more time before the weight of duty fell to him." The words slipped out, then he downed more of the water.

King Cedric's devotion was to Celiana. Everything else was second. It was that devotion Alessio tried to mimic with the Princess Lottery. It was that devotion that Sebastian continued to fail to meet.

Alessio was doing the best he could. But he wasn't the king.

Alessio swallowed and choked on the thoughts. He was number two. He'd always been number two.

"Sebastian does have a lot going on." Brie kicked her legs, water splashing up onto the T-shirt she wore. "But that doesn't mean you can't be angry about him joking about his demise. Or be angry that you have to step up. You are allowed to be angry."

Anger was emotion and emotions were normal, but if he gave in to them, he wasn't sure he'd stop.

"Sebastian expresses enough emotions for the both of us."

Leaning over, Brie cupped some water then splashed it in his face. "Nope. One person does not get to express the emotions for another. Try again." The water splashed in his face, again, but this time he was ready.

"Brie, it's all right."

More water. "Seriously—"

More water.

"Say 'I was angry.'" She dumped more water on his head.

"I'm already wet!"

More water dropped on his head. It was coming quickly now.

"Fine. I was angry."

Brie beamed. "Why was that so hard?"

"I don't know." Except he did. He'd let his emotions rule once, and the consequences were catastrophic.

"Ugh. You're lying." Brie shook her head and let out a soft sigh. "If you don't want to tell me, just say it's not up for discussion. So much is not up for discussion with you anyway. I don't get it but…fine." She crossed her arms, tears hovering in her blue eyes. "See, anger. It's an emotion and you can give in to it."

He hated causing her tears and the acknowledgment that he was holding back. "I show emotions."

"The easy ones." Brie gripped the edge of the pool. "Joy, happiness or excitement. Fear, anger, hurt…those emotions are just as valid."

"I know." The words felt wrong on his tongue. Since returning, he made sure no one saw his anger or his hurt.

How he'd yearned for something he could never have. He was a prince, born with a literal silver spoon in his mouth. How could he want more?

What kind of person did that make him?

Brie's brow furrowed, but she didn't call out the lie or splash him again.

"Do you need to swim more laps, work off the emotions I caused?"

There was no way to work off the feelings she brought out in him. In the two weeks she'd been at the palace, his world had shifted.

He'd expected that. You didn't get a lottery bride without everything changing, but he'd expected to still feel in control of himself.

He'd expected it would take time to know her, to be comfortable in her presence. Instead, his soul was dancing to a new and unknown rhythm.

"I killed my father." The words slipped into the open in the pool. They were words he'd never voiced, not even alone.

"No, you didn't." Brie slipped into the pool.

"You don't have on a swimsuit."

"Don't care." She wrapped her arms around him. "You didn't kill your father."

"I did, though." Alessio pinched his eyes closed. "King Cedric's plan for Sebastian's foreign bride fell through. So he dreamed up the Princess Lottery—for me. He was sure it would fix tourism. And he called me in Scotland, demanded I come home. Do the duty I'd refused for so long. I said…" His voice trailed off. He couldn't say the words. Couldn't give them voice.

"I said something I can't take back. Then he had his stroke. He never woke up. Never saw that I'd come home to do my duty."

"Alessio—"

"I am sorry that you got caught in the royal cage. Though with luck, you won't have to stay in it."

"We don't have to stay in it. You can still be whatever you want. Go back to Scotland."

There was a hesitation in her voice on the word *Scotland*. Or maybe he just hoped there was.

Sebastian needed him. He'd known that since before his brother's coronation. He'd seen it the first time everyone in the hospital room bowed to the new king as the old one was pronounced gone from the mortal plane. Alessio wasn't going anywhere. It was best to simply accept that.

"Enough about me. We have to get to Ophelia's. You're trying on wedding dresses and 'choosing' my suit."

Alessio made air quotes on the word *choosing*. He planned to enjoy the make-believe time. He might never see Brie in a wedding gown, but for today, today he could almost believe she'd be his.

"Nope." Brie kissed the tip of his nose, then swam away from him and started floating on her back.

"This morning was a lot, so I shifted the schedule. There are benefits to being best friends with the shop owner."

"What about the rumors? The articles. Do we need to take a photo of us in the pool? It will look sweet."

She floated over to him, her gaze locked on his. "What if today is just for us? And we don't think about the show part of it. We splash each other in the pool and have breakfast and watch a movie or take a walk where no one can see us. What if today we're just Alessio and Brie?"

Brie was so close to him, her eyes bright with an emotion he wanted to believe was hope that he'd say yes.

Like he'd ever say no to this.

"That sounds like heaven." It would be a little slice of perfection. Then he cupped a hand and splashed some water at her.

"You call that a splash?" She pushed an enormous wall of water toward him.

"Really, really, Princess. Is that how you want to play?"

Her giggle echoed behind another huge splash, and his heart exploded as she smiled at him.

Pulling her close, he was very aware of her body next to his.

"It's hard to splash you when you're holding me." Brie's cheeks were pink, but she didn't pull away from him.

"You want me to let go?"

"No." Brie captured his mouth.

Her fingers tangled in his wet hair, and he tightened his grip.

"Alessio."

His name on her sweet lips anchored him. Nothing mattered in this moment but her touch, her heat, her presence.

"Brie."

His fingers flirted with the edge of her wet shirt. He'd been her first kiss. They'd kissed so many times in the last fourteen days. It brought him joy each time.

But now, in this moment, his body ached to lift her from the pool, carry her to his rooms and forget everything else.

Her breasts pressed against him. She only had to say the words, and he'd do it. Lose himself in her.

She pulled back, desire blazing in her eyes, but the hint of hesitation was there, too. She pulled farther, and he didn't try to hold her. He wanted her desperately, but not before she was ready.

Alessio blew out a breath, then ran a thumb along her cheek. "Thank you for finding me."

"Anytime, Prince Charming."

She splashed more water, her laughter echoing around the pool, and he joined in the fun.

CHAPTER SEVEN

"PRINCESS! PRINCESS!"

It was weird to hear the title called out. The first time she'd heard it, Brie had nearly cried. Every other time, she'd used it as her focal point to make sure she kept her ideas on point. Today, though…today it felt different.

Her gaze flitted to Alessio, clearly getting into his role of dutiful heir to the throne. She understood now the reason the rebel returned the ever-dutiful heir to the throne. It was tragic.

But knowing it made her feel closer to the man beside her.

"Princess! Princess!" They were calling out for her. It should make her nervous. It always had before. That title symbolized the loss of everything she'd gained.

But it also meant Alessio. What if she could work and be a princess? What if the connection she'd believed was just the aftereffects of the lottery high was real? What if he was her match?

No. No. She wasn't traveling that path. This was a show. And they were getting far too good at the optics. That was all.

That didn't explain the pool or the meals they shared. No one was watching them then.

"So many people. I still have a hard time believing they're showing up."

"Everyone believes we're prepping for the wedding of the century, Brie. Trying on gowns—that's a can't-miss event. Our union is a big deal today. Tomorrow, we focus on some other tourist location." He held up his hands. "I know you sent me the schedule. I think it's an art gallery."

It was. And she knew he was playing with her. Alessio knew their schedule down to the minute.

"Right." It was the only word her tongue seemed capable of forming.

Our union.

Why had those words felt so right to hear, even when he was joking? This wasn't the life she'd planned for...the life she'd fought for.

If she turned her head, the flashing lights she could see in her periphery were all the reminder she needed. This life was the opposite of freedom.

Alessio would look delectable in a wedding suit. A wedding suit he'd wear when he pledged his heart to another.

Her heart raced and her stomach turned. He'd meet another at the altar, maybe in Scotland. Someone he chose, hopefully. And she'd be working in her downtown office, proving to her parents and everyone else that she didn't need them to accomplish her dreams.

Each was getting what they wanted...

There was no need for jealousy. This was a show. A role-play. A marketing campaign for the best Celiana offered. Nothing more.

Morning coffee...and kisses.

And why wasn't he saying anything! He was just staring at her, his deep green eyes holding hers.

Lifting a hand, he caressed her cheek. "You all right? You look as though you've seen a ghost."

Tiny bolts of electricity slipped along her skin. His mouth was so close to hers. They needed to pull apart, to get the show started. But she couldn't make herself move.

"Fine." Her voice quavered, and her breath seemed caught in her throat. "Just having a think on the agenda."

"Your brain is always spinning with ideas." He brushed his lips to hers.

The touch was so light, nothing like the passionate kisses they'd shared in the pool. Yet somehow it felt deeper.

The door to their car opened. She could hear the click of cameras, photographers capturing the perfect moment.

Except it hadn't been for the cameras. She saw the frown form on Alessio's face before he wiped it away. It was good they'd been caught in an organic kiss. But part of her wished the moment was just for them, too.

There is no us, Brie!

"Time to go, Prince Charming." She plastered on a smile as he leaned closer.

"You got this." Alessio's words were soft against her ear. Sweet and kind, but the worry wasn't for the crowd.

No. The crowd she could deal with. Her feelings for Alessio... She wasn't quite sure how to handle those.

"A kiss for the camera." Lev's voice was haughty and the first thing she heard upon exiting the car.

"We are engaged, Lev." Alessio smiled. It wasn't the full, beaming one that caused crinkles to show on the sides of his eyes, which was the smile that made her heart and soul dance when he showed it to her.

She squeezed his hand, then slid her arm around his waist. "Do you have an actual question?"

Lev's eyes lighted on hers. "You're supporting your best friend's shop. Do you plan to stay at your brother's new hotel for your honeymoon when it opens? Will any of Celiana's citizens not tied to you personally reap benefits from this—" Lev gestured to their joined hands "—union?"

Beau had a new hotel? So the rumor was true. It didn't surprise her. Their father had extolled the virtues of owning land, buildings and businesses at the dinner table. No time was spent on the children's days, other than admonishments if they'd fallen short of expectations. And they'd fallen short so often.

Still, she'd hoped that Beau would find his own way.

"I haven't spoken to my brother in years."

Each word felt like a tiny knife against her tongue as she

voiced publicly what she'd barely admitted in the privacy of her own home.

Alessio's hand tightened on her waist. Not much, just a touch tighter to remind her that she wasn't alone.

When they stopped this charade, she would be solo again. And the knife the question created cut even deeper.

"I wasn't aware that he was opening a hotel. As far as my dress goes, yes, Ophelia will design my wedding dress, but Alessio and I have plans for as many citizens as possible to participate in our wedding."

Our wedding.

She'd not actually meant to say that. In fact, Brie had carefully scripted her words to ensure she never actually said *wedding*. She hinted at it with marketing euphemisms designed to highlight where they were, not the nuptials they didn't plan to have.

"Will the press get that list?" Lev was calling her bluff.

"Of course." Alessio kissed the top of Brie's head. "I'll have it sent over this evening. Now, my fiancée and I have an appointment to get to."

Alessio nodded to the crowd, raising his hand to wave as they made their way to Ophelia's door.

"Why is the shop so dark?" Alessio's question echoed in the empty room. "Did Ophelia run off?"

"Without me?" Brie chuckled, though she was as surprised as him to find the lights off and the blinds drawn. Usually the room was bright with natural light. "She better not have."

"I didn't," Ophelia called from the back. "I typically use natural light for these fittings. However, with all the camera flashes and such…" she offered as she came into the main room. "I've set up the back for you two. I told the press when they asked that the dress was a state secret."

Her friend beamed, clearly enjoying being in on the actual state secret.

Brie stepped into the back room and knew her mouth was

hanging open. The storeroom was transformed. How much work had Ophelia put into this subterfuge?

The plan was to try on dresses and suits. That way they looked rumpled when leaving. Not disheveled but clearly tousled from trying on outfits. But the room looked like a real bridal setup.

Gauze hung over walls she knew were a dull gray. The boxes of materials usually stacked back here had vanished. The soft sofa she'd seen many brides' mothers sit on was back here, too.

She looked at the bright purple couch. The vibrant color popped against the gold gauze on the walls. Her mother would never sit there. No aunties would watch her try on dresses.

The walls seemed to close as she looked at the couch. What a silly thing to care about. Her mother hadn't been in her life in years. She'd not even reached out since Brie's name was drawn in the lottery. Maybe Lev asking about Beau had triggered the memories.

In her family's world, Brie no longer existed. If she crawled back, they'd take her. But the strong woman she was…that woman wasn't welcome. As she looked at the empty couch, the reality that this was just one more experience she'd lost hammered through her.

"Brie," Alessio and Ophelia spoke in unison.

Her eyes darted to her friend, then to Alessio.

"My family isn't here."

He stepped to her side, pulling her into his arms, holding her. It felt perfect and it also reminded her of the illusion. Still, she couldn't step away.

"I'm sorry, Brie," Ophelia said. "The mothers, aunties, the family usually sit there. I didn't think when I pulled it back here."

"Why would you?" Brie let out a laugh that was far too close to a sob as Alessio stroked her back. "It's a couch. This shouldn't matter. It's just a couch."

His lips pressed into her forehead. "It represents what

you've lost through no fault of your own. You are allowed to be upset by that. Even angry."

"Now anger is acceptable." Brie swallowed the lump in her throat.

"I thought you pointed out that it was always acceptable."

"Using my words against me, Prince Charming?"

"No." His lips brushed her forehead again as she looked up at him. "Just trying to help."

"Thank you." Stepping from his arms, Brie shook herself. "Well, that was quite the dramatic bridal moment!" She wiped a stray tear from her cheek. "But now we have a fashion show for the prince!"

"Yes." Ophelia looked from Brie to Alessio, a thought passing over her friend's face as she met her gaze.

Brie tilted her head, waiting for Ophelia to say whatever she was thinking.

Instead, she nodded to Alessio. "A fashion show for a prince. In my shop."

Brie smiled as Alessio sat on the couch and she followed her friend into the dressing area… She'd talked to Ophelia about finding her most outrageous dresses, the ones she'd designed because the idea just wouldn't leave her but she knew might never leave her racks.

Ophelia was an artist. Most of her designs were meant to sell, which meant they followed similar patterns: mermaid dresses, tight on the waist but flaring at the bottom, poufy princess ball gowns, sleek A-lines in shades meant for a bride.

But there were other dresses: over-the-top creations that fit on a runway or a magazine shoot. Those were dresses that Ophelia loved but doubted would ever sell. Brie had made Ophelia promise to pull as many of them as possible for this escapade.

The first dress did not disappoint. It was an actual mermaid theme, the blue bodice fading to sea green as it spilled past her feet.

"You are a dream in that gown. A mythical being. I swear,

if your hair was wet, it would look like you just stepped out of the ocean."

Alessio grinned as she stood before him, but there was the hint of something in his eyes.

Disappointment.

She struck a pose, trying to bring out his real smile. The one she craved.

The dress hugged her in all the right places. It was beautiful, but there was no place for Brie to wear it. And it certainly wasn't a wedding dress.

And he'd expected to see one, expected to see her playing the part. She'd not counted on that. Her plans, her expectations for today, all vanished.

"Next one!" She dipped from the room and met Ophelia. "Can we put a few wedding dresses, like actual ones, in the rotation? Alessio—"

Brie cleared her throat as Ophelia raised a brow. "Like a dress you might wear down the aisle?"

"I mean, I'm not walking down the aisle, but he…" Again her throat closed as she looked at the closed door of the dressing room.

She could picture Alessio sitting on the couch. Picture him waiting, hoping that she'd step out in a wedding dress, even for a fashion show he knew was fake.

The fact that she wasn't, the look on his face, the acceptance hiding hurt…

"I set aside a few earlier. I'll grab them."

Brie nodded, ready for the next few hours of dress-up.

After an hour of trying on dresses, playing princess, Brie couldn't take her eyes off herself. The image in the mirror *was* a princess, a woman she could see walking toward Alessio.

The soft gold glimmered on her skin. The scalloped bodice hugged her breasts as the A-line dress slipped over her hips. The simple cut contrasted with the delicate flowers embroidered from the bodice to the train. They were the flowers of Celiana.

This dress…

His mouth would fall open. He'd smile, a real one, dimples, creases around his eyes. He'd beam as she walked toward him.

It was easy to imagine. Easy to see.

"I can't show him this one." The whispered words hung in the dressing room.

Ophelia wrapped her arms around Brie. "I've seen this moment many times before with my brides."

"This moment?" Brie placed her hands on her stomach, staring at the image in the mirror.

"When they find the one. This is your wedding dress."

Except she didn't need a dress. Even one as perfect as this, which she could see herself wearing while standing next to him. His hands were reaching for her over the altar as they promised forever.

"I'm not marrying Alessio. I'm not." The words were soft, barely audible. Brie wasn't even sure she'd managed to push them out.

"Who are you trying to convince? Me? Or yourself?" Ophelia squeezed her shoulders.

"I have my company."

"Maybe you could have both…" Ophelia met her gaze in the mirror.

"Princesses don't have careers." Brie hiccuped as she looked at the gown. "This isn't my gown. It's beautiful, but it isn't mine."

"Brie—"

"This isn't real. I'm not the protagonist in a fairy tale. Alessio and I have a deal and a goal to *not* meet at the altar. We aren't in love."

Aren't in love. Why did saying that out loud hurt so much? It was a marketing scheme—her best plan ever. But it wasn't real.

Apparently her heart would need her brain to remind her of that more often.

"Honey." Ophelia's gaze was full of questions Brie didn't want to answer.

"Time for Alessio to try on suits. My turn on the couch." The words were rushed, and her emotions were spilling everywhere as she looked at the gown in the mirror one last time.

This was a dream.

Alessio and she got on well. He was sweet, and he was kind. And his kisses awoke places in her body…

In another time, another place, maybe they'd have found each other. Found happiness.

But that wasn't this time. It wasn't this place. And her heart felt like it was cracking as Ophelia helped her out of the wedding dress.

"You look like you stepped from a fairy tale." Brie clapped as Alessio stepped from the dressing room.

"You've said that about the last three suits." Alessio playfully crossed his arms. "I know there isn't as much difference in these as your dresses, but still…"

Brie laughed and he moved toward her, dropping a kiss on her lips. "Do you like this one more or less than the last two?"

"Can I be honest?"

His heart pounded against his ribs as he looked at her. She'd not shown him the last dress. He didn't know why. She'd said that it hadn't fit right. A lie, he suspected, but something had shifted.

She was laughing at all the right moments, clapping and having a good time—she'd even posted a picture of him in the first suit and asked people to weigh in—but there was a look in her eye, like she was assessing him each time he walked out. It was like she was actually looking for a suit.

Of course she wasn't. And he shouldn't want her to. Though that didn't stop the rebel from wishing that maybe she was thinking of staying no matter what the marketing scheme produced.

He tried pushing those selfish thoughts away.

"So what is your honest feeling on these suits, Briella?"

"That you looked delectable in each of them, but they are very similar. Each of my dresses was different. The mermaid gown to the last..."

The last.

She'd hesitated. What was the last dress, the one she'd refused to show him?

Brie looked away, so he focused on the other part of her sentence.

"Delectable?"

Her cheeks darkened but she met his gaze, desire burning in his eyes. "You know you're attractive, Prince Charming." She shook a finger at him playfully. "Searching out compliments? Really?"

He knew he was conventionally attractive, that he met society's definition of handsome.

It wasn't society's definition he wanted, though.

"It's still nice to hear." He kissed her again. Since opening up in the pool, they'd kissed so freely. It was a gift he didn't deserve, but he couldn't stop worshipping her lips. "Ophelia has one more option. Though it sounds like you could pick any of these options and be happy with the outcome."

"Alessio—"

He captured her lips before she could argue that there was no need to pick out wedding attire. He knew that. It was a slip of the tongue, a wishful thought. But he didn't want the reminder right now.

"Go!" Brie pushed at his shoulders after he broke the connection. "Maybe the next suit will be magic."

He stood and headed back to the dressing area. The suit he'd seen on the rack was gone. Alessio looked in the dressing room. Nothing.

"Ophelia?"

She rounded the corner, a dress bag slung over her arm. "I don't think the final suit I picked before is a good fit."

"Oh." Alessio didn't quite know how to respond. He didn't

think of his clothes that much. It was a statement of privilege, he knew, as was the fact that he had a personal shopper who knew his tastes and the clothes appeared when he needed them.

His mother thought more about her outfits. He'd heard her argue that people were going to talk about what she wore, how she wore it and when she wore it, so she might as well make the statement she wanted with the clothes on her body.

"The suits seem fine." He pulled a hand over his face. Those were not the words to give a designer, but what else was there to say?

"*Fine* is not what we are going for." Ophelia sucked in a breath, then looked at the closed door. He knew she was seeing beyond it to the woman on the other side.

The best friend she'd offered aid to flee the island.

"*Fine* is not what one wears to a royal wedding, Your Royal Highness."

He shook his head. "Ophelia?" She knew this wasn't real. Knew they were here only because the hints of rumors were bothering Brie. Hell, the only reason they were trying on outfits was because Brie was worried if they came out looking too perfect, people might suspect they'd only sat and chatted with Ophelia.

That was a worry that would never have crossed his mind. Her brain saw all the patterns, the questions people might ask, like his saw the potential in glass.

"Just humor me." Ophelia pushed past him into the dressing room and hung the bag on the wall hanger.

Alessio waited in the hall, not wanting to crowd the woman. Brie's family was gone—not from the mortal world, but from her life. Ophelia was her sister, not by blood, but in all the ways that mattered.

Ophelia nodded as she stepped from the room. "If you can give her choices, then maybe there will be a royal wedding."

Choices.

The word hung in the silent hallway. Choices were not what

royals got. The country came first. What royals wanted came in a distant second.

Brie deserved more than that. Still, Ophelia's words hung in his soul.

Brie deserved all the choices. He could give her that, behind the palace's closed walls. In public, they'd be supporters of his brother, beholden to the people of Celiana. In the palace... His brain ceased the conversation as his heart screamed that it wasn't enough.

But what if it was?

Rather than try to voice anything, Alessio stepped into the room and quickly donned the suit.

It was a charcoal gray, with a gold tie. The cut was similar to the other suits, highlighting his broad shoulders and slim waist.

It wasn't all that different from the black and navy suits Ophelia had shown him, but it felt right. That was a weird feeling for a suit.

He stepped into the hallway, and Ophelia raised a hand, covering her mouth.

"I take it you think this is the one, too." Alessio chuckled and reached for the door handle. "Shall we see what my Brie thinks?"

He stepped into the room and saw Brie's mouth open, then shut. Her eyes flicked behind him. He wasn't sure what the silent communication was, but he didn't stop looking at her.

"What do we think of gray and gold?"

"Perfect." Brie pursed her lips, tilted her head, took a step toward him, then stopped. "It's a perfect wedding look."

"Brie?" He closed the distance between them. She looked happy, but also terrified. Two emotions he'd never seen together. "What's wrong?"

"Nothing." She shook her head against his shoulder. "Nothing is wrong. Why is nothing wrong?" Her nervous laugh echoed in the back room.

He looked to Ophelia and then back, unsure what to say. "You want something to be wrong?"

"We're picking out wedding outfits."

"Not really." He pressed a kiss to the top of her head. "We're playing dress-up." That was such a bitter truth.

"We're weeks into this charade."

Charade.

His soul rioted against that word. It was a charade. And he hated that. This wasn't what she'd planned, but they were having fun together.

Her kisses were not what he should be focusing on in this moment.

"We're picking out a gown and a suit and it should feel *wrong*. This isn't supposed to make me—"

Her words cut off and Ophelia's words echoed in his mind. *If you can give her choices...* Could he keep her? Could he actually have her as a partner in the life he hadn't wanted? Would she stay?

"Brie." He pulled her into his arms, unsure what to say but needing her with him. Her body relaxed into his. He rested his head on hers, soaking in the moment.

CHAPTER EIGHT

"BRIE!"

"Briella!"

"Princess!"

Calls echoed from around the market stalls. Everyone wanted to see Celiana's future princess.

Brie was doing great. She'd waved when they'd exited the vehicle. Then she'd answered a few questions and taken so many floral offerings he suspected their vehicle would smell of pollen, sweetness and leaves on the way back to the palace.

People were snapping photos, and he'd heard more than one person mention how they'd never have thought to come to the markets if Brie wasn't here.

She was a hit. And her idea was working. What would happen when she left? Would the excitement continue without her?

And would he be able to keep going?

Of course he would. He had to. Still, Alessio knew it would be fake smiles greeting the people then—even if they never realized it.

"Prince Alessio." Lev's voice echoed behind him. The royal tabloid reporter, despite his claims of hating everything about this "spectacle," was at each event.

His father had taken the position of answering Lev's questions in the past, granting him access like all other journalists. Sebastian had questioned the policy but left it in place.

Lev hated the royal family, even though they were the reason people clicked on his opinion pieces, the reason he made as much money as he did. Whether his antagonism was for website clicks or a true dislike, Alessio didn't know. Nor did it matter.

The man was going to write the articles he wanted; at least this way the palace got a little control.

"How does it feel to be third now?" Lev looked over Alessio's shoulder, clearly watching Brie with the crowd. "Always second fiddle to someone, huh?"

Second fiddle.

He felt his jaw twitch and he saw the gleam in Lev's eyes. *Second fiddle. Spare. Extra.* Those were words his father used constantly. And they were words Alessio hated, words he never heard when he'd left.

"Briella is doing a lovely job. I'm proud that my fiancée is so loved by the people." The bite of jealousy in his heart had nothing to do with Brie.

She was a natural. But a lifetime of second fiddle, a lifetime of hearing the phrase, from those he loved and those he very much did not, still stung.

"People think this is more of a marketing stunt than a love story. Any comment?"

Alessio tilted his head and wanted to curse. Reacting to such a statement was a tell, one he was usually very good at controlling.

Technically, everything the palace did was a marketing stunt. They used their image for power, but Brie was elevating the game.

"I don't really think that needs a comment." Alessio smiled at a small boy who handed him a picture of him and Brie.

"What about people who say that Sebastian should be the one doing this? That you're stealing your brother's spotlight? The spare rising above his position."

"*King* Sebastian." Alessio emphasized the title the reporter had omitted, enjoying the hint of color invading Lev's cheeks. It was one thing to disparage the royals at the keyboard, another to do it to their faces.

"King Sebastian is busy taking over from King Cedric. He didn't plan to take the crown so suddenly." So suddenly. The stroke, brought on by Alessio's argument. Or at least elevated by it. No matter what Brie thought.

Sebastian seemed to wilt as the crown he'd been raised to wear landed on his head. Alessio wasn't sure what had happened, and the few times he'd brought it up, Sebastian had changed the subject or just walked away.

Sebastian was the one their father loved, the one he'd doted on. Of course his grief would take a different course from Alessio's.

So he'd done what he hadn't before. He'd stepped into his duties. It was as simple—and complicated—as that.

"You didn't answer my question." Lev raised a brow.

"What question?" Brie's sweet voice was tinged with fire, though he doubted Lev realized it, as she slipped her fingers into his. "What question?" she repeated as she looked from Lev to Alessio.

"I asked if he had any comment on people saying that Alessio was overshadowing *King* Sebastian."

"Are people saying that or are you typing it and hoping they'll agree?" Brie's voice was steady as she squeezed Alessio's hand. Then she pointed to a stall. "I want to see that."

She pulled Alessio away without waiting for Lev to comment. He looked over his shoulder, unsurprised to see Lev make a note on his phone.

"He's going to stir that into some kind of rumor." Alessio made sure his words were only for her ears. To others it would look like he was whispering sweet nothings.

"Probably." Brie's bright blue eyes held his. "But we'll deal with it."

We. He loved that word when it was applied to them.

Brie leaned her head against his shoulder as they made their way through the crowded area, the security team a few feet behind and in front of them.

He kissed the top of her head; he loved touching her, getting close to her. The motions weren't for the cameras he knew were everywhere, not anymore.

"Brie!"

"Brie!"

"You're quite popular, my dear." He let the endearment run off his lips.

Brie's cheeks tinted pink, and he put his hand around her waist. "Popularity is easy. Keeping their focus on the important things is harder."

She kissed his cheek, then pulled him toward the stalls. "Come on."

"Of course." Brie was right. Today was supposed to be about highlighting the stalls, not them.

She leaned over a stall with a few handmade bags he was sure she'd pointed to randomly when she dismissed Lev. "These are lovely."

"Thank you, Princess. I'm glad I came this weekend. I almost didn't with prices for travel—" The seller cut off her words. "Anyway…"

"You've struggled?" Brie's voice was even, and Alessio looked over a few bags in the stall to give them at least the appearance of privacy.

"Who hasn't?" The woman sighed. "I mean, I guess you—"

"My parents disowned me a few years ago. I spent days living off coffee and stress as rent came due. My upbringing was very privileged—I can't deny that—but I've also known what it feels like to be terrified that I'd lose my tiny studio apartment."

The woman reached over and gripped Brie's hand. "My parents passed two years ago. I've taken over the care of my teen sister. I started making bags to sell to supplement the income as tourist visits dipped at our family restaurant.

"But since the lottery," the woman continued, her tone instantly brightening, "it's been quite full. I don't need to be here, but these—" She looked at the bags. "My mother always called it a hobby. But it…"

"It makes you feel whole." Brie grinned.

She really was in her element here. Alessio saw the young woman relax, Brie's calming presence giving her something he couldn't describe. If she stayed, married him, she'd be such an asset to the royal family.

And that was exactly why she should leave.

No one should be an asset.

"They're just bags." The woman bit her lip as she looked over her wares.

"No." Brie picked up a small white leather bag that looked big enough to carry a cell phone and maybe a tube of lipstick. It wasn't practical, but Alessio could see the craftsmanship.

"That's part of my bridal collection—guess you're drawn to it."

"I guess I am." Brie grinned. "I'll take it."

"Oh. No, it's my gift to you, Princess."

Brie shook her head. "I appreciate the kindness, but lesson one in business—don't turn away paying customers. Even if they wear a crown."

She laughed, then looked to Alessio. "Except, who has our money?" Her cheeks darkened as she looked from the purse to the woman behind the small counter.

By rule, the royal family didn't carry wallets or cash on them. People sent their bills to the palace. Or they did just as the woman suggested and offered things as a gift.

Alessio handed the woman a card. "Send the bill here, and the palace will make sure you're compensated."

"Thank you."

"And I'll check," Brie added. "Send the bill!"

"Yes, Princess."

Alessio wrapped an arm around her waist as they left the stall. "You are amazing. Just so you know."

Brie hit his hip with hers. "I am. But the reason her hobby has a chance to become a business is because her restaurant is thriving again."

He heard the hesitation in her voice. "The lottery did what

I intended. Your marketing…" He paused, barely catching himself before the word *scheme*. Her marketing was more than a scheme, and there were ears and cameras all around. "It's working."

"If we don't meet at the altar…" The whispered words vanished into the commotion of the crowd.

But he didn't need to hear the end of the sentence. If they didn't meet at the altar, would the kingdom continue to thrive? Brie's plan was brilliant. It should have been instituted years ago. But was it sustainable without the wedding? He wasn't sure. When they separated, shattered the illusion, would the kingdom suffer?

All were questions to consider, but his brain was focusing on one word. *If.*

If we don't meet.

Not when. It shouldn't bring him so much pleasure, but damn. His heart felt like it wanted to jump out of his chest.

"Oh!" Brie brightened as a glasswork stall came into view. The light struck the handblown glass; it was a sight to see.

"Did you make this?" Brie stepped into the stall, her mouth hanging open as she looked at the art on the shelves.

The man's weathered hands had held the tools for molding liquid glass into the most beautiful pieces for over forty years. Emilio taught a class at the college Alessio had attended. And Alessio had been fascinated from the moment he'd shaped his first piece.

He'd learned everything possible from the master glassworker.

"Emilio is the island's only master glassblower." Alessio looked over the art, amazed, as always, at his friend's ability. The glass pieces molded in his tools, whether dinnerware cups or ornamental works, were masterpieces.

"Not true. You are here, too." Emilio stepped from the booth and reached for Alessio's hand. "What have you made recently?"

It was his standard question. Not *How are you?* or *What's new?* but *What have you made?*

"I've been a bit busy."

"You said you were a glassworker but…" Brie's eyes were bright as she looked at Emilio's art. "You blow glass? Like this?"

"Not anymore." Alessio bit the inside of his cheek, fighting the urge to ask Emilio if he'd seen the recent exhibit in Paris. The images Alessio had looked at on his computer made his hands itch to craft something. But he'd put that world behind him.

"Alessio?" Her voice pulled him back.

"Let me introduce you to my fiancée, Brie Ailiono." He smiled, ignoring the questions he didn't want to answer in Brie's eyes.

Emilio reached for her hand, but Alessio saw more than a hint of reservation in his eyes.

"I was at your family estate last week," Emilio said to Brie.

Brie's body shifted as she leaned toward Alessio—reaching for him, seeking him.

"I'm not in contact with my family."

"They said as much." Emilio pursed his lips, then clicked his tongue.

Alessio knew he was weighing his words. He'd heard the click so many times in the man's workshop. It was a tell Emilio knew about but was unable to stop. Except there wasn't a piece of artwork needing critique.

"Emilio—" Alessio wrapped his arm around Brie's waist. If his friend had heard something important, they needed to know. The Ailiono family was powerful; anyone who doubted that found out at their peril.

"What am I missing?" Brie's gaze met his.

"Emilio clicked his tongue. I was his student for years. It means he's weighing a tough set of words." Alessio squeezed her. "What aren't you saying, Emilio?"

"Your family hired me for a big piece of art. In your old

room. Told me to throw everything out. Not what I was paid for, but some clients…" He cleared his throat.

Some clients were entitled. Alessio had run into more than one during the three years he'd run his own shop. One client screamed that the art he'd commissioned was too big. When Alessio reminded him that it was the exact measurements he'd requested, the man had become apoplectic.

"I'm surprised my stuff was even still there." Brie smiled but her eyes didn't light up. The bouncy spirit she'd had with the woman in the previous stall was absent.

"They said marrying the prince in a lottery was beneath an Ailiono." Emilio's words were direct.

Beneath an Ailiono. Only that family would think having a royal bride was beneath them. Sure, the lottery was different, but it wasn't like the Ailionos' unions weren't also arranged. That was why Brie had fled.

"Your mother said that if you followed through with it, there was no hope for you."

Brie's breath hitched but she didn't say anything. Was she mourning that loss or realizing a door she thought closed forever had a crack? At least it had, until her name rose from the lottery drawing.

Until this moment, Alessio had never understood the phrase *I saw red*. The color danced across his eyes. He was mad at the Ailionos, mad at Emilio, mad at the situation as a whole.

"Emilio—" His voice was harder than intended. It was the tone he used as Prince Alessio in the rare cases where a strong royal persona was necessary. Brie wrapped an arm around him, squeezing his side just like he'd done for her.

Emilio held up a hand. "I do not say this to hurt you, but I wanted to explain why—" he looked over his shoulder "—why I brought something to the market this weekend."

He turned and went behind the bench that served as his checkout stand. "Your campaign to showcase the island makes it easy to know where you'll be."

Campaign.

He saw Brie shift. The rumors were still there, not as squashed as she'd hoped. But that was a worry for another day.

Emilio pulled out a box overflowing with pictures and trinkets. "I managed…" He cleared his throat. "I'm sure I didn't get everything important to you, Princess, but these things looked loved."

Brie took one step toward the box, paused, then quickly closed the distance.

Her fingers reached for the box, her shoulders shaking as she looked over the trinkets of her girlhood. She'd mentioned leaving, but this box meant she'd truly fled. She'd left behind nearly everything.

She lifted pictures, holding them up to show him. Some people in the images he recognized, while others were acquaintances that moved in similar circles. She flipped through a few notebooks and journals, laughing to herself.

"These were my secret dream journals. I had to hide them under my bed."

Emilio nodded.

And her parents were throwing everything out, all the things she might have cherished.

Brie ran a hand over one of the journals. Her face was so full of excitement over a secret dream journal.

It was a secret because she couldn't be Brie. Until she'd left their home, she'd been Briella, the daughter of the wealthiest man in the nation, but not a loved child. She'd been an object for gain. It was only when she left that she became herself.

Freedom.

Worry pressed against his chest. He didn't want to steal that from her. But he also didn't want to give her up. If he gave her choices, perhaps he could find a way to make her want to stay.

Brie was so much more than a pretend lottery bride. She was the woman who listened to his darkest secret, comforted him, then splashed him with water. She was the woman who could take a simple outing and turn it into a viral marketing campaign. She was the one he was falling for. Truly falling for.

A small bumblebee stuffie rose and she let out a sob. Alessio pulled her to him without thinking. If she was upset, then her place was in his arms.

"My brother gave this to me when I was five or six. He used to joke that I was always buzzing around him. When I left, I was so alone, no one to bother. I always wondered if Beau missed me. Or if he was grateful the annoying sister was finally gone."

He kissed the top of her head, holding her tightly, reminding her that she wasn't alone. Not as long as she was with him.

He held her for several minutes, letting her gather herself.

Finally, Brie pulled back and walked around the bench, pulling Emilio into her arms. "Thank you. Thank you so much."

"Consider it an early wedding present." Emilio hugged her.

"No one will be able to top it, Emilio." Alessio winked. This was a gift Brie would remember for forever.

Brie stepped back and wiped a tear from her cheek.

"Make me a promise, Princess." Emilio tilted his head as he looked at Alessio. "Make him show you his studio. Don't let him give up his gift."

"I plan to see it. As soon as we return to the palace." Brie nodded, determination clear in her features.

"Wow!"

Brie couldn't believe the "small" studio she was standing in was Alessio's glassworks studio. It was organized chaos. Designs covered the walls, sketches that were gorgeous on their own but that he could craft in glass in their image. The man was a master.

"Alessio." She whispered his name as she walked past the drawings and then saw a completed piece on the table. Twisted flames licked up at an indistinguishable human figure. Whether the man was beating the flames or consumed by them was up for interpretation.

"That was the second-to-last piece I created." His eyes hovered on the piece, a frown hinting at the edge of his lips. "I haven't been in the shop as much this year."

Consumed by the flames.

He'd put all his efforts into saving Celiana through the bride lottery. And it was working. She'd heard that throughout the market stalls today.

People were seeing improvements. They were smiling and happy to have the prince and future princess in their places. And just like in Ophelia's shop last week, it felt natural. It felt like where she was supposed to be.

It's because I've been doing it for over a month. I've been living and breathing this life. That's all.

And maybe fear. She'd lost nearly all the jobs she'd lined up during the bride lottery. No matter what line she gave, no matter the hints she dropped, they all assumed when she wed that the princess wouldn't work. And she couldn't come right out and say she was planning to leave Alessio. Not yet.

The idea of walking away from him, from the man that understood her need for freedom, understood the craving, grew more painful with the passing days. This was a fake relationship; it was. And it was impacting the company she'd built.

If she didn't have her business…what did she have?

Alessio. She had Alessio. If she wanted him. If she was willing to step into this life, hold his hand and walk this path.

So many ifs…and yet none of them felt insurmountable. They felt…they felt perfect. And that was terrifying.

They could continue as they were, marketing Celiana. It was different and not a traditional job. There'd be no penthouse suite…but the success might be more meaningful.

He was grinning as he walked to his furnace, his hands running along pipe-looking fixtures next to it. This was his happy place. This was the place the real Alessio loved most.

The pool was where he worked off unsettled emotions. This…this was his sanctuary.

"You should have seen my shop in Scotland. It was this

tiny cottage. I sold my wares in the front and the back was my workshop."

"Scotland. You had a shop there?"

Alessio turned, his face lit with happiness. "It was the best place. Mine. I was a glassworker. No one even knew I was a prince of Celiana. Three years I got to take orders and live as a creative."

"You could do it again."

Alessio shook his head. "No. My place is by Sebastian. I might get to play in here more—after all your plan is working. But my own shop full-time—that dream is over."

He reached for her hand, squeezing it before stepping away. "The glass ball everyone put their lottery tickets in was my last major piece. I knew that when I made it."

"You made that?" It had been large, so large. She took her phone from her back pocket and pulled up her social media page. She scrolled back and found an image she'd taken in front of the entry post.

The large ball was on spinners. She'd joked on more than one occasion that the intricate hearts traced in the ball were over-the-top, but she'd privately admitted that ball was lovely. On sunny days, rainbows formed in the glass. Press releases had talked about how it was a sign of good fortune.

And she'd have never guessed that it was sculpted by Prince Alessio.

"Why didn't you tell everyone? That is a story the press would have eaten up!" The marketeer in her wanted to scream at the lost opportunity. The stories she'd have spun in Ophelia's dresses...

Plus, it added depth to Alessio. It let the world see the man she saw.

"Because." He wrapped her in his arms. Time froze as his green eyes held hers. The urge to tickle him, to make him laugh, nearly overwhelmed her, but she wanted to hear his answer. "Then they would have wanted to see my workshop. There'd be pressure to film me creating something."

"True."

Everyone would want to see it. Would that be so bad? Prince Alessio had a secret creative side. The dutiful prince was so much more than just the image he projected. More than the interviews projected, more than the crown. More than the re-formed rebel.

Alessio was funny, kind, silly. He was a full person, but the rest of the country didn't get to see that man. Why?

"Heaven forbid that the world should learn that you are a master glassworker."

Her fingers brushed along his jaw, enjoying the feel of his beard.

Alessio leaned his head against hers. "This is mine. I didn't want to share it. But if you want to post about it, I can strike a pose."

It would be the perfect story. But she knew she'd never post a single image in here. As long as he wanted this to be only his, that was how it would stay. He'd given so much up for Celiana already; she could give him this space.

"It can be our little secret, Alessio."

He kissed the top of her head. "Want to make something?"

"Make something? How would I even do that?"

Alessio pulled back and pushed a few buttons on the wall. The furnace made a few loud noises that must be normal since he didn't blink an eye at them, then it kicked to life.

"I taught classes in Scotland on the side. Taught others the craft. My shop was the one place in the world I was number one."

Brie's heart turned on his words. "Alessio."

He held up a hand. "I didn't mean anything bad, Brie. Want to give it a go?"

She was torn. She wanted to see him in this place, witness the true artist emerge. But she wanted to touch the hurt spot in his heart, too. That was the place that claimed he was only the spare, the man caring for the new king, the one who felt responsible for his father's demise.

He was so much more.

"Yes."

He flipped a few more switches and grabbed supplies from around the shop. She watched his face relax and the stiffness leave his shoulders. She watched him come into himself. His face was open, free of duty.

"All right, come here."

She moved to the furnace, letting him guide her. He handed her safety goggles, then directed her behind a small metal-and-wood table beside the furnace. His hands were firm on her hips as he shifted her slightly.

"Relax, Brie."

That might be possible if his hands weren't resting on her hips.

"Trying."

Alessio grabbed a blowpipe and fitted it against the hole in the furnace before coming back with the molten glass.

"Whoa." It was one thing to know he did this with such skill, another to see the red-orange glass.

"I got you." He placed the pipe on the table, the glass hanging off, and wrapped her hands around the pipe. Then he stepped behind her again, pressing his body against hers.

He whispered instructions in her ears. Brie did her best to follow them, but all her mind could think of was the man behind her, the feel of him against her, the promise of what might be.

Her life had changed, altered completely. The idea of leaving, escaping, no longer felt like an absolute necessity. If she was honest, the thought of leaving hurt.

Together they molded the glass, turned it, twisted it, made it into something new.

That was what this relationship was. Her heart rate pulsed in her ears; she felt her face flush and it had nothing to do with the heat of the room. It was him, the man whose body made her sing with promises she'd never sought.

The man she was falling for.

Her brain had tried to ignore the attachment.

"See?"

She blew out a breath. As she looked at the molten blob he'd pulled from the furnace, it transformed into a heart. It was weird how one second it was nothing, but now it was something.

Just like us.

They were something now.

But what did that mean for the future? Brie wasn't sure, but for tonight, she wanted to pretend they weren't the prince and his lotto bride. Just Brie and Alessio.

"Ta-da!" Alessio's lips skimmed her neck before he took the pipe from her hands. It was a glass heart with a yellow one inside. Beautiful.

"Nice work, Brie." He dropped a kiss on her cheek before taking the heart to a little box in the corner. "Needs to cool."

"Alessio—" she walked toward him "—I did very little of that. It was all you."

"It was us." His eyes glittered.

She couldn't stop herself from moving. She wrapped her arms around him, capturing his lips. Tomorrow she'd start to figure out the conflict between what her heart felt and her mind wanted. Tonight, all she needed was the man before her.

Need, desperate to make him hers, completely wrapped through her.

"Take me to bed, Alessio."

Take me to bed.

Alessio lifted Brie in his arms, the weight of her body a thrill on his already warm skin. Standing behind her, holding her hands as they molded the glass, had been as blissful as Alessio ever thought to get. But her words and her lips, they dragged him even further toward heaven.

Her lips pressed against his neck, her fingers ran along his chest, and it took every ounce of attention to ignore the

flames licking at him to ensure they made it to his bedroom
as smoothly as possible.

Brie laughed as he kicked open the door. "I swear that is a
movie move, Alessio."

"Maybe." His mouth lowered, drinking her in, savoring
the moment.

He laid her on the bed and her hands immediately flattened,
her face changing.

"Brie…" Her whispered name burned on his lips. "If you've
changed your mind—"

"No, but—" she pursed her lips and he saw her swallow
"—what if I'm bad at this?"

"Not possible." Alessio lifted her fingers, placing a soft kiss
against each one before dropping her hand. "Tonight is yours,
Briella." He opened his arms and saw his words register.

"Just like my first kiss." Brie sat up on her knees, her hands
threading under his shirt.

This would be the most blissful torture. But Alessio would
not deny her the moment.

Her hands explored him. She lifted his shirt over his head,
a smile radiating across her lips. "You are so magnificent."

Alessio's fingers found the edge of her top and his body
quivered as she raised her hands. Her red lace bra nearly
brought him to his knees.

"You are the magnificent one, Brie."

His lips trailed along her collarbone, and she reached behind herself to unhook her bra.

They explored each other, and he made a mental note at
every breath change, every sigh. Bringing her pleasure and
driving her to wonder were the only thoughts in his brain.

When she lay beneath him, Alessio dragged his lips across
her thighs before finding her inner core. Brie bucked under
his dancing mouth as he devoured her. She was sweet and fire
and everything he needed.

"Alessio!"

Her cry as he felt her body tighten turned him on even

more. He'd not thought it possible. He stroked her with his fingers, bringing her to bliss again. Then he pulled the condom down his length.

The urge to drive himself to the hilt pulsed against every nerve, but he held himself steady as he pressed into her folds.

Brie wrapped her legs around him, pulling him deeper. She took a long breath.

"You are so beautiful," Alessio whispered against her ear, holding himself steady until she started moving against him.

They found their rhythm and he lost all thoughts of anything besides the woman with him. This was as close to heaven as he'd ever get and he was savoring every moment.

CHAPTER NINE

BLOND HAIR SPILLED over his chest, and Alessio gently stroked Brie's back. The urge to touch her, to convince himself that she was here, that he'd spent last night worshipping her body and was not trapped in one of his dreams, cruised through him.

He'd once heard a friend say the afterglow of being with his girlfriend, now wife, was the best feeling in the world. It was how he knew he wanted to propose, to ensure he spent the rest of his life with a person who made him feel so whole.

Alessio, like many of the guys in attendance, had laughed. The stereotype that women enjoyed snuggling, but men moved on, ran deep in their youthful subconscious.

Now though, as he held Brie in the early hours, he knew what his friend had meant. He knew how deep the feeling was, and the rightness of being exactly where you belonged.

But what did belonging to a prince mean for her?

"What time is it?" Brie mumbled as she lifted her head. The hair spilled over her eyes, and her lips were luscious and calling to be kissed.

"Just after six. I found a way to keep you in bed." He grinned, then brushed his lips over hers. "How are you this morning?"

He'd been gentle and made sure she reached the heights of making love, but that didn't shift that last night had been her first time. Mentally, and physically, that was a big deal. And it was the only reason he hadn't woken her this morning with kisses trailing along her magnificent body.

"Deliriously happy." Her fingers danced along his chest. Pink rose in her cheeks and her smile radiated straight to his heart.

"Deliriously happy." He kissed the tip of her nose, unable to keep from kissing her. "I love the sound of that."

He loved her.

The words hovered in the back of his mind. It hadn't been intentional, and suddenly all the things she'd have to give up by his side hit even harder. But her marketing plan was working. She could get her freedom…and what would that mean for his heart?

"We need to get breakfast." Brie rolled over and sighed.

"And you want coffee," Alessio teased.

"How well you know me." Brie laughed. "I'm going to head to my room. I'll see you soon." She dropped a kiss to his lips, then slid from the bed, grabbed her clothes and headed through the connecting door to her room.

It was the first time she'd used it, and he couldn't describe the burst of happiness that floated through him to see it open now.

Alessio rose from the bed and grabbed his phone. The text from his assistant, Jack, made him smile. They had a state function tonight. It would be his brother's first; he was welcoming a foreign dignitary from Europe. The staff had worked hard on the function, but it wasn't his concern.

Brie and Alessio were attending as ornamentation only. The spare and his future bride, they'd have the night mostly to themselves while everyone was focused on King Sebastian's first state dinner. But he had a surprise for her. And it had been delivered this morning.

He quickly donned some slacks and a comfortable shirt and went in search of Brie.

She was sitting on the bed, and he saw a tear slip down her cheek.

"Brie?" He moved to her side, sitting beside her and pulling her to him. "What's wrong?"

"Nothing. It's nothing, really." She hiccuped back a sob and shook her head. "I'll manage."

His stomach dropped. "What will you manage?" *And why?*

"Another job I set up before the lottery draw just canceled. I've kept a few clients, but everyone believes that when I become a princess I won't work, so…" She laughed but there was no humor in the sound.

When I become a princess.

Those words shouldn't matter, but his heart wanted to cling to them.

"Royalty works all the time."

"I know. But not an actual job. I worked so hard on the floor of that tiny apartment and in the rented office I had. The life I'd planned for myself, the life that was supposed to keep me safe, that was supposed to build a life away from my family name—it's slipping through my fingers."

She sucked in a breath and pressed her hand to her chest. "It was my purpose. What I was good at. I can't draw or create beautiful dresses out of my imagination. I don't feel called to write or work in a glass studio. But I can see other's visions and I can make it a reality for them. Take their hopes and dreams and create the path to success for them. Princesses don't run businesses is all people can see."

"What if you did run it?" Alessio ran his hand along her back. "What if you had your marketing firm and the crown?"

"What?" Brie looked at him, her eyes bright with so many questions.

There was no reason she couldn't work. No law prevented a princess from running her own business. He should be telling her that she could end this experiment now, end the relationship, but he didn't want to let her go.

"I love you." The words danced from his mouth. "You are my other half. I never expected that. I don't know what you feel or…"

Brie's hand landed on his lips. "I love you, too. I'm not sure how it happened or when. But I love you, Alessio."

"What if we announce later this week that you plan to run your marketing business from one of the palace's office suites? It might not be as big an operation as you planned before. We'll still have royal duties, after all. But I guarantee you clients will flock to your inbox."

"You mean it?" Brie wrapped her arms around his waist, leaning her head against his shoulder.

"Yes. You are a royal, or you will be. But that doesn't mean you can't be your own person." It didn't. Not for her. He'd find a way to make that the truth.

"So if I wanted my first client to be a glassworker whose art is magnificent…"

She could have a different life inside the gilded cage of the palace. He couldn't, but he wasn't going to argue that point now.

"Your first client will be Ophelia and she would definitely agree with me."

"She would." Brie laughed.

A knock echoed at his door.

Brie looked through the open door between their rooms. "Someone is looking for us."

"Jack. He has coffee, and a surprise for you."

"A surprise?"

"Yep. Do you want that or coffee more?" He winked, hoping the joke would make her smile.

It did.

"I always want coffee."

"Want or need?" Alessio grabbed her hand and pulled her through the door.

"Good morning, Your Royal Highness. I have coffee and—" Jack looked up from the coffee cart, pausing as he saw Brie standing next to Alessio. "Good morning, Ms. Ailiono."

"Brie, Jack. Just call me Brie."

Jack nodded, and Alessio watched Brie roll her eyes. The man's family had served royalty in European courts for more than a century. When they married, he'd call her Princess or

Your Royal Highness. He was raised in old-school protocol and would never shift.

Jack stepped back out of the room, and Brie headed toward the coffee tray. She poured herself a cup, added two sugar cubes and a dash of milk, then took a deep sip.

Alessio watched her sink into the morning ritual, knowing it was grounding her. Coffee was a thing Brie claimed to live for, but he suspected it was really her liquid safety blanket. A routine she needed.

"All right, I have the dress here." Jack stepped back into the room, carrying a dress bag that he quickly hung on the door of Alessio's closet.

"Dress?" Brie's eyes flew from the bag to Alessio.

"For tonight, Ms. Ailiono." Jack stepped up to the dress, but Alessio waved him off.

This was his surprise. Maybe it was selfish, but he wanted to do the reveal. Jack took the hint, offered a quick bow and left them alone.

"I have a dress for tonight. A simple blue dress your mother found. She said it matched my eyes."

"And she wasn't wrong." Alessio stepped to the dress bag. "But this one was made for you. I knew that the moment I saw it."

Brie raised a brow as she set her coffee cup down. "Saw it…"

He unzipped the bag.

Brie's breath hitched.

This was the moment he'd wanted. The realization. The understanding.

"The mermaid dress." Her hand was over her mouth.

"My mother is right—blue is lovely on you." He looked at her. Her eyes were so full of emotion, so full of love.

"It's over-the-top. I might get more press than King Sebastian." Brie giggled as she moved toward the dress.

"I suspect Sebastian would enjoy that. But in truth, it is his first state dinner. We are mere ornaments to this play."

Brie wrapped her arms around him, holding him. "You are always more than an ornament, Alessio. At least to me."

"That's more than enough."

That's more than enough.

Brie had replayed Alessio's words all day while she was prepped for the state dinner. Today was the first time she felt like she was truly acting the role of princess.

It was the role she'd play for the rest of her life. And she'd get to keep her business, too. She would stand beside the man she loved and work the career she craved. Alessio was making dreams she'd never considered come true. She didn't mind being the lottery bride, helping the country, if she still got to be herself.

"Wow."

Alessio's voice echoed in her soul as she turned to look at him.

"You look—"

"Not like myself!" Brie's giggle was too high-pitched.

Her body was a work of art, but she was a ball of nerves. Tonight was the first night in the real role she'd play as Alessio's life partner. It needed to be perfect.

A beauty technician had worked on nearly every part of her today. Her toenails were bright blue in the peep-toe shoes. Her fingernails were a light green.

The makeup artist the palace had hired had looked at the dress and squealed with excitement. The woman had spent nearly an hour highlighting and contouring while palace staff went over protocols with her.

"You look mythical."

"Mythical."

She looked in the mirror one last time. Her hair wasn't wet. In fact the braid looked almost like a crown, though she wouldn't wear one of those until they were married.

Still, she looked like a mermaid. It was what the dress was designed to do. Ophelia was truly an artist.

"Protocol talked with you?"

Ad nauseam!

The woman had prefaced that this was King Sebastian's night so many times that Brie had almost asked if she and Alessio could just skip the thing altogether.

"Yes. I run a tight ship on the outings I plan, but when the palace is in control…" It was next level. Tonight was not about Brie and Alessio. That had been made clear. "I promise not to outshine King Sebastian."

The tips of his lips tilted down, and Brie wanted to yank her words back.

This was Alessio's lived experience. He'd grown up the spare, always walking behind his father and his brother. There was a protocol for who was highest in the family.

"I'm sorry." She stepped toward him, reaching for his hands.

"You don't need to apologize. I'm sure that is what the office said. Though perhaps more diplomatically."

"*Diplomatically* is cutting." The words were out before she could think them through. Again.

"I just mean…" She blew out a breath. If this was a movie, she'd have a loose piece of hair to push out of her face or blow away. Instead, she was literal perfection. "Their words are very sweet. Controlled, yet…" She shrugged, not sure why she was trying to describe how listening to the protocol officer felt.

"Yet biting. A reminder that you aren't supposed to shine too brightly."

It was this attitude that had chased him to Scotland, but she was not going to let it happen around her.

"Alessio." She squeezed his hand. Today was the first time she'd heard the words *be smaller* since she stood by his side. Everything about her marketing campaign for the country was about blending into the background—but that was for a different purpose.

"Are you all right?" His fingers ran along her chin.

"Careful, you'll get glitter on yourself." She looked beautiful, but was it too much? Protocol had told her the lotto bride was taking a back seat this evening.

Lotto bride.

It was what she was and was the title she'd used with everyone before she and Alessio agreed to make it real. Now that their relationship was a fact, the tag felt like a slight.

And not just to her. But to Alessio.

"I don't care about some glitter." His thumb traced her jaw.

"I'm fine." It was true, but anger was overtaking the nerves she'd had all day. "But we need to find our own place after the wedding. We can still serve the throne, without actually living next to it. And I'll have my business to handle."

And he'd have his glasswork. He'd deflected her comment this morning, but she was going to find a way to get him regular time in his shop.

His eyes brightened and his smile made her want to strip the suit from his shoulders and spend the night luxuriating in the warmth it drove through her soul.

"I think that can be arranged, Princess."

A knock nearly made her jump. This was really happening.

"Ready, Your Royal Highness and Ms. Ailiono?" Jack's voice echoed from the other side of the door.

"Showtime." Alessio dropped his lips to hers.

They needed to get going, but Brie wrapped her arms around him, deepening the kiss. The world could wait a few moments longer. Alessio's hands stroked her lower back as she drank him in.

The glittery world she was about to step into was just for show. Her and Alessio, and the life they built away from the cameras, from the palace, from duty—that was reality. The reality she craved.

He broke the kiss as another knock came. "Duty awaits."

"So it does. Stay by me." Brie's skin felt slick as she wrapped an arm through his. She'd been in front of the cameras for weeks. There was no reason for tonight to feel different.

It did, though.

Because I love him.

"You are going to do great. I won't leave your side."

He'd be by her side. Brie could do this, and royal events would get easier...right? The shine would leave the lotto bride, but Brie was still enough. She was. *Right?*

She smiled and fell into step beside him. "I'm holding you to that, Prince Charming."

The room was warm—like all crowded events—but Alessio was hyperaware tonight. All eyes had flown to Brie when she stepped into the room. His heart had nearly exploded watching everyone's heads turn as she walked in.

Brie, his princess.

"Your fiancée is quite lovely." One of the ambassador's entourage smiled as he looked toward where Brie was talking to a few other dignitaries.

She looked over at him and nodded. He made sure that he was never more than a few feet from her.

"She is beautiful inside and out, and brilliant."

Brie was the most beautiful woman he'd ever seen. And her family had hoped to capitalize on that beauty by marrying her to a business associate. That was only one piece of her. One tiny, tiny piece.

Alessio loved every part of her.

"She will be the talk of this evening. The gown is something—a show." The man's words were cool, but Alessio heard the statement in them. Brie was the star.

That was a problem.

Sebastian was hosting. Sebastian was meant to be the focus.

"I am surprised she didn't post it on your social media page. It has been less active lately."

The man's gaze focused on Brie and the direction of the conversation gave him pause. It wasn't that it was less active; it was that there was less of him and Brie. It hadn't been conscious, at least he didn't think so, but as they grew closer, sharing private moments, kisses, felt off.

That was a worry for another day. Right now he needed to find a way to refocus the evening on his brother's success. This was Sebastian's event. Alessio nodded to the dignitary, his eyes moving subtly around the room.

He'd lost track of his brother.

Once, it had been Alessio ducking out of these events and Sebastian covering for him when he said something flippant. Since his return, Alessio had protected his brother, offering a response when Sebastian froze or said something glib.

His role was to support his brother, a role he wouldn't have yet if Alessio had stayed in Celiana. Still, Sebastian knew how to play this game. He'd been good at it, too. Once upon a time.

Heat flashed up his neck and Alessio took a deep breath. It wouldn't do any good for people to see his frustration.

Where was the king?

"Everyone will be talking about the princess tomorrow."

The words struck him, and he looked again for Sebastian, still not finding him. Would he be in one of Alessio's old hiding spaces or someplace new?

"And her dress! I've never seen such a creation."

The conversation floated over him as he kept looking over the crowd. Where was the king?

"Will you excuse me for a moment?" Alessio waited for the dignitaries to offer a polite response, looked toward Brie and was relieved to see she was fine. It was Sebastian he needed to find.

Alessio moved through the crowd, searching for the tall, dark-haired king. He should be easy to find.

"Alessio." His mother's voice was soft but urgent as she captured his arm.

He saw the same panic in her eyes that he was feeling. Sebastian had slipped away. From his first state dinner. This was…this was a nightmare.

"Can you please tell the ambassador about Celiana's tourism goals? It's one of my youngest's pet projects." Queen Mother Genevieve smiled, but Alessio knew she was close to breaking.

"Pet project?" The ambassador raised a brow.

His mother had already wandered off. Alessio shrugged. "My mother downplays my interest a little."

It wasn't intentional. He just wasn't the king. As the heir, he helped, but there was no expectation that he'd sit on the throne. So his projects became "pet projects," even if they were literally the saving grace of the kingdom.

"My fiancée and I are heavily invested in ensuring Celiana's future." Alessio saw his mother disappear through a side door. "Let me tell you all we've accomplished."

"Where have you been?" Alessio strode to his brother's side as he saw him enter the ballroom from a side door.

"I had some business to attend to with the ambassador."

"Really?" Alessio wanted to shake him. The lie was preposterous, and Sebastian had to know that. "I've been with the ambassador for the last hour. He is interested in discussing trade options with parliament tomorrow."

"Then I wasn't really needed anyway, was I?" Sebastian nodded and started to walk off. "You and your bride-to-be had everything handled."

Brie.

Alessio's body went rigid. He'd been so focused on the ambassador and finding Sebastian, he'd wandered away from her. She'd been on her own for more than an hour now, all because he'd had to play the role that was meant to be Sebastian's.

"You're the king." Alessio's tone was harsh. "Act like it."

"Baby brother." Sebastian clicked his tongue. "What would our father say to that?"

It was a low blow. A consequence of boys who were close, at least once. They knew where to hurt each other. Which was why it was so easy to respond.

"What would he say about the man wearing the crown after him?"

Sebastian's face blanched but he didn't back down. "I suspect we'd both be disappointments."

The words were soft, but Alessio heard the hurt under them. He opened his mouth, but no words flowed.

"Enough of whatever this is," the queen mother said as she stepped toward them. "Sebastian, the ambassador is ready for dinner. And Alessio, Brie is handling herself well enough."

Well enough. Palace-speak for something was wrong, but they weren't going to speak of it here.

"This is Brie's first official function besides the day of the lottery. I think she's done exceptionally well." Alessio saw his mother's eyes widen. Since returning, he'd never pushed back. Never did anything more than fulfill his duty.

Which he'd done tonight to cover for the king's absence.

"Celiana comes first." The queen mother's words were tight. "You both need to remember that. Remember your father's expectations."

Sebastian made a noncommittal noise and wandered to the door leading to the dining room. A small bell rang, and the crowd turned to look at the king.

His father's expectations were the reason Alessio left...and the reason he was back.

"It is my pleasure to welcome Ambassador Ertel. If you will follow me, I know the staff has prepared a delicious dinner."

Alessio moved quickly to Brie's side. She linked her arm in his, but her face was devoid of the excitement he'd seen earlier. Her jaw was tense, her shoulders were tight and he was nearly certain that she'd rubbed some of the makeup off her face.

"Brie?"

"I'm fine."

The words were quick and an answer to a question he hadn't asked.

There were too many ears here, but as soon as he had her someplace more private, he was going to discover what had stolen the light from her eyes.

CHAPTER TEN

BRIE OPENED HER EYES, knowing there was still at least an hour before the sun rose. Alessio snored softly on the pillow next to her. They'd arrived back from the state dinner long after midnight.

Exhausted physically and mentally, she'd washed the remainder of her makeup off and they'd fallen into bed. Alessio had wrapped his arm around her, and she'd bit back her questions as he slipped into dream world.

The questions were pointless anyway. She knew the answers. That was the problem.

It was a problem the morning made even more difficult to ignore.

Slipping from the bed, she padded softly back to her room. She needed to get dressed, make coffee and settle her nerves.

He'd broken his promise last night. He'd left her. And the wolves had feasted.

Making it clear that the public might love the tourist uptick from the princess lottery but the aristocrats—the ones who'd spent a lot of money to try to make their daughters princesses—were not as pleased.

People had whispered, in just a loud enough tone to be overheard by her, about everything. How much makeup she was wearing—clearly too much. The dress she'd chosen—an obnoxious choice suited to her *social media*. The words were whispered with such viciousness they'd made her ill.

She'd not posted the dress or the process of getting ready.

She'd thought of it, but it seemed too personal. Alessio had gifted her the dress because of their private time in Ophelia's shop. She'd wanted to hold to herself all the emotions that brought out. Perhaps that was a ridiculous statement for a princess.

More than one person had mentioned that she looked like she'd been trying to overshadow the king's event. The upstart lotto bride.

They insinuated she was stepping out of her sanctioned palace role to make herself and Alessio bigger, grander than they should be. Like she wanted to upstage the king.

And the king had disappeared…making her wonder if somehow, despite knowing how ridiculous it was, the words were true. Of course they weren't, but that didn't stop the pain of hearing them.

Her dress, the beautiful piece of artwork, was the talk of the event. She'd heard more than a few whispers and seen people with cameras snap a few shots when they thought she wasn't looking.

She'd been asked more than once if the palace had paid for the dress. She assumed the answer was yes, or perhaps Alessio had asked Ophelia to borrow it.

Then there'd been the not-so-subtle insinuations that she was nothing more than a stunt for the royal family. Those statements had flowed far too freely with Alessio's notable absence from her side.

Because of his absence.

The problem was that there was no way to deflect the "jokes," not when they were the truth. The fact that they'd fallen in love didn't change the fact that he'd pulled her name from a glass ball in a princess lottery that she'd joined as a marketing manager. That was the role she'd played for weeks now—blasting herself and Alessio across multiple social media platforms.

Without the princess lottery she'd still be in her tiny apartment, in comfy clothes, the rebel daughter of the Ailiono family. She'd have grown Ophelia's business, and her own, in a slower fashion. Hopefully.

The coldhearted truth of business was that success was not guaranteed, particularly when the most powerful business family in the country refused to talk to you. That meant she had a limited pool to prove success. More than half of new businesses collapsed within two years. Ophelia's was stable because of the lottery.

The reason everyone talked about Brie today was the lottery. And the words were less than kind when Alessio wasn't around to soften their tongues.

She left her room and headed for the media room. There was coffee there, and she needed to run some business plans past the few customers who'd stuck by her after her name was drawn. In a week or two she could tell them the plan for her to work as a princess. And there were videos to review of her and Alessio dancing last night that would work well for the social media campaign. With any luck one of them was relaxed enough for her to upload.

People had left more than a few comments that they wanted more of the prince and princess-to-be. A few weeks ago, Brie would have easily uploaded a playful kiss, or a video of them laughing. But as she grew closer to Alessio, those images—and she had many—felt too personal to give up for gossip.

She needed to do some marketing, though, a way to highlight the Ruins of Epiales they were visiting at the end of the week.

Turning the corner, she nearly ran into Jack. The man was flushed and holding several papers. A lifetime of reading body language made the hairs on the back of her head stand up.

"Ms. Ailiono."

"Jack." She watched him look at the papers then purposely away from her. "What's wrong?"

"Nothing." He was lying, trying to protect her.

"My brother always looked away when he was hiding something." At least he'd been that way when she'd seen him years ago. Perhaps now...

Focus, Brie.

"Ms. Ailiono." Jack's voice was so soft. But he didn't say any more.

"What's in the papers?" Brie crossed her arms. "Alessio is still sleeping, so why don't you accompany me to the media room? I need coffee, then you can tell me what I did wrong last night."

Pink invaded his cheeks as he pursed his lips. The truth was radiating from him.

"You need to work on your tells, Jack."

He didn't offer a retort, but he did turn and follow her.

She entered the media room and immediately headed for the coffee bar. "I'll assume this is a 'strongest blend I have' kind of morning?"

"I suspect it is, Ms. Ailiono."

He waited as the pot brewed and she doctored the blend. Turning with the mug in her hand, she pointed at the papers that were still in his hand.

"What's the damage?"

Jack looked at his feet, then back at Brie. "The dress."

"Was lovely," Brie stated, hating that Alessio's gift, the mythical creation he'd chosen just for her, was causing problems.

"Yes." Jack moved to one of the tables and started laying out the papers. All online posts, from blogs, gossip sites…and finally the most reliable paper in the country.

Ailiono Family Taking over Palace!

Soon-to-Be Princess Spends over One Hundred Thousand to Outshine King!

Princess Briella—Royal Stunt Turned Royal Money Pit!

Jack had even printed the first slide of an online video breaking down Brie's sparkly makeup. It included commentary about how a princess did not sparkle, at least not more than the king. In one night, she'd gone from Alessio's beloved fiancée to an upstart.

The lottery bride turned villain.

Because of a dress.

It was ridiculous, but women had been torn down for so much less. A feel-good story earned hundreds of clicks, while a hit piece earned thousands, sometimes millions. As a marketeer she understood the dynamics.

As the focus of the stories, they stung. What would happen when they announced her plans to work outside the palace? Would that be seen as an upstart move?

She moved the papers and saw one other post under the others.

"Oh, I didn't mean to include—"

She read the headline.

Prince Alessio Already Tiring of His Lotto Bride?

The first paragraph of the article was direct.

Prince Alessio was noticeably absent from his fiancée's side last night. Our sources can confirm that the prince spent less than three minutes beside his future wife during the cocktail hour. One source remarked that Briella looked for him several times. No doubt she is learning that having her name drawn from a crystal ball does not actually make a princess.

The door to the library opened but Brie didn't look up. Tears coated her eyes, and she didn't want Alessio to see them. Today was already going to be hard. They needed a plan, a strategy to make sure that their plans for Celiana didn't unravel.

And to clear my name.

"Brie! I was hoping to—" His voice cut off, likely because he registered Jack in the room.

"Your Royal Highness. There were some reports about last night."

"The press noticed Sebastian's absence." Alessio's voice was tight. "I tried to cover."

"No." Brie wandered to the coffeepot, poured herself another cup and made one for Alessio, mostly to give herself something to do. To collect herself.

"The press didn't notice the king's absence."

Brie's fingers shook as she waited for Jack to finish his statement, to drop the hammer.

"The commentary is about Ms. Ailiono."

"Oh. Not Sebastian?"

"No. Not Sebastian." Brie's voice was tight as she turned to look at him. She knew he was his brother's keeper. Sebastian was the reason he was home, the one he felt responsible for.

But he'd given her his heart…or at least that was what he'd said.

"Brie…"

"The press is quite focused on the dress."

"I'm sorry. All of this is over a dress? I mean, that sounds like a win, considering what they could be printing."

"What!" Brie turned, pressing her hands behind her against the counter, mostly to keep herself in place.

Alessio raised his hand. "I just mean that if we have to choose between them running reports about a missing king or getting too focused on a dress, the choice is easy."

Brie walked to the table, grabbed the report about him tiring of her and one discussing how much she'd spent of the palace's coin. She marched toward him, slapped the papers against his chest, then left.

Rationally she knew that he'd not seen the articles. She knew he was reacting to what sounded like a silly idea. But he'd broken his promise. She'd been nervous. She'd asked him to stay by her side. If he'd been there…

This was what they'd printed over a dress. This was just the beginning, and he was blowing it off to protect his brother.

Because that was why he'd come home, why the rebel had become the dutiful.

But where did that leave Brie?

Prince Alessio was noticeably absent from his fiancée's side last night.

The first line of that article cratered his soul. He'd left her. That was true. The rest of it was absolute rubbish.

He wasn't tiring of Brie. The exact opposite. He looked forward to each moment, craved her touch. He loved her.

And the dress. He pushed his hand through his hair as he stepped into yet another room where Brie clearly wasn't. For a woman who'd rarely exited the media room over the last several weeks, she'd found a way to make herself remarkably scarce.

The dress was his gift. No citizen's funds had paid for it. Hell, Brie hadn't even planned to wear it. It was a surprise, his gift to her on what was her first true royal engagement— at least in her mind, even if the country never realized she'd planned to leave.

His surprise had blown up in their faces.

Another door, another empty room. Was she purposely hiding from him?

But what was he to do? If Alessio was honest, there was nothing he could have changed about last night. Sebastian's absence was a bigger problem than a dress and observations about them not standing together in the hour before dinner officially started.

"Brother."

"Have you seen Brie?" The question was out before he'd even turned around.

"Good morning to you, too." His brother's brow furrowed as he moved toward him.

"I'm in no mood to play games, Sebastian. Have you seen Brie?"

"Not since last night."

"Do you even recall seeing her?" Alessio's tone was sharp, but he couldn't stop the frustration filling him. "After all, you weren't in attendance for a sizable portion of *your* event."

Color coated Sebastian's cheeks.

He'd aimed his words and they'd landed. His brother should have been there. It was his responsibility. Whether he wanted it or not.

"You covered well." Sebastian crossed his arms.

Righteous anger seemed to boil in his soul. He tried taking a deep breath but that did nothing to stop the fury. The man he'd been warred with the man he'd become after his father passed—and the first won.

"Where the hell were you?"

"I needed a break." Sebastian shrugged as though it was nothing.

"A break. A *break*!" Stars exploded in his eyes. What the hell?

Sebastian rocked on his heels but didn't step away. "Don't you ever need a break, brother? A break from the pressure pushing against your chest, shaking fingers, each breath more ragged than the next."

"Not since I returned." Alessio heard the deep wounds in his brother's description, and maybe if he knew where Brie was, if he knew she was all right, if he knew she hadn't left him, he might feel more understanding.

"Well, I don't have the benefit of getting to run away!"

Run away, pushed away, left for nothing until the crown wanted something of him. All those were words the man he'd been wanted to scream at Sebastian. But none of that was his brother's fault.

"You were born to be the king." They were their father's words, which Alessio had heard him state so often to his brother. They were whispered with as close to affection as their father got.

"What a prize." Sebastian looked at his feet, then back at

Alessio. "If there was a path for abdication, the crown would be yours tomorrow. Then we'd see what you think of it." Then his brother turned on his heel and walked off.

"Sebastian!" Alessio understood the pressure. It wasn't the same for him, but he wasn't the person he wanted to be, either. Not anymore. At least he'd gotten a three-year reprieve. Sebastian would never get one.

"I'm sorry. I just need to find Brie. The press... I need to find her."

The king paused, and for a moment Alessio feared he wouldn't turn around.

"What did they say?" Sebastian started back toward him.

Rather than answer, Alessio held out the papers.

Sebastian read them, his brows rising at certain points. "These aren't nice, but—" He shrugged. "The palace's response is not to comment."

He knew that. The standard response was no response... unless it was about the king. The palace had squashed a few stories about their father, and more than one story about Sebastian's recent playboy lifestyle.

Alessio and Brie were not given the same treatment.

"I know. But Brie still needs comfort." She needed him this morning, and his mind had gone to where it always went since he returned home. The throne.

"Your bride is in the gardens. In tears," his mother said as she stepped from her rooms. Only her presence made him aware of where he was. He'd clearly been too focused on finding his fiancée to realize that he was so close to his mother's suite.

"Palace sources?" Sebastian sighed.

"Sources? Please, Sebastian. If you paid attention, gave anyone but the women you chase attention, people would tell you what you needed to hear, too." Genevieve had cultivated her staff well. She was their queen mother and employer, but she treated each member of the staff with absolute respect. It earned her their respect.

Alessio was trusted, too, but he was the spare, the one people bowed to but never paid as much attention to. It was the position he'd grown up in, the one he'd finally accepted when he came home.

"Which garden?" Alessio asked.

He didn't need to stay for whatever dressing-down his mother planned for his brother.

"Main courtyard."

"Thanks." He took off.

"No running in the halls."

He heard his mother's call but didn't slow his pace. He needed Brie.

Now.

He heard her sob before he saw her. She was sitting under a cherrywood tree, the stuffed animal Emilio had returned beside her. A set of notebooks was in front of her.

If she wasn't crying, the scene would be almost picture-perfect.

"Brie? Sweetheart?"

"Come to apologize?" Her voice wavered but the words were clearly a demand.

"Yes." He should have registered that she was upset, should have taken a few moments to comfort her before gently explaining that this was part of their role, too.

Sometimes he was the distraction—if it benefited the crown.

It was what he had to do. But by tying herself to him, she'd be expected to have the same role. The idea was a bitter pill as he slid to the ground, taking in her tearstained cheeks and red eyes.

"I'm so sorry, Brie."

She looked at him, her blue eyes still swimming with tears. Cocking an eyebrow, she raised her chin. "For...?"

"For not taking a moment to read the situation. For rushing to say that it was better that the press discusses a dress than Sebastian."

"Are you sorry for saying it, or sorry that it's true?"

"Brie—"

"I'm an Ailiono, whether my family wishes to claim me or not. I've been a sacrificial lamb before. How often will I have to do it here?"

Her words were daggers, sharpened weapons that struck with such precision.

"I don't know." Hiding that truth was not going to work.

"And what about when I'm working—will that be a host for gossip to redirect eyes from the palace?"

Working. Her company.

That was what this was really about, and there was more than a bit of jealousy in his chest that she'd asked about it. This wasn't really about them.

Maybe he should let her go, let her chase her dreams, relish the fact that he'd gotten more time than he deserved with a woman who made him feel whole.

The words to release her refused to appear. Instead, he said what was truly on his mind.

"You're my heart, Brie. All of it will work out. There will be hiccups and days that the barbs hurt. We just have to let the noise float away."

"Float away. Sticks and stones can break your bones, but words can never hurt you." She wrote something in the journal in front of her without looking at him.

"Words hurt. That schoolyard rhyme was made to make bullies feel better, not because it contains an ounce of truth." He leaned forward and put his hand on her knee. "Brie, look at me."

She raised her head. Shadows hovered under her eyes. She was clenching her teeth but there was a hint of something in her gaze. A hope.

"I can play games. I grew up in them." She held up a hand before he could say something to that sad statement.

"Some might even say that as a marketeer, I'm a professional game player, making people believe that they need something or that their life will be better with such and such product. It's a skill, and I am good at it."

"Brie…"

"What I will not accept is being second with you." Her bottom lip trembled. "With you, I need to be first. *Our* dreams and goals need to be first. I could have come with you last night. If the headlines were 'Prince Alessio and Briella Ailiono Taking Too Much of Ambassador's Time' or 'Spare and His Lotto Bride Stealing King's Show,' I'd shrug my shoulders."

She reached for his hand. It was warm as she squeezed him, grounding them in the garden.

"I spent my childhood as a pawn to my family's ambitions. I fell for you, Alessio. I want to be by your side, but we get to have our own dreams, too."

"We do. We do, Brie. I promise."

He should have pulled her with him last night. He should have stayed by her side. She was right; they could have talked to the ambassador together. The stories likely would have read exactly as she stated.

"We are a team. Promise."

"All right. Apology accepted." She pressed her lips to his. "Now we have to focus on the next problem."

"Next problem."

"Yep." She flipped the notebook around. "You were noticeably absent from my side."

"I read the article, Brie."

"Good. Then you know that in the first instance we had that wasn't controlled by us, you looked like you didn't want me. We'd posted less on my social media as…"

Her cheeks brightened.

He dropped a kiss to her lips. "As it became real?"

"Yeah." Brie ran her hand along his jaw. "So how do we shift the narrative back to the lovebirds, without throwing your brother under the well-deserved bus?"

* * *

"What is this I hear that Briella will work when she puts on the crown?"

His mother's words weren't harsh, but he could hear the steel in them. He wasn't sure which of the queen mother's staff had overheard and passed on the conversation, but it hardly mattered.

Alessio looked to the media room. He'd only just patched things over. She was planning their next steps and he was getting her coffee. This wasn't the time for the conversation, but one rarely got exactly what they wanted behind the palace walls.

Brie would, though. Somehow, he'd find a way to give her the choices she needed and the dreams she deserved.

"Brie plans to run the marketing firm she had before all this. It won't be for profit, though she plans to complete the work for the companies that have already contracted her."

Brie had told him that the few companies who'd taken a risk on her, and stayed on following the lotto bride announcement, deserved her to finish what they'd contracted. After that, her focus would be on the tourism industry and nonprofits.

It was a brilliant idea. One that would endear her to the country even more.

"That is not a good idea."

"Mother—"

She held up her hand and Alessio bit his tongue.

"Maybe in a few months. But right now, after last night, it will look like she is seeking freedom from the palace."

Freedom.

The thing Brie had craved her entire life. The thing she deserved.

"I fail to see how working during our union is seeking freedom from the palace."

Except he knew how the optics would look. Rather than doing "royal" duties, Brie would focus on her company. He could argue that the nonprofit work was an excellent royal duty, but it was different. And different was not something the royal family sought out.

"She will have too many duties. Your father took on too much. If you had stepped up sooner…"

Her words trailed off, but Alessio knew the ending. *Your father might still be here.*

The queen mother looked at the day calendar she carried, despite the staff switching to phones and tablets years ago.

"I have to see to some things. Let Brie know it won't work, Alessio. Your brother needs your help. It's not fair to give her dreams that cannot be delivered."

His mother turned and glided down the hall, the sweep of her shoulders just a hair off. *What dreams had she given up for Celiana?* That was a question she'd never answer.

But Brie was going to get her dream. It might take him longer to figure it out. A delay was necessary. That was all.

Or I could set her free.

The thought rocked his soul. Maybe it was the right answer. She could still have her dreams, outside the palace, without the royal life holding her back.

Alessio looked to the door of the media room and shook his head. No. There was a way for her to have it all. Maybe just not right away.

CHAPTER ELEVEN

"HERE WE GO!"

Brie waved to the camera as Alessio held her close. It should feel nice, should be lovely. Maybe it would, if it felt real. When the camera was off, they did fine—sort of. Alessio had pulled away since the state dinner earlier this week. It felt like there was an answer he wasn't giving. Or maybe she just hadn't asked the right question.

No matter what she tried, it felt like there was a wall between them, and she had no idea how to strip it down.

"Will that one work?" Alessio's sigh echoed in the car as they pulled up to the Ruins of Epiales.

They hadn't had as many redo moments since the first week. Brie looked at the video and knew it wouldn't work. They looked like robots, not two people in love. It would just fuel the conversations already running wild.

"No." She bit her lip and kissed him. He softened in her arms. The two of them were becoming as close to one as possible in the back of the car. This was the moment they needed to capture, but she also hated sharing it when it felt like the only time they were close was when the camera wasn't an option.

"How about you do one as we head to the moors?"

She nodded, kissed him again, knowing that wouldn't be best but it was better than the video they had. She stepped out of the car and shivered.

The Ruins of Epiales always felt chilly to Brie. The old palace and fortress of Celiana had been built around the same year as the Roman Colosseum. It was in worse shape than the giant structure in Italy, but there were still identifiable walls and a sanctuary.

Epiales, the personification of nightmares according to the Greeks, wasn't worshipped here, but according to legend, the ruler of Celiana had dreamed of invasion in the year AD 300. It was a nightmare he hadn't believed until it had come true.

"We're at the Ruins of Epiales today!" Brie waved to the camera, then panned to the ruins, making sure to capture a shot of Alessio while avoiding the security detail that was always just far enough away to give the illusion of aloneness.

The ruins' historical records were minimal, though archaeologists agreed that the area had been ransacked and burned. The place certainly harbored nightmare energy, but whether anyone had experienced nightmares before the area was destroyed, no person walking the earth for generations had known.

"This is an impressive site." Brie turned the camera back to herself and tried to ignore the unease. It *was* an impressive site, but its vibes always felt off to her. It wasn't something Brie could put into words. "Into archaeology? Or hikes in unique locations? Then this is the site for you." Brie smiled, then shut off the video and hit Upload.

That would have to work.

Whatever the general dread of this place was, it felt stronger today. She ached to wrap her arms around herself as she and Alessio followed the guide.

She had to pull away from the creeping dread that had followed her since the day after the state dinner three days ago.

The seismic shift had rattled the very foundation of her soul.

A week ago, she'd have stepped into Alessio's arms, walked hand in hand with him, joked about the icky feeling this place gave her or made some silly, or spicy, joke to lighten the creepy mood of the ruins.

Now, though…

She looked ahead. He was only a foot or so in front of her.

Brie could reach her hand out and touch him. The small physical distance was highlighting the chasm she felt growing between them.

The worst part was that Brie knew she should do it. That was the plan they'd hammered out in the garden: ignore the press and be as they were. She should reach for him, make the jokes, put the smile on. Play the game. After all, the papers were already running wild with speculation that the lottery stunt was coming to an end.

And once more the papers were focused on one thing. The mermaid dress was old news. Now all the press could talk about was the lack of a ring on her engagement finger.

Even now she absently rubbed the empty finger. Alessio had offered her a choice of rings when they'd started this stunt, but she'd not wanted one. Somehow that would have made this real.

Now that it was real, now that everyone was noticing, Brie couldn't help but feel the slight even if Alessio hadn't meant anything by leaving her without an engagement ring. In fact they'd discussed it last night. And he'd worried how it would look if they chose one while all of this was going on.

He was right.

But he'd also recommended holding off on announcing that she'd be keeping her marketing firm. Just until this blew over. There was no need to spin up more scandal.

They were the right words, too. She knew that, knew that it would be more illustration that their relationship was nothing more than a glorified marketing campaign for the country.

The irony that this was how it had started was far from lost on her.

Still, it felt like there was more to the story. There was something he wasn't telling her. Or maybe she was looking for cracks. Whatever it was, they weren't the same as they'd been.

And everyone was noticing. They'd not been acting before, not trying to tell a story. It had come naturally, a gift she'd not recognized until it was gone.

Now they needed to tell the story. They needed to quash the rumors, the cutting looks, the whispers. Now was the time to play the role of prince and future princess.

And it should be such an easy story to tell. They didn't have to pretend.

"This place is glorious." Alessio breathed in as they stepped to another section of the ruins. "Sad, but glorious."

"Yes." Brie nodded, happy to have some conversation other than the thoughts her mind was supplying.

"You can envision how beautiful it must have been just after it was completed." Her words were right, but they felt off. Stiff. Like she was talking to a tourist rather than the man she loved.

Alessio moved, and for a moment she thought he was reaching for her, looking for her hand.

But before he connected, the tour guide stated, "If you close your eyes, you might even feel the spirits."

Alessio turned and a chill slipped down Brie's back. As a rule she didn't put much credence in ghosts. However, she never quite ruled them out, either.

It would be nice to pretend it was the ghouls sending cool air racing across her skin, rather than the empty feeling of watching Alessio stuff his hands back in his pockets as he followed the guide's instructions.

Closing his eyes, he stood perfectly still. The wind blew his hair, and Brie drank him in. He was gorgeous, though the wear of the last few days was visible, too.

The lines around his eyes, the hint of darkness under them and the pinch of his jaw… The image he showed the world of the relaxed, dutiful prince was absent.

At least to her knowledgeable eyes.

Neither of them were sleeping well.

Her brain refused to turn off. It kept replaying the horrid headlines that graced websites and the few printed papers still around. It whispered terrible things, usually in the sound of her mother's voice.

She'd gone from the lotto princess bride to the interloper in one night. With one dress.

And the palace had said nothing. Alessio had said nothing. They didn't want to throw the king under the bus, though Brie wouldn't have minded doing it.

But couldn't Alessio have said that he bought her the dress as a gift? Couldn't they have issued some joint statement, been a team united instead of the quiet pair they'd become?

Their silence just fueled the questions she now heard peppered through crowds meeting them. The frowns she saw were difficult to ignore. And they seemed to chase slumber away.

As a result, Alessio was constantly shifting with her movements. She'd even mentioned moving back to her bed if her tossing was keeping him up. He'd declined each offer. That warmed her heart. He wanted her in his bed.

But that didn't chase the worries away that he was hiding something.

"I don't feel anything." He opened his eyes and grinned.

"Really?" Brie found that difficult to believe. Maybe he didn't feel ghosts, but the air felt…heavy, like the general vibe between them. There were so many things to feel.

"Do you?"

"I feel cold." The words came out before she could think them through. She bit her lip and tried to force a smile, tried to make things feel normal between them.

"The wind off the ocean is a bit biting."

Alessio tilted his head and looked at their guide, who'd given them a little space. It wasn't a lot, not enough privacy that they could have a real conversation. And the Ruins of Epiales were not the right place anyway.

He stepped closer and she waited for his arms to wrap around her. She waited to be pulled close…but the moment didn't come.

"We can leave. The press got a few pictures of us arriving, you put up the video and this is probably a pretty niche tourist location. Not sure anyone is visiting Celiana just for this place."

The ruins were interesting, if you were already on the island, but tourists seeking these kinds of places had far more exceptional locations to visit.

"Do you want to leave?" She buried her hands in her pockets. If he wasn't reaching for her, then she wouldn't reach for him.

"Brie—" Alessio shifted, opening his mouth and closing it before saying whatever was on his mind.

Then looked back at their guide. "The princess is a little chilly. I think we're going to cut this outing a bit short."

"Of course." The guide nodded, but Brie saw the hint of something in his eyes—a note of glee, or excitement. It was wiped away by a soft smile so fast she was sure she'd misread it.

Stop looking for worries, Brie!

If only her brain would listen.

The guide started back down the path to where their car was waiting. Alessio looked at her, his jade eyes seeming to bore into her soul, then he stepped to the side and started down the hill after the guide.

She sucked back a sob. Something needed to shift, needed to change; they couldn't continue like this. But what if asking the questions shattered her heart?

What if it's already shattered?

Brie looked out at the ruins one last time. The once beautiful location had been worn away by time and fire. She wrapped her arms around herself, then straightened her shoulders.

She was in charge of her life. That hadn't changed just because she'd fallen in love with Prince Alessio.

Turning, she followed the path Alessio had taken. Had he even noticed that she wasn't right behind him?

Alessio stared at the empty path and tried to determine if he needed to go after Brie. Or would that make the already uncomfortable divide between them larger?

He'd thought she was right behind him. After all, she'd said she was cold.

And rather than pull her close, I said we should leave.

Because pulling her close felt off, like it was for show. Behind closed doors they were better than in public, but not as good as they'd been. She'd agreed to delay announcing her plans to work, and he hated that he hadn't told her what his mother had said.

Alessio felt like he was acting. He felt like everything was for a show he no longer wanted to star in. He wanted Brie, not the drama, not the pain he suspected the palace would inflict on her someday.

And the guide was clearly planning to sell the story of today. Alessio had seen it in the man's eyes. He should have acted for the guide, should have pulled Brie close, but to do it just for the show... No, he hadn't wanted to give the guide anything.

Throughout his life, he'd gotten good at telling who was genuinely interested in talking with him, hanging out with him, and who was looking for a way to earn a few quick bucks selling royal stories. Maybe it wasn't fair to the tour guide, but from the second he and Brie had stepped onto the path, the man had watched them. And not in the friendly manner he'd seen on so many of their trips.

There'd been no questions and no friendly banter. Instead, it felt like the guide was memorizing the story he wanted to sell. And the Brie and Alessio that had been on display a few weeks ago had vanished. They needed to be the fun-loving couple they'd been, but the pressure to show it had sucked the joy from their love.

And that reminded him why he'd run from this place to begin with. The palace could start a narrative, could seed the story, but it was ultimately out of their hands how people received it. And by loving him, Brie was trapped in the same web he'd spun himself.

That wasn't fair.

"Prince Alessio, I thought Brie looked gorgeous in her gown last week."

The small voice in the crowd made him smile. Turning, he saw a teen leaning over the barrier.

"I thought she did, too."

A reporter stepped in front of the teen. "Do you think your father would have approved? Would he have been happy that your brother's first state dinner was refocused onto your lottery bride's fantastic expenditure?"

"My father always put Celiana first. I am sure he would be happy that his sons continue to do the same."

It was a stock answer. There was nothing Alessio and Sebastian could do to please their father. Or maybe they could have, if they'd done more. Sebastian might not have been able to do more, but his mother was right. Alessio could have stepped up sooner.

"We want a real answer, Prince Alessio. Would your father have approved of Princess Briella Ailiono?"

No. Brie wanted her business. He wanted that for her, but his father would not have understood. She wanted choices, and he was dreading how many the palace would strip away.

"Briella is *my* princess." It wasn't a lie and not an answer, either.

"Then where is she?"

She rounded the bend in the path, and he felt his body relax a little. Once again, he'd left her. And once more it wasn't intentional. He'd started walking and reached the car before realizing she hadn't followed. It wasn't nefarious. That didn't remove the shame, though.

"She was enjoying a few private moments in the ruins." Alessio pushed off the car and closed the distance between them.

He reached for her and saw her eyes widen as he took her in his arms. "You enjoy a few moments alone?" He dropped a kiss on her nose, then squeezed her tightly.

It was the first time that he'd held her in public in days. His soul was thirsty with need, but his heart was also raging at the injustice that their relationship had shifted.

Brie smiled but didn't answer as they walked back to the car. He moved to put his hand around her waist, but she stepped away. "Brie—"

She waved to the crowd, then opened the door and slid into the car.

Alessio offered another wave to the crowd before following his bride.

"Brie, I thought we were supposed to be trying to reignite the love story. Make them believe. People are asking hard questions…"

Were there worse words to speak?

"I am not a pawn. You reached for me because everyone was there—"

"No. I was worried."

"And yet you didn't come looking for me. Because then they would have asked about that, right?" She leaned her head against the headrest. "We get to decide our story, Alessio. Us!" Her blue eyes flew open as she gestured between the two of them. "Even if they misread it. It's our story. Ours!"

"I'm sorry, Brie. That was the worst way to say that. I just…" He paused, then decided to just go with the truth. "I'm lost."

"Lost." Brie repeated the word. "I guess that's as good a word as any for whatever is happening."

"So what do we do about it?"

"We talk." Brie laughed, though there was no trace of humor. "About real things. We stop worrying about the cameras…at least as much as we can."

"What do you want to talk about?"

She opened her mouth, then closed it.

He watched her shift, watched her battle back her discomfort.

"What aren't you telling me?" The words were soft, but her hands gripped his. "What are you holding back?"

Alessio took a deep breath. Of course she'd noticed. "My mother doesn't think you working, you keeping the company, is a good idea." The words were out. Now he waited for the anger, the frustration.

Brie nodded. "So the delay is more a not-happening if the queen mother has her way? Does your mother have that power?"

She didn't look angry, just concerned.

"Not directly."

"Does your brother?" Brie tilted her head. "After all, you left the island for years."

It wasn't that simple. Not anymore. He owed Sebastian. Royal duties took up time, and his brother didn't have a spouse to carry the load. He didn't want his brother to feel like he had to do everything. Maybe that wasn't fair, but it felt like a debt he needed to pay.

"I will find a way to make it work."

That was a promise he was keeping. He wasn't sure how yet. But Brie was going to work in marketing. She was. He loved her and she was great at this.

Maybe he'd gone into the bride lottery only looking for a bride willing to play the role, but he'd found a partner. He didn't want to lose that.

"I don't need a way to make it work, Alessio. We can make it work, just by saying it, if *we* say it—as a team."

"A team," Alessio repeated.

He wanted it to be that easy, but the palace...the duty he'd stepped back into... Alessio didn't control his own destiny. He never really had.

"Yes. As a team. But you must focus on the next thing. You deserve freedom, too. I know that doesn't look like Scotland anymore. But you have to be you. Your own person, not Sebastian's helper or the dutiful prince."

Brie raised a hand to his cheek. "What is your next thing? The thing that you choose when this is over? Your glass—"

He couldn't think of his glass studio. Not now. This was his life. It was what he owed his family, not the dream he'd had once upon a time. "That dream is over. I know you look for the next thing. Because you had to when your family threw you out."

"My family did not throw me out. I left. I chose a new adventure, and I am begging you to choose one, too. We can't be Prince Alessio and the lottery bride forever. So what's next, Alessio? What does our life look like for us?"

"I don't know."

"I know." Brie leaned over and kissed his cheek. "But you need to find your dream outside the title of Prince Alessio. The dutiful heir can only be one part of the story. We deserve to carve our own path. Together."

He raised his hand to her face, like he could magically force the touch to remain forever. Like he could chase loss and fear and everything else away.

CHAPTER TWELVE

ALESSIO ROLLED OVER, his hand brushing Brie's empty pillow. He stretched and looked around. Had she not slept here?

She'd been watching a reality television show when he'd yawned last night. She'd said she'd come in shortly, but…

Alessio slipped from their bed and started to head through the interconnecting door when a knock echoed through his room. He glared at the door. Early morning knocks never meant anything good.

He considered ignoring it. Finding Brie was all his heart wanted to do, but duty stayed his desires.

"Jack." Alessio wasn't surprised to see his assistant at the door. Nor did the mountains of papers the man was carrying shock him. The trip to the ruins had been a nightmare.

At least they'd lived up to their name. He wasn't a giant believer in prophecy, but perhaps that place truly was cursed.

"Where is Ms. Ailiono?"

"I don't know." Alessio pinched the bridge of his nose, hoping she might step through the door connecting their rooms. Or sprint in with a mug capable of carrying a full pot of coffee. Anything.

"The papers are all running some variation of the same story." Jack laid out several articles on Alessio's desk.

An image of Brie standing alone at the ruins was at the front of each story. Her hair was whipping in the wind, and it looked like a tear was falling across her cheek.

She looked lonely. Terribly lonely.

"Each article has the same statement from Ms. Ailiono."

"Statement from Brie?" Alessio grabbed one of the papers Jack had printed out, his heart sinking as he read.

On the day of the lottery draw Briella Ailiono intentionally chose a dark dress for the occasion, when most of the potential brides were wearing white, gold or cream. She was quoted as saying that "Dark colors are best when love dies."

When the reporter joked with the marketeer, "Guess you won't cry if your name doesn't come out today?" Ms. Ailiono stated, "I'll cry if it does."

The princess-to-be never wished to join the royal family. If this picture is any indication, the first weeks of the "romance" were a show.

Prince Alessio deserves a bride who wishes to be by his side. It's clear Briella Ailiono is not a good fit.

Something her estranged family found out years ago.

The last line was a low blow. Most of the island looked at the Ailiono family with a mixture of fear and disgust. The rich patriarch and matriarch cared little for the island, except for how to invest for their own benefit.

They'd thrown their daughter's stuff out without thought when redoing her room. Only Emilio's kindness had saved some of her precious things.

But the article was full of truth, too.

She'd never wanted to be his princess. Or anyone else's. She'd not hidden that fact from him. He'd been that person before.

He'd stood alone.

It would only get worse. He knew that. Brie was in love with the man who'd never sit on the throne, the one destined to be the spare as soon as his brother married and produced an heir. Then Alessio would slip further down the line of succession, but his duties would still be to the family.

He was not the prize the lottery had made him out to be. He'd unintentionally turned the woman he loved into a villain by focusing on his duty to Sebastian and the memory of his father. Brie deserved so much more than that.

I'll cry if it does.

He ran his finger over those words, then over the image of her crying. She'd not lied.

What's next?

Her question from yesterday had haunted his dreams and it seemed to echo from the paper.

It was time to respond. Forcefully. He had to demonstrate that the palace was behind her. Behind them.

There was another knock…or rather a pounding…at the door.

"Come in, Sebastian."

His brother entered, with their mother close on his heels.

"I used to knock like that. I thought you had more decorum, brother."

Sebastian stretched his arms. "I think you have enough decorum for us both now."

The joke fell flat as their mother crossed her arms. "This isn't the time for jests."

"Any time is a time for a joke." Sebastian yawned.

"That just wasn't a very good one." Alessio looked at his phone. There was no message from Brie.

"Boys."

Both Alessio and Sebastian straightened quickly. They might be grown men, but that didn't stop their inner child from responding.

"We need to draft a response. Brie can help craft it."

It would be a first. The palace would be responding to gossip, but it was time.

Alessio looked to his brother—the king of Celiana. Sebastian knew their father wouldn't have approved of commenting. He'd have ignored it completely or privately encouraged the discourse to distract from Sebastian's lackluster start to his rule.

But Sebastian sat on the throne now.

"I was married to your father for forty-three years." Their mother sucked in a deep breath. "He would have told you what a foolish statement that was."

She was right, but Alessio's eyes never left his brother. He was the king now. That didn't come with political power, but influence. Influence he could wield.

If he wanted.

"The lottery is being called a stunt, a scam, and now Briella is on record saying she never wanted to be the princess." Sebastian pulled his hand across his face, the same motion their father had made when frustrated. "We do need to issue a response. One that shuts all the narrative down."

Alessio could see the old Sebastian returning before his eyes, could see the man trying to finally step into their father's shoes. Why did it have to be this moment?

"You called it a stunt first. I seem to remember you being happy when Brie said she wouldn't marry me the day after the lottery."

"It was a stunt. If you two hadn't played the lovebirds so well, extracting yourselves would be easier. But hell, you made them believe the two of you were in love. Made them believe the story—either this is a lovers' fight or far worse. A scam on the island's goodwill."

We are in love.

Alessio kept those words buried.

"We move the marriage up." Sebastian pulled out his phone, typed a few things, then pulled up a calendar. "Does three weeks from tomorrow work?"

Alessio knew his mouth was hanging open. Those were words he'd never expected from Sebastian's mouth.

"No words, brother?"

His brain was full of words, but none that wanted to push their way into existence.

"We rush the wedding. Should anyone ask, it's because the two of you are tired of this kind of press. You just say you can't wait any longer to be man and wife."

"Husband." Alessio pulled his hand over his face.

"Excuse me?"

"It's husband and wife. Not man." Alessio didn't know why Sebastian's wording disturbed him so. But it wasn't just Brie taking on a new title. It was Alessio, too.

"Brie—" Alessio tried to find some words. "What if Brie doesn't want to rush the nuptials? She and I had a deal." Sebastian had laughed at their agreement when Alessio told him.

But that was his brother, the man uncertain of the role thrust upon him. And that man was no longer standing in front of him.

"She signed a contract. And you told me that the deal was off if it brought scandal to the island. We are dangerously close to that. Tourism is how our people survive. You didn't have to come back, but you did. You are the heir to the throne and sacrifices must be made."

"I came back for you. I came because I thought I owed Father."

"And you did. You owe a duty to the crown. Like it or not. You weren't here to help your father. He took on everything for this country." His mother's words were tight. The strain in her eyes ripped through him. Maybe she had loved him.

"You were born royal. That is who you are. The path you walk." Her fists were tight. "Your father gave you both as much time as he could. Step into the roles he wanted for you. For this kingdom."

The path he'd been born to—this was why Alessio didn't make wishes. His destiny had been laid out before he'd taken his first breath.

Sebastian straightened, raising his chin. Now it was his king before him. He was truly stepping into the role, and Alessio wished he wasn't. "If lovebirds can visit the Ruins of Epiales and break up, then we are a cursed island. You reawakened the imagery of an island of love—so if this fails, then we will watch parts of this island fail. Our people may have to emigrate. They might lose everything. Heaven knows her family will gobble up any property they can get."

Sebastian took a deep breath. "So, get her on board. Or come up with another brilliant plan to fix this."

With the final command, his brother stepped out of the room.

His mother looked at the door. Sebastian hadn't slammed it shut; instead, he'd closed it with cool effectiveness. Just like their father.

"He's right." The queen mother stepped to Alessio's side. "You chose this, and so did Brie. Maybe she didn't expect it, but the contract was nearly ironclad."

She kissed his cheek. "Your father and I made do. You two will, too."

"Celiana comes first."

She smiled as he repeated the mantra he'd heard from his earliest memories.

"I need to find Brie."

His mother nodded and stepped out of the room. Alessio looked to the pillow where she'd not rested last night, and his heart broke.

He wanted to meet Brie at the altar. He wanted her to be his wife, but this…

Perhaps a rushed wedding was right for Celiana—but that didn't mean it was right.

The best thing he could do for the woman he loved was set her free.

Brie sighed as another text came in from Ophelia.

Last night she'd fallen asleep in the chair while bingeing reality television. She'd been trying to relax and clear her brain—but it hadn't really worked. Ophelia's first text broke the barely there slumber she'd achieved.

It had a link—the first of many her friend sent. The reporter's words worried Ophelia, and she even offered to break Brie out of the palace.

The article didn't worry her. No, it was pure fury racing through Brie as she read each line. She'd sent a note to Nate, off the record, to let him know how low it was to sell her statements without at least reaching out for comment.

He'd reached out for comment then. Brie had laughed and hung up.

So far this morning, she'd gotten more than fifteen texts and three phone calls, and her email inbox was full. Several of the accounts that dropped her were letting her know that they'd be willing to renegotiate the contracts if the wedding was off.

In other words…you're going to be a big story and we can profit off it since it looks like you might have some free time coming.

As a marketing strategy, it wasn't half bad.

"Brie." Alessio's voice was strained, so he'd seen the articles.

It was cowardly to have hidden away, but she'd been trying to figure out a plan. Something to fix the blazing headlines. Something to help him figure out what was next. Something to let him see a path besides being the scapegoat for things he couldn't control. His father's death wasn't his fault. He'd returned and done a good job.

Alessio still needed something more than the crown. He needed his own thing. The lottery bride scheme would always be tied to what he felt he owed his father. And his life was bigger than that.

"So, it's been a morning, huh?" Her phone buzzed, and he looked at her pocket.

"Everybody and their brother seems to be reaching out this morning. I even had a company offer me a position, if I wasn't getting married." That email had been wild. The staffer had indicated that she could come on as soon as she liked.

We already have the press release written.

"Maybe you should take it."

Brie blinked; her mind was blanking on his response. He couldn't be serious. Yes, there were bad headlines, the image worse, but together they could fix it. Together.

"No." Brie was going to keep a calm head. She wasn't going to shout or scream or demand he take back that hopefully flippant statement. "We release a statement."

Her phone dinged again, and she grabbed it from her pocket. "Ophelia is texting every three minutes." Brie didn't plan to read the note, just silence the phone. But her eyes caught the words wedding in three weeks, followed by angry emojis.

She opened the text, read it, then looked at the man she loved. "Why is Ophelia asking if I am getting married in three weeks? She says the king reached out personally."

"Sebastian says that this is a scandal. That if lovers can visit the Ruins of Epiales and look as we did, then the island is cursed."

"That is a reach." However, given the headlines, she understood the king's concern. At least partly. It was why she'd been working all morning to find a solution.

Getting married in three weeks was not the solution.

"Well, since that isn't happening, what are we going to do?"

"I was born a prince."

No. His words pierced her soul. No. No. No. An *I* statement. When they were meant to be *we*.

"You are more than that. You are."

Alessio shook his head. "This is my thing, Brie." He gestured to the palace. "The role I play. There is no next for me."

"It doesn't have to be." Brie shook her head. "It can be part of it. But not all. We can figure this out. As a team."

"I read your comment." Alessio's words were soft, even, with almost no emotion to them.

"Words spoken the day of the lotto, before us." She'd meant them when she'd said them, but that didn't mean they were accurate today.

"So you are fine as the lotto bride? You want this?" He gestured to the palace.

That was a complicated question.

She looked at Alessio. She wanted him, wanted to be part of his next thing.

What's next?

She'd never considered that it wouldn't include her. She'd told him at the ruins that they made decisions. She got to have control. Her family had never allowed that, but Alessio had promised to make decisions with her.

"I want you."

"I am this." Alessio's smile was the formal one, the one he'd worn in so many interviews. The dutiful heir to the throne was standing before her.

"Are we a team?" They could weather this—as a team. They just had to choose a path together.

"I release you from the contract. I sent a note ahead of this discussion to a few news outlets, nothing fancy but just to beat Sebastian's press release of the wedding. I'll give a press conference in a few hours. I am giving you your freedom. You deserve it."

The words she craved hearing six weeks ago were knives to her soul now. "You released a statement? And organized a press conference, too."

Wow. He'd been busy. Her chest felt like it was caving in, like the air in the entire world had vanished. Stars danced in front of her eyes, but she was not going to crash—not here.

This wasn't a team discussion. He'd made the choices and she wasn't part of them. Just like her parents had decided everything. Alessio knew why she needed a say in the decisions. That didn't mean she wanted everything her way; there were always compromises. But she'd asked to be a teammate. A partner. And the most important choice—the one deciding her future—had been chosen for her. Again.

"All right." It was a chore just to get two syllables out. She could do a lot of things, but she couldn't be with a person who wouldn't even discuss such choices with her.

She looked at her hand, her ring finger empty. "I can't give you back an engagement ring, since I never had one." A sob pulled at the back of her throat, but she didn't let it out.

"So—" she stepped to him."—I'll just say that I hope you get to be yourself. That you get what you really want. What you truly deserve." She pressed her lips to his cheek. "Goodbye, Prince Alessio."

She turned and walked away, not sure where she was going.

"Brie." Alessio's call echoed at her back, but she didn't turn around.

If she looked at him, she'd run to him, beg him to reconsider. And no woman wanted to beg a man to choose her.

CHAPTER THIRTEEN

ALESSIO STARED AT the smart board in the media room. Brie's block words outlining the plans, the expectations and how her marketing plan would benefit Celiana were all still in place. He'd held the eraser in his hands more times than he wanted to admit and hadn't erased a single word.

Her books, the coffee she liked, the way she'd arranged the pillows on the couch… He'd not changed a single thing. It was his homage to the woman he loved, the woman who deserved more than duty and a gilded cage. She deserved a world of choices, not select ones governed by security and history and duty and things that never seemed to be in a royal's control.

This was the life he'd been born to, the path he walked. He deserved this, not Brie.

"Alerting the press to your breakup was certainly one way to get around my suggestion of pushing the marriage up."

Suggestion.

Alessio let out a dark laugh. "It felt much more like an order."

His brother hadn't seen him in the last three days, though his presence was felt. He'd sent, or rather had his assistant send, Alessio's packed royal schedule to him every morning.

Alessio wasn't sure if Sebastian needed the help or was trying to distract him.

"It was." Sebastian's words were cool as he stepped beside him. "Imagine my surprise when my now oh-so-dutiful brother disobeyed."

"Since taking the crown you haven't been exactly the pinnacle of duty."

Alessio didn't feel like playing games. His duty was to the crown now, to his brother, but that didn't mean that Brie's life had to be that way.

The expectations, the sacrifices…

"I haven't." Sebastian sighed.

Alessio waited for him to expand on that, but instead his brother started toward the coffeepot and poured himself a cup. He took a deep sip, then returned his attention to Alessio.

"We did a one-eighty, you and I. The rebel king and dutiful returned heir."

"Do you have a point, Sebastian?"

"No." He crossed his arms. "But your former fiancée left her binder of ideas for the tourism board. Her company now takes the tourism board's phone calls whenever they have questions. The woman got right back to the work she loves. She is brilliant at it."

Alessio's soul wept for himself, but his heart soared. This was what he wanted for Brie. Her own life.

"She is brilliant." The words were barely audible, but Sebastian didn't press him.

"On to today's dealings. I have you slated to do an opening for the arts council tomorrow, and there is a board meeting for the tourism council this afternoon. Also, I was thinking of sending you as my representative to the UK for a state function at the end of the month. And there are two ribbon cuttings I need you to attend as the royal representative this evening—ribbon, not ideal, but the businesses didn't ask me. Still, we don't want anyone to think we are shirking the duties Father had."

Alessio didn't want to spend the rest of his life in council and board meetings, even for things he liked. He hadn't had a second to breathe while mourning the end of his engagement.

"No."

The word slipped out and Alessio waited for Sebastian to

argue. They didn't need to be King Cedric. Yes, some things were important, like the arts council. And someone should attend the state function, but they did not have to do everything King Cedric had.

His brother only tilted his head, a motion eerily like their father. "No to which part?"

"All of it." Alessio looked at the board with Brie's notes. Marketing was part of her, the thing that made her feel whole. "I mean, I can do some things, but I want my own life, too." That was something he should have realized when Brie asked him what was next.

Brie.

Her face floated in his mind. He needed her. And glasswork. Alessio didn't want half a life. He needed more.

Sebastian smiled. His brilliant grin spread across his face. "I was actually worried it was going to take at least three state trips, but I was prepared to sacrifice you." His brother clapped and looked around the room, his shoulders straightening.

"You don't owe the crown or the memory of our father a lifetime of sacrifice." Sebastian sighed. "The crown is mine and it is past time that I wore it fully."

"Sebastian—"

"Don't interrupt your king." He winked. "I am not our father. Your happiness, your choices, Brie's choices…they get to be yours. Your role is the one you decide."

"You couldn't have decided this before you ordered me to marry Brie immediately?" Alessio squeezed his brother's arm, color creeping up his cheeks.

"I'm still learning."

"You're going to wear the crown well."

His brother would find his way, and he'd be a good king.

"I'm getting there." Sebastian put his hands on Alessio's shoulders. "I release you. Not that I need to, but I do. From whatever role Father set for you. From whatever argument he had."

"Sebastian, we argued and then…"

"And then he had a stroke. I know." His brother held his gaze. "Or rather I suspected that was the reason you returned. But that was bad luck. If there was fault, it was his—not yours. He worked himself to death for the crown. You will always be my brother. But it's time that I took over the role I was raised to have."

He was his own person…if he wanted to be. A weight fell from his shoulders, and he looked at Sebastian.

"You kicking me out of the palace?"

"You will always be my brother. But yes, I am kicking you out. Find your path, Alessio."

Alessio looked at the smart board one more time, then at his brother. "Thank you."

He raced past him. There was only one place he wanted to be. Next to Briella—wherever that took him.

She was his next.

His last.

Brie looked at the art studio, and it was impossible not to think of Alessio. The tourism council had asked her to look at the place for an art exhibit and class space they thought they might be able to market. She'd nearly said no, but the proposal had taken over her plans for Celiana in the last week. Even adding to them.

Part of her hoped Alessio might be here. Such a foolish hope. The man was busy. It seemed he'd been at nearly every event since the press conference where he'd announced that their engagement was off.

The simple words had been given at a press conference that happened a few hours after she'd left the palace. He'd taken no questions, just thanked Brie for the time they'd spent together. He'd told the nation it was precious, and he'd hold it close for the rest of his life.

He'd said nothing else. So people had reached out to her. Her phone had rung off the hook for the first twenty-four hours. And she hadn't turned it off because she was hoping Alessio might call.

A foolish hope. She knew that, but the phone still buzzed at least once an hour and she still looked at it, hoping to see his name.

Instead, it was customers. Her marketing firm was booming. But she was taking on very few clients. Most of them were the nonprofit clients she'd planned to engage with as Princess Briella. She'd never sit in a fancy penthouse with that clientele. In fact, her business would likely only be a moderate success, if you only looked at the amount of coin it brought in.

It wasn't work that would make her family wish they hadn't thrown her away. But it was rewarding, more rewarding than just trying to prove she was more than the tossed-away Ailiono daughter. That was a label she hadn't realized she was fighting against until she relaunched her business. Like Alessio, she'd been chasing something she didn't actually want.

She loved marketing, but she'd proved herself to herself and that was all that was needed. At least the work kept her busy enough to only think of Alessio every other hour, instead of every minute.

She'd replayed the conversation after their visit to the ruins so many times. She'd thought of other ways to say she wanted him, wanted to be his next. Wanted to be a team.

When they were, they were unstoppable.

Hell, in her dream last night, she'd screamed "Choose us" when he'd told her to take the job. He'd done it, too. In her dream, he'd pulled her so close, held her tightly and told her they'd figure out everything together.

She'd woken in her small apartment and sobbed.

He'd sent her away, released her from the contract...without talking to her. That was the part that stung. But she also hadn't responded when he'd called her name.

She'd likely spend the rest of her life wondering if she should have turned around, told him she loved him, told him that she'd stand beside him at the press conference and set a wedding date. Not in three weeks, but in a few months. She should have offered him the chance to choose them.

Brie closed her eyes. She'd told him he needed to find something, but not offered her ideas. Not a great teammate there. She could have told him she thought he should focus on glasswork. If she could have a business outside the palace, so could he.

He could teach children or use it to encourage the arts. There were so many options, options she hadn't voiced because she wanted him to choose it himself.

What if I had? What if I'd asked why he was releasing me instead of just agreeing to what he thought I wanted?

Brie wiped tears from her cheeks. There was work to do. She had a lifetime to second-guess the choices she'd made with Alessio.

This building was out of the way for tourists. But locals could benefit from the classes. And a few artsy tourists might find their way here. She made several notes about brightening up the front of the building with a mural and flowers to make it more welcoming. Then she opened the front door.

Alessio stood in the middle of a large room. Boxes were strewed around the room and his furnace was already set up in the back corner.

"What—" Brie blinked as she looked at the large, nearly empty room and the prince. "I thought this was a marketing meeting."

"It is." His eyes found hers, and he started toward her. "Brie. I wasn't sure you'd answer if I called, but the tourism board said…" He let out a nervous chuckle. "This is my new studio."

Brie's hands moved to her chest. His new studio. She wanted to scream with joy and launch into his arms. But she kept her place. "It will be a perfect studio."

It felt like a lame statement, but all her other words seemed to have vanished now that he was in front of her.

Alessio pushed his hands in his pockets as he blew out a breath. "I had a whole speech, and it's flown from my brain.

So here's the main points. This is my next. And you are my next. You're my partner. I should have asked what you wanted instead of pushing you away. The palace was my prison for so long. I felt like I let my brother down by arguing with my father and that I deserved to stay. I didn't want you trapped with me. I wanted you to have the choices, but I didn't give you a say in those choices. I let my fear rule me, and I hurt you."

"You should've let me choose my path." Brie reached for his hand. "I never felt trapped when I was with you."

"I love you, Brie." He shook his head. "We are a team, period. If you still want to be. I am stepping back from my role with the palace but not away completely. There may be times we don't get to make all the choices, if Sebastian really needs—"

The world brightened. The pain in her chest, the ache in her heart, vanished as she stood before him.

"Shush." Brie put her finger on his lips. "I love you, too. But I let my fear of being controlled like I was at home rule me. Life means some choices are out of our hands. I should have pushed back the other day. I should have turned when you called instead of running. Us, us is what I choose. Even knowing there may be times when some choices are out of our control."

He closed the distance between them but still didn't reach for her. "I want you to be my wife. Meet me at the altar. As Brie and Alessio, nothing else."

He slipped to one knee and pulled a ring box from his pocket. "Marry me, Brie. Not for Celiana or tourists or anyone else. Just for me and you."

The ruby sparkled in the light.

"I love you. Yes!"

He pulled the ring from the box and slid it on her finger. A perfect fit.

EPILOGUE

ALESSIO LOOKED AT the twin-flame glass design. It was even more perfect than the image that refused to leave his brain for the last week. He'd made this in his mind so many times, shifting the glass design, but now that it was real, now that it was here…

"Alessio?" Brie called before she walked into the studio. The back half of the warehouse he'd proposed to her in was his studio, but the front was her office space. It was perfection.

He felt like he had in Scotland—like himself. Except even better than that, because he wasn't alone.

"I have a meeting to look over the marketing for the non-profit you set up, and Ophelia wants—" She stopped, her eyes falling on the glass.

Bright blue flames wrapped up through green flames.

"Alessio." Brie's blue eyes, the exact color of the blue flames, caught his. "That is…"

"Us."

"Us." Brie pulled up her phone and quickly tapped something out before looking back at his art.

"Our teamwork." Alessio stepped beside her. "Two flames, burning brightly on their own, but wrapped together, something magical." He kissed the top of her head.

"We are pretty perfect together." Brie leaned her head against his shoulder. Her hand reached out, touching the glass. "Emilio will want to see this."

"He'll want to put it in his gallery. It might fetch a decent price."

"It's priceless." Brie shook her head, turning in his arms. "And not for sale. It will be on display in *our* home." She brushed her lips against his.

Alessio deepened the kiss, pulling her tightly. "If you want to go see Ophelia, Princess, you need to pull back now."

Her eyes flashed with pure desire, and Alessio's heart exploded with the knowledge that Brie was his. Nothing in life would ever be more perfect than her by his side.

"That was Ophelia I was texting. Letting her know I'll be late." Her lips captured his.

"I love you." He breathed the words against her neck.

"I'm the luckiest woman in the world."

Brie's giggles echoed through his workshop. He was the lucky one. In a glass ball of hundreds of slips, he'd pulled the name of his soulmate. One lucky slip that led to her. Alessio wouldn't change anything.

* * * * *

COMING SOON!

We really hope you enjoyed reading this book.
If you're looking for more romance
be sure to head to the shops when
new books are available on

Thursday 4th January

To see which titles are coming soon, please visit
millsandboon.co.uk/nextmonth

MILLS & BOON

afterglow BOOKS

Introducing our newest series, Afterglow.

From showing up to glowing up, Afterglow characters are on the path to leading their best lives and finding romance along the way – with a dash of sizzling spice!

Follow characters from all walks of life as they chase their dreams and find that true love is only the beginning...

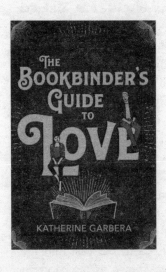

Two stories published every month. Launching January 2024

millsandboon.co.uk

MILLS & BOON ®

Coming next month

PART OF HIS ROYAL WORLD
Nina Singh

'My name is Eriko Rafael Suarez. I'm the man you rescued from nearly drowning the other day.'

Her hand flew to her mouth. 'Oh! I didn't recognize you! You're so…'

He nodded. 'Yes, I imagine I looked quite different. For one, I'm a bit less unconscious now.'

As far as jokes went, it was a rather bad one. Still, the corners of her mouth lifted ever so slightly. His attention fell to her lips, full and rose pink. Her hair was a shade of red he'd be hard-pressed to describe. Arielle Stanton was a looker by half. Riko didn't know what he'd been expecting, but he hadn't been prepared for the jolt of awareness coursing through his core that hadn't relented since she'd opened her door.

'So, I don't mean to be rude. But why are you here?'

'I'm here to personally thank you. For myself and also on behalf of the king and queen.'

She gave her head a shake. 'The king and queen?'

'Of the kingdom of Versuvia. It's a small island nation a few nautical miles from Majorca to the east and the Spanish coast to the west. We're known as the Monaco of the Spanish world.'

Her brows furrowed once more. Again, she eyed him up and down. 'Right.' She dragged out the word pronouncing it as if it were three syllables. 'Listen, I don't know how to break this to you, but I think you might have suffered some type of head injury during your accident. Probably wanna get that checked out.' She began to shut the door.

'Please wait. I know it might be hard to believe, but it's the truth. I'm Eriko Rafael Suarez, heir to the Versuvian throne. Firstborn son of King Guillermo and Queen Raina. My friends call me Riko.'

She stuck her hand out. 'Pleased to meet you. I'm Arielle Trina Stanton, the duchess of Schaumburgia. Daughter of King Alfred III and Queen Tammi, MD.'

He simply stared at her, completely at a loss for words.

For the life of him, he couldn't figure out why he was still standing there. He'd felt obliged to thank her in person, and he'd done so. But something kept him planted in place where he stood, unable to walk away just yet.

Continue reading
PART OF HIS ROYAL WORLD
Nina Singh

Available next month
millsandboon.co.uk

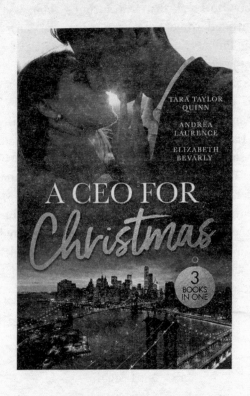

OUT NOW!

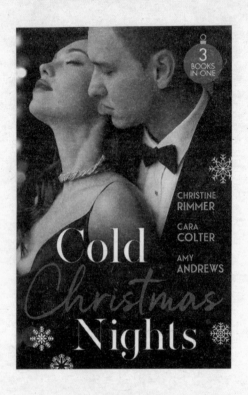

Available at
millsandboon.co.uk

MILLS & BOON

LET'S TALK
Romance

For exclusive extracts, competitions and special offers, find us online:

 MillsandBoon

 @MillsandBoon

 @MillsandBoonUK

 @MillsandBoonUK

Get in touch on 01413 063 232

MILLS & BOON

THE HEART OF ROMANCE

A ROMANCE FOR EVERY READER

MODERN
Prepare to be swept off your feet by sophisticated, sexy and seductive heroes, in some of the world's most glamourous and romantic locations, where power and passion collide.

HISTORICAL
Escape with historical heroes from time gone by. Whether your passion is for wicked Regency Rakes, muscled Vikings or rugged Highlanders, awaken the romance of the past.

MEDICAL
Set your pulse racing with dedicated, delectable doctors in the high-pressure world of medicine, where emotions run high and passion, comfort and love are the best medicine.

True Love
Celebrate true love with tender stories of heartfelt romance, from the rush of falling in love to the joy a new baby can bring, and a focus on the emotional heart of a relationship.

Desire
Indulge in secrets and scandal, intense drama and sizzling hot action with heroes who have it all: wealth, status, good looks... everything but the right woman.

HEROES
The excitement of a gripping thriller, with intense romance at its heart. Resourceful, true-to-life women and strong, fearless men face danger and desire - a killer combination!

To see which titles are coming soon, please visit

millsandboon.co.uk/nextmonth